ABOUT THE AUTHOR

Danny Rhodes grew up in Grantham, Lincolnshire before moving to Kent in 1994 to attend university in Canterbury. He has lived in the cathedral city ever since. After a number of his short stories appeared in magazines on both sides of the Atlantic his debut novel, *Asboville*, was published in October 2006. Well received by critics, it was selected as a Waterstones Paperback of the Year and it has been adapted for BBC Films by the dramatist Nick Leather. Rhodes' second novel *Soldier Boy* was published in February 2009. *Fan* is Danny's third novel, and he continues to write short stories in a variety of genres.

Fan

a novel

DANNY RHODES

ARCADIA BOOKS

Arcadia Books Ltd
139 Highlever Road
London W10 6PH

www.arcadiabooks.co.uk

First published in the United Kingdom by Arcadia Books 2014

ISBN 978-1-909807-80-8

Typeset in Minion by MacGuru Ltd
Printed and bound by CPI Group (UK) Ltd., Croydon CRO 4YY

This is a work of fiction. Names, characters, places and incidents are either
products of the author's imagination or are used fictitiously.

Arcadia Books supports English PEN *www.englishpen.org* and
The Book Trade Charity *http://booktradecharity.wordpress.com*

Arcadia Books distributors are as follows:

in the UK and elsewhere in Europe:
Macmillan Distribution Ltd
Brunel Road
Houndmills
Basingstoke
Hants RG21 6XS

in the USA and Canada:
Dufour Editions
PO Box 7
Chester Springs
PA 19425

in Australia/New Zealand:
NewSouth Books
University of New South Wales
Sydney NSW 2052

The day trip over
A tangerine sun
Becomes blood red sun splashed horizon

Ian Brown, 'Always Remember Me'

To the lads, wherever they are

In memory of James Quinton, poet and editor

Remembering the 96 and all of the others

I can never go back on what I've written. If it was not good, it was true; if it was not artistic, it was sincere; if it was in bad taste, it was on the side of life.

Henry Miller

The Shortt Report of 1924.
The Moelwyn Hughes Report of 1946.
The Chester Report of 1966.
The Harrington Report of 1968.
The Lang Report of 1969.
Lord Wheatley's Report of 1972.
The McElhone Report of 1977.
The Popplewell Report of 1986.

The Green Guide of 1973.
The Safety of Sports Grounds Act 1975.
The Green Guide second edition of 1976.
The Green Guide third edition of 1986.

Monday, 20th September 2004

Cold September turned colder when he caught the evening news. Marooned in a forgotten room of some cavernous hotel, his little window served him a featureless rectangle of English Channel, of slate-grey sea etched with off-white breakers. The beach below was a shelf of deposited pebbles above another shelf and then another.

The edge of the world.

He struggled to the water on his arrival, slid on his haunches down each steep bank, satisfying some urge to stand at the shoreline, to hear the water gathering and dragging at the stones. Looking seaward he took in the miserable hue of ocean and sky, the distant hulking form of the power station out on the spit, and fuck all else. The air was fresh and zestful though. He sucked in a great lungful of the stuff, released it slowly, revelling in the act. But his calves still succumbed to cramp as he made his way back. He was forced to use his hands, to drag his frame up the shelf like a sea turtle, emerge breathless and flush-cheeked at the top.

A posse of golfers were making their way along the links course, dressed in garish yellow. A white van was parked on the kerb, two lads in the front stuffing their faces with service station sandwiches, copies of the *Sun* propped on the dashboard.

The sports pages.

Naturally.

He fought to regain control of his breathing. Out of order, knees fucked, his thirties catching up with him, attending a teachers' conference he had no interest in. He'd asked if he could opt out, landed a certain look from the personnel manager. Apparently it wasn't acceptable to stand still. He'd asked when that had changed, when it had become a sin to tread water.

'You can't tread water for long before you sink...'

The door had been politely closed in his face.

The students kept him grounded. He couldn't resent them with their pie-in-the-sky ideas, even if most were lazy bastards who wouldn't amount to anything. His job, he understood, was to make them believe anything was possible and to help them on their way by ensuring they reached their quota of acceptable grades. Truthfully, it didn't matter much what happened to them after that. Sometimes he ran into one five years down the road, kid in tow, on the way to the supermarket or back from it, ciggie in hand, pushchair laden with nappies, lads three steps ahead of their girlfriends, tense enough to snap. But they smiled at him and called him Finchy, asked him if he was still at the school and some of them apologised for being little pricks and he lied and told them they weren't so bad.

He sent them out each year with their little brown envelopes; sent them to get on with the rest of their lives. Somebody somewhere totted it all up. The gears shifted a notch. Another cohort dropped into place. It really didn't matter.

But the news on the TV mattered.

Football Legend Clough Dies

The images on the screen mattered. There was the man in his baggy shorts banging in the goals for Middlesbrough and Sunderland and there he was again in his trademark green pullover on the dog track at Wembley, two arms raised above his head, thumbs up, playing to his people. There he was escorting a clown from the hallowed City Ground turf, cuffing some bloke around the ear, shooting two fingers at the Trent end boys for calling a stricken Charlie Nicholas a wanker. There he was with the Division One trophy, the League Cup, the European Cup, side by side with Peter Taylor. There was Trevor Francis stooping to head the winner against Malmö, rolling over the concrete shot-putt circle in the Olympiastadion. There was the mischievous grin as he fielded questions from reporters, gave Motto the runaround, messed with Ali. There was the beetroot-coloured, pockmarked face that signalled his final days in management, the wretched alcoholic. And there he was at the end, the old man in the cloth cap sat in the stands at Burton Albion.

Husband, father, grandfather.

Legend.

Brian Howard Clough OBE, 21st March 1935–20th September 2004.

Brian Howard Clough.

He felt like he'd been kicked in the stomach, stared out of the little window at the water, gulls arcing against the wind, spatters of rain on the glass. He had an hour to kill until dinner. He'd planned to go for a swim but his breath was well and truly knocked out of him. He fell back on the bed and stared at the ceiling instead, thinking about Kelly. She wouldn't be home. It was too early. He didn't want to speak to her anyway. He couldn't speak to anybody. He turned on to his side and stared at the wall, closed his tired eyes.

Piss-flooded terraces and asbestos-roofed covered ends. Testosterone-fuelled foot soldiers and brutal police escorts. Soul-destroying defeats and ecstatic celebrations that suggested life really did depend on it all.

A procession of memories.

Arse-ache coach trips across the Pennines, to the Black Country, to London fucking town. Up the country and down again, week in, week out. Thatcher's bloodied Britain coughing up its innards. Smokestacks and drizzle. Retching fucking suburbs. Moss Side. Toxteth. The Meadows.

Bradford. Kenilworth Road. Heysel. The *Herald of Free Enterprise*. Kegworth. Hansen strolling around at the back.

Quarter to five on a Saturday. Ron bloody Atkinson. John fucking Aldridge.

And the boys. Bob's bus. British Rail. The most boring town in England. The Brilliant Corners. Cud. The Wedding Present. The Stone Roses. High-school girls. A grammar school for boys. A new-build primary in 1976. A teacher who stood six feet six, who spent his weekends watching Nottingham Forest take on the whole of Europe and beat the fucking lot into vile submission.

Twice.

Two golden stars.

All of this spitting at him out of the past.

A torrent.

BJ, Jeff, T-Gally, Hopper, Gav, Stimmo, JC and Sharpster. The whole fucking bunch. He'd not seen any of them in years. He could see them in the gloom now, though, all of them, sixteen years old, seventeen, eighteen. Formative years dominated by one shared obsession. A way of life.

Nottingham Forest.

The mighty Reds.

Up the country, down the country, week in, week out.

No fucking excuses.

And something else. Something shifting in the silt of his memory. Twisted crowd barriers. Lads lugging makeshift stretchers across a pitch strewn with the injured and bewildered. The dead lined up in rows on the turf. Twisted minutes. Twisted metal. Twisted news reports. Everything twisted.

Scarves draped over the gates at Anfield.

Scarves hanging from the goalposts at the Kop end.

A carpet of colours.

Twisted fucking memories.

Him in full darkness now, removed from the present yet part of it still, the hotel pipes clanging, the far-off sound of doors closing, lifts humming. The distant echo of laughter. A clap of false thunder from the military range along the coast.

A cold dread seeping through him, starting in his toes and rising. The things he'd buried coming back again. Everything kicked up. The silt lifting.

He switched on the lights, turned on the TV again, avoiding the news at all costs. He closed his eyes, painted himself a pastoral picture, a pleasant Sunday, a meadow, a barn and a blue sky.

The fens in summer.

He fought with all his might to block the bad memories out.

But they came anyway. Of course they did.

A broken heart. A broken girl. A broken summer.

A naked body dumped in a hedge beside a set of kiddies' swings.

He sat up, desperately fending them off.

It was too late.

The barn door was open.

The black mares had bolted.

It was the City Ground.

It was your City Ground.

It was Anfield.

It was St Andrews and Villa Park.

It was Highbury.

It was White Hart Lane.

It was Ayresome Park and St James' Park, Old Trafford and Goodison.

It was The Den and Plough Lane, Filbert Street and the Baseball Ground.

It was grounds that survived and grounds that died.

It was Highfield Road.

It was Maine Road.

It was all of these grounds and dozens more.

It was the 1980s.

Tuesday
Wednesday
Thursday

A hat-trick of torturous days.
Of excruciating days.
The black mares in free gallop.
Running amok over field and furrow.

Say 'fucking' at every opportunity.

Pronounce it 'fookin'.

For this word is the glue that binds every Nottingham sentence together.

Aye, meh duck.

Aye.

Friday

Early. Only Harding and Brompton in before him. No fucking surprises there. He walked the empty corridors, grabbed a mug from the cupboard in the Inclusion room and filled the kettle.

7.15 a.m. Quiet hour. Deathly still. Into his classroom. No fucking heat from the radiators, staring into the courtyard at the pathetic trees, the hard-packed earth, a lonely Bic biro, the torn-off cover of a kid's planner. Hunched over his mug, motionless, searching for motivation. Footsteps passed by his doorway. McCarthy, white shirt and black tie, like he was heading to a funeral. No hint of the week in his face.

McCarthy the machine. Smiling.

'Shit the bed, John?'

'Thought I'd take a leaf out of your book.'

'Grand. See you in briefing then,' said McCarthy. 'You can say a few words about that course we sent you on.'

Fuck.

Fuck, fuck, fuck.

It's the winter of discontent. The rail workers are on strike. The public sector workers are on strike. The engineering firms, the heartbeat of the town, are floundering. Your dad works in one of them and there's no money in the house. Your dad's struggling to make ends meet. But so is everybody else. It's 1979.

The streets are littered with uncollected rubbish.

Crisis? What crisis?

Your school closes because there's no oil to heat the building.

Crisis? What crisis?

Twenty-nine million working days are lost in industrial disputes.

Crisis? What crisis?

You're eight years old. You spend your days at school and your week-ends kicking a football through a 1960s' estate, locating grass wherever it grows, a patch here, a patch there. When there's no grass there are ramshackle asbestos garage blocks and splintered panel fences.

What do you know about anything?

Nothing.

How do you know?

They fookin well tell you, don't they? Every fucker you speak to.

It's 1979.

A change is coming, a change with roots once bound to your own.

Where there is discord, may we bring harmony. Where there is error, may we bring truth. Where there is doubt, may we bring faith. And where there is despair, may we bring hope.

But if you're a working-class boy from a working-class estate with a working-class father you'd better brace yourself.

Because those roots are long since severed.

And you are fucked, mate.

Well and truly.

7.50 a.m. He stared at his planner, at the blank pages, at a full day in the classroom, five fucking lessons in a row, hardly time to take a breath.

Kirsty Watson the first in, as always. She only lived across the street but was one of the rarities, happier in school than out. And here she was, leaning against the door frame.

He set her off changing a display. She was glad enough doing it.

'Did you see your mum lately?'

Without a blink.

'I never see my mum.'

Enough said.

One by one the rest of his form dribbled in. He left them to it, fucked off to briefing.

Mullholland. Irish. Fit as fuck. Her and the rest of the English honeys huddled in the corner. He attached himself to their edge, listened to their stories of Thursday night shenanigans until attention fell his way.

'How was the training?'

'Like a slow death.'

'At least you had an easy few days.'

He shrugged, brushing the training under the carpet. But the carpet was threadbare, on its way out.

Silence.

So he told them all about it, or what he remembered about setting meaningful targets, difficult conversations, the importance of self-evaluation and the appraisal of others. When he thought back to the hotel everything was monochrome.

Even his face in the mirror.

'Did you hear about Cloughie?' he asked.

Two of the girls looked at him.

'Who?'

Simultaneous fucking ignorance.

At least it was Friday.

P1–Year 8. Fucking mad bunch. He stuck a DVD on, kept them in their seats. Animated Chaucer. *The Pardoner's Tale*. Fucking Chaucer to that crowd. Fucking education system.

P2–Year 9. Testosterone and hormones. It hardly mattered what he planned. Ten minutes handing out pens. Ten minutes ridding the room of mobile phones. Ten minutes chasing homework. Ten minutes issuing instructions. Ten minutes repeating them. Ten minutes blocking the door to prevent the fuckers getting out to break early. A healthy routine that suited both sides.

P3–Year 11. All boys. It was Friday. There was the weekend's football to talk about. Chelsea. Arsenal. Spurs. West Ham on the TV. Hardly any of the fuckers had ever been near a ground. He pitied them for it. He really did. He showed them some video footage of Cloughie in his prime. They laughed at the length of his shorts.

P4–Year 12. Lazy bastards. Literature students with not the slightest interest in English fucking literature. Pick a poem. Any poem.

P5–Year 7. Drama. Fuck me.

Duty at break. A mug of tea outside the toilets, the reek of piss, discount perfume and teenage sweat. Lunch in his room, ham sandwiches wrapped in tinfoil, a packet of crisps, an apple. Kelly's killer cuisine. Department catch-up after school. Tea and biscuits. The girls calling him a miserable bastard each time he risked a contribution. At least Davies didn't piss about or pontificate. They were done in a half an hour.

He drove home in the forlorn twilight, past the leafy grounds of the local grammar school half a mile up the road, felt the familiar resentment and a faint glimmer of pride in himself. He hadn't succumbed. He still had his principles in place.

Not that it fucking mattered.

A tall, stooping man. Fuzzy hair. Glasses. A bigger smile when he spots the shirt. Not Liverpool. Not Manchester United. The Major Oak with the three lines, the little curve on the extended 'R' in the word 'Forest'.

Your parents buy you the away strip, yellow with a blue trim. It sets you apart. You love it for that reason, even then. You love to pull it on, to feel the crackle of the fabric against your skin, love to run out on the school field in it, to smack the brown leather ball around, love to imagine you're John Robertson jinking this way, jinking that way. You're in love with a girl at eight years old but you love your football more. You will always love your football more. And you respect this teacher, this tall, willowy man who reads you chilling stories by Roald Dahl while East Midland sleet raps at the windows of the classroom and dark clouds race across February skies. This teacher who is a bit of a maverick and popular with the mums, who you spot on a street corner with a group of other excited souls one early morning during a May holiday, his neck draped in a red Forest scarf.

'Isn't that Mr what's-his-name?' asks your dad.

You nod your head in wonder.

'I know where he's going,' says your dad. 'Lucky bugger.'

The European Cup Final.

You're old enough to stay up and watch it but you don't really understand what it means for a provincial club like yours to have made such a step, to have swept aside Liverpool (the Champions of Europe), AEK Athens, Grasshopper Zurich and FC Cologne on their way to Munich to take on the unlikely Swedes, FC Malmö. You're eight years old. You do not know that just two years earlier your side were playing in Football League Division Two. You do not yet appreciate the genius of Clough and Taylor. But you adore Trevor Francis for that goal. Just like your adoration for John Robertson grows when he shimmies and sways past Manny Kaltz to win the trophy again a year later against Keegan's FC Hamburg.

You are Nottingham Forest.

You don't quite understand that yet, but you are.

Saturday

He spent the day on the sofa, watching the tributes to Clough, listening to the updates from grounds he knew and grounds he'd never know. In the evening he collected Kelly from her shift, fetched Chinese food, shared it with her whilst staring at the TV, the two of them shirking the subject of where they were heading, their elephant filling the space between them on the sofa, in the bedroom, in their double bed.

Together apart.

Later, he wrestled his mares in the darkness.

Sunday

He took himself out along the river, trudged up the path, hands in pockets, sometimes stopping to stare at the rolling water, sometimes looking down at his reflection, not liking what he saw, wondering what was coming next, how long it would be before Kelly brought the subject up again, where it might lead them.

Because she would do.

Five years and all the associated baggage, the good times and the bad times. Five years in this singular relationship. The road ahead paved with expectation. Him floundering, tripping on the flagstones.

Mares and elephants.

Elephants and mares.

How the fuck had it come to this?

Monday

Monday morning blues.

He couldn't face work, got Kelly to call in sick for him, tell them his voice had gone. And it had. He wasn't fucking lying about it. He lay under the covers listening to her move about the house, tense until he heard the door slam and her footsteps disappearing down the garden path and away.

He collapsed in on himself.

Dark clouds trooping in. He shut his eyes against it all.

When he woke later the house was fucking freezing. He cranked up the heating, made himself a mug of the good stuff and retreated to bed with a handful of ginger nuts. He sat there propped against the pillows, dunking each biscuit and savouring the sheer indulgence. He looked at the time and pitied the poor bastard that had been taken to cover him. Well, fuck it, he needed a rest. He stayed in bed until lunchtime, ignoring the phone twice, hearing the post land on the doormat, half dreaming these things, slipping in and out of consciousness. When the phone rang the third time he was in the kitchen, trying to make himself a sarnie. It was Kelly.

'You're up then.'

'Just.'

'Feeling better?'

'Not really.'

'Have you called the doctor?'

'No,' he said.

'Are you going to?'

'No.'

'He'll give you something.'

'I don't want anything.'

A pause.

'So you're okay then?' she asked again.

'I have a bad throat.'

Another pause.

'Are you going to fetch me?'

'If you like.'

'5.15, the usual place?'

'Yep. All being well…'

He heard her sigh.

'Stop being so morose,' she said. 'What are you going to do now?'

'Take it easy,' he said. 'Revel in my freedom. Be the life and soul…'

'Fuck your sarcasm,' she said. 'Are you going to make some room in the attic? You said you were.'

'If I feel up to it,' he said.

He didn't bother with a sandwich in the end. He made himself soup instead and stuffed the bread into it, sat in the living room watching the Boating Channel, thinking about buying a canal boat and fucking off into a netherworld. When the soup was done he went upstairs, opened the hatch to the attic. He carried the ladder up from the garage and set it in place, switched on the light and peered into the fucking shambles beyond.

Boxes of shit. His and hers. He hoarded stuff like he hoarded memories. Wasn't that the fucking problem? The immediate passed him by but the past lingered.

On his hands and knees, shuffling about, his shadow forever blocking the way. Suitcases full of clothes. Her clothes. Her handbags. Her shoes. More clothes than fucking Elton. All as good as new. The box of tricks they'd collected and had fun with in their livelier days, now consigned to the attic. Another fucking life. What if he called her now, ordered her home, told her he had the box out and wanted to try a few things? He sat with his legs dangling from the attic hatch, pondering the thought. Given the circumstances it was best to leave it.

Crawling. Forcing his way into the darkest corners. Somewhere. Fucking somewhere. Boxes. Another life. Before Kelly. Before teaching. Before all the middle-aged mediocre bollocks. Uni files. Before those. A box in the corner. Cardboard. Taped shut. Maybe. Just maybe.

They were piled together, a couple of hundred at least. Two hundred games. Two hundred days. Two hundred great adventures. Home and away. He dragged the box into the light, down the ladder, down the stairs, out into the garden, out to the summer house. He kicked away the summer chairs, the wheelbarrow, the gardening tools, cleared the worktop. It wasn't meant to be a shed. It was never meant to be a shed.

He raised one from the box, lifted it to his face, buried his nose in it, breathed it all in, the agony and the fucking ecstasy, the magic and the mayhem. His first forays into manhood played out in squalid away ends, on dirty British Rail trains and tired city streets. It was all here, written on these pages. He could smell it. He could fucking well reach out and touch it.

In the bottom of the box, an enamel badge, a subtle thing, the simple tree, the heraldic treatment of water, red, white and gold, a centimetre square. He rested it on the worktop, placed it there with precision and reverence.

He started sorting the programmes, season by season, match day by match day. Virgin trips to Anfield, Old Trafford, Highbury. Chaz and Dave at White Hart Lane. Short-sleeved on a pitch-level terrace at Goodison in August. Huddled with the others at Upton Park in dark November. There were implausible gaps and omissions, games he remembered not evidenced by a programme, games long forgotten with a programme to prove he was there.

Snakes and ladders.

There was one complete pile. One full season. Every single minute of every single game.

88–89.

A season to remember.

A season to forget.

And not forget.

To never, ever forget.

Eight years old.

Nottingham?

Aye, meh duck. Nottingham.

The old Market Square rammed with people.

Your fookin people.

The players on the balcony of the council building, high above the two lions. The European Cup glistening in the sunlight.

The crowd at the barricades, swaying and rocking. Eight years old, on your dad's shoulders, three hundred yards away but feeling like you can reach out and touch it. The crowd surging against the barriers, a heaving mass of joy. Flags waving, banners flying in the sunlight, in the city.

The envy of Europe.

The pinnacle.

And singing.

Everybody singing.

A great mass of people becoming one, celebrating one thing, living as one, breathing as one.

The players on the balcony.

Clough and Taylor on the balcony.

You and your dad.

Your dad and you.

The whole world in your hands.

He was waiting in the car park when she finished work, sat with the engine idling watching the other women. When she opened the passenger door he was miles away, lost in a dream of slender ankles and tight arses.

'Alright now?' she asked.

He shook his head.

'I've felt better,' he said.

'Well, thanks for coming out,' she said. 'I didn't fancy the bus.'

'Couldn't any of these have given you a ride?'

'Maybe,' she said. 'But I wanted you to do it.'

She leant over and kissed him on the cheek.

'Can we talk later?' she asked him. 'Just talk.'

'You know we can,' he said.

He felt a tinge of affection for her, a stab of guilt too. She was like that, able to catch him off guard. For a few moments, as he pulled out and joined the queue of cars shifting towards the ring road, he felt his spirits rise. But it was stop-start after that. All headlights and tail lights. Rain too. Spray and mist. The wiper blades made a poor job of it all, had him squinting through the smeared windscreen, the lights a blurred collage, his head pounding, Kelly talking through all of it about work, about women he didn't know and processes he had no interest in. It took a lifetime to reach their driveway, to slip the car on to it, to unlock the doors and get into the house.

She disappeared upstairs for a shower then.

Mercifully.

He lifted the key off the hook in the hall, slid open the French windows and stepped outside. Beyond the gardens, the sound of evening traffic on the High Road. He floated across the lawn to the summer house, stared through the beads of water on the glass at the neatly stacked piles, slid the key into the lock. And then he stopped. He stared at his dark reflection in the glass, stared at a seventeen-year-old version of himself, gazed into the eyes, fought his way behind those eyes, searching for a sign, not knowing what parts of himself were shaped by the things those eyes witnessed one day in April long ago and what parts were not, but knowing they were coming at him all the same, galloping freely through the fields, heading his way.

He braced himself against them. There was nothing else he could do.

And they didn't talk, not about anything.

It was the Trent end at 3 p.m. on a Saturday.
It was your Trent end.
It was the central pen to the right of the goal.
You can see it now, packed to the rafters.
You can feel the ebb and the flow.
You can see your people.
You can hear their songs.
Your skull is a symphony hall.
The music resonates within it.

Tuesday

Munching on toast, the phone erupting in the hallway. He waited for Kelly to get it.

'It's for you,' she said.

'Not work...'

'No, I don't think so. It's nobody I recognise.'

He didn't get up.

'Not a fucking sales call.'

Kelly moved across the kitchen to the sink, flushed her mug under the tap.

'He asked for John,' she said.

He lugged himself out of the chair and barefooted it across the cold tiles to the phone, lifted the receiver, listened, waited a moment.

'Alright?'

A voice on the other end. East Midlands accent. A voice from the old town?

'Alright—'

'Remember me?'

'Who is it?'

'You don't remember?'

'No,' he said. 'No, I don't.'

A fucking fruit machine, the images revolving and flashing. This face. That face.

'Black Jack,' said the voice.

His felt his stomach drop away.

Reels dropping into place.

'I've some news, mate.'

'Right.'

'It's not easy…'

Dead tone. Monosyllabic.

'It's Stimmo.'

Stimmo.

'He's only gone and done himself.'

A chill in his bones, a raking down his spine.

'Hello?'

'Yes, mate, I'm here.'

'The service is on Friday. I know it's late notice. Took me a while to find you…'

'Right. Cheers. For letting me know.'

'10 a.m. at the crem.'

'Right, mate.'

'We thought you'd want to know. We're all in shock. Right fucked up, to be honest.'

'How did you…'

'T-Gally. His mam called your mam. Friday. See you there.'

'Right. Cheers, mate. Cheers for calling.'

Silence at the other end.

'Hello?' asked Finchy.

'Yes, mate.'

'I said thanks for calling.'

'I heard. I said we'll see you Friday.'

Finchy paused.

'Aye,' he said, at last. 'I'll be there.'

The reels at a standstill. Him at a standstill, in the kitchen, bare feet on the cold tiles.

Stimmo. Stimmo. Fucking Stimmo.

The black mares in free gallop, running wherever they fucking pleased. The black mares trapped in a mass of bodies.

Kelly came into the kitchen. He stared ahead of himself, feeling her in his peripheral vision. A blur. A shadow.

'Are you okay?'

An absent nod of the head.

'Who was it?'

'An old mate of mine. A bloke from years ago. Nobody you'd know.'

She stood there watching him. He didn't say anything else.

'I have to go,' she said.

'Yeah,' he said.

'Will you be okay?'

He nodded.

He spotted the twist in her lips, knew what she was thinking. And then he said, 'Tonight. We can talk about it tonight. We can talk about everything tonight.'

After she'd gone, after she'd shut the door behind her, he went upstairs to get ready for work. He pulled on a shirt and stood at the window doing up the buttons, looking down on the little patch of lawn, the scattered leaves, the cluster of houses.

The Close in autumn.

Stimmo ahead of him in the queue for the Trent end, the turnstile clicking and counting them in. The two of them slipping in the side of the end pen, along the fence, into the centre pen, up behind the goal. Into the action. Stimmo at Derby giving the sheep-shaggers grief. The rain pelting down. Stimmo piling on top of the others at Tottenham as Forest nick a late winner. Stimmo on the train on the way back from Hillsborough, staring out of the window, blanking the guard when he came for the tickets, telling the guard to fuck off, telling each and every one of them to fuck off. Stimmo at the bar in the Hound during Italia 90, older than his years, yet a lesser being. That was the last time he saw the guy. He'd stopped going to football, worked every Saturday, said he had to, said he had no fucking choice. Maybe it was true.

Or maybe it was bollocks?

He pulled a tie out of the wardrobe and placed it around his neck, thinking about method, wondering, imagining, trying not to imagine. The postman came up the drive. He watched him sort the letters in the bundle, pick out a couple. He heard the letter box snap. The woman at number nine was in her window, standing looking in his direction, there in just her bathrobe. She pulled the curtains shut. The postie was two doors down already. Finchy looked at the clock on the dresser. Time was ticking on. He had to get going. He coughed. He wasn't sure he wanted to go anywhere.

Town was busy, the streets rammed, the sky full of charcoal clouds. It was raining again. Everything was blurred streaks. When he reached the school he sat in the car park with the engine idling, watching the kids meander through the gates and scatter in all directions, watching the buses pull in and kids flood out. He looked at the school building, bent out of shape by the water droplets on the windscreen. He sat there for fifteen minutes trying to drag himself in the direction of his classroom, lost in a fog.

He'd go up after work, stay overnight, get it over with and come home again. And tonight he'd give Kelly what she wanted. Because if he was anything, if he was man at all he'd do that at least, sit down and talk it all through, tell her honestly what he was feeling about the two of them, about babies and fatherhood, what he felt their next steps were. Not that it would make a difference. She was set in one direction. There was no fucking doubt about that.

Maggie's settled in Downing Street. Maggie's got a second term. It means nothing to you except that she comes from where you come from, was born where you were born. But it means something to your town.

Your town is floundering and forgotten, ransacked and ridiculed.

The most boring town in England.

He's taking the morning register while his form stare absently out of the classroom windows, stare absently at their mobile phones, stare absently at the blank desks in front of them. He can't blame the fuckers, not on this dismal day. He's hardly with it himself.

A crisp packet blows against the window and he momentarily loses himself. He forgets where he is on the list, whose name he's called out and who he hasn't. He can't be arsed to start again. Besides, the bell is ringing for the end of registration, for the start of period one.

He turns to Kirsty Watson.

'Can you count up before we go?' he asks.

And without question, without comment, she takes on the job, rising to her feet, counting each body rising from the chair, each body moving towards the door.

'One, two, three, four…'

Cars lined bumper to bumper.

'… nine, ten, eleven, twelve…'

Ashen faces and blank expressions.

'Sixteen, seventeen, eighteen, nineteen…'

Adidas Sambas pounding the concrete.

Adidas Sambas on the Penistone Road.

'Sir? Are you okay, sir?'

The classroom is empty save for Kirsty Watson, Kirsty Watson and her eager to please smile. Her sweet smile.

'Twenty-four, sir,' she says. 'All except Becca Smith.'

He nods.

'Are you sure you should be back in, sir,' asks Kirsty Watson, who is thirteen years old. 'Only you don't look too good.'

'I'm fine,' he says. 'I'm fine and dandy.'

But the first two lessons of the day are bastard trials and

today it is his break duty. Things can only go downhill from here.

2 p.m.

Finchy's in the head's office.

He's staring at a monitor, staring at an incident that happened two hours earlier, living a moment from another lifetime.

The camera shows a narrow corridor, a set of stairs leading away, an extra down-step, vending machines, kids huddled in the corner, paying homage to the vending god. At the top of the frame, the double doors leading to the playground, a splash of pale light beyond.

The pinch point.

Kids are moving to and fro, in dribs and drabs, in twos and threes, in larger groups. Girls linked with girls. Lads marching shoulder to shoulder. Much posturing.

The camera shows a northern city, a street deviating at an outer concourse leading to a set of turnstiles.

The slender elbow of Leppings Lane.

It's 2.30 p.m. on match day.

There are fans in the ground and fans not in the ground.

There are fans who've been delayed on their journey.

There are fans leaving The Five Arches pub, The Horse and Jockey, The Dial House, The Park Hotel.

There are fans who've been enjoying the sunshine on this warm spring day in April.

A football crowd like any other is descending on Leppings Lane well in time for kick-off, moving through the Hillsborough gates and into the outer concourse.

But something is wrong in Leppings Lane. There is no filtering system in place to direct fans to where they need to go, no system to turn fans away, no system to manage their arrival.

And once they're in this cul-de-sac there's no obvious way out. The mass of people congeals to form a clot in the outer concourse. There's no way of passing the message back to those that can alleviate the pressure. Not at 2.30 p.m. on match day. And so the crowd swells, becomes a compression, becomes a melding of exposed flesh, becomes a crush of bones.

Occasionally, the back of Finchy's head appears in the picture, there and not there, joking with Carly Edmunds, having a go at the lads with trainers and the two little shits kicking at the vending god for not delivering their dreams. Break duty like all break duties. A disruption to his day. A pain in the fucking rear.

It's 2.40 p.m. on match day.

Mounted police are imprisoned within the coagulation, unable to manoeuvre. A police horse is lifted off its feet in the swell. Police are waving their arms in helpless abandon, eager to move the crowd back. But there is nowhere for this crowd to move to. People are pressed against the brick wall. People are pressed against the blue concertina gate. People are pressed against each other, suffocating each other where they're stood. The ageing turnstiles creak and click under the strain. The ageing turnstiles jam. The ageing turnstiles are overwhelmed.

The clock ticks towards kick-off.

The camera shows a scene of chaos, shows a swaying, fluctuating mass of people. The camera shows perplexed faces, aggravated faces, the face of a fan desperate for help, the face of a policeman bewildered by an impossible problem.

The camera shows fans clambering over the wall to escape the confusion.

The camera records the cacophony of sound, exuberance becoming frustration becoming anger becoming pain, becoming the helpless mewing of the injured and the afraid. It records the indecipherable tannoy announcements that are lost in the dissonance, the growing sense of urgency, beginning as one sound, becoming something else.

Get back! Get back!

But they can't hear. And they can't move. They're trapped in the outer concourse of Leppings Lane, trapped between their brothers and their sisters.

Open the gate!

Open the fucking gate!

Nobody opens the gate.

Break is over. The camera shows a growing swell, shows dribs and drabs thickening in that space between the vending machines and the bottom of the stairs. Kids struggling to get in, kids struggling to get out. The biggest laughing and joking.

'I told them,' he says. 'There, see that one look back over his shoulder? That's Billy Stubbs. He's looking at me. He's heard me having a go. I bloody told him.'

But the daft bastard's not listening, not acknowledging him at all.

2.48 p.m.

The concertina gate is opened to eject a supporter. One hundred and fifty fans spill in. The gate is closed.

2.50 p.m.

The camera shows the back end of the Leppings Lane turnstiles, the inner concourse, shows fans waiting for their mates, lost to them in the melee. Blokes are filing through, shaking their heads. Girls are filing through shaking their heads. Kids are filing through, clinging to the shirt-tails of their dads. These people file across the screen from left to right, preparing themselves for a football match, for the biggest day out of the season, a game that will kick off in ten minutes' time, in six hundred seconds from now, because the opportunity to delay the kick-off has already passed.

These people file across the screen from left to right, across the concourse and into Gangway 2, under the sign that reads 'Standing' because where else should they fucking go? They file across the screen from left to right. Nobody stops them.

The tunnel should be closed but it's not.

The fans should be re-directed but they're not.

Nobody directs them anywhere.

They file under the sign that reads 'Standing'. Into the central pens. Into pens 3 and 4. Into pens that are already full to capacity.

Lambs to the fucking slaughter.

More kids come through the doors, fighting the tide. A tiny blonde thing is caught up in the flow. There are big lads in the foreground now, the last to leave the canteen. In their fucking element. Bodies press against bodies, press against plaster, press against glass, until the artery is blocked. The little blonde thing's there one moment and gone the next. He is simply engulfed. And there are three or four on the ground now. But Finchy can't see them. All he can see on the screen is a collection of heads and shoulders, confused, anguished faces. They're down there, though, down amongst the boots and the trainers and the heels and the knees.

That's why he's here.

In the head's office.

In the fucking shit.

2.52 p.m.

Open the gate before someone is killed!

Open the fucking gate!

The police open the concertina gate. Fans flood through it. But there's nobody telling the poor fuckers where to go and nowhere for the majority to go except where momentum and common sense takes them.

Across the concourse.

Under the flaking blue-and-white sign that reads 'Standing'.

Into tunnel 2.

Into the tunnel with the 1 in 6 gradient.

Into the valley of death.

2.57 p.m.

The gate is closed.

A voice from far away.

'What are you doing now?'

A voice on the fringes.

'John, are you listening to me? What are you doing now?'

'Eh?'

'In the video. What are you doing?'

He's frozen to the spot.

A statue.

A useless cunt.

He opens his mouth to speak but no words come out.

3.00 p.m.

They're moving through the re-opened gate. They're eager, urgent, keen to get a vantage point because it's gone 3.00 p.m. and the game has fucking started.

They don't know what's happening in pens 3 and 4.

They don't know the pens are overfull.

They don't know that people are dying in those pens.

They don't fucking know.

They can't fucking imagine.

And the tunnel is dark. Dark and dank. It stinks of piss and shit.

At the end of the tunnel a blue sky is beckoning. At the end of the tunnel is the far-off sound of a football match.

'Two minutes,' says the head. Says Chris. Says his mate. 'Two fucking minutes of inaction, John.'

He shrugs.

'Fucking hell, John. We could have a serious problem here. We've three kids in hospital.'

The camera shows pens 3 and 4 of Leppings Lane. The camera shows a compacted multitude of heads and shoulders. A crowd full of turbulence. People are lifted off their feet. People are carried down the terrace with no free will. People are facing in every direction. People are trapped between the torsos of their neighbours. They're shouting or trying to shout, but even that's becoming too much. Breathing in deep to shout means not breathing out again. They're floundering. There are people on the ground, people underfoot. There are lifeless bodies with bleached faces propped against the living. Limp heads rest on lifeless shoulders. People are killing people simply by being. With each second that passes the pressure grows. The barriers designed to protect are transformed into rudimentary killing machines. One fan's arm snaps against the metal, another's ribs cave in.

A barrier gives way, a barrier designed to withstand 400lbs per foot of pressure, a barrier with too much work to do, a barrier displaying corrosion visible to the naked eye, a barrier later found to contain a rolled-up copy of the *Yorkshire Telegraph and Star*, 24th October 1931.

Fans tumble down the terrace. Fans tumble on top of other fans. There's a pile of bodies at the bottom of the terrace, set upon set of wide staring eyes, of vacant expressions, a tangled mass of limbs. There are bodies covered in bruises, blue bodies, bloated bodies. There are bodies pressed against the perimeter fencing. There's vomit and saliva and mucus and God knows what else.

Some are clambering up and out of the pens to safety.

The lucky ones.

Some have nowhere to go and no way of getting there.

The sky is perfectly blue.

The dead are propped against the living.

The symphony of a football match has been replaced by the desperate dirge of the dying.

'John, are you listening to me? Do you understand what I'm saying?'

He's not listening.

He's fifteen years away, crammed into his own little space on the Spion Kop at Hillsborough. 15th April 1989. He's seventeen years old. He's watching a Liverpool fan dance a jig in front of the bank of Forest Fans, watching the guy being led away by stewards in bright yellow bibs.

The clarity is extreme.

He's feeling the crowd swell in number as kick-off approaches. It takes him a while to find his footing, to find his voice, to find his place in it all.

He's watching the players enter the pitch. He's singing his songs. He's watching the game take off at a tremendous pace, watching Clough dispossess Ablett on the halfway line, watching Forest force a corner and then another, watching Forest pass the ball clean and true, watching the Forest players bite into tackle after tackle. He's believing, like all the rest around him, that this is Forest's season, that they're in the form of their lives and ripe for revenge.

Why fucking not?

And then he's watching Liverpool fans scale the fencing to gather on the track behind Grobbelaar's goal, gather behind the advertising hoardings for Bic Razors, Coalite and Fly Thai, watching a solitary St John's Ambulance steward leading one fan away, watching Liverpool fans tumble now over the fences of Leppings Lane, to gather in clusters at the edge of the pitch, a growing mass of fans, watching police-men filing along the perimeter in the direction of Leppings Lane. He's watching Liverpool force a corner of their own, watching Beardsley's rasping effort crash back off the bar, watching Forest manoeuvre the ball to the Liverpool end, watching the black shape of a single policeman race across the 18 yard box towards the referee.

Everything changes.

Everything.

Forever.

'John, John. This is a serious business.'

Tell me about it, Chris. Fucking tell me about it.

He's listening to Forest give it to the Scousers for ruining it all. He's giving it himself, shouting 'you Scouse bastards' with everybody else. He's not seeing. He doesn't under-stand. He's watching hundreds of bewildered insects scramble over the fencing, hundreds more climbing into the stand above. He's watching a dark shadow spread across the green baize.

A dark shadow that will engulf him.

There are scuffles on the Kop, Forest with Forest. There are scuffles between the drinkers and the non-drinkers, the sensible and the senseless. All around him, bemused faces are struggling to comprehend what is happening in front of their eyes.

And he's watching the living carry the lifeless on make-shift stretchers made out of advertising hoardings, watching a line of police lock together across the playing surface to deflect a threat that's not even there.

They're doing fuck all.

Fuck all.

He's watching a bunch of lads in tracksuits trying to give the kiss to a mate, trying to do that when they've no fucking clue, witnessing their desperation as they frantically seek help where there is no help, watching them cover the face of their mate with a leather jacket.

He's hearing a bloke behind him mutter something to another bloke.

'He's fucking dead. They're all fucking dead.'

'The governors want to know what happened,' says Chris. 'The parents are demanding answers…'

Lost within the veil.

Lost in darkness.

'And it isn't just the parents and governors, John. I've had members of staff complain too, about the language you used.'

That brings him back.

'The language?'

'The swearing.'

'Did you see what was happening?'

'Regardless…'

'They were in danger, Chris. They were all in danger.'

A row of bodies in the goalmouth. The row lengthening, becoming six, becoming eight, becoming a dozen. Row upon row of bodies in the goalmouth.

The dead and the living.

The living and the dead.

3.10 p.m., Semi-Final Saturday.

At 3.15 p.m. a solitary St John's ambulance tries to force its way across a field littered with the stricken and the exhausted, the dead and the dying, pathetic in its isolation.

At 3.20 p.m. a second ambulance makes it no further than the corner flag at the Kop end.

The clock ticks forever onward. He and the others trapped in limbo, wanting to help but penned in, helpless, not able to help. A veil of silence falls over Hillsborough and everybody in it, a veil that settles as realisation and awareness surface in the mind. There are fifty-four thousand people in the ground but he can hear his own shallow breath.

It's 3.36 p.m. on 15th April 1989 before a third ambulance reaches the stricken of Leppings Lane.

It is the end of one era and the beginning of another.

He's still in the office an hour later. In Chris's office, waiting for the telephone, waiting for the hospital.

'You've not been yourself lately, John,' says Chris. Says his mate. 'Why don't you take a few days?'

'I like being busy—'

'Just until you're feeling better.'

Sleet rattling the windows, the head's beloved flag billowing, threatening to tear itself free.

'They'll think you've suspended me.'

'I'll assure the parents you were only concerned with the safety of their children. I can't suspend you for that. So take a few days. Take a week. Then we'll reappraise. Go to the doctor. Get signed off.'

'I'm not ill,' he said.

'Just a week or two. To see you right.'

'Chris…'

'Please, John. The governors will be furious.'

He left the cunt to it, walked back to the Department Office feeling like the whole world knew his business. He closed the door to his classroom and wandered over to the window, stared out at the clouds tumbling in from the coast, at the trees whipping in the wind, at the squalls of rain tearing across the playground. He picked up his briefcase and shut off the lights. Fuck setting cover. They could deal with it. He went to the stockroom, dug out a box of cellophane zip files, nicked the fuckers for his own purposes.

He was wet through by the time he reached his car, a drowned fucking rat scurrying away.

They were talking about Cloughie on the radio again, about legacy and longevity, about forty-four days at Leeds, about why he never got the England job. Talking bollocks. He turned the radio off. He didn't want to hear about it. He sat in the evening traffic, the wiper blades raking at the window, listening to the repetitive motion, drifting away, thinking about his teaching career and how a week or two of sick leave was no great event in the grand scheme of things. There were fuckers in the place who couldn't get through a week without taking a day to get over themselves.

A car horn sounded. The road ahead of him was clear, the traffic stacked up behind. He lurched himself awake, stalled the fucking engine. Another fucking horn. He re-started the engine, turned in the direction of the surgery.

'All fucking right,' he shouted. 'Alright!'

And then he was off up the road in pursuit of another traffic jam, away into the dregs of autumn and its haunting fucking endings.

Nottingham Forest 1 v 0 Sturm Graz
City Ground

Bright lights, big city. It is these things to a twelve-year-old.

The UEFA Cup Quarter-Final.

Fried onions. Cigarettes. People. Lots of people. More than you've ever dreamed of. Bustling. A lot of stairs.

A panoramic view.

The lush green turf. The red and white. A goal. A 1–0 win.

You've never seen anything like it and now that you've seen it you want more.

Germinating seeds send out their little tendrils.

An addiction takes root.

In the car on the way home your dad is listening to the news on the radio, news about the National Coal Board. In the car on the way home your dad is swearing at the radio.

'Bastards,' he says. 'Bloody bastards.'

He walked in to find Kelly sprawled on the sofa. Split fucking shifts.

'What are you doing home?' she asked.

'Signed off.'

'Signed off?'

He gestured his incredulity with a shrug.

'What's the matter?' she asked him, not getting up, not taking her eyes off the shit on the TV. The same old Kelly. All aggression, no fucking sympathy.

'Stress,' he said. 'Let's call it stress.'

'Stress?'

'Fucking hell, Kelly. Stop repeating everything.'

He dumped his bag, wandered through to the kitchen and the kettle, filled it.

'You didn't say anything.'

'Eh?'

'About feeling stressed.'

'I don't feel stressed. I've just been signed off with it.'

'You said you had a sore throat.'

'It's nothing to do with that.'

He clicked the kettle on, took off his jacket and shoes, went to the cupboard and picked out two mugs. She appeared in the doorway.

'Are you having one?'

She nodded.

'Did something happen?'

Kelly. A dog with a bone.

'I swore at some students,' he said. 'In the corridor. At break.'

'Is that all?'

'I shouted in their faces. I pinned one against the wall – the head called me in.'

'And then what…'

'We talked and he suggested I get signed off.'

A roll of the eyes.

'How long?'

'A week. The doctor said a week. To begin with.'

'You've been to the doctor?'

'Briefly,' he said. 'She gave me this.'

He pulled the leaflet out of his back pocket.

Coping with Stress.

'And school gave me this.'

Another fucking leaflet.

Managing Conflict.

Kelly grabbed the thing, laughed, threw it on the table.

'What were they doing?'

'Who?'

'The students.'

'Crushing each other.'

'Something dangerous, then?'

'Yes.'

'And you stopped it?'

'Sort of.'

'And now you're signed off with stress.'

'One of the parents phoned in.'

She shook her head.

'This fucking country's gone mad,' she said. 'You should leave that profession.'

He stiffened.

'It's fucking true. What are you doing if you can't discipline them? There's a fucking real world out there…'

He didn't say anything. What was there to fucking say? He squeezed the tea bag against the side of mug number one, watched the liquid darken, binned it, moved on to mug number two, watched the liquid darken…

'They'll not last five minutes.'

He nodded. He stared at his mug. He stared at the tiles.

'Get a job with adults,' she said. 'Deal with adult situations. Every day you come home with these stories.'

She took her mug and moved into the living room. She was animated, wound up. She placed the mug on the table. Some of the tea spilled over the side of the mug. Her way of caring, to get angry and slam about the place. Her only way.

'I could do with the break,' he said.

'Couldn't we all,' she said. 'Anyway, I have to get ready.'

She picked up the mug again and disappeared upstairs. He heard the bath running, the sound of her footsteps on the landing, in their room, in the spare room, in the room that might one day become the nursery. Her footsteps stopped there for a time, then moved on. He looked down at his bag, at the pile of essays squeezed between his diary and his sandwich box, already knowing the content of each one of them, wondering how much longer he could let the valiant efforts of the few able students carry him through the desperate ramblings of the rest, his mind drifting to the summer house and cardboard boxes. And to Friday, to somewhere he was expected to be, somewhere he didn't want to be.

He heard the bathroom door slam, the lock slip across its runner. He could picture her, staring into the mirror, checking herself out, turning sideways, imagining a different profile. And he needed to talk to her about it. The two of them really needed to sit down and talk about it.

There are places you recognise on the TV every evening, Bilsthorpe and Newstead, Cresswell and Babbington. In these places miners are fighting with miners, miners are fighting with police.

There are mile-long convoys of police vans on the A1. You stand on the road bridge with your pals and watch them pass. You flick the V sign in their direction.

You scarper.

You laugh with your mates.

You're twelve years old.

There's fuck all else to do.

You live in the most boring town in England.

Finchy drove Kelly to her shift. Then he drove her home again. On both journeys, during both legs he waited for her to bring up the subject that was pulverising them, but she didn't. She was fucking thinking about it, though. Of course she was thinking about it. It was all she ever thought about. It wasn't like he had to be a fucking mind reader.

Anderlecht 3 v 0 Forest
(Aggregate 3 v 2)
City Ground

In your little bedroom, portable radio by your side, you are listening to Peter Jones' commentary, to Tottenham squeezing past Hadjuk Split, but hearing only the updates coming from Anderlecht where Forest are toiling in the protection of their 2–0 lead. Lying in bed in the darkness hoping and praying and dreaming, you take the body blows as Forest concede one-two-three goals. You feel the gut-wrenching disappoint-ment as the reporter relays the news of Forest's exit. You're crushed by the harsh cruelty of the penalty that wasn't, the goal that is disallowed, the acrid stench of injustice. You will one day come to learn about the referee, about him being on the take, about the corrupt nature of the game you love. But that day is a long time away.

You are not yet tainted.

You are not yet stained.

You cry yourself to sleep.

It won't be the last time.

Wednesday

He sat up into the small hours, her upstairs and him down-stairs. Fuck all between them sometimes, two isolated lives under one roof.

When he was ready for bed he switched off the lights, went to the back window, looked out at the block of darkness, at the summer house nestled in the shadows.

He felt the creeping of fifteen years.

He climbed the stairs and went to the bathroom, blinked in the brittle light, cleaned his teeth, took a piss, washed his face and hands. Routine, the seam that held a life together. His fucking anchor.

The bedroom was dark, just the glow of the digital radio. 1.23 a.m., the sound of Kelly breathing beneath the covers. He undressed and slipped into bed beside her, lay there on his back, acutely aware of his own heartbeat, the coursing of blood through his veins.

The dark hours, when the door opened a crack and invited him to consider it all.

The black nothingness.

It chilled him. Of course it fucking did. He turned on to his side, to face the wall, closed his eyes, waited for sleep to come.

And inevitably he got to thinking about the back door, about locking the fucking thing, or not locking it.

He resisted the urge. He'd tried the handle before climbing the stairs. He always tried the handle. He had a picture in his mind, of reaching out, of taking the handle in his grip, of feeling the fucking resistance. But was that tonight? Or was it another night? Nights melded into other nights until he couldn't separate one from another.

11th May 1985

Bradford City v Lincoln City
Valley Parade

It's the end of another season. You're at the City Ground and Everton are in town. Everton have just secured the First Division Championship. Up and down the country teams are winning promotion and falling into the relegation mire.

There's a promotion party in Bradford.

Bradford City are Division Three Champions.

It's their first trophy in fifty-six years.

Fathers and sons are there to witness this moment. Grandfathers and grandchildren. Generations of families.

Football as it used to be.

A spring day. The Main Stand full to bursting.

Valley Parade, eleven thousand strong.

Warnings from the council unheeded.

Warnings from the police unheeded.

Warning after warning unheeded.

Bradford City Football Club should clear the litter from under the Main Stand.

The timber construction is a fire hazard. There is a build-up of combustible materials in the voids beneath the seats. A carelessly discarded cigarette could give rise to a fire risk.

Exit from the ground should be achievable in 2.5 minutes.

A club with no money to deal with such things.

A club with part-time owners doing what they can.

The Green Guide is filed away, lost in darkness.

Letters from the County Council are filed away, lost in darkness.

Plans are in place for the future. Plans are in place for major works on the main stand after promotion is secured.

Plans are in place.

But there is a game today and over three and a half thousand people are situated in the Main Stand.

At 3.43 p.m. a single spark is all it takes.

And now smoke is rising from the void beneath the seats.

Black smoke is billowing from the void beneath the seats.

Funnelling.

Toxic.

The wooden Main Stand is a tinderbox.

The Main Stand is seventy-four years old, constructed from wood. The seats are made of wood…

A club with no money.

A spring breeze blowing.

The people that have come to a promotion party are now in serious danger.

… the existing felt roof covering and the areas of decayed boarding…

In the Main Stand the fire is spreading beneath their feet.

In the Main Stand the fire is spreading above their heads.

… an unacceptable fire hazard and should be rectified as soon as possible.

And it takes just four minutes for the fire to engulf the Main Stand.

Four minutes of hell on earth.

Fire above, below and beyond.

… the available exits insufficient to enable escape…

Raging heat.

Burning timber.

Burning bitumen.

A rain of fire.

They die in their seats.

They die in the walkway behind the stand.

They die in the toilets.

Fifty-six die.

On the same day, a fifteen-year-old boy is killed when a wall collapses during rioting between Leeds United and Birmingham City supporters at St Andrews.

On Bob's bus, traipsing back to the old town along the A52, you listen to the radio as it relays its sombre messages. At home that evening you sit and watch footage of the fire on television. You watch again and again and again.

You watch the fans spilling from the stand on to the pitch, hopping over a waist-high perimeter wall.

Like ants from a nest.

You watch a policeman paw at his burning scalp.

You watch grown men rolling on the turf while flames lick at their clothes.

You watch an old man emerge from the flames, a man on fire.

A bewildered burning man.

You watch all of this and you fight back tears.

You have never seen anything like this before and you never want to see anything like this again.

But you will.

Football in 1985.

No place for kids.

But you go anyway.

It's part of what you are and without it you are nothing.

Popplewell publishes his interim inquiry into 'Crowd Safety and Control at Sports Grounds'.

The problem right there in the remit.

Popplewell caught between safety and control, between two incidents that do not bear comparison.

Preoccupied with hooliganism following the incident at St Andrews, comparing the scenes to the Battle of Agincourt.

But lacking understanding.

Urgent consideration should be given by football clubs to introduce a membership system so as to exclude visiting fans.

Unable to square the circle.

Fences around the pitch need not come down though perimeter fences need to have gates in them and the facility to open them in an emergency.

And ignored.

Evacuation procedure should be a matter of police training and form part of the briefing by police officers before a football match...

Bradford.

A 1968 copy of the Telegraph and Argus *pulled out of the cinders.*

Sweet wrappers produced before decimalisation pulled out of the cinders.

Seventeen years of inattention.

A time bomb quietly ticking.

A time bomb exploding.

But no blame for Bradford from Popplewell. No culpability in his report despite the ignored warnings. Bradford City FC and Bradford City Council only forced to take responsibility by the private actions of the victims' families.

The Popplewell Interim Inquiry.

Safety lost to control.

An opportunity missed.

1:40 a.m.

He was wide awake now, more awake than he had been when he came to bed. He pulled the covers off his skin and made his way, naked, exposed, across the room to the landing.

'What are you doing?'

Kelly, agitated. Always fucking agitated.

'Checking the back door,' he said.

'It'll be locked,' she said. 'It's always locked.'

'It might not be.'

'What time is it?'

'It doesn't matter. Go to sleep.'

'I was asleep.'

He heard her sigh, heard her swear under her breath. He reached the top of the stairs. No fucking need to drag this out. No fucking need to make an issue of it. He trotted down the stairs two at a time to the back door, reached for the handle, forced it down, met the resistance.

It was locked then.

He cursed, climbed the stairs, got halfway up and felt the urge to go and check one last time. He fought that urge, knowing how ludicrous it was, ground out two further steps then turned and made his way back down again. Drifting across the carpet he reached into the darkness, took the handle in both hands, wrapped his fingers around it, took a mental photograph of the moment, two hands on the cold metal, fingers interlocked, a grainy image of his naked self in the French windows. He turned the handle with all the energy he could muster, felt no give at all. Of course there was no fucking give. Of course there wasn't.

He climbed the stairs again, reached the landing, stopped there, his head full, a blur of thoughts.

There are hordes of bodies, you at their centre. Blue-lipped people with swollen faces stare into your eyes, through your eyes, at a place beyond. There's a tightening, a constriction. You wake gasping for breath, your chest on fire.

But it isn't over. They come out of the darkness, out of the walls, out of a black tunnel. They pile into you in unending numbers. They collapse on to you. They call your name in desperate, weakening voices.

Naked, tracing his fingers up and down the backs of his arms, across his shoulders, feeling his skin, picking, busying himself with blemishes, drifting off into some netherworld where thoughts wrestled for attention without ever becoming thoughts and memories surfaced without ever becoming memories. Time became timeless, meaning meaningless. He remained like that, naked on the landing, shivering with cold, arms and shoulders scratched and reddened, muscles tight and twisted, cock shrivelled to nothing, his head running at incredible speed, repeating itself, reaching overload. There was just the automotive action of his busy fingers.

And he wasn't there.

He wasn't fucking anywhere.

The summer after Hillsborough.

Top floor of National Express, en route to Torquay.

Just you and the boys.

The Stone Roses on the stereo.

I Wanna Be Adored.

'What the fuck would you want to be a door for?'

'Adored you daft fuck. Adored.'

Or is it Newquay?

No fucking sunshine either way, just football on the beach, endless fucking crazy golf and pissed-up evenings.

And birds. Chasing birds. On Fistral and Tolcarne, down Bank Street and Central Street, into the early hours, a relentless quest to make the holiday mean something, for it to carry some of the burden.

Or is it fucking Torquay?

Hanging out at Castle Circus, chasing the foreign birds. Seeing it in the fucking papers and magazines each and every day.

Story after story.

Image after image.

Bloated faces pressed against wire mesh fencing.

Seeing it and thinking 'I was there. I was fucking there' and telling the girls at Castle Circus and nobody giving a shit and showing them the pictures and the girls turning their faces to the ground and telling you to be a happy boy and the lads calling you a miserable bastard for dwelling on the subject and chasing the girls away.

Memories swamping your head. Memories threatening to sink you.

The rot setting in.

Even then.

He snapped out of himself, shuffled in the direction of the bedroom. The hall light came on. Kelly appeared, on her way to the bathroom.

2.10 a.m.

'You should see someone about that,' said Kelly when she climbed back into bed. 'Sixteen fucking minutes you were stood there. I sat here and watched you. It's not fucking normal.'

He blinked in the darkness.

Sixteen minutes lost to a slice of something that was nothing.

3.05 a.m.

The sound of a freight train inching its way through the city. The clack and clank of the trucks, the whine and squeal of the brakes. He listened to them dissolve into the darkness, listened to his own beating heart.

Years passing like days, a life racing away.

He turned on his side, watched the breeze flirt with the curtains, the window open to let the air in, Kelly's pet hate, his unconditional need. Alongside all of the others: his routine at bedtime; cleaning the house prior to leaving it; tagging 'all being well' on to every arrangement; sleeping on the right side of the bed. He told himself it was his broken nose but he knew the truth of it.

Averseness to sleep.

Sleep reduced to necessity.

He climbed out of bed, his bare feet nestling on soft carpet, wandered silently down the stairs to the dining room, to the French windows, slid them open, reached high on the shelf for the cigarette packet Kelly kept there, fumbled for the lighter. He didn't smoke, had never smoked, only the odd drag when he could think of nothing else to do with himself. And so he lit the cigarette in the doorway, stepped outside on to the decking, felt the chill in the air.

He took a drag on the cigarette, coughed, took another, coughed again. He looked across at the shed, thinking of the box and its contents, its collection of translucent days. He thought about the lads and how long it had been since he last thought of them. He thought about Cloughie.

A man amongst men.

Cloughie shooting two fingers at the Trent end when Nicholas was stricken versus the Arsenal.

Cloughie and his fucking random programme notes.

Cloughie and his presence.

No fucking nonsense Cloughie.

The night was cold. He was stood on the decking with a cigarette he didn't want. There was fuck all else happening, no fucking moon, no fucking stars. He half-willed Cloughie to turn up, Cloughie in his fucking green sweater, the scruffy bastard.

But nobody came.

He took a final drag on the cigarette, coughed, stared down at the lawn. Nothing stirred. There wasn't anything in the darkness except his past. He retreated inside, locked up and climbed the stairs, went back to bed.

'What are you doing now?' asked Kelly.

'I can't sleep.'

'Go downstairs then.'
'I've been downstairs. Now I'm back.'
'You stink of fags.'
'I had—'
'Fucking disgusting habit,' she said.
'… one of yours.'

29th May 1985

Liverpool v Juventus
Heysel Stadium, Brussels

Wednesday. You ride your bike up through the estate to Gav's place. A quiet evening bathed in soft sunlight, full of the promise of summer. You're breathless with excitement, set fully on the spectacle.

Tonight will be Tardelli, Platini, Rossi and Boniek.

Tonight will be Grobbelaar, Hansen, Dalglish and Rush.

And Heysel.

Tonight will be Heysel.

One word.

Heysel.

A word that will blemish the English game.

But you're thirteen years old tonight. You are glued to a portable TV in your mate's bedroom. You are just boys, staring at the TV, waiting for a football match, staring instead at running battles on decrepit terraces, at missiles raining down on cowering policemen, at a wall collapsing and people dying.

You're numb with shock, numb with shame.

The game is an afterthought. You're not sure what to do, whether to watch it or turn away from the screen.

You cycle back as night's coming on, the estate quiet now, full of menace. You go to bed feeling bemused, understanding there is no way of knowing what's coming at you, no way of preparing.

In the darkness the thought chills you to your bones.

You're just a boy.

The blackest days are ahead.

Because there are episodes where some horrific calamity plays out before your eyes. You're locked in a cage, your eyes taped open, forced to witness it all, unable to do anything, unable to influence the outcome. Anguished people beg you to help them but you are powerless to come to their aid. One by one they collapse in front of the metal bars that contain you. They lay, row upon row, on a carpet of green baize.

The clock reverses an hour.

The episode begins all over again.

Another day mooching about the house. Kelly at work. Kelly home. In the evening everything kicking off again.

'I spoke to Mike,' she said.

'What?'

'I spoke to Mike, about the other day. I called him.'

'He's walking on eggshells. He'll exaggerate everything,' he said. 'You know how these things work.'

'Mike said they have it on film. Mike said it wasn't very pleasant. Those were his exact words.'

He moved away from her, across the room towards the sofa, keeping his distance.

'Not-very-pleasant,' she said, stressing each syllable like it meant something.

'Fuck off, Kelly,' he said.

'It's a miracle it hasn't made the papers,' she said.

Mike's machinery clicking into gear. Closing fucking shop on him. He puffed out his cheeks.

'That's over-dramatic,' he said.

In truth, he couldn't remember much about it, just the big lads, the rest toppling and tumbling into one another, legs, arms, torsos. And screams. Shrill, involuntary screams. Hollowed-out fucking screams. Swimming-bath screams. Him a helpless bystander. The big lads laughing, cracking up, two of them legging it but the third holding his ground, gagging for a confrontation, him shouting down the corridor, the lad bigging it up, the two of them chin to fucking chin.

Him and the lad.

The lad and him.

Billy Stubbs and John fucking Finch.

In the corridor. In the camera's eye.

And then everything falling away. A void.

Dark fucking matter.

Kelly standing in the doorway to the kitchen, looking high and mighty, like he had some burden to bear that would damage the both of them, like she was tied to his shame.

'It'll not be a week,' she said.

'It'll be fine.'

'It might be weeks and weeks.'

'It won't be.'

'What if they sack you?'

'They won't sack me.'

'What if they take your teaching licence away?'

'They won't do that either. Nothing happened.'

He could see her dropping out, see the faraway look in her eye. He was pushing all the buttons, aggravating her to 'tilt'.

But he couldn't fucking help himself.

'Whose side are you on, Kelly?' he asked at last.

'How about the mortgage? Or the fucking credit card? How about I'm on their side? And you being the man I moved in with instead of the miserable bastard you've become.'

He felt the bad stuff rip through him, the two of them adept at crucifying each other.

'Something's going on,' she said. 'I've not seen you like this before.'

'Nothing's going on.'

She turned away from him.

'Kelly,' he said. 'Kelly…'

He could tell her now, he realised, tell her everything. Tell her about the phone call, about Clough and Stimmo, the whole fucking mess. Maybe she'd listen. And perhaps if she listened she'd understand. But she wouldn't fucking listen and she wouldn't understand because people didn't understand. They carried the burden on their own terms, slotted it in a neat little place of their own design and chose to leave it there. It didn't matter if that person was a pal, a parent or a fucking fiancée.

Brussels
   A hot day in May.
   Serene outside Brussel-Centraal station.
   Peaceful on rue de la Montagne.
   Not so in the Grote Markt, the central square.
   The Grote Markt occupied by two thousand fans.
   Fans bathing in the fountains of the Grote Markt.
   The Grote Markt swamped with beer.
   The Grote Markt littered with broken glass.
   A carnival atmosphere or the first sparks of a riot.
   One drunk fan in a dress-up police hat directing traffic.
   Fans robbing. Fans pillaging.
   A stand-off with the police.
   Tear gas and trouble.
   In the streets surrounding the stadium.
   A ban on the sale of alcohol not enforced.
   Bar upon bar making the most of the opportunity.
   Fans drinking their beer.
   Fans singing their songs.
   The police watching on.
   Two cordons of token security checks.
   Fans with genuine tickets.
   Fans with forged tickets.
   Fans without tickets.
   Two cordons of nonchalant, blasé policemen and baying police dogs.
   Too easy.
   At the turnstiles.
   Fans using their tickets.
   Fans passing tickets back to fans waiting outside.
   Fans paying cash for entry.
   Holes in the cinder block perimeter wall, holes big enough for
grown men to push through.
   A fractured water pipe.
   A sea of mud.
   A mess.

Inside the stadium.

The Liverpool sections packed to their limit.

Two sweltering cesspits.

Belgian police pelted with missiles by Italian fans.

Twenty-seven Belgian police injured by flying debris.

The temperature rising as the temperature falls.

Fans with genuine tickets.

Fans with forged tickets.

Fans without tickets.

Liverpool fans.

Juventus fans.

And neutral fans.

Neutral sections for neutral fans occupied by the partisan.

Neutral section Z occupied by Italian fans.

Neutral section Z placed beside Liverpool sections X and Y.

Cricket-ball-sized stones littering the crumbling terraces.

Perfect ammunition for those inclined.

An exchange of missiles.

From section Z into section Y.

From section Y into section Z.

Flares and rockets.

Rockets and flares.

Provocation and fighting on the terracing.

A free-for-all.

Three waves of assault on section Z from section Y.

A wall collapses.

A poorly constructed wall.

Thirty-nine people die in the crush.

Thirty-two Italians, four Belgians, two French people and one person from Northern Ireland die.

Hooligans are to blame.

History is to blame.

Twenty years of terrace culture is to blame.

Indiscriminate ticket touting is to blame.

Poor policing is to blame.

Poor crowd management is to blame.

Poor stadium maintenance is to blame.

But UEFA absolve themselves of ignoring the warnings, of staging a match in an arena unworthy of the role.

A condemned structure crumbling to pieces.

A ground in an advanced state of decay.

Such a stadium hosting the centrepiece of the season.

The European Cup Final.

Chicken-wire fencing separating rival supporters while Rome 84 still burns in the blood.

A request from Liverpool CEO Peter Robinson to have the game moved due to safety concerns filed in a drawer.

The Belgian police absolve themselves of not employing the manpower, of inertia, of not knowing how to handle a football match on such a scale, of not understanding what the fuck to do when two sets of fans turn on each other.

English football is on its knees, bruised and bleeding from open wounds.

UEFA observer Gunter Schneider sticks the boot in and the bitch in the blue dress draws the knife.

Liverpool FC shoulders responsibility for the actions of hooligans.

The city of Liverpool shoulders responsibility for the actions of hooligans.

English football shoulders the blame for the actions of hooligans.

English clubs are banned from European competition.

Up and down the country fans are treated with contempt. They're the scum of the earth, the dregs of a nation. An honest supporter is a thug taking a day off.

There's a war on football.

Much, much later a Belgian judge concludes that blame should not rest solely with English fans and that some culpability lays with the police and authorities.

Fourteen supporters are convicted of involuntary manslaughter.

UEFA officials are threatened with imprisonment but receive conditional discharges. A member of the Belgian Football Union is charged with regrettable negligence. A Belgian police captain who made fundamental errors is charged with negligence. Both receive a six-month suspended sentence.

But this is much, much later.

And the damage is already done.

In all sorts of ways.

Thursday

When he reached the bedroom she was sleeping. Of course she was, it was 3 a.m. for fuck's sake. He slipped into bed next to her, lay there for ten minutes unable to find any sort of restfulness. Lying on his back he felt the weight of the duvet against his chest, the obvious presence of his beating heart. He felt the blood rushing through his body, felt it in his limbs, his toes and fingers. He heard it racing through his head in pulsing torrents. He thought about cut-off points, about when a life starts and when a life ends, about when a life is and when a life isn't. He looked at the clock on the dresser.

3.13 a.m.

He thought about a solitary St John's ambulance threading its way through a disaster zone, a policeman lifting the corner flag from its berth, a second policeman tearing along at the ambulance's flank. A solitary St John's ambulance soon mobbed by the desperate and the distraught.

A single St John's ambulance.

He pictured the Liverpool skyline, the two Liver birds, the monolithic cathedral, the gates of Anfield draped in scarves that hung like tears, a carpet of grief on the sacred turf.

The dark of the room unsettled him. He listened to the trains shunting around the station, tried to search for an away day, any day that wasn't that day, a day with a happy ending. He couldn't locate one.

He turned to look at Kelly, the familiar outline of her turned-away shoulder.

The two of them lost in the darkness.

Again.

Tragedy after tragedy.

Warning after warning unheeded.

Stairway 13, Ibrox. 1961.

Two fatalities.

Stairway 13, Ibrox. 1967.

Eleven injured.

Stairway 13, Ibrox. 1969.

Twenty-nine injured.

Stairway 13, Ibrox. 1971

Sixty-six fatalities.

Judge Smith's chilling verdict.

'The board would appear to have proceeded with the view that if the problem was ignored long enough it would eventually go away.'

Tragedy after tragedy.

Warning after warning.

Kelly sniffed. He noticed her breathing had changed, that she was awake as he was awake, locked in her own thoughts.

'Kelly...' he whispered.

'What?'

Agitated. Again.

'Kelly?'

'What do you want?'

'I want you to love me,' he said.

He just came out with it, like that, could hardly believe it himself.

'What does that mean?'

'I want you to empathise with me,' he said. 'Just the once. I want to know that it's possible for you to do that.'

The darkness had him. Somehow it was spiralling and hurtling around him, a fucking maelstrom. He was trapped at its centre. He could hear the discomfort in her voice as she responded, Kelly thrown off balance, the two of them teetering on the brink of two different lives, two separate pathways, neither of them prepared for that.

Not yet. Not yet.

'You're incapable of loving me,' she said. 'Why should I love you?'

'No,' he said. 'I'm just incapable of saying it.'

'So you love me?'

'Fucking hell, Kelly,' he said.

'Tell me you love me…'

'Shut up. You're not listening.'

'Say it,' she said. 'If you really feel it, then say it.'

'You've fucking turned it around,' he said. 'You always turn it around.'

And that's what she did. Just like Cloughie, turned defence into attack in the blink of an eye. Slick. Sublime. Ruthless. The irony was fucking blinding.

He climbed out of bed, pulled on his T-shirt and boxers, moved across the room, out on to the landing, down the stairs, heard her shouting after him.

'Say it! Say it!'

He pushed open the doors and stepped out into the garden, took himself off to the summer house, shut himself away. For a while he was alone with it all, his head a mess, his hands shaking, his heart beating at ten to the fucking dozen. Then she appeared in the doorway, wrapped up in his Paul Smith cardigan, quieter now, calmer, almost understanding.

'Why can't you say it?' she asked him.

He shook his head. He stared at the box of programmes, picked his way absently through the pile that was 88–89, seeking it out. The FA Cup Semi-Final 1989. Liverpool v Nottingham Forest. Hillsborough. He turned it over in his hands, considering that this item and nothing else in his possession had witnessed what he had witnessed. He almost forgot Kelly was there.

'John,' she said.

'It's not in me to say it,' he said. 'Not to you or anybody.'

'That doesn't make it better,' she said. 'How does that make it any better when you're talking to your fiancée?'

He felt himself shaking. He stared at his quivering fingers, at the pages of the programme shivering in the damp air. He couldn't leave them out here, he realised. He had to bring them back inside, look after them, allow them access to the world he inhabited.

'Look at you. Look at how cold you are. Come inside,' she said.

'It's not the cold,' he said, but she was already on the garden path, already walking away from him, back towards the house. He replaced the programme in the pile, packed the piles back into their boxes, carried the boxes across the garden into the house. When he reached the lounge she was waiting for him.

'What the fuck do you do out there, anyway?'

He walked past her into the kitchen, placed the boxes on the table. She followed him.

'Come on. What do you do out there that's so fucking interesting it's better than sitting in here next to me.'

'I don't want to watch TV,' he said.

'What?'

'You watch TV and I don't want to watch it.'

'Except that when I fuck off to bed, then you'll come inside and watch the thing.'

'It's just on,' he said. 'I don't watch it.'

'No, you just sit up half of the night, staring into space. You could come to bed with me.'

'I don't need much sleep,' he said. 'You know how I am.'

He felt exposed in the brightness of the kitchen, the subject of a fucking lab experiment. He opened the fridge and fished about, not really looking for anything, simply trying not to look at her, not to have his eyes meet her eyes, expecting her to go to the boxes on the table, fish about, start asking questions. But she didn't.

'You're a useless prick these days,' she said. 'A fucking useless prick. I'm not talking about sleeping!'

And then she was gone. He heard her storming up the stairs, heard the bedroom door slam shut.

He went into the hallway, grabbed his school bag, dug out the pile of cellophane zip files he'd nicked from the stockroom, carried them back to the kitchen. He sat at the table and started the job of filing his programmes, one cellophane wrapper for each, a protective cell to keep everything in place, to prevent the past from spilling everywhere and making a mess, to protect the present from the things coming its way. He turned his head to look at the kitchen clock.

It was 3.50 a.m.

It didn't matter what the time was.

Are there fifty thousand others like you?
    Fifty thousand souls going through this again and again?
    Night after night when the lights go out?
    Fifty thousand living it over and over again?

In the morning. Kelly on afternoon shift. Kelly slamming around the house, making her fucking statement. He stayed in bed out of the way, drifting in and out of himself, fighting the rushes when they came. A war of attrition. Later, when he ventured down, she was sat in the living room watching Jeremy Kyle. He wondered what the fuck had happened to her, the woman who once kept him up all night analysing the set design and social commentary of Fritz Lang's *Metropolis*. Kelly who once loved the movies of David fucking Lynch.

Kelly and her adult situations. She worked in telesales for fuck's sake, managed a bunch of lads and lasses in their twenties, managed their behaviour, their absenteeism, their prospects. Or lack of them. There was hardly a difference between his job and hers. And now their routine was set out of joint, neither of them knowing what to do with themselves, fresh wounds festering.

But Jeremy fucking Kyle. It niggled at him until he couldn't help himself.

'This is what you get up to on your day off?'

'It's not my day off. I'm in at eleven.'

'Even so…'

'It's just on,' she said. 'Background noise.'

'While you do what?'

'While I wonder what happened to my fucking life…'

Just like that. A short and sharp stab to the ribs. Kelly at her cutting worst.

Multiple fucking stab wounds on his person, on his wretched cadaver.

He left her to it, took the bus into town, wandered in and out of bookshops and charity shops, killing minutes, playing for time, running down the clock, one minute after another, acutely conscious of their passing. When he was done, when he had no imagination left to play with he took himself back to the house, made himself useful by cooking up some pasta, left Kelly's in the fridge in case she fancied a bite when she got home. Humdrum stuff. Nothing extraordinary about any of it. But trying. Trying to retreat his ten yards and forget about Stimmo and every fucking thing else.

He watched his own daytime TV, observed the clock on the Sky menu tick on and on towards nightfall, watched the sky darken beyond the French windows, considered where the fuck another day of life had disappeared to.

To the local pub then. To a replay of some Premiership game on the TV. Villa versus Palace. Hardly fucking inspiring. A smattering of souls in the place, the football an afterthought. In between glances at the barmaid, he watched the match over the top of his pint, trying to claw back some interest. But it wasn't the same, would never be the same, would only be different in ways that made others baulk and laugh and pour scorn because they didn't know about the edge, the raw energy, the chipped paint, the crumbling concrete, the cages. They didn't know about Derby at the Baseball Ground in clinging drizzle, crammed into the away end, piss wet through but pissing on the fucking sheep. They didn't know about Maine Road on a filthy Wednesday evening, 0–3 down at half-time, Loftus Road when the chips were down, Selhurst Park in the snow. They didn't know. They hadn't lived those days. They weren't fucking there.

And so he watched Villa versus Palace and watched the barmaid until he'd had enough then wandered back home to find the house empty. He nipped upstairs, pulled out the laptop, clicked through to some pictures of Kelly displaying her wares, worse for drink and up for a bit, thought about what his chances were of taking more pictures like that, a fresh batch, knowing it would be a while, knowing it might be never, knowing that the way they were he'd be lucky to catch a glimpse of her bare arse, let alone have the thing shoved in his camera lens.

And all he was really doing was delaying the inevitable, delaying packing his bag, folding his suit into it, stepping out of the house and out of the close in the direction of the station, delaying a journey he'd put off for fifteen years. With nowhere left to turn he found himself searching the boxes for his old DVDs, Goals of the Season, Champions of Europe, stuff like that. He carried them back to the living room, laid himself out on the carpet, slipped the first one in the pile into the machine, dropped seamlessly into another era.

In the past it might have been a porno.

In the past.

The Football League receives £6.3 million for a two-year TV rights deal.

Conservative Member of Parliament and Luton Town chairman David Evans introduces a membership scheme at Kenilworth Road.

Luton Town bans away supporters for the start of the 1986–87 season instigated by hooliganism during a home game versus Millwall in 1985.

But you live for your away days.

You hate David Evans and you hate Luton Town.

You hate their plastic pitch.

There is talk of the ban spreading to all football clubs.

There is talk of banning away fans from every ground in the country.

But football strikes back.

Luton Town are thrown out of the League Cup.

And you obtain a membership card for Luton Town.

You visit Luton Town to support your team.

You applaud your team off the field at Kenilworth Road.

You have defeated David Evans and you will defeat him again because some things are worth fighting for. The membership system will not be forced upon you. You will not allow that to happen.

You're a fucking working-class hero.

By five he'd made his decision. He'd shoot straight up to the
old town that evening, get a hotel, attend the service and shoot
home again. He packed his bag and stuck it in the hall, fixed
the enamel badge to the lapel of his suit and folded it away. He
was contemplating writing a note to Kelly when he heard the
key in the lock.

Fuck.

He considered making a bolt for the back door, sneaking
around the side of the house and legging it. Instead he listened
to the sound of her heels coming to a halt on laminate, the
sound of her muttering to herself.

'John?'

He kept his mouth shut, uncertain whether to make light of
it or lay it on thick. From the living room came the sound of
the TV, still showing the goals of the eighties, Psycho banging
one in from outside the box versus Ipswich.

'John?'

'Yep?'

Casual. Forced. Ridiculous.

She opened the door, looked him up and down, saw straight
through him.

'What's the bag for?'

'The bag?'

Pathetic.

'The bag in the hall.'

'Just some things,' he said.

'Some things?'

'Some things I need.'

'For what?'

'I'm going away...'

'Fuck off.'

'I have to,' he said.

Liberated. Shit scared.

'Where?'

Her posture stiffened. He imagined how it would be if he

tried to push past her, if he went for the bag and the door. He didn't move a muscle.

'Just away,' he said.

'For how long?'

He shrugged.

'Forever?'

He shook his head. Not forever. Surely not forever.

'If it's not forever you can tell me where you're going.'

His head a pitch invasion now, cunts running in all directions, climbing the floodlights, clambering over the scoreboard, dangling from it. A fucking mess.

'It's for a few days,' he said.

'If it's another woman you can fuck off now and not bother coming back.'

He glanced out of the kitchen window. Two kids were kicking a football up and down the street in the twilight. He could hear the smack of leather on tarmac.

'Is it?' she said.

'Is it what?'

'A woman.'

'No,' he said. 'Of course it's not. It's no big deal.'

She clocked the notepad on the table.

'Were you going to leave without telling me?'

He shook his head.

'You're a liar,' she said.

She looked him up and down, really seeing him now, really taking him in.

'Why are you wearing that?'

She pointed at his shirt.

'You never wear things like that.'

He shrugged.

'I found it in the attic.'

'You're going to football? Is that it? What is this, some lads' weekend? A stag do? You don't have to keep it a secret.'

'Can I tell you when I get back?'

She pursed her lips.

'Do what you like,' she said. Then she turned and slammed the kitchen door behind her. He heard her thundering up the stairs. Somewhere in that whirlwind moment, her heels must have come off.

He wondered what the hell he was thinking.

Warning after warning unheeded.

Hillsborough 81. Leppings Lane.

The FA Cup Semi-Final.

Tottenham v Wolves.

Congestion at the Leppings Lane turnstiles and crushing on the confined outer concourse results in the opening of exit gate C and serious crushing on the terraces.

Thirty-eight injured.

The police suggest reducing the capacity of Leppings Lane.

'Bollocks,' says Wednesday Chairman Bert McGee. 'No one would have been killed.'

The introduction of lateral fencing reduces movement into the side pens.

Inadequate and poorly recorded inspections.

No revised safety certificate.

The introduction of further lateral fencing creates two central pens.

Sideways movement is reduced.

Recommendations to feed fans directly from designated turnstiles into each pen are not acted upon, rendering the turnstile counters irrelevant. The 1 in 6 gradient tunnel breaches the recommendations of the Green Guide but is deemed not to be a safety risk.

No mass admission anticipated.

No information available regarding crowd distribution between pens or the capacity of each pen.

The width of the perimeter fence gates well below the standard recommended in the Green Guide.

And warning after fucking warning.

Hillsborough 87.

The FA Cup Quarter-Final between Sheffield Wednesday and Coventry City. Tightly compressed away supporters in the central pens of Leppings Lane are pulled to the safety of the upper tier.

The FA Cup Semi-Final.

Coventry v Leeds.

Leeds fans unable to raise their arms above their heads due to crushing on the Leppings Lane terrace. Leeds fans pulled to the safety of the upper tier.

Hillsborough 88.

Liverpool v Nottingham Forest.

Your Nottingham Forest.

No updated safety certificate.

Access to the tunnel closed prior to kick-off.

Fans redirected to the side pens.

But there's still crushing in the central pens.

Fans collapsing.

Fans fainting.

It's impossible to breathe.

In April, 1988.

Considerable concern for personal safety.

Some Liverpool fans vow never to enter Leppings Lane again.

At Hillsborough.

On the Leppings Lane terrace.

In April, 1988.

The Safety Certificate's stuck in a drawer, out of date and out of mind.

Nobody wants to be reminded of the Safety Certificate.

Nobody's listening.

Heading north through the heartland, north through the patchwork. Heading to the old town. Kelly's screams in his head. The two of them in the bedroom. That cutting tongue of hers. Her in that towel. Fresh out of the shower. Her naked shoulders. Her wet skin. Her wrists slipping from his grip.

The two of them in the bedroom, wrestling, grappling, fighting.

Truly fighting.

The same piece of track. Sunday, 9th April 1989. Heading home from Wembley. League Cup Winners. First trophy in a decade. With the boys all the way, Chester, Coventry, Leicester, QPR, Bristol fucking City, a sun-drenched Sunday in London town, stuffing the holders, stuffing the Hatters.

Psycho in his little white hat.

Forest on a fucking roll. Confidence soaring. Tearing all and sundry to shreds. Seventeen wins in twenty-two games.

Cloughie clasping his hands, punching the air. A lone figure on the dog track, skirting the celebrations, slipping down the tunnel and away.

One job done.

They'd criticised him, the daft bastards, for sloping off like that, but they didn't fucking understand. They didn't see the bigger picture. Let the players have their fifteen minutes, then get on with things. There was so much more. There was Hillsborough for fuck's sake, the FA Cup.

One big job left to do.

Kelly naked on the bed, the towel at her feet, her head buried in the pillow. Him breathless in the doorway, shocked at himself.

Lads on the 19.00 out of King's Cross, revelling in it, the stuff of dreams. Spilling into the aisle, dancing the miles away. Conga up and down the carriages, blokes joining blokes, strangers united, five, ten, twenty deep, up the train and back again. Even the fucking guard joining in, the rest of the passengers laughing along, a party on the 19.00 King's Cross to Leeds.

Sunday evening. 9th April 1989.

Party time.

'Let's all have a disco, La la la la La la la la…'

And they did.

Fifteen fucking years. He could see them all, half expected the door to slide open, the lads to come barrelling down the carriage, lads and lads and lads and lads, each in their colours, loving the crack.

He could see them all.

A train full of ghosts.

A movie reel beyond the window. Lights flashing by. The train thundering onward. A tin of lager at his lips.

The bittersweet taste of what once was and what is.

Invisible death looming on a black horizon.

A perpetual shadow.

Then and now.

Now and then.

And in another dark corner, their bedroom door shut fast. Him on the dark landing, retreating down the stairs, leaving it behind.

Leaving Kelly behind.

The landscape gathered itself in. Familiar villages he recognised by patterns of street lights, the meandering river somewhere in the darkness, the red warning lights on the waterworks, the old factories convulsing in their death throes, the glow of halogen spotlights protecting the asset strippers' bounty from the pilfering hands of the discarded and forgotten. Rows and rows of dark terraced houses beyond the window on his side of the train, well-lit commuter estates beyond the other.

Polarised fucking opposites.

The old town.

Dismantling the bedrock. Burying its foundations. A twenty-year process of decay, of living and dying … and dying … and dying.

A legacy of ruin in the manufacturing heartlands.

A mirror to the soul.

He walked out of the station, down the incline and into the old town, his footsteps leading the way, the rest of him following, straight to the hotel, straight to his hotel room, his hotel bed, exhausted from his journey, from his week, from the news about Stimmo, from all that had happened with Kelly.

He stroked the scratches on his forearms.
He winced with pain.

You're fifteen years old. You are travelling to Leicester. You have a ticket
to the biggest derby game of the season.

And there's no fucking love lost either.

It's a nasty day to watch a football match. It's a nasty fucking place.

And it will rain burning toilet rolls.

Off the stinking train, out of the station.

Get in, get out, fuck them about.

Into a wall of police. Penned against the station wall, pressed into half
a pavement. Held there for an hour.

'Let us go…'

'You're not going anywhere.'

'We're here for the game.'

'You'll watch the game when we say so.'

A bitter, antagonising hour.

'This is a joke.'

'I can't see anybody laughing. Stand there and shut up.'

Treat them like animals. Herd them like animals.

Down the fucking High Street. Shoppers cowering in doorways.

Strangers in a strange land.

Invaders and raiders.

Through the industrial estate, floundering, on its knees. Lads and
more lads, blokes and more blokes. Wound up. Acting up. The escort
rocking and rolling, pulsing, throbbing. The fucking buzz of it. The noto-
riety. The adrenalin rush. Black fucking polo shirt, scarf covering the
face, bellowing out the Forest sound.

The mad fuckers with their missiles.

The bricks and the mortar.

The splinter of windows.

The shiver and shatter of glass.

The cheers.

The laughter.

Singing working its way down the line, voice catching voice.

Red Army! Red Army!

'Stop singing or I'll arrest you.'

'What for?'

'Because I can. And take that scarf off.'

2 p.m. on a Saturday.

'Wipe that fucking grin off your face.'

We are Nottingham, I said we are Nottingham..

Penned by great fuck-off horses and dogs and big fuck-off policemen. Marched like prisoners.

To the turnstiles. The click and the clack. The rust and decay. Into the guts, into the away end. A terrace fit for dogs or the criminally insane. All metal and wire mesh. Cigarette smoke, beer, piss, the home fuckers baying for blood. Three hours of chanting, at the pitch, at the home end, at life itself.

The throat red raw.

Every fucking Saturday.

Penned like fucking fish in a can. Forest scoring. Forest going mental. Leicester scoring. Leicester going mental. Leicester scoring again and again.

Windows at the back of the away end.

Prime fucking targets.

Police in the pen. Everything kicking off. Police dragging some poor fucker down the concrete steps, his clothes riding up, dragging him down the pen on his backside, hearing the poor bastard shriek, seeing the skin tear clean to the bone.

Somewhere beyond the heads and the mouths and the fists, somewhere beyond the fences and spikes and mesh, a football match on a green velvet carpet.

No fucker taking any notice.

You are fifteen years old. You go to Goodison Park, to Highfield Road, White Hart Lane, Carrow Road and Villa Park. You visit Selhurst Park on a cold Wednesday evening, a two hundred and forty mile round trip, six of you crammed into a Ford Granada. You go to Vicarage Road, Old Trafford and Anfield. Up the country, down the country, through the streets and alleys.

The broken-backed blur of Thatcher's Britain beyond the windows.
Week in, week out.
Living for football.
Living for the crack.
The foookin crack.
School on the Monday. What a fucking joke. A bunch of naïve virgin fucks who don't have a clue about life or how to live it.

'What did you do at the weekend?'

'I was at Filbert Street and in the dirty Leicester streets with five thousand Forest, watching fuckers bleed for the cause.'

'Why, what the fuck were you doing?'

Friday

The same weather, bright and cold, the same fucking chapel. He'd not been there since a road accident killed an ex-schoolmate. He'd not had cause to go back.

But BJ and that fucking phone call. Cunt.

We're suffering here so you can suffer too.

And fuck me, he was suffering.

He had every best intention, got up in plenty of time, ate breakfast in the hotel, got his black suit on, pulled his tie straight, strolled purposefully down into the old town, over the river and past his old gaff, altered now, the clock shop gone, developed as a flat, an extension of the ground floor where the Scotsman used to live, some fucking modern planning arrangement designed to squeeze people into spaces and money into fat wallets. And it was just a hundred yards from there, the length of a fucking football pitch. He could see the black gates, the driveway leading up to the arch, the chapel beyond, and if he'd been pressed for time perhaps he'd have headed straight up there, found himself a seat at the back somewhere, made himself part of something he really was no longer part of. But he wasn't late. He was too fucking early by any measure. He had time to think and to revisit his doubts.

They strangled the life out of him.

He continued down to the river instead, stopping at the bridge, wrestling with guilt, telling himself it was better this way, to take a moment, to gather his thoughts, to arrive at the last minute and avoid the inevitable onslaught of bitter glances and barbed questions.

Bitter and barbed for what? For fucking off down south and leaving them to it?

Too right, serri. Too fucking right.

The river was deathly quiet, no sign of life on the water, some old guy in the allotment burning off the dead and the dying, the rotten and the wasted, black smoke rising in a thin plume, drifting up and away. An old gal came down the path. He felt her eyes on him, him in his suit, his shined shoes, his dew-glazed hair looking like fucking Brylcreem. But he wasn't a ghost. She could see him better than that, he realised. She knew what he was and what he fucking wasn't.

He looked down at the water, at the sluice gates holding everything back. Black thoughts started spilling in, trapping him between moments.

Dark water rising.

The river become a river of people moving inexorably towards a tunnel, trailing into a dark space where there was no space, filling an area that was already full, compressing and solidifying there.

The dead and the living, the living and the dead. The dead standing up. Blue lips. Vacant expressions. Lifeless eyes. The lights going out.

And Stimmo shouting over his head, shouting the same fucking thing over and over.

'That one's dead, mate. I'm telling you he's fucking dead.'

A look on Stimmo's face then, a look that etched itself on to him, became part of the person Stimmo was after that day, if he remembered it right, if he could be trusted to comprehend anything about the life he'd lived.

Stimmo. There and gone.

He didn't go to the service. Did he fuck as like. He wandered the streets of the old town instead, feeling the separation of fifteen years, registering the changes.

For better.

For worse.

The corner garage transformed into a drive-through take-away. Half the factory site already given over to housing association dwellings, clean bricked, neatly shrubbed, soulless.

The fleapit nightclub, his old stomping ground, gone. No trace of its shell or its footing in the earth but the topography the same, the stretch up to the town hall littered with the old and the new, with names he recognised on shop fronts and pub signs and vans, and names he didn't know at all. A supermarket where the old town football ground used to stand. Nothing to remind him except the chip shop they used to visit at half-time. All other traces swept away.

Time moved relentlessly onward, the hour of the service passing into oblivion like everything else, leaving him untethered, without anchor in a place that had been his anchor for over half a lifetime.

And he should have gone home then, got himself on the train and made his way back, tried to get the wedge back in. But he didn't. He couldn't get past that bedroom door, couldn't see beyond it. He was a daft bastard, really, a let-down to himself, a disappointment to others. So he really did have to stay. He had to explain himself, see the people he'd not seen, find out what the fuck it was all about, Stimmo doing himself in like that, discover if he was barking up the right tree or poking about in dark places he had no business with.

He returned to the hotel and booked himself in for the weekend, closed the curtains, switched off the lights and crashed on the bed, knowing he had to call BJ, to avoid being the one they'd all say didn't give a fuck.

To be forgiven.

He raided the minibar, sank the whisky and the wine then drifted off into a vision of himself, sinking a six-pack of Fosters on the bank of the Trent, the churning river at his feet, the fucking Trent end looking like it might collapse into the water, tilting against the clouds, threatening to fall on top of him, crush his sad bones. Some woman on the bridge turning down the steps, carrying a wreath under one arm, turning down the alley in the direction of the ticket office. Others following behind, little ants crossing the bridge, turning down the steps, wandering along the far bank, disappearing into the alley, an endless string of people in ones and twos and little clusters, him on the far bank watching them all, trying to build up the courage to do the same.

A drunken reverie.

Still he fancied himself following them down to discover a red brick wall decked in scarves, the cross of St George, that name 'Brian Howard Clough', those dates 1935–2004, the freshly daubed message 'you did it your way'. He dreamed he stood there in the silent car park paying homage whilst his brothers and sisters drifted past him to lay their own messages, flowers, hats, scarves, ghosts to rest.

A car park full of memories. A sad fucking ending really. Couldn't they have opened the gates, let the cunts on to the pitch, offered some sense of affiliation?

Because he was dreaming of the same colours draped over a goalmouth again now, Anfield in the aftermath, a carpet of condolence, a terrace bathed in remembrance, a different type of loss, but one connecting to the other, drawing fifteen years together so they might not have happened at all, his adult life bracketed by two moments, the death of one, the death of ninety-six. And then there was Stimmo, the spark that put a light to it all. He'd let that fucker down, well and fucking truly.

He was, as he'd often been called, a selfish bastard.

He woke in the dark, struggled to locate himself, floundered for a while in a room he didn't recognise amongst anxieties he couldn't control. And then he saw the golden church spire beyond the window, recognised the old town's sombre silhouette, dropped back into the pillow, clicked on the TV, buried himself in mediocrity.

Somewhere amongst it all he dialled BJ's number. BJ picked up on the second ring.

'You're a cunt.'

'I couldn't face it,' he said. 'I thought I could but I couldn't.'

'So you're a cunt. And now you want to try and make it better.'

'I guess so.'

'I'll be at the bank tomorrow.'

'Eh?'

'Sincil Bank. You daft bastard. 2 p.m. outside the Shakespeare.'

'Are you fucking kidding?'

'No, mate. Why would I kid about a serious thing like you buying me a pint?'

The phone went dead.

Barely sixteen. Finished with school. Sixteen and a day on the Government Youth Training Scheme. None the fucking wiser. Dead hours. Dead days. The barest fucking interest in the job and the job with the barest fucking interest in you.

£27 a week.

£32 a week.

£70 a week.

An idiot's progress.

A day a week in college. On the bus at the crack of dawn, sleeping on the back seat as it rattles its way through village after village, heading to the cathedral city.

Learning nothing and having nothing to offer but the vaguest awareness of the skills required to work in a dying industry.

Two fucking years of cheap labour then dumped back into the world.

Redundant.

Twice.

Seventeen and on the scrapheap.

Getting nowhere fast.

A summer of fuck all. Sat with your feet up. Mam and dad on holiday. Family home to yourself. But no spends. Six fucking weeks on the giro. The season coming around, and no fucking spends. Your dad on your case. The world on your shoulders. Down the jobby on a Friday. The jobby with the dead heads. Hating that more. Hating that the most. Patronised. Sneered at. Laughed at.

Your ex-schoolmates starting out at Oxford and Cambridge and Durham and LSE.

Hate and resentment brimming. Hate and resentment bubbling. You with your O levels in English and Geography and fuck all else.

Not what you know but who you know and you don't know any fucker worth knowing.

Except your dad knows someone, someone at Royal Mail. Maybe. Perhaps. Just to tide you over. Just for a few weeks, that will become months, become years, threaten a lifetime.

But that first morning, up at the crack, down to the Sorting Office, out on the streets in the bright summer sunshine. It isn't so bad. Not bad at all. You and the bike. You and the morning. You and your thoughts. No fucker bothering you. No fucker asking for anything. Nothing to get bored about. You in your shirtsleeves. House to house, street to street. You by the river. You in the park. You in your uniform. You with an identity. Mr Postie. The girls loving it. Loving you. You loving the girls. Home by mid-morning. Home with the day to devour.

Just the fucking evening shifts to get through. Three hours at the facing table. The clock crawling. You part of a machine, doing a job a machine could do. The mail coming at you from all quarters, bag after bag. Pile upon fucking pile.

The good and the bad. The rough and the smooth. The rough and the fucking smooth.

But money in the bank. Real money, not fucking pocket money. More than you need. More than enough. Summer fading. Autumn falling away. Winter coming on. The season ticking by. Forest ticking off the wins. Getting to games no trouble. No fucking trouble at all. You and the boys, a band of merry men, of merry lads, traipsing up and down the country, eating up the burgers and the miles, road and rail, rail and road, following the Tricky Trees.

Over land and sea.

And Leicester.

Because it is steep banks of concrete and steel crowd barriers.

FAN

It is metal cages.
It is wide-open terraces exposed to the elements.
It is taking whatever mother nature and the world can throw at you.
And throwing it back.

Saturday

Lincoln fucking City. A Saturday afternoon smeared with rain. BJ munching a steak and mushroom pie, the two of them huddled in the Stacey West Stand.

In memory of Bill Stacey and Jim West.

In memory of Bradford.

'You should have come. You should have made the effort,' said BJ.

'I couldn't face it,' he said.

'None of us could. But we faced it.'

'It brought back too many memories.'

'Aye, well we've all got those memories, mate.'

BJ brought his pie up to his face, bit out a chunk of steak. A thick globule of gravy dripped into his lap.

'Fucking pies,' he said.

'Fucking prawn sandwiches more like,' said Finchy.

'Not here mate,' said BJ. 'Not in this fucking league.'

'Do you watch it much?'

'The Premiership?'

'Aye.'

'I don't go to games. I've no cause. There's something not right about it. Fucking Premiership and fucking Sky TV. All that money sloshing about. All those foreign fuckers. And don't get me started on fucking all-seater stadia.'

Finchy looked out across the ground, thinking '*this* is all seater'.

'A bloke pissed on me in the Trent end once,' he said.

'We all got pissed on. Some of us did the pissing. That was part of it. But they fucked with it, didn't they? Fucked with it so that every fucker and his dog wants to watch it and every fucker, his dog and his wife has an opinion on it. Fucking genius bit of marketing that. I'd like to see some of today's lot at an eighties' game, see how they'd cope. Remember Highfield Road? Remember the fucking away end? Fucking rammed. I was nearly cut in half against a barrier in that cage. Remember Ashton Gate, getting piss wet through in the sleet, coined for one hundred and twenty glorious minutes?'

BJ, chuckling to himself.

'Remember Filbert Street? That was when football *was* football. That's why I come here these days. It's the closest I can get to those times.'

Finchy looked out at the scene before him, at the pitch cutting up, the slanting rain, at twenty-two players, journeymen and also-rans slogging it out, at three thousand hardy fucking souls bearing the weather, the away fans tucked in the corner, the home end giving them stick. In some ways it felt like the eighties.

'The same fucking buzz,' said BJ. 'Just the numbers lacking.'

The visiting centre-half booted the ball over the stand. Everybody cheered. The centre-half puffed out his chest, pointed and bellowed his orders. Football fucking League Division Two.

BJ laughed.

'Before you say it, I know the quality's shit. But at least we're not watching a bunch of fucking prima donnas. Fucking corporate boxes and nonsense ticketing. They did the same to fucking Glastonbury.'

'Glastonbury?'

'All that security. It used to have a fucking edge.'

'You paid to go to Glastonbury?'

'Did I fuck. I climbed the fucking fence like everybody else. Then I nicked a tent. Glastonbury 2000, mate. Fucking legend. I haven't been since they tightened up.'

BJ laughed. The same boyish laughter. Just the fucking same. Older. Fatter. The same.

'We were lucky,' he said. 'Lucky to be a part of it.'

'Do you reckon?'

'I fucking know it. How can young lads like we were go to football these days? They can't unless they come to watch this. But this is alright. This'll do.'

4.30 in the afternoon. A black sky above. Brilliant light below. The ball in the air, the ball in the stand, the ball anywhere but on the fucking ground where it belonged.

The two of them laughing.

'Cloughie would be tearing his hair out.'

'At least it's real, mate. At least it's honest.'

Nil fucking nil honest.

Shuffling out of the stand. Floodlights shimmering in puddles. The smell of Bovril. The smell of burgers and onions. The smell of a quarter to five on a Saturday.

The smell of fifteen years.

BJ recalling past endeavours.

'Had a couple of good knocks over the decades. Before the fucking banning orders. Now I have to be careful.'

'You still find trouble then?'

'Only if it finds me...'

'Does it?'

'Does it what?'

'Does it find you?'

BJ looked Finchy up and down.

'Who are you,' he said at last. 'The fucking old bill?'

Another pub. The bar full to bursting. BJ nodded to the landlord, led Finchy to a booth in the corner of the lounge.

'Always quiet around this side,' he said. 'No fucker wants to settle in. A quick pint, a quick moan about the fucking game and this place'll be dead. But we'll be here, son. We'll be here. Reminiscing. You and me...'

'I want to ask...'

'About Stimmo?'

'Is it that obvious?'

'What else is there? We haven't set eyes on each other for over a decade.'

'I dunno. Impending middle age?'

'You always were a reflective bastard. Teacher. I might have bloody guessed.'

'It's partly about Stimmo.'

'I'm going to let you down on this. I know nothing about it. The guy did himself in a week last Thursday. That's all I've got.'

'Wearing his Forest shirt.'

'Spot on.'

'Which one?'

A moment's hesitation. BJ supped his pint and stared across the lounge towards the frosted glass and the bar on the other side.

'A fucking home shirt,' he said.

'Which one?'

BJ shrugged.

'Come on. Some fucker must know.'

'I see where you're heading…' said BJ.

'It was fucking Shipstones. I'll put my life on it. It was Shipstones and it was too fucking tight after fifteen seasons and it made him look like a real fat prick hanging there.'

'Fuck off, mate.'

BJ slammed the table.

'You always were a depressing bastard.'

'Well, it's been on my mind,' said Finchy.

Another mouthful of beer. Another elongated stare at the frosted glass.

'I hadn't seen him for about five years,' said BJ. 'Other than the odd nod of recognition in town. I didn't see him socially at all, not since he stopped going to football.'

'He wasn't going to Forest then?'

BJ shook his head.

'He stopped a couple of years before I did. We had the Europe thing. That was alright. Then it all went sour, didn't it. We were overtaken by fucking Wigan. For fuck's sake. Wigan.'

'Do you know his missus? I feel like I should … you know.'

BJ sunk the rest of his pint and wiped his mouth.

'*You* know his fucking missus.'

'Eh?'

'Fuck off, John. Don't pull that one,' said BJ, restless now, agitated, the fuse lit.

'Who?'

A look.

'Seriously?'

'Fucking seriously.'

'Jen White, mate.'

Almost knocked him flying.

'Never.'

'Long after you fucked off. Don't worry about that.'

'Fuck,' said Finchy. 'I had no idea.'

'Hardly fucking surprising. You're two hundred miles away. You've been two hundred miles away for fifteen fucking years.'

BJ took another sup of his pint.

'And now you're back…'

BJ shifted his weight. BJ with his signet rings and his thick curly hair. A boy rolled into a man. A dangerous bastard. The old stare was back. He was watching the frosted glass and the bar beyond, looking like he wanted to disappear into that crowd, put this whole sorry fucking business to bed.

Or kick its fucking head in.

'Stimmo's not the first to go,' said BJ. 'We lost Nev last year.'

Finchy stared at the bar, sorting faces, sorting names. Mismatching and matching.

'Everton fan,' he said at last.

BJ nodded.

'Aye, mate, Everton. Just like us, though. Home and away. North, east, south, west.'

'I remember him,' said Finchy. 'But not the way Stimmo went?'

'No, not the way Stimmo went. Just living,' said BJ. 'Just life …'

BJ put down his empty glass.

'I need another pint,' he said.

'I'll get these,' said Finchy.

'The least you can do,' said BJ.

Finchy got to his feet. Fuck all happening in the lounge so he pushed through the door into the bar proper, met a wall of noise, familiar accents bemoaning familiar failings, 'lack of quality, lack of pace, never lack of effort, mate, never lack of effort', pushed his way shoulder to shoulder, back in the crowd again, back on the fucking terraces. He ordered two pints, slinging his words at the barman, planting his feet and stiffening his shoulders, bracing himself, fighting for his little bit of space. In his head, Forest songs, away day songs, songs on steeply banked terraces, songs on unfamiliar streets. And then, behind him, the sound of shattering glass, some sort of ruckus, away fans at the door, landing punches on home fans. BJ came wheeling in from the lounge, barrelling his way through the place, arms fucking flying, punches finding the mark, leading the fucking charge as the away fans legged it over the threshold and up the road, home fans flooding out, giving chase, until, in the blink of an eye, the bar was empty. There was just Finchy, the landlord and a floor decorated with broken glass.

The landlord raised his pint.

'Cheers,' he said. 'Cheers to you and no fucker else.'

Finchy stood surrounded by spilled tables and spilled pints. The gambling machine was flashing with credit. Pool balls were still bouncing around on the fucking baize. Half a cue was resting there, one end splintered and jagged, the other half no fucking where to be seen.

'Every fucking home game,' said the landlord. 'You'd think they'd get bored of it, but they don't.' He wandered over to the door. 'Still, it pays the fucking bills.'

From somewhere down the street came the sound of singing, a hundred voices baying for blood.

'Can you hear, the Lincoln sing, the Rochdale ran away…'

'Run, run, run you bastards…'

'Fuck off Dale, fuck off Dale…'

Finchy grinned, imagining BJ at the head of the mob. BJ, the grandaddy. The grandaddy of his own fucking crew.

Why the fuck not?

He withdrew to the station, took a train back to the old town, retreated to the hotel, to his room, a snail in a shell, checked the football results, thought about who else he needed to see now that he was here, now that he was fully up to his fucking neck. He thought about Kelly, the night before he left, the slings and arrows, piled pillows and muffled screams, bedroom doors and dark landings.

It was all a blur.

Everything was a blur.

His whole fucking life.

You travel back.
    You can't help yourself.
    It's all around you.
    It's in your flesh and your bones and your blood.
    It's in your heart and soul.
    The past is the present.
    The present is the past.
    They're indistinguishable.

Where? The most boring town in England

When? Saturday, 5th December 1987

Why? You tell me, you bastard…

Still morning. One degree above zero. Head throbbing from the night before. Midnight curry stirring in the belly. No time for breakfast in the fifteen minutes between seventeen-year-old John Finch's alarm clock sounding and dragging his bike from the alley.

The iron gate squealing on its hinges.

Up before the lark. Pedalling through the silent streets, racing by his old scout hut, sleeping, shuttered, redundant. Skirting the print works that dumped him, the Telecom exchange, the rows of yellow vans, heading inwards, scooting under the arches of the railway bridge, the great scar connecting north to south, the town to everything else.

He slips into the yard, slams his cycle in the rack, checks his postal bike. Number twenty one. No punctures. No trapped chain. He pats the saddle. Good to go.

A voice in the darkness.

'You're fucking early.'

Webster. Union man. Always something to say.

'Away day—'

'Bob's fucking bus?'

Finchy shakes his head.

'Train,' he says.

'Where?'

'Wimbledon.'

'Because no fucker wants to go there except daft bastards like you.'

Webster glances at the clock.

'I don't want to see your ugly face on this ramp before 9.30 a.m.,' says Webster. 'Don't fuck up twenty-one walk.'

'It's already fucked,' he replies.

Because it is.

He makes to get on. Webster calls after him.

'King's Cross?'

He nods.

Webster sucks the chill air through his teeth, shakes his head.

'Rather you than me,' he says. 'But that's up to you. Just don't come back before 9.30.'

Finchy strides to the frame, full of purpose, starts prepping his delivery, hands moving in a blur, on automatic, a machine. Just him to begin with but others joining their own frames until one by one all of the frames are occupied.

Distractions coming at him from all sides.

'Where are the mighty Reds today then?'

'Is Clyde Ave yours?'

'Jesus, you're in early. On a promise?'

Old blokes. New blokes. Blokes who could do better. Blokes who can't believe their luck. A job for characters. A job for blokes who don't mind being outside in all weathers, blokes who are happiest on their own, blokes who like to get up early, get a job done and have the rest of the day to themselves. Model aeroplane enthusiasts. Petrol heads. Blokes with allotments to tend. Blokes that have their fingers in other pies. Ex-firemen. Ex-squaddies. Ex-drinkers.

And drinkers.

And dreamers.

All and fucking sundry.

A job for life if you look after it, if you don't fuck up.

And he's becoming one of them, part of the fabric. He enjoys their company, the banter, the hours of ripping the piss. Only he hates the early mornings. He hates the rain. His fingers can't manage the cold. He isn't fully adjusted to this life. He never fucking will be.

Blokes are already on the ramp when he steps out the door, his bag fit to bursting. But one bag means he has a fighting chance, if he gets his arse into gear. He stands for a moment, looking up at the sky. It's still dark. The stars are masked by low-slung clouds. Next to him, a bloke's smoking a cigarette. Nobber Harris. Nervous type. Always fidgety. Not an ounce of fat on him.

'Looks like rain,' says Harris. His breath reeks of alcohol. Six months earlier, just a few days after Finchy started at the place, Harris collapsed from a heart attack in the street. At forty-three. Now he's back, none the fucking wiser.

'I fucking hope not,' says Finchy.

'You're alright,' says Harris. 'You can nip in to your mam's place.'

'No time for that this morning,' he says.

He lugs his bag off the ramp and over to the bike stand, straps it in place and then heads back inside for the box keys. That's how it works. Mail out, mail in.

Every day, bar Sunday.

Every fucking day.

He looks up at the clock above the door.

6.20 a.m.

Harcross catches him at the bike shed. Harcross. Millwall fan. Eastender. Up from London, one of the boys and then processed to shift manager. Now he's caught between two worlds, struggling to know where to place himself. The bikes aren't meant to move until 6.45 a.m. It's policy.

But Harcross travelled to Mexico 86, was one of the boys doing the conga in the 3–0 win over Poland. Such relief in that procession. So nearly a wasted trip. Portugal. Fucking Morocco. Wilkins chucking the ball at the ref, getting his marching orders. Captain Marvel and his shoulder. Bobby 'is my fucking tie straight?' Robson. They'd almost blown it, teetered on the brink and then come home wounded heroes, beaten by Maradona's genius and the hand of God. There was that miss from Lineker. John fucking Barnes squandered on the bench for eighty minutes. The silly cunts.

Harcross understands it's Saturday. Harcross knows what that means. Football day. The boss isn't in. The boss isn't coming in. He shoots a wink at Finchy and a blind eye at the clock.

Out of the yard then, legs pumping, hunched over the handlebars. The bike all top-heavy from the mailbag. His breath leaving trails behind him like a puffing fucking steam train.

6.45 a.m. on a Saturday. The clang and clatter of the market traders setting up their stalls.

Twenty-one walk. One of the bastard walks. A walk no fucker wants. Council houses. Council flats. Thatcher's forgotten families. Forgotten youth. He's one of them. It hasn't dawned on him yet how expendable he is. His life's about earning a few quid, getting out of the house with a bit in the pocket, pool and snooker clubs on week nights, pubs at weekends, girls when he can get them.

And football.

Football at the heart of it all.

Forest home and away every fucking Saturday.

A reason for living.

The Royal Mail job makes it all possible.

The Royal Mail job makes it all so hard.

The estate. Saturday at 7 a.m. Primitive signs of life behind grubby curtains. Fifty calls in. Five hundred to go. In the flats. Up and down the stinking stairwells, the reek of putrid nappies. Single-mum suburbia. Six months on the job and not one proposition. So much for the stories. Perhaps he isn't old enough. Perhaps he's too fresh-faced.

Perhaps it's a load of bollocks.

The estate smothered in darkness, just the bark of dogs and the whine of the milk float for company. Pounding the stairs. Getting the flats out of the way. Propping the bike against the doors and carrying the bundles in, making quick work of it while his legs are fresh.

The clock ticking.

And after the flats, the rest of the warren. His old primary school, the black iron gate padlocked, shut for the weekend, taking a well-earned break from the squealing and bleeding knees. On to the retirement bungalows, the disremembered, never much to deliver here except on gas and electric days when every fucker gets one. He dashes up and down the pathways, anxious not to get stalled by one of the oldies. No desperate single mums in negligees but plenty of oldies with a story to tell, yearning for company at any price. They're always up, stalking the mailbox.

But not today. He slips silently in and out of each garden, doesn't give them an opportunity.

The sky pale now. Light filtering through the cloud, spilling over the horizon. A paperboy scoots past with his bag of twenty papers. Jammy bastard. He'll be home with his brekky in no time, all done for the day. There'll be Saturday ahead of him, no school, a wander around to his mates, perhaps a kickabout in the park, home for the footy results, tea on the table, a chance to do it all again the next day. He doesn't know what's waiting for him around the corner. He doesn't have a clue.

Thank fuck for small mercies.

8 a.m. One third complete. At his parents' place. A cup of tea on the table, the biscuit tin full to the brim after the weekly shop. He grabs a handful of digestives, gulps the tea down. He could kill half an hour here, bury himself in the sports pages, lose the will to venture back out. But not today. He's back on it before the pulverised biscuits reach his intestines.

'You're going then?'

His mam, as concerned now as when he was ten years old and heading off fishing with the lads. '10.10 to King's Cross.'

Spitting biscuit crumbs.

'Is it open?'

'What?'

'King's Cross.'

'I should fucking well hope so.'

She looks at him.

'But the fire…'

'It's a big place.'

'There's no bus?'

'No, there's no bus.'

He's still her boy, always will be. She wants to stop him. But she can't. She's done it before, a long time before, Villa away to be precise, but he was younger then, still beholden. He'd no money of his own. Now he has money. And if she still has the right, she no longer has the will. Villa away. It still fucking irks him. Villa 0 Forest 5. He fucking missed it, sat at home listening to the score rack up on the radio. The house was a fucking warzone that day. A fucking warzone.

The home straight. Council semis all lined up in rows, some facing the street, some facing other semis across bare patches of earth that were once seeded with grass. A maze of alleyways dissects the lot, severing them apart. Some face on to the metal fence that marks the boundary of the high school. The steel fence with the spiked top is a new addition, a replacement for the wire fencing that lost its battle with the kids of the estate years ago. Now there are no rabbit runs through the undergrowth. No way in, no way out. He's a product of the local grammar himself, a nameless entity. Here he is delivering his letters in his postie uniform. None of the other fuckers in his year at school are doing anything like it. They're wrapped up warm in their beds, enjoying a day off from the sixth form, another day on their long and prosperous journey through academia. But they don't have football on a Saturday. They don't have that.

The last letter, the last letter box.

9.20 a.m.

Fucking A.

Fifty minutes to change, drop off his bike and the mailbag and launch himself up to the station where the others will be waiting. Fifty minutes to become the man. He pushes open the bag and fishes around inside it. His hand comes to rest on a packet no bigger than his fist. He turns it over, reads the address. A top-floor flat. He looks at the sender's address. Fucking Persil. A free fucking sample?

Fuck!

No, fuck it.

He buries it in the fold of the bag. It can wait until Monday. If Harcross checks his bag on the way in he'll plead the innocent, pretend he hasn't seen it. It's hardly fucking urgent, a fucking free sample of Persil for a single mum in a top-floor flat. She'll hardly be pacing the fucking hallway in anticipation.

He stops at the mailbox, takes the key from the cloth bag and pulls open the door, empties the contents on top of the fucking Persil packet, cycles home, changes into his Pepe Jeans and Pringle polo shirt.

Casual.

Always casual.

He takes his Forest scarf too, for later, picks up his railcard, shoots out the door again. Then it's back on the bike, back to the PO, legs a blur. He passes Jeff on the way, Jeff all Best Company denim, all bristle and aftershave.

'See you at the station, you fat bastard!'

'Gahhhhhhhhhhhhhhhhhh!'

He swings the bike into the yard, slams it into the cycle rack. 9.45 a.m. Plenty of time.

'Funny how you can make it back on Saturdays.'

Harcross on the ramp in crisp winter sunlight.

'It was a light day. Just the one bag.'

Harcross smiles. He knows the fucking score.

Finchy pushes through the plastic doors into the office,

chucks his bag on the facing table and turns it over. Mail spills out. Longs and shorts. Firsts and seconds. Packets on the belt. Persil packet well hidden, heart pounding all the same, in his nature to please, to be a good lad despite himself. He turns to look at the door. Harcross is miles away, staring at the signing-in sheets. Other blokes are ambling back in, blokes that didn't start early, blokes who aren't sweating, blokes that never seem to rush. Either they have it easy or he's fucking useless. He chucks his bag into his locker and makes for the door. 9.52. Eighteen minutes. Plenty of time if…

Webster's waiting for him.

'Nicely does it,' says Webster. 'Don't sweat, son. One day you can kiss twenty-one walk's backside and take your pick of something more leisurely.'

Finchy nods, tries to manoeuvre his way past.

'Not so many single mums mind. Any luck yet?'

He shakes his head.

'Fuck me,' says Webster. 'You're a slow cunt at everything.'

Two other blokes are on the ramp, chugging at cigarettes, laughing when Webster laughs, bleating when Webster bleats. Fucking sheep.

He looks at his watch. 9.54 a.m. He doesn't have time for this bollocks.

'Fucking Wimbledon away,' says Webster. 'It's a pity you haven't got anything better to do.'

Is there anything better? At 3 p.m. on a Saturday? Anything better than an away day with the boys? A better place to be when the ball hits the back of the fucking opposition net? It's better than sex. They've all long since settled on that.

The highest of highs.

And Webster's being a cunt, pure and simple. Finchy can see the look in his eye, the poison.

'I'll be off then,' says Finchy, dismissing the bastard. He jumps from the ramp, marches over the yard and out of the red gates, not looking back, not giving Webster another chance.

'2–0 to the Crazy Gang,' shouts Webster. 'Fashanu double.'

He shoots the cunt the finger, races across the street between the cars, up the alley that cuts through the terraces, to the station, arrives there with three minutes to spare. And they're all there waiting, BJ, T-Gally, Jeff, Hopper, Stimmo, each with eight hours in the sack behind them and a full fucking brekky in their bellies, each spruced up for a Saturday in the smoke.

Cunts.

Sunday

You traced your fingers over these walls.
You ran through these fields.
You played in these parks.
You grazed your knees on these streets.
You laughed on these corners.
You wept on these benches.
You drank in these pubs.
You pissed in these alleyways.

A morning choked with rain and peeling bells. He went to breakfast then sat about the hotel, read the Sundays, only half interested, thinking about BJ, seeking out a report on a violent showdown between rival fans at the Lincoln v Rochdale game. But there was nothing. It was Division Two for fuck's sake. Nobody in the nationals gave a shit.

By eleven he was lost in himself, aware only that he wasn't checking out or heading back south, not yet. He requested another night instead.

'You can have all week if you want,' said the girl at the desk.

'I might need it.'

'I'll book you in until Friday,' she said. 'If you want to check out at any time just let us know. A sort of daily arrangement.'

'You'd do that?'

'It's a forty-room hotel and we've got twenty rooms empty,' she said. 'I think we can be flexible.'

He went back to his room, changed and headed into the old town, letting his legs carry him, spent an hour drifting around the market streets, the narrow lanes, before traipsing up the hill in the direction of the estate. It didn't take him long to wind up at the hulking new sports complex, the third-generation football pitch, the deserted car park, the soulless athletics stadium where Town played their games. He peered over the fence at the pitch, marooned as it was beyond an expanse of running track and run-off, shallow, partially covered terraces, a characterless concrete stand. It was meant to be better than the old place. It was cleaner, safer, up to scratch, but better? Was it fuck. A grand athletic stadium maybe, but it was no place for a football match. And this is what they'd discovered, the diehards from Tamworth and Guiseley, Matlock and Whitley Bay, a bland, windswept nothingness. A place to visit, tick off and instantly forget.

Somewhere in the distance, the sounds of men shouting, the dull thud of a football. He climbed a grass embankment, stumbled upon the remaining grass pitch, sandwiched between so much concrete and tarmac, a tragic encounter, the pitch cut and bruised by wet autumn, tufts of longer grass in midfield, twenty-two blokes huffing and puffing, a couple of hardy spectators, a boy on his bicycle, an old guy with a dog, one team decked out in odd shorts and socks, manager-less (the bare eleven), rudderless, all at sea. They conceded two goals while he stood there. He watched them asking helpless questions of each other.

The ball bobbled and deviated its way across the surface. The nets had seen better days. The goal area was a sea of mud, the goalposts a multicoloured array of torn-off tape, the remnants of a thousand Saturday afternoons and Sunday mornings. The referee stood in the centre of the pitch watching it all take place around him, good for twenty quid plus expenses, good for nothing except keeping things in order, his face the picture of boredom. Beyond him, the changing rooms, daubed in graffiti, the windows covered in metal sheeting, some of the brickwork chipped away, a couple of beer bottles by the door, a third smashed into pieces. One of the corner flags was bent at the middle, lopsided, falling over. When a player tried to pull it loose to take a corner, the ref ordered him to put it back. There was a scrape of dog shit near the touchline where Finchy was standing, turds scattered by his feet, out of play, out of mind.

Beyond the bedlam, beyond the mounds of earth, the metal fencing that separated the sports complex from everything else. He could see the empty 3G pitch more clearly from here, pristine in its unemployment, silent, dew on the fibres, a million tiny water drops. Another cheer erupted from the side that were leading. The losing keeper bellowed his disgust, hammered the ball back towards half-way. One of his teammates threatened to throw the towel in, headed for the touchline, telling his keeper to fuck off. The ref stepped in, pointed to his pocket, pointed at the sad excuse for a changing facility. The bloke thought better of it. He pulled his socks up, surrendering authority to the man in black, went steaming into the next tackle that came his way, missed ball and man, ended up on his arse in the smear of dog shit, his actions punctuated by cries from both sides, cries of 'well in' and 'calm down'. The leading team were popping the ball about now, loving their morning, the losers a tragic, shambolic metaphor for the state of the game and England's sad exit from Euro 2004.

As he was leaving he heard the old bloke talking to the manager of the decent lot. He was pointing at the shit on the player's back and at the 3G pitch through the fence.

'You're fucking joking,' he said. 'At £100 a pop? We get the grass for half that.'

'Aye, and the shit to go with it,' said the old bloke.

They both laughed. The bloke with the shit up his back had stopped somewhere near the centre spot. The ref headed his way and blew his whistle. Twenty-one blokes turned to look at the guy with shit up his back but no fucker went over to help him remove it.

Finchy stuffed his hands in his pockets, remembering this

place at 3 p.m. on a Saturday when he was a boy, a wide open space, no sports centre, no athletic stadium, no fucking indoor bowling club, just six pitches laid out in a grid and six matches, the spaces between each pitch lined with people, him and the lads playing football behind one of the goals, using the back of the net, winding up whichever keeper was occupying the goal, racing on to the pitch at half-time for five minutes of goal-mouth action, looking at the players like they were fucking heroes. He could smell the embrocation oil, the well-spent sweat, the leather of his boots. All of this to the sound of a transistor radio that barked the scores from north and south, east and west, listening out for the Forest score, listening out for Liverpool, hearing that Paisley's boys were behind, laughing about it, shuffling home for tea at 4.30 p.m., arriving in time to watch the vidiprinter on Grandstand, watching the scores come in, Liverpool winning now, Liverpool always fucking winning.

He wandered down the alley between the sports centre and the school, an alley formed by two twelve-foot-high metal security fences, each metal strut topped with a fuck-off spike. They might have been two prisons placed side by side, but they weren't fucking prisons. They were anything but prisons.

He didn't intend to linger outside the house he'd grown up in for any great lapse of time but he did. It took a kid on a bicycle shooting past him and telling him to 'fuck off' to drag him out of himself, drag him to the line of shops where he wrestled with visions of the old and the new. The hairdressers, once the launderette, where his mam earned a few quid each week. The co-op, swallower of the newsagents where he'd earned his pocket money as a paperboy. The squalid council flats above. The little car park.

He traipsed to the top of the street, on through the bollards into the jitty, made his way to the courts, feeling as conspicuous now as he'd felt when he'd first ventured beyond the threshold his parents administered when he was a child.

He could hear his mam's words.

'Go anywhere you like but don't go there.'

It stuck tight for a while and then it loosened. Like everything. Of course it fucking did.

Fuck all had changed. There were still houses displaying the damage of a warzone where no war had been fought. There were still gateposts without gates, fence posts without fencing, windows without glass, kids without clothes, lawns without grass. More satellite dishes, more cars crammed into too few spaces, more dialects, more languages, too many to mention. So that had changed.

That and nothing else.

The deadland was harder to locate, much of it eaten up by concrete and metal. There were modern units, clean edges, neat lines.

And fences. There were fences.

Fences where there had been no fences.

Patches of the deadland. In the small unoccupied spaces the sprawl had missed. Remnants. And they responded when he stumbled upon them, spoke out to him in a quiet whisper, told him not to forget or forsake them

Not to let them be squeezed to nothing.

There was no fucking danger of that. To dispose of them was to dispose of himself.

In 1980 they were going to build.

Eight years old, trampling through the deadland, the place where the estate petered out and the great beyond began.

The place where everything reached a standstill.

Chewed-up fields.

The deadland in the height of summer. Rabbit runs through the scrub. Haphazard mounds of earth.

They were going to build.

An unintentional landscape. The 'mud hills', the industrial tyres, the canisters and the timber, the discarded carpets, the pallets, the tarpaulin-covered dens, the stink, the dirt, the fucking ferocious freedom of it all.

The money dried up.

A dumping ground.

Pushing through the undergrowth. Dragging bits of wood. Dragging bits of carpet. Hammer and nails. Porno mags. Ciggies.

No, you can't have any spends.

Crawling deep into the growth. In groups. In gangs. Days in the deadland. Dawn to dusk. The dry heat of summer. The old town baking in the dry heat of summer.

It doesn't grow on effing trees.

The deadland.

Brown in the heat.

Worn through.

A deferred landscape.

Interrupted. Forgotten. Abandoned.

The whole fucking town and all of its people.

The money dried up.

He worked his way through the maze of alleys and cut-throughs towards the canal, worked his way down to the canal bank that was clotted with algae, all detritus and stink.

He felt his heart break.

Kids in the deadland. Traipsing through the dead growth to the canal. Scrambling and scrabbling at the bank, flirting with the dark water.

Children of the deadland.

'An honest day's work for an honest day's pay,' said Maggie.

But there were no fucking jobs.

He dropped in on his parents. The least he could do. The two of them pleased to see their eldest but the undercurrent always there. He was thirty-three years old. He'd been with Kelly a while now. There was still no sign of a wedding. There was still no sign of…

He refused them access, joined them for Sunday lunch pleasantries instead, for beef and Yorkshire pudding, for apple pie and custard, then he slipped away, promising a proper visit at Christmas, him and Kelly, for a few days, so things weren't such a rush, so his mam could get the house ready, so they could all sit down and have a good chat about everything.

His dad accompanied him to the garden gate.

'I heard about your old mate,' said his dad. 'So did your mother, though she didn't want me to mention it.'

'That's why I came up,' he said. 'It was meant to be a flying visit.'

He closed the gate behind him, stood there, his dad on one side, him on the other, the autumn wind buffeting the trees, his fingers on the cold iron, his dad's fingers on the cold iron, drops of water shivering on the cold iron.

'It's about time you sorted yourself out,' said his dad. Not a question. Never a question. 'You're thirty-three years old.'

He nodded.

'I am,' he said. 'I am.'

When he was done with it all, when he was spent, he made his way back towards the hotel, breathing in the malt from the maltings, breathing in another clutch of memories, cutting through the tunnel under the railway, piss alley, into the town centre and on to the park where the river ambled, over the white bridge and towards the hotel, stopping off at The Lion to catch the Sunday game, eyes roving from face to face, seeking out familiarity, finding none, considering how it was possible to become so detached from a place that had raised and nurtured him at its bosom for so many years and yet so attached that he felt he could take just one unremarkable step backwards, wind up where he'd started and not even know the fucking difference.

And he called his place again, of course he fucking did. The phone rang.

And rang.

And rang.

He pictured it, crying out in the kitchen, yearning for a palm to clutch it.

It clicked to answerphone, to Kelly's ghostly voice.

He didn't bother to leave a message.

It was Lacoste and Ralph Lauren, Barbour and Burberry.
It was Lyle & Scott, Paul & Shark.
It was Fila and Benetton, Ellesse and Adidas.
It was Pringle and Patrick.
It was Nike.
It was all of these things.

King's Cross.

Saturday, 5th December 1987.

Seventeen days.

The dead smell. Human fucking flesh. He catches scent of it the moment he steps off the train. Perhaps it's in his head but he catches fucking scent of it all the same. It's melded into the walls, into the charred metal and melted plastic. Two fucking weeks and it's still there. One fucking cigarette. One discarded match. Piles of rubbish, rat hair, fluff, sweet wrappers. A wooden escalator, sixty years old. And tunnels, draughts from passing trains, tubes and shafts, solvent-based paint, a bastard blowtorch.

A funeral pyre. A cremation pit.

Choking black smoke.

Death by asphyxiation.

But the station's open for business and here they are about their business, lads, taking the piss, looking out for colours, wearing their own in little ways, the tucked-away scarf, the subtle enamel badge, the East Midlands accent.

Forest till I die.

Underground, overground. Edgware Road. Earl's Court. Parson's Green. City to suburb. Concrete metropolis to leafy lane. SW19. A stone's throw from the dog track. No sign of the fucking tennis. A right fair walk from the station, mind. No fucking crowd. No sign of a Div One ground or football match. Just a December day. No fucker about. It might as well be the fucking Simod Cup.

And there it is.

Plough Lane.

'A shithole.'

'Fucked if I'm coming here again.'

'Where's Bob's bus when you need it?'

He's seen this many people at Meadow Lane. And that on a Tuesday. A better atmosphere at the Lane as well. But here they are watching Forest trying to stroke the ball around whilst the Wombles lump it. Here are Carr and Rice shitting bricks on each wing, looking like kids against Sanchez and co. Here's Fash the Bash bruising it out, giving Chettle an elbow, a knee, a fucking hard afternoon. Here's Clough Jnr nervously twitching each time he receives the ball with his back to goal. Tackles come straight through him, raking studs, swinging fists, no fucking protection. Clough Snr motionless on the touchline. Only Psycho looks up for it, in his element, carrying the others. Not for the first time. The Forest end uninspired. Tail ends of half-engineered songs drift up and out over the back of the open terrace, disappear into the December air.

Plough fucking Lane. There are more exciting ploughing matches.

Half-time. Nil fucking nil. He can hear his dad chuckling in the kitchen, the radio droning away.

'When have you been to a fucking ploughing competition?' asks Jeff.

'I dunno. When I was a kid, maybe.'

'Sad bastard.'

'At least we got outside. You and your fucking darts.'

'Plenty of tits.'

'When you were seven?'

'I've always been a tit man, mate. Gaaahhhhhhhhhh.'

'Fuck off, Jeff.'

Black Jack. Capable of fluctuation. Good to have on your side.

'Plenty of tit in the Shovel last night.'

'Don't get started on your fucking barmaid stories.'

'Nope. Donna. Barmaid's best mate. Her bloke's in the nick until New Year. Gagging for it.'

'And you're the man to supply it.'

'If she wants it.'

'Well, she won't want it from you.'

'Not what she was saying last night.'

'What's her bloke inside for?'

'GBH.'

'Ha ha. You fucking idiot. RIP Jeff-er-y.'

Laughter. Always laughter.

Some of them fuck off for burgers. The rest shuffle about on the terrace in the December gloom, flicking through the programme.

'At least Courtney's not reffing.'

'Cunt.'

The second half no better than the first. Webb strolling about.

'Do some work, you lazy bastard!'

Psycho flexing his muscles, puffing out his chest. Wilkinson up top, hands on hips.

Minutes tick by like hours. Stoppage after stoppage. The ball in the air. The ball in the stand. The ball lost in SW20.

A Wimbledon corner. An unchallenged header. One fucking nil to the Crazy Gang.

'How much for this shit?'

A late equaliser. A 1–1 draw.

Forest we love you...

For better, for worse.

Even on days like this.

Even in places like this.

Back through the city, back through the blackened station. Stevenage. Peterborough. Lager from a can. All the way home. Geordie fans in the next carriage. Mad as fuck. Wanting to be like them.

'With an N and an E and a Wubble U C...'

BJ in his element, lapping up the banter.

'He's not Black and his name's not Jack...'

Their hometown, emerging out of the darkness.

'Straight down the Bell?'

Fuck that. He's knackered. It's home for tea, to change, to do his hair, to get himself looking presentable. No wonder the other fuckers never pull. And he needs something inside him, something to soak up the beer. He isn't like them. He can't sink it like they can. It always comes up again.

He's three pints behind when he gets into town but that's alright. By half-eight he's in the Hound, programme neatly folded in his back pocket.

A badge of honour. A validation.

Catching up with Lincoln and County and Portsmouth, sharing stories.

'At least you cunts got a point.'

'It was shit.'

'Not as shit as 0–3. What a fucking shambles.'

'Bury? Rather you than me, mate.'

At closing he shuffles home, worse for wear but not so bad, not really, munching on kebab and chips, keeping his place in line amongst the late-night revellers on the long road back, not wanting to overtake or be overtaken, not wanting to gain on anybody, not wanting to be gained upon.

Happy to be invisible.

Monday

A leafy cul-de-sac, dead still in the grey afternoon. Not a fucking soul about, not a breath of the living anywhere. He felt it when he reached the end of the close, felt the anonymity, twelve detached, four-bedroom houses, twelve neat tarmac driveways, twelve double garages, twelve freshly mown front lawns. He could picture the scene, twelve fucking lawnmowers on Sundays, the whir of machinery, the unravelling of hoses, sponges and chamois leathers, twelve pristine people carriers for twelve wives and twenty-four perfect fucking kids. He'd almost arrived at that place himself. Almost. He'd been teetering on the brink of it for months. And then the proverbial shit had hit the fan.

The shit of fifteen years.

He scanned the numbers, thinking it could only ever have been this way for Neil Hopley. Number nine. Our Nigel's number. Our fucking Nigel.

He walked up the drive. Two o'clock on a Monday afternoon. A couple of doves on the telephone wire. No sound. Not a breath of wind. The old town living up to its mediocrity, almost revelling in it.

The most boring town in England.

The iron bitch's roots hung out to dry. Her ignominious burden.

Lower middle class and from the provinces. Embarrassed and irritated by her origins. She turned her back on the place, struck through her history.

Fucking elocution lessons.

He pressed the doorbell. Somewhere inside the place he heard it sound, quiet, reserved, polite. The patter of feet. An image of a child behind the frosted glass, a child's voice calling out. A girl? He couldn't tell just yet. And then a second image. A mother. Hopper's wife.

'Ellen, come here.'

A girl.

Somewhere in the house, a baby crying.

He saw her hesitate, Mrs Hopley, not expecting anyone, probably thinking he was one of those men who turned up on doorsteps in the middle of nondescript afternoons like this one to hawk household products, five dusters for a pound, the latest revolutionary aid to clean, well-ordered living. He thought about Janet Allen coming home to her perfect suburban dwelling to find death waiting in her kitchen. The summer of 89 rearing its ugly fucking head, choosing the opportune moment.

Fifteen years.

Fifteen fucking years.

A breath away.

The lock clicked open and then the door, to reveal a beige carpet, magnolia walls, the scent of pine-fresh.

To reveal Mrs Hopley. Neil's missus. Neil's lady wife.

A look. Suspicious. A foot resting against the frame. A nod all the same. A quiet voice.

'Can I help you?'

Prettier than he expected, but burdened, by motherhood, by a four-bedroomed house in a cul-de-sac, by keeping up the fucking pretence.

He realised he was nervous, ridiculously nervous, looking guilty, feeling guilty. He shouldn't have fucking come. He really shouldn't.

'Is Neil in?' he asked.

'He's at work.'

Of course he was at work. It was two o'clock on a Monday

afternoon. Every fucker was at work. Every fucker except John Finch.

'Can I ask who you are?'

'An old friend,' he said. 'We went to school together.'

'Okay?'

'And we watched football…'

She was still looking at him, seeking more, wanting answers to questions a wife wants to know about a husband she thinks she knows but sometimes wonders about. At times like this, times like now.

'I'm up for a few days, from down south,' said Finchy. 'I just thought I'd catch up…'

… to ask your husband about the day we went to a football match and witnessed a fucking tragedy, to ask him how he's dealing with that after all these fucking years, how he's coped, how he's managed to get himself a wife and two kids and a fucking people carrier and a lawn that looks fit for the 18th green at Wentworth, how he's managed those things.

The little girl pushed past her mum's legs. He looked down and smiled at her. She stared up at him.

'He'll be in this evening,' said the mother, Mrs Hopley, Neil Hopley's fucking wife. 'Can I tell him your name?'

He hesitated. He wasn't certain. He hadn't thought things through.

In the end he said, 'John. Tell him John called.'

'A surname?'

'He'll know me as John. John from football.'

He retreated after that, back down the drive. He could feel her eyes on him, working him out, calculating the risks involved in allowing this man to rekindle a relationship with her husband, thinking about what it might jeopardise, what skeletons it might unearth. He wondered how it might have panned out differently if he'd turned up with Kelly and the children they were yet to have, a dog perhaps, turned up in a great fuck-off people carrier, the latest fucking model and all the trimmings, called Mrs Hopley by her first name, trendily kissed her on each fucking cheek.

Curtains twitching as he wandered back into the estate, on to the lane, into town, back to the fucking hotel, the church spire bearing down upon him, the room shrinking, his head shrinking with it until there was no room for anything of the present, only memories that pressed against his consciousness, seeking recognition, demanding attention.

And the room was too warm. There was no air.

DO NOT OPEN THIS WINDOW plastered on the glass.

What the fuck did they think he was planning to do? He thought about complaining but he didn't have the energy. He flicked the TV on and stared at that instead, trying to get himself back in the land of the living, desperately fending off the memories threatening to tumble out and bury him.

Doncaster.

Wakefield.

Leeds.

North to Geordieland.

Hopley and BJ off to the café together.

BJ and Hopley in the bar at Darlington station.

Bosom pals.

Inseparable.

Fogged-up windows. Yorkshire and Teeside swamped with rain.

Grey skies. Low-slung cloud. The train rocking and swaying.

Soporific.

Knackered.

In need of a kip.

The longest away day of the season.

And then some.

At seven he ambled down to the hotel restaurant. Nobody there. Monday evening, dark October chill in the room, Polish waitress smoking a cigarette in the doorway, blowing smoke into the night. When she saw him she took one last drag, threw the cigarette out into the darkness and pulled the door shut behind her. He picked up a menu, scanned it briefly. He wasn't hungry. He dropped the menu and made his exit. The waitress stared after him, brushing ash from her uniform.

Out into the night then, fog descending on the old town, clinging to the trees, an eerie glow from a solitary street light. A car traipsed past, a silent ghost. He thought about faces pressed against wire mesh, blue lips, the dead propped against the living, bodies on advertising hoardings, bodies laid out in rows along the touchline like fucking stewards at ninety minutes, frantic CPR, sirens wailing but no fucking ambulances, heads covered by jackets, jumpers, football flags that read Liverpool FC, the Liver bird. He thought about being penned in, forced to watch it all unfold before him.

Take it all in. Take it all in because you are never ever going to put this to bed. Run, hide, do what the fuck you like but don't try to forget, don't ever try to forget because you can't. It will find you. It will fucking find you.

He made his way down the Parade and into town, turned up towards the commuter estate that transformed the old town in the eighties. A heart transplant. For better and worse. The old town's heart still beating but it wasn't the same. The commuter estate grew, a malignancy, until it hit the railway line and then it stopped, nowhere left to go. Another estate popped up somewhere else, commuterville in the bloodstream of the old town, altering the fabric of the place, bringing its money, its aloof superiority.

Bad blood. Death in the veins.

Janet Allen, arriving home in the middle of the day, into the big house with the big driveway, not knowing what was waiting in the kitchen, who had let themselves in through the French windows that backed on to the railway. The roar of the 11.35 to Leeds smothering her screams.

A second car in Hopper's driveway. Lexus. Smart. Parked

behind the people carrier, boxing it in. Curtains closed. Warm light beyond the curtains, the cul-de-sac transformed now, a snug security blanket. Him at the end of the driveway, half in and half out, uncertain of himself. Beyond the porch, beyond the light that snapped on when he stepped on to the drive, Neil Hopley. Hopper to his mates. Fellow fucking witness number two, rising from the sofa at the sound of the doorbell, puffing out his cheeks, sharing a look with his wife, knowing only too fucking well who would be standing at the front door when he opened it, why the fucker was there after all these years.

John fucking Finch, no less.

He'd aged. Of course he fucking had. The same round face, the same glasses, but taller, much taller than Finchy remembered. And more confident. More at ease. Obvious from the start.

Hopley didn't say anything. He just stood in the doorway, guarding it.

What the fuck are you doing here? What the fuck are you doing outside my house?

'Alright, Neil?'

Nothing.

'You haven't changed.'

Not a thing.

'Nice car. Nice house. Your parents still around the corner?'

Somewhere up the line, a train sounded its horn.

'Before you begin, I'm not interested.'

Hopley. Some sort of fury behind his eyes. Steadfast in the doorway, protecting his own. Everything to fucking lose.

'Why are you here?' he asked.

Rhetorical question.

'T-Gally tells me you're engaged,' said Hopley.

Finchy nodded.

'Then why aren't you at home with the missus?'

'I came to talk…'

'I don't want to talk. Not about any of that.'

What might that be?

'I thought you might fancy a drink,' said Finchy.

'I don't. I don't want to talk about Stimmo either. I haven't seen him in fucking years. He's just a name in the paper...'

'He was our mate...'

'He was a stranger from another lifetime.'

Train thundering through the old town. The air reverberating. Lights flickering through the dead growth. Hopper giving it some. Train hurtling through the old town, sucking the oxygen after it.

'You come here, set my wife off asking questions, cause a row, upset my fucking kids.'

'Sorry, Neil...'

'It's not their fucking burden. Do you understand? I don't want anything to do with you or anything to do with what we used to be. You stopped going before any of us. Do you remember? You weren't part of the Cup run in 91. You weren't with us in Europe 95.'

'I couldn't be a part-timer, could I?'

'So what the fuck does any of this have to do with you?'

Hopley shifted his weight. The doorstep creaked under it.

'Fucking turning up here after fifteen years. I take my eldest to games. He loves it and he knows nothing about any of that shit. Why should he? It was a different time. A different fucking world.'

'Old habits die hard,' said Finchy, forcing a smile.

'Go and do your dying somewhere else,' said Hopley.

'I was just—'

'Fuck off back down south, John, Fuck off and deal with whatever you've got to deal with. If you need help, go and get counselling.'

'Neil?'

A woman's voice calling from the end of the hall.

Hopper, over his shoulder.

'Coming love.'

Hopper turning back. Barely a whisper now.

'See?'

Mouthed words through gritted teeth.

'You're a cunt. A cunt for coming here, ploughing that shit out of the fucking ground. It's buried. Fucking leave it there and fuck off.'

The sound of the train faded into the distance, the sound that punctuated his life through nights as a kiddie, nights as a young man, mornings on the papers, mornings on the post. Summers and winters. Every fucking weather. Hopper didn't move. He was still stood in the doorway, seeing him on his way.

'And keep off my fucking lawn.'

Short fucking shrift.

Finchy backed away into the night until Hopper closed the door and the hallway light went out. He crossed the road in the direction of the embankment, pulled himself up over the fencing and dropped down on the other side. He traipsed up the slope, stood there looking at the rails, the darkness bleeding in from both directions. North and south. The old town somewhere in between. He considered stepping on to the rails, laying himself prone across the fucking tracks. If the live rail didn't take him the next HST would. But hadn't he read somewhere that fast trains were bad for suicide? Hadn't he read that a person was more likely to be mauled than killed outright, more likely to wind up a paraplegic, wind up with a head, a torso and nothing fucking else?

He laughed at himself in the darkness, laughed at the black slab of darkness, laughed in its sorry-arsed fucking featureless face.

He was losing his fucking mind.

Up the country, down the country.
   Every fucking week.
   This is what you live for.
   You with your decent job.
   You with a place of your own.
   A flat furnished with cast-offs but yours all the same.
   You with an ad in the paper, a room going spare.

It was quiet when he reached the hotel car park. A single light in the lobby. No one on reception. He was two steps from the revolving doors when two shadows appeared from the darkness.

'John Finch,' said one.

Hoods up, scarves tight to noses. No fucking faces.

'How've you been, matey?'

The two of them blocking the doorway. One a big fucker. The eyes of the first vaguely familiar.

But it had been fifteen years.

'Alright,' he said. 'How's yourselves?'

The two of them dancing from one foot to the other, ants in their fucking pants.

'What you been up to?' He knew the voice too. He knew the fucking voice...

Names and faces.

Faces and names.

'Nothing much.'

Rings on their fingers. Big fuck-off signet rings on the big fat fingers of the big fucker.

'Try to keep it that way,' said the smaller one.

'Who's fucking asking—'

One to the ribs from the big fucker, doubling him up. One to the side of the head. He felt the signet ring gouge his scalp. Pain exploded as a third punch struck his ear. He dropped to his knees on the steps of the hotel thinking 'daft cunts', thinking about searing fucking pain, thinking about nothing. Big hands on his collar then, big hands turning him over on to his back so he was looking up at the moon, a fucking football in the night sky behind them. The big fucker planted a trainer on the side of his face.

Thank fuck for casuals.

The smaller one leant in close, hissing in his ear.

'Fuck off back down south. Stop giving people grief. You soft southern cunt.'

And then they were gone and he was on the stone steps, on his back, looking up at the sign for the North Hotel. The revolving doors were spinning. He heard a rushing sound, felt the air tremble. It might have been a late-night HST tearing through the old town, the Edinburgh sleeper, or it might have been the blood pumping around his fucking skull. He dabbed a bloodied paw against his head, felt the stickiness there, crawled through the revolving door and into the lobby, pulled himself to his feet and dragged himself up the stairs.

In Room 11, thinking about Brian fucking Rice and a magical day at Highbury, he turned on the shower and undressed, stepped under the hot water. He felt the sharp sting as the jet of water struck the side of his head and watched the water turn pink about his feet. He stood like that in the shower for ten fucking minutes, hardly moving, shivering with shock, considering heading back where he'd come from, to a different kind of life, knowing it wasn't an option, not yet.

Too much was unfinished. Too much hadn't even fucking started.

A full year and more before Hillsborough.

New Year's Eve. Her in a group, timid, sheltering amongst the rest. Him catching her eye, holding on to it.

Asking for a name.

Jen White.

Walking her out of the pub at last orders, walking her to the taxi rank. Standing on the corner of the street in the chill evening air, lads and lasses planting New Year's kisses on each other, too fucking nervous to make his move even as the taxi driver calls her name.

Asking to see her again.

You find yourself a flatmate.
   A friend of a friend.
   He works all night and sleeps all day.
   You never see each other.
   In many ways it's the perfect arrangement.

Halifax Town 0 v 4 Nottingham Forest
The Shay

The Shay in January. Bleak, brutal January. The Bus Garage end. A speedway track. An amphitheatre. Lifeless, bare branched trees. The proverbial banana skin. But not this year. Not fucking this time. Too early to get excited but not too early to dream.

Because there is only the league and the FA Cup to play for.

Leyton Orient 1 v 2 Nottingham Forest
Brisbane Road

In the seats at Brisbane Road. Calvin Plummer netting the winner against the run of play.

One-nil down, two-one up.

Jammy bastards, riding their luck.

A sense of something in motion.

On the bus, on Bob's bus, on the way home, you dare to talk of a Cup run. You dare to imagine such a thing.

Rock City on the Thursday evening. The Wedding Present. Finchy, Gav and Stimmo rammed into T-Gally's mini. Parking up in the Broadmarsh multi-storey. Pushing through the crowd, pushing right to the fucking barrier to watch Gedge play at one hundred miles an hour. Gedge singing for the broken-hearted, pouring out his soul.

Granadaland.

Brassneck.

A high-speed world of melancholy.

Clever, witty, beautiful bastard.

Blur of wrists on guitar. One hundred minutes of ecstasy thinking, 'This is it. This is who I am.'

Out into the winter evening, slick with sweat and the sweat of others. Buzzing. Fucking buzzing. Ears ringing. Feeling the cold coming on, no fucking jacket, just a rag of a T-shirt, arguing over the set list and the merits of an encore.

Their breaths trail behind them in the midnight shadows.

And that fucking mini. They clamber back into it, Finchy and Stimmo in the back, Gav in the passenger seat, T-Gally turning the ignition and lifting the gear stick into reverse, the thing coming away in his fucking hand like a Laurel and Hardy sketch. Breaking into fits of laughter. T-Gally climbing out of the car, standing there in the empty multi-storey with the gear stick in his grip, open-mouthed, not wanting to laugh, unable to stop himself, scrawling a note on the back of the Weddoes ticket and shoving it on the dashboard, the four of them sprinting for the last train, tearing through the Nottingham streets, work just five hours away, crashing on the train, waking at the old town station, slipping into the flat and into bed, wishing Jen was sleeping over to keep him warm.

On a night like this.

Waking at five with a pounding head, thinking about Gedge singing 'I'm not always so stupid', heading out into the morning, already late, hating the bastard job for its lack of consideration. Fingers burning with cold, hating that too, but picturing the moment, the fucking gear stick coming away in T-Gally's grip, arriving at the depot with a grin tattooed on his face, a fucking story to tell, Harcross at the signing-in book, marking the time.

'I'll make it up.'

'I know you fucking will.'

'I was at a gig. Wedding Present. Rock City.'

Harcoss nods, knowing his stuff.

'Rock City. I saw The Specials there...'

Sliding away in the direction of his frame. Harcross calling him back.

'My mate's car broke down.'

He starts laughing again. He can't help himself.

'The fucking gear stick came clean off in his hand. It's not funny but...'

Harcross laughs louder still.

'Not funny? It's fucking hilarious.'

Harcross shouts down the line of frames after him.

'Half an hour on the table when you get back in.'

Half a fucking hour.

He turns to the frame to see Spence there, grinning, the frame piled high with shit.

'Afternoon.'

Head still ringing from the music and the beer, he sits at the frame doing his thing, watching the other men drift out of the office, until there's just him there, stuffing the bundles of letters into bag number two, trying desperately not to let it get to three of the fuckers.

'Still here?'

Harcross.

'Look at it all. And you want me in for half an hour when I get back?'

'Half an hour keeps your poor time-keeping off your record. Unless you'd rather…'

'Nope.'

'And you owe me for tomorrow.'

'Tomorrow?'

'Aye.'

'What about tomorrow?'

'Southampton?'

'Too fucking right.'

'10.08 train?'

'If I'm lucky.'

'You're not.'

Harcross points to a pile of sacks in the corner.

'What are they?'

'What do you think?'

Harcross runs a finger across his throat.

'You're joking.'

Harcross shakes his head and mouths 'phone bills'.

'On a Saturday?'

Harcross shrugs.

'So what do I owe you for?'

'Letting you take them out Monday.'

'Serious?'

'Who wants a bad-news bill like that on a Saturday? You can take them out Monday. That'll cheer the bastards.'

Harcross.

One of the management but forever one of the boys.

Tuesday

Tuesday. Lunchtime. Big new pub on the fringe of the old town.

The deadland.

Insipid shrubbery. Bedding and borders, parking and playground.

Stained October light. Sombre sky. Sat in a booth nursing a pint, the table littered with meal deal leaflets.

He heard the belly laugh before anything else.

Jeff-er-y.

'John fucking Finch. How are you, serri?'

More belly laughter. It carried him back to happier times, to sun-kissed terraces, to season-ticket Saturdays in the Lower fucking Tier.

City Ground, Oh mist rolling in from the Trent…

'Jeff.'

He stood up, shook the hand of a long-lost brother.

The waitress came over.

'Hello, love,' said Jeff. 'A pint of your best, please. We'll order food in a bit.'

'Your local?'

'My pub mate. Or one of my pubs. I work for the brewery. They know what I like because I sold it to them!'

Jeffery. A lifetime in ale.

'You were in insurance…'

'Fifteen years ago, mate. Fifteen years ago. It was shit. This is better. What about you?'

'Teacher.'

An exaggerated ingestion of air.

'I'd kill them or shag them,' he said. 'Either way I'd end up in the nick.'

More belly laughter. No fucker noticing. No fucker caring. Some bird in heels tottering past, carrying her better days with her.

'Remember that one?'

Finchy looked over his shoulder. He didn't remember. He couldn't remember.

'Sally Watson? Smithy's ex?'

Smithy. Another name stirring in the silt.

'He caught her with Wilt.'

A blank canvas.

'Wilt. Sheep shagger. Fat cunt.'

Finchy shook his head.

'Imagine your missus done over by a Derby fan. The fucking shame.'

Jeff fell to silent pondering.

'You haven't changed,' said Finchy.

'None of us change,' said Jeff. Jeff-er-y. 'We just get older.'

Finchy thought about Hopper, his blurred shape behind the frosted glass.

'Anyway, what brings you up this way?' Jeff asked. 'I thought you'd defected south.'

'I came up for the funeral,' he said.

'Funny,' said Jeff. 'I didn't see you there.'

'I didn't go,' he said. 'I couldn't face it.'

The waitress brought a beer over. Jeff took a mouthful, wiped the froth from his top lip.

'It was alright,' he said. 'Considering what happened. Stupid bastard.'

A lull. A moment. The two of them supping their pints. Two kids laughing in the booth behind them. Hardly a place for mourning the living or the dead.

'I should have gone,' said Finchy. 'I meant to go.'

'Aye, but you didn't. Anyway, now it's done.'

'Did you see him much?'

'Only around town. He stopped going to football years ago.'

'You still go then?'

'Aye. Sixteen season-ticket years and counting. Impressive stuff, eh?'

Another mouthful of ale.

'Gasping,' said Jeff. 'He was with that ex of yours. Did you know that? What's her fucking name?'

'Jen.'

'Aye. What she saw in him I'll never know. Mind you, she went out with you. Pair of cunts.'

More laughter. Infectious laughter that got others laughing. Laughter punctuating everything. A soundtrack to a life.

'Are you married? I'm fucking married. Shouldn't complain, though. 'Er indoors looks after me. Sticks my tea on the table. Top bird. Got any kids? I've a daughter. Light of my days...'

'Fiancée,' said Finchy. 'No kids...'

'You'd best get on with it then, mate. Before she fucks off with someone who will...'

Finchy thought of Kelly, of their house in the close, the spare bedroom, an empty shell.

'I saw BJ the other day.'

'The notorious BJ. Fat cunt. He knows some hard fuckers.'

'Took me to watch City.'

Mocking laughter.

'He's still fucking going there? You know why? They banned him. He goes to City because he can get away with it. He doesn't go for the football. Not these days. Every fucker knows what he goes for.'

'His ban's expired. He says it's more honest.'

'That may be. Still shit, though.'

Another lull. The supping of pints. The two of them off somewhere distant, a northern train station perhaps, a face-off with some random fucking crew, BJ piling in, the rest of them keeping their distance.

'Tough about Clough,' said Finchy.

'Aye. I went over last week. Paid my respects.'

'I need to do that,' he said. He recalled his dream, the endless procession of people on the banks of the Trent. Had he dreamed it? Could he be certain he'd dreamed it?

The waitress came over. In the nick of time…

'Steak please, love,' said Jeff. 'Medium.'

'Same,' said Finchy.

The waitress wheeled away.

'Look at the arse on that,' said Jeff.

The same roving eyes.

'I'm still a dirty bastard,' said Jeff. 'I haven't changed. Women, beer and Forest, that'll do me. Not necessarily in that order mind. Oh and her indoors. And Lilly. Fuck everything else.

More laughter.

Jeff-er-y, a never-ending source of amusement to himself

There were things Finchy wanted to ask but it wasn't the right time, not today. It was enough just to be there, to sit opposite this bloke from his ponderous past, to drag the years back, to help each other seek out lost moments, to chew the fat off some long-lost away day neither of them could truly remember yet neither of them could truly forget.

'Are you going to pay her a visit?' asked Jeff, when all seemed done with, when all the vaults were opened. They were stood in the car park amidst the rush of distant traffic.

'Jen?'

'Who else?'

Finchy shrugged.

'Do you know where she lives?'

Jeff nodded.

'Yes, mate,' he said. 'I was there on Friday. For the wake. I think you should. I think it's the least you can do.'

Some day.

One day.

Jen's birthday.

Rain and wind.

Wind and rain.

The walk is a two bag bastard. The walk is an estate mired in a bleak nothingness. The walk is a sopping-wet card in a pink envelope, crushed red roses.

She's waiting on the doorstep when he reaches the flat, a drowned flower. His heart swells.

'How long have you been here?'

She looks at her watch.

'Forty minutes,' she says.

'Do you not have college?' he asks.

'I'm not going in,' she says.

He lets her in the flat. They climb the stairs.

'I'll stick the kettle on,' she says. 'And I'll run you a bath.'

He undresses in the bathroom, sinks into the hot water. She brings him a mug of tea and undresses herself.

'Why not?' she says.

She climbs in and sits opposite him, all soft flesh and soap suds. He lifts the mug of tea to his lips.

'You're amazing,' he says. 'I should be looking after you.'

She smiles.

'I do my best,' she says.

They spend the day in the flat. They could go out but they stay in, comfortable in each other's company.

It's like that.

It's effortless.

John Finch and Jen White.

An inseparable item.

His mates taking the piss and him not caring.

His mates on the piss and him not bothering.

Days becoming weeks becoming months.

A beautiful thing.

Another street, another doorbell, the old part of the old town. Terraced houses laid row upon row around the shell of the factory that wasn't, the factory that died a slow death through his early years, dumping men like his father, skilled men.

Nervous as fuck outside this two-up, two-down, nervous of how she might respond to finding him on her doorstep.

All these years later.

She came to the threshold in jogging bottoms and a sweat-shirt, smoking, the air behind the door thick with the stuff. He coughed. Before he could speak she was on to him.

'I fucking knew you'd turn up,' she said. 'Not at the service. I knew you wouldn't have the guts for that.'

'I was going to come,' he said. 'I couldn't...'

Weak in spite of himself.

'Couldn't what?'

He bit down on his bottom lip.

'Do you think *I* could? Do you think any of us could? But we fucking well did...'

'I'm sorry,' he said.

'I don't give a fuck,' she said.

He didn't move. He didn't say anything. He didn't leave either. The smoke found the open doorway, escaped into the evening.

Stalemate.

'You'd best come in then,' she said.

Tuesday evening. *Coronation Street*. Cigarette smoke. Alcohol. A living room distorted by loss, at odds with itself.

'Drink?'

She pointed to a half-bottle of vodka on the fireplace. He shook his head. He realised she was older.

'I'm not a drinker,' she said. 'Someone left it here after the wake...'

Lost for words.

'What brings you back this way?'

Was she fucking kidding?

'I'm visiting a few people,' he said. 'After what happened I thought I should.'

'You should have been here Friday.'

'I'm sorry,' he said. Again.

Just the TV. The sound off. Water shifting in the pipes.

'I didn't know about you two,' he said.

'Fucking hell,' she said. 'Is that what this is about?'

'I'm just saying.'

'If you spoke to your mate you might have found out. Or if you spoke to me...'

'I lost touch,' he said. Then he added, 'With everyone.'

'You cut us off,' she said. 'You forgot about us.'

'I didn't forget. I remember everything...'

Everything.

He looked at her. She was staring at the TV. She'd put on weight, become a woman. Of course she had. It was fifteen fucking years.

And she looked tired. She looked strung out.

Who fucking wouldn't?

'He never said anything,' she said. 'I didn't have a fucking clue.'

'It's not your fault,' he said.

'Five years. Two in this house. Sharing this sofa every night. Getting ready for work. Coming home. Going out. Shopping. Holidays. Visiting parents. Breakfast. Dinner. Tea. Bed...'

'Jen...'

'... and I didn't have a clue. Nobody told me. Nobody fucking told me.'

'Jen...'

'Fucking Forest shirt. He was never interested in football. He always let me have my telly on. He never went to games. He never played...'

'It might not have been that.'

'What?'

Anger welling behind her eyes.

'I'm just saying.'

'Don't fucking say. Don't you dare.'

She took a swig of vodka, grimaced, took another.

'I don't even like this shit,' she said.

'Do you want me to put the kettle on?'

'There's no milk,' she said. 'There's nothing to go with it. Only this.'

She raised the bottle.

'I could get some…'

'You'd like that, wouldn't you? A chance to fuck off again…'

'I'll come back.'

'I might not want you to come back. I might not want you here. But you're fucking here, aren't you?'

He got up. She shook her head.

'Don't you dare fucking go,' she said. 'Not until I say so.'

He sat back down again. In the almost silence he could hear *Coronation Street* ending, not in this house, in the house next door, the misery-laden soundtrack to a life. For a moment he was eight years old again, away to bed, his dad on nights, his mam settling down with the TV, the sound creeping up the stairs, him trapped in darkness, the clock in the living room chiming. And winter. Always fucking winter.

'You'd think someone would have said something. *Watch for that. Keep an eye out.* You know. His mum. His dad. His mates. Nobody said a fucking thing. So how was I supposed to know? When the police came, when they started asking questions, I felt like a fucking idiot. A fucking Forest shirt? I thought they'd got the wrong bloke. I told them to go and check again. I even thought it might be you…'

She laughed.

'No such fucking luck…'

She coughed into her glass, took another drag of the cigarette.

'He kept it in a suitcase, in the garage. He got up, left me in bed, brought me a cup of tea, went into the garage, put that fucking shirt on and off he went. I heard his van like I always do, thought, that's him gone for the day, time to get myself up. Except he didn't go to work. He went to that fucking hut instead. The selfish fucking bastard.'

She threw the glass across the room, started bawling.

He got to his feet, went to hold her. It was all he could think to do with himself.

'Don't you touch me,' she snarled. 'Don't you fucking touch me.'

But he held her anyway, gripped her tight, hooking his arms around her, shushing her, rocking on his heels, rocking them both until she stopped struggling, stopped fighting, until she was only whimpering in his arms and he held her like that for an age more, refusing to let go, not wanting to let go, feeling fucking useful at last, feeling like a fucking human being for the first time in weeks, since it all kicked off with Kelly about kids and family and the seemingly impossible idea of a future together.

20th February 1988
FA Cup Round 5

Birmingham City 0 v 1 Nottingham Forest
St Andrew's

Dismal, dull February.

Drab and dire February.

St Andrews. Birmingham B9. Heading down Garrison Lane and across the waste ground to the back of the away terrace.

Ripe for fucking ambush.

The police on their horses.

The police in their white vans.

The police and their truncheons.

Everything kicking off on the waste ground.

A battleground.

Amidst naked trees and naked skies.

The Tilton Road end steep and wide, packed to the rafters. Ten thousand mighty Reds. Bitter atmosphere on a bitter afternoon. No love lost. Not here. Not today.

And not much between these two Midland sides, not much separating one from the other, just a classic Forest counter-attack, a loose ball dropping to Gary Crosby, Gary Crosby firing home the only goal at the Railway end.

You delirious on the Tilton Road terrace.

You and BJ and Hopper and Jeff and T-Gally and Gav and JC and Sharpster.

And Stimmo.

All of you delirious.

The reds go marching ON, ON, ON...

Somehow he found himself propped on the sofa, her leant against him, a film on the TV, light-hearted, irrelevant, easy. He felt her drop into sleep, relax into regular breaths. He sat watching the screen, sipping vodka because there was nothing else, trying not to think, trying to remain in the moment and not slip backward through fifteen years to nights like this one on the yellow sofa in his upstairs flat, her over for the night, the borrowed furniture, the mismatched lampshades, empty cupboards. His first forays into independent living. He told himself he wasn't guilty of anything, told himself that over and over. He'd come to pay his respects. That was all.

To pay his respects. He could hardly fucking believe it.

When the film ended he sat for half an hour, not wanting to move, not wanting to wake her, using the remote to flick through an endless stream of channels, unable to connect with anything. And so he sat for another hour, eyes half shut, drifting where the vodka took him, until she stirred, sat up, grounded herself.

He looked at the clock. It was almost 2 a.m.

'I'd best go,' he said.

She got to her feet, disappeared upstairs, left him sitting there, awkward, wanting to leave now, wanting to leave in the right way, satisfied he'd achieved what he came for, offered some empathy. He heard the toilet flush, her footfall on the stairs. She returned to the living room, came right out and said it.

'You can stay here.'

He didn't move. She laughed at his awkwardness.

'Listen,' she said. 'That's the first time I've slept since this nightmare started. I need someone here.'

'Your family?'

She shook her head, laughed.

'If you want...' he said, '... I can sleep here, no trouble.'

He patted the sofa.

She shook her head again.

'No,' she said. 'Sleep next to me.'

He realised his head was spinning. He glanced at the empty vodka bottle.

'Please,' she said.

'What if somebody finds out,' he said, pathetically.

'I don't fucking care,' she said. 'I don't give a shit what anyone thinks. They can think whatever they like.'

She turned her back to him and walked out of the room. He heard her climbing the stairs.

'Do what you want,' she said.

He got to his feet, stood there in the living room, staring about himself, thinking of Stimmo at Leicester, steaming in with BJ and the others, Stimmo on Bob's bus, Everton away, laid out on the back seat covered in his own puke, Stimmo a dead weight in a dark shed by the railway tracks, the quiet creak of the rope against the beam, a passing train sending him rocking into a crack of daylight. And he thought of Stimmo on the steep terrace at Hillsborough, those three words falling from his mouth, the very moment he changed to somebody with whom none of them were able to correlate.

'He's fucking dead.'

And now Stimmo was dead.

He thought about Kelly. He pictured the spotless kitchen, the meticulous living room, the narrow staircase, the dark landing, the bedroom door. He tried to picture beyond it but came up against his barrier.

Time and time and time again.

He looked at the front door, his exit point, heard the wind buffeting the wood, considered the blustery street beyond. He imagined himself trudging back to the hotel, collar up, his footsteps echoing through the old town's narrow lanes, out on to the High Street, up the hill to that bed in the room with the windows that wouldn't fucking open. He was pissed for fuck's sake. He wasn't sure he'd make it. And what if those two nasty fuckers were about, eager to give him another seeing to?

What then?

All excuses of course. Because he couldn't do it to her, not again, couldn't leave her so coldly, so fucking selfishly.

Not tonight.

The bedroom window was open. Did she remember? Did she open it for his sake? She was already beneath the covers. He took off his jeans, slipped in beside her, lay there for a minute staring at the ceiling, wondering if she'd changed the fucking sheets since...

... and then she moved closer to him, pressed herself against him. He pulled her in until she was wrapped up in his warmth, closed his eyes.

Scared shitless.

But she fell asleep in seconds, left him marooned in darkness and staring at the gap in the curtains, listening to the rain drumming against the roof tiles. He tried to let himself go, to feel the same as she did perhaps, as though the world beyond the window had retreated a notch, just for a little while, just for a few hours, that it didn't matter if it was 1989 or 2004, that fifteen years had compressed to form a seamless stretch of a moment they could inhabit as their own.

But if there was such a place he couldn't reach her there. He lay awake in a black vault instead, watching grainy scenes repeat themselves on the ceiling above him, shameful acts of heartless selfishness in black and white, splashes of colour for the odd times he made her smile.

And he does make her smile. Through a winter and a spring. Nights at hers with her mam and dad, her sister, her brother.

Nights in his flat, just the two of them.

Sometimes, afterwards, she falls asleep with her head on his chest. He lays awake and strokes her hair, breathes in the scent of her perfume, feels the warmth of her body against his own.

He has yearned for this, a connection like this, a wholeness like this one.

For a time he feels himself wanting for nothing else.

He can't imagine a scenario in which they won't be together forever.

That's how young he is.

That's how much living he's yet to experience.

Wednesday

He was awake when dawn broke, as still as death itself, staring at the crack in the curtains, willing the new morning to come, terrified of hearing a knock at the door, the click of a key in a lock, imagining any number of visitors; her mum; her sister; her brother. One of Stimmo's lot.

But nobody came.

She was still sleeping, pressed against him. He felt sick in the stomach, imagining her waking from futile dreams to find him there and not Stimmo.

He shouldn't have stayed. He should have looked after number one.

Ever the selfish bastard.

When the sun came bleeding through the curtains he put some space between the two of them, eased his skin free of her skin, manoeuvred his body to the edge of the bed. She stirred and he closed his eyes, pretending to sleep, to be comfortable where he was. She rose from the bed with her back to him. Through narrowed eyes he watched her naked silhouette against the curtain. He closed his eyes as she turned to face him, felt her watching him. He lay there wanting to believe that when he opened his eyes again he'd be back in Room 11 at the hotel, that all of this was a desperate fucking dream of his own.

He heard her leave the room, heard her pull the door shut quietly behind her, heard the rush of a tap in the bathroom. He tried to sit up in Stimmo's bed, feeling the room spin, his stomach burn, the vodka returning to punish him. He placed his bare feet on the carpet, prepared himself, shifted his weight on to his legs. The rush of blood caused him to stumble forward into the chair his clothes were draped across. He reached out an arm, steadied himself against the wall. Then he fought to dress himself. It was all he could do to keep his balance as he stepped from one leg to the other, to stop his head from swimming, to prevent his stomach from going into spasm. He managed everything except his socks.

Footsteps on the stairs. She came into the room in her dressing gown carrying two mugs of black tea, passed one to him, sat on the edge of the bed, staring at that same crack in the curtains, at the same slice of sky beyond. He watched her, uncertain what to do with himself.

'Thanks,' she said at last.

He didn't say anything. He was lost for fucking words.

The two of them, sipping at steaming black tea in silence, her on the edge of the bed, him sat upright, his back propped against the wall.

'You left so quickly,' she said.

'Jen…'

'Shut up. Just let me get all of this out,' she said. She brushed at her knee with the palm of her hand. 'It took me a long time to get over you leaving the way you did.'

'It was eight months,' he said. 'February to October. All drawn out. I didn't just…'

She turned to look at him.

'Don't,' she said. 'Please, don't. We were still sleeping with each other in August.'

'You wouldn't leave things…'

'I was barely eighteen.'

'Your sister…'

'My sister?'

'She came to the flat.'

'My sister.'

'I had all that coming at me, wedding plans, bridesmaids' dresses, your mam and dad…'

She shook her head.

'It was the engagement party,' he said. 'That's what started it. They were all asking about us.'

'You daft prick. Do you think I wanted what she wanted?'

He stared at his socks on the chair.

She stood up, went to the window and pulled the curtain open, stood there looking down on the street. 'I just want you to listen,' she said. 'I don't want you to say anything, just fucking listen. Then you can do what the fuck you want.'

She turned to look at him. He nodded silently in her direction.

'When you left I threw myself at someone else,' she said. 'I ended up moving in with him.'

She looked down at herself, seemed to consider her appearance for the first time then dismiss the thought with a knowing laugh. Or something like that. He was no fucking expert.

'I lived with that bloke for three years,' she said. 'And I spent a lot of that time thinking about you, even though you were miles away living another fucking life, even though you were a bastard to me in all sorts of ways. I'd get up and stare out of the window at the same fucking streets morning after morning and I'd think to myself *you know something, he was right to do it, right to fuck off*, but then I'd hear another voice telling me *he could have taken you with him, he could have saved the both of you* and that was enough to make me hate you for an hour or so, just long enough to get another day kicked off, then the whole sorry scenario would repeat itself...'

'Saved?'

She looked directly at him, shook her head.

'When that sham ended I had to move back home. It was a disaster. My brother was kicking off big time, everybody this close to murdering each other. I saw you one Christmas around then. You were home for the holidays, out with your old mates. You sailed right past me, didn't even bat an eyelid...'

'I didn't see...'

'Shut up,' she said. 'I know you didn't. I remember thinking to myself *he didn't fucking look at you. What the fuck have you done to yourself?* I gave up for a while after that, stopped going out, stopped bothering. I tried the 'concentrate on a career' thing. That was a joke. I ended up having meaningless flings with blokes at work, did my fucking reputation the world of good. Another fucking story. And then, when I finally got to going out again I met Stimmo and would you credit it, he was another shadow of the fucking past.'

She smiled an ironic smile.

'I met him in town,' she said. 'I didn't know who he was. He came straight up to me. He said he knew me as your ex and that you were a fucking silly prick for breaking up with me and fucking off.'

He supped his black tea, tried not to grimace.

'I nearly didn't bother. But he was a perfect gent,' she said. 'I told myself I could do with a bit of that, a bit of fucking appreciation for a change. Nobody treated me like he did. I've been on a pedestal for the past five years...'

He forced a smile. He couldn't remember a time when he'd been so aware of himself, of his movements, of the expression he was exhibiting, of how someone might read those things.

'I fucking hated that pedestal,' she said. 'I saw other men behind his back. I blame you for that.' She pointed to herself. 'So this isn't some broken body wracked with grief for a dead boyfriend. It's someone who's riddled with guilt over what they did to a good man. Or what they didn't fucking do.'

He saw anger welling in her eyes again, the same anger surfacing and re-surfacing.

'I could lie to you,' she said. 'I could tell you I stopped thinking about you, got over you in a flash, but I didn't. You were always fucking there. Even when I had a man that would do anything for me I had to keep him at arm's length. I tormented the poor bastard really. I don't think he ever felt he truly had me. And now this...'

'What he did has nothing to do with you,' he said

'How the fuck do you know?'

He made a move to get out of the bed, felt the same sharp pain behind his eyes.

'Oh no,' she said. 'You aren't fucking going anywhere.'

She moved across the room to the doorway, slammed it shut, stood there with her back against it.

'Let me tell you something,' she said. 'This has everything to do with me. I'll live with this for the rest of my life because I should have cared more, made him feel wanted, made him feel loved.'

'Maybe he was happy loving you.'

She shook her head.

'I should have married him. He asked me enough times. Soon, I kept saying. Soon. And in my head I was thinking just one more night with someone else, one more encounter that wasn't what he was laying on the table, which was solidity and settlement and a future together. And he must have known. He fucking must have. This town's too small to keep those things quiet. But he never fucking challenged me, never said anything. And then he goes and does this to himself and people tell me it's all because of a fucking football match.'

He stared at her.

'Even if it is I should have known about that because I should have been open to him telling me. But I wasn't. I didn't fucking listen to him and I didn't know anything about it. I should have made the connection, but he wasn't like you. He didn't bother with football.'

'He never said anything?'

'About what?'

'About football? About Forest?'

She shook her head.

'Do you know something else?' she said. 'Do you want to hear something truly fucking horrendous? Do you want to know what sort of person I really am?'

He didn't say anything. He didn't do anything. He just sat there on the bed, marooned in the covers, his back against the wall.

'I've had this thing going through my head,' she said. 'This thing that keeps telling me I don't even get the satisfaction of knowing he did what he did because of me. I get questions instead. Questions and more questions, about fucking football and that fucking day you all went to a match and came back changed. Everybody's been telling me about it. And all I can think about is you. You not calling me to tell me you were okay. Me hearing it on the radio and not even knowing what fucking end you were in. Waiting and waiting by the fucking phone, becoming more and more convinced that something had happened to you, that you were in the midst of it all. Fuck, when I picture that day and what you put me through I can hardly believe I'm stood here speaking to you, that I forgave you for putting me through that anguish. And my mam, and my dad. All of us. But you didn't give a fuck.'

She crashed the door with her fist.

'I blame that day,' she said. 'I blame that day for everything that happened between us. You were happy before and miserable after. You were satisfied before and restless after. You were one person and then you were someone else. But I didn't know Stimmo was there too. Nobody told me. He never told me. So I got it twice, didn't I. Once and then again. You and Stimmo. What are the chances?'

He sat there in silence. Truly found out. Truly exposed.

'Kenny Dalglish,' he said at last. 'Three fucking times.'

'What?'

'Nothing,' he said. 'Sorry.'

They fell into silence. The curtain twitched in the breeze. He thought about the street below, encroaching footsteps.

Eventually she asked him, 'What's it like down there?'

'Where?'

'Down south.'

'The same,' he said. 'More expensive. The people aren't so friendly...'

'But you're happy you went?'

He shrugged.

'It was fifteen years ago. I had to...'

She stared back at him.

'I had to do something,' he said. 'Before it was too late.'

'Because your life was so fucking awful?'

'Because I could see the next forty years in front of me, the lifers at the PO, intelligent blokes just going through the motions. I wanted more than what they had...'

'And?'

'And nothing. I'm not sure what they had was so bad, not now, but then ... then I was certain...'

He put his tea down.

'... and frightened,' he said. 'Of what people wanted for us.'

'My sister. My perfect fucking sister.' She spewed laughter at him. 'So now you're back...'

'To sort some things,' he said.

He could remember her now. Scenes were flooding back, the dam well and truly breached. He could see the uncertain seventeen-year-old, see her in the town pubs in the early days, him all stoked up with jealousy, terrified of losing what he'd discovered, and he could see her naked and unwanted in his bed eighteen months down the line, how she'd come to represent the very thing he needed to escape from, the town and everything in it, everything that had happened. He remembered the things he'd done to her in those desperate months when he didn't have the fucking decency to turn her away from his door, always inviting her in, throwing down crumbs of hope, making a fucking mess. And here he was all these years later propped up in her bed, wondering once again how the fuck he was going to slide away, knowing it had to start with him getting his socks on and getting out of the bedroom, knowing there was that and then everything else to get through before he returned from whence he came ... or crawled back under his fucking stone.

He saw the woman she grew into before he left, how he'd aged her. And he saw her looking at him now, staring across the room at him.

'I'm sorry,' he said.

'What for?'

'Everything,' he said. 'All of it.'

'We're all sorry,' she said.

She followed him down the stairs to the front door. He stopped there, waiting to be shown out, not wanting it to look like he was running away again, both of them clear that it was exactly what he was doing, still terrified the door might burst open, that he'd be discovered there in his old mate's house with his old mate's girlfriend.

His old mate's fucking widow.

And then he was out of there, back in the light, staring across the old town at the grand old church spire, thinking of the hotel and a cooked breakfast, thinking of Kelly, thinking how long this whole fucking charade might be set to go on for. Kids were making their way to school, the same uniforms, the boys in their black blazers heading one way, burdened with bags, urgent in their steps, the brown-jacketed others heading in the opposite direction, sauntering, hands in pockets, hardly a bag between them.

And never the twain shall meet...

Nothing changing in the old town.

And why the fuck should it have? It was fifteen years, the blink of an eye. Or it was half a lifetime. It was one of those things.

When he turned to look over his shoulder to see her still stood in the doorway in her dressing gown, her eyes red from crying, he knew he'd see her again before the mess was cleaned up. He couldn't leave things half-baked with her again.

He just couldn't.

12th March 1988
FA Cup Quarter-Final

Arsenal 1 v 2 Nottingham Forest
Highbury

Monday lunchtime. The Cup draw on the radio.

Not Arsenal away. Not Arsenal away. Not fucking Arsenal away.

'Arsenal ... will play ... Nottingham Forest'.

Arsenal away.

You're straight to a phone, making your plans.

A week later you take a train to the City Ground. You queue in the car park. You queue with the lads. You queue for hours. You hold the ticket in the palm of your hands. You kiss the ticket.

You are going to Highbury with eight thousand brothers.

And here you are, at Highbury in March.

Incessant rain.

The Clock end rammed with a solid fucking mass of dreamers. Wilkinson rifles one in from twenty-five yards to ignite incandescent ecstasy and a dream becomes something tangible. The tricky trees are in full flow, soaking up pressure and springing from deep, caressing the football, keeping it on the turf. The beautiful, beautiful game. Clough Snr the master, Clough Jnr the apprentice with the vision of a seer, slipping Brian Rice in on goal. Brian Rice all on his own in the Arsenal half. Brian Rice bearing down on the Clock end, bearing down on the Arsenal goal.

Not Brian Rice. Not fucking Brian Rice. Any fucker but Brian Rice.

The *Sunday* fucking *People*...

Going, going, gone! Rice springs the Arsenal offside trap, lifts the ball over Lukic and the Gunners are out of the Cup.

Three photographs. Your fans erupting in stages behind the goal, grainy faces etched in anticipation, in wonder, in delirium.

The cult of Brian Rice is born.

Brian Rice, journeyman, born in Bellshill, Lanarkshire, a Nottingham legend in his time. Robin Hood, eat your fucking heart out. All together to the tune of 'Yellow Submarine':

Number One is Brian Rice, Number Two is Brian Rice, Number Three is Brian Rice…

Highbury in the rain. Drenched to the bone in the Clock end. Sambas soggy. Gooners not happy. Your coach pelted with bricks and mortar. Your coach attacked by a thousand angry fists.

Cocooned. Not giving a shit. Face pressed against the window, aggravating the fuckers with wanker signs and middle fucking fingers, not even flinching when the blows come at the glass.

Because you are there, at Highbury.

And you are on your way to an FA Cup Semi-Final.

Knackered. Sick to the stomach.

Guilty of nothing. Guilty of everything.

He slept for six hours, cocooned in the room with the windows that wouldn't open, sunlight streaming in. The room too hot, robbed of air. Unable to breathe. His head pounding, his legs numb, his arms two dead weights.

Unable to breathe.

Unable to breathe.

The sound of screaming woke him, high-pitched, incessant screaming. He opened his eyes, sucked in a lungful of nothing. The phone in his room was ringing. It took him a moment to locate it, the phone on the dresser, out of reach. He dragged his forlorn body across the space, lifted the receiver, confused, uncertain, hardly with it.

'Hello?'

His voice a dry croak, the taste of vodka still lingering, his stomach lurching.

Starving.

'Mr Finch. It's reception. There's a call for you.'

'A call?'

'Shall I put it through?'

'I suppose so...' he said.

A click. A crackle. A voice he didn't recognise.

'John Finch?'

'Yes,' he said, more alert now, imagining the fucking police or something, thinking of Kelly, a tragic discovery, the fucking madness of that evening.

But it wasn't the police.

'Can you hear me? Can you hear me good and clear?'

Hard-edged. Local. Threatening.

'I can hear you,' he said.

'Stay away from Jen White, you sick fucking cunt.'

The line went dead.

He sat up, his heart beating ten to the fucking dozen, trying to rouse himself, to put voices to faces, not having a clue where to start. He felt the convulsions then, the bile in his throat, struggled to the bathroom, threw up in the toilet. On his knees in the old town, vomit on his lips, vomit in the toilet bowl, the bitter smell of vomit and vodka all around him. He vomited again, planted his forehead on the cold toilet bowl, ten thousand nails in his skull. Ten thousand nails and ten thousand hammers.

Guilty of nothing.

Guilty of everything.

He milled about in the hotel room for the rest of the afternoon, a living corpse, thinking about Jen and Stimmo, about trouble pouring through an open door. He thought about other doors too, closed fucking doors and the secrets they contained. He thought about Duckenfield and Bettison and the SYP. He flicked through the TV channels, stuck the racing on, the two-thirty from Kempton, the rain drilling down, the steamed-up camera lens, the mad bastards cheering their rides home.

Horses for fucking courses.

At five he traipsed through the hotel corridors to the bar. It was empty, the shutters down, tables stacked against the wall, the carpet damp from cleaning. He tried the dining room instead where the tables were set for breakfast. There was no fucker in there either. The whole place was deserted, save for the girl on reception, tapping away at a keyboard. He made his way to the desk, waited in dumb silence like a spare prick at a wedding.

'Are you okay, sir?' She flashed a bored-looking smile in his direction.

'Fine,' he said. 'Yourself?'

'I'm well,' she said. 'What can I do for you?'

He shook his head.

'Nothing,' he said. Then he said, 'Is there food tonight?'

'The chef's not coming in,' she said.

She went back to the keyboard, to the PC screen, to a list of numbers and symbols.

'It's just that I'm hungry,' he said.

'We have sandwiches,' she said. 'Sandwiches, crisps and peanuts. Or there's the contents of your minibar.'

The fucking minibar. Home to a solitary Twix and fuck all else.

'I thought I'd be able to get something,' he said.

She shook her head.

'Evening meals are reserved for pre-booked coach parties,' she said. 'We have no coach parties. If we did I could squeeze you in. There are restaurants in town. It's a ten-minute walk.'

He considered what restaurants the old town might have to offer on a Tuesday evening in October. He smiled at the tragedy of it all.

'I know,' he said. 'I used to live here. I lived here for a long time.'

She smiled back at him.

'But not any more.'

'No,' he said. 'Not any more.'

'Why did you move away?' she asked him.

He shrugged.

'To escape?' she asked.

'Maybe,' he said.

'To find somewhere better?'

'Perhaps.'

'Is it better?'

'Is what better?'

'The place you live now,' she said.

'In some ways,' he said.

'I feel the same about my country,' she said. She wasn't looking at the PC screen any more. There was some life about her.

'You're Polish, right?'

'Yes,' she said.

'Do you miss home?'

'Sometimes.'

'How long have you been away?'

She held up three fingers.

'Three years,' she said.

'Will you go back?'

'One day,' she said. 'When the great migration ends.'

He stood beyond the desk, looking down at her in her uniform, thinking she might be pretty, not entirely decided on the fact.

'When I left here there were no foreigners,' he said.

'That's why they hate us,' she said.

'Who hates you?' he asked.

'The local people,' she said.

He laughed aloud at that, couldn't help himself.

'They hate people from the next town,' he said. 'I shouldn't worry too much about that.'

'It's strange,' she said. 'They hate us just for being.'

'You should try coming back after fifteen years,' he said.

'It could be nice here,' she said. 'If the people were more accepting.'

'They're okay deep down,' he said. 'But if you don't like it, why stay?'

She held up her hands, waved in the direction of the empty foyer.

'I go where they send me,' she said.

'You live in the hotel?'

She nodded.

'Eventually I will get a move to London,' she said. 'Then we'll see.'

'London,' he said.

She looked at him then, expecting him to say something perhaps. But what the fuck was there to say?

Back in the hotel room, back in his own world, he called the house, listened to the phone ring, let it run its course, put the phone down, rang the number again. He did that for twenty minutes with his arse perched on the edge of the bed, images of the evening he left wrestling for attention.

The two of them in the living room, Kelly spread out on the couch, him in the chair. A row about his intentions. His fucking bag in the hallway.

Waiting.

'What happened to us?' he asked.

There was a moment when she didn't say anything, when she seemed to be sucking it all in, setting things up for what was to come.

'What happened to you?' she said at last.

'No, us, Kelly. What happened to us?'

'I know what happened to me.'

'I'm not talking about that.'

For whatever reason she didn't follow that familiar fucking route. For whatever reason she clambered off the sofa and crawled across the carpet, draped herself over the arm of his chair, placed one hand on his knee.

'I just want to take us to the next step,' she said. 'You know what I want.'

'And then everything will magically sort itself...'

'I think so,' she said.

She moved on to his lap, placed her forearms on his shoulders.

'You realise you'd get to fuck me incessantly,' she said. 'Night after night, time after time.'

A new fucking tactic this. He wondered what she'd been reading, who she'd been talking to. He could see the bitches at her work, lining up with their fucking tips and methods. But for all that his cock was stirring. Of course it fucking was. He had a face full of tit. She had her cunt pressed against his thigh. He could feel the fucking heat there. She kissed him, stuck her tongue in his mouth.

Fuck it.

He kissed her back, grabbed her arse and pulled her up his lap so that her cunt was grinding against his cock. She squirmed with encouragement.

'Upstairs,' she whispered.

He followed her to the bedroom, three steps behind, her arse in his face. She shimmied when she realised. He pressed his nose against her crotch, made a show of breathing in the scent of her, heard her gasp, the two of them in the zone now, the outcome inevitable.

In the bedroom she sat on the bed and pulled him towards her, went straight for his belt, unzipped his flies, pulled his cock out of his boxers, started slobbering and licking at it. He gripped the back of her head, knowing full well her strategy but not bothering to second-guess it, focusing on his own thing, fully fucking loaded.

And then he was splayed on the bed, and Kelly was riding him, grunting, moaning on top of him while his hands squeezed her arse and tits. Breathless, frenzied fucking, just like the old days. And somewhere in that, eyes closed, mind desperately seeking obstruction, he found himself at Ashton Gate, Garry fucking Parker ramming the ball in from the edge of the box, six thousand Forest going fucking mental on a rain-drenched terrace, punched and kicked and dragged in all directions, transported from one point to another, a sperm in a shoal of sperm, rising and cresting a wave.

Better than sex. Better than fucking sex.

He came to his senses with milliseconds to spare, pulled out of the challenge and fell to earth, sprayed on Kelly's stomach so that she came crashing down along with him.

'You prick,' she screamed.

He felt her fist strike his nose. Her fingernails gouge his chest.

'You fucking prick!'

And then he was rolling off the bed, scrambling out of her reach.

'We're supposed to be waiting,' he shouted.

'Waiting for what?'

'We agreed, to wait.'

'It's what you agreed.'

'It's what the doctor advised.'

'Six months,' she yelled. 'It's nearly a year. Do you think I'm fucking you for the fun of it?'

'Keep it down,' he said.

'Fuck off. Fuck the neighbours. I'll yell fucking rape. I'll yell fucking rapist.'

She was gone from him. She was somebody else.

All he could think about was the last time, of getting off the hook. He ran to the bathroom, tried to piss, couldn't manage it, listened to her breathing behind him.

'You know how I feel,' he said at last. 'You know I'm not sure about it.'

'Then I'm not sure about us,' she said.

'Kels—'

'Don't call me that. You've thrown away the right to call me that.'

'Kelly...'

'Kelly what? Kelly, let's wait and wait until you're too old?'

'You're thirty-three.'

'And I've lost one child already. How do I know it's not going to happen again?'

A thick channel of shadow separated them. It might as well have been the widest fucking ocean. To break it she turned on the bathroom light, sat herself on the toilet, grabbed a wad of toilet paper and started wiping herself.

'You're supposed to want this as much as I do,' she said.

He started out of the bathroom. He didn't want to watch her wiping his spunk from her stomach.

'Where are you off to?' she asked.

'Somewhere else,' he said.

'I'm sick of you,' she said.

She got up from the toilet, pulled him back by his wrist.

'Now what?' he shouted.

But she didn't answer. She just opened the bathroom door, switched off the light and slammed the door behind her, left him in pitch darkness, pondering another fucking defeat.

In the end he followed her back to the bedroom, climbed on to the bed, lay down next to her. She wasn't having that. She rolled out of bed again, dragged the duvet to the floor, turned on the light and positioned herself in the middle of the room.

'Turn the light out,' he said. 'For fuck's sake.'

She shook her head.

'No,' she said. 'Look at me. Fucking look at me.'

She stood there, naked and exposed in the middle of the bedroom.

He shielded his eyes.

'Look at me,' she said again. 'Why is this not good enough for you? Why am I not good enough?'

He sighed.

'I just can't do it,' he said. 'That's it. I've said it.'

That's when the shit really hit the fan.

Twenty minutes later, bloodied and bruised, he grabbed his bag and made his way out of the place, out into the night. He looked back at the house, at the darkened windows, at the sudden stillness, feeling the sweat on his skin cooling, feeling the breeze at his collar. And he thought about going back, retracing his steps, climbing the stairs, pushing the bedroom door open. But he couldn't do it. There had been a breaking point and they'd finally reached it. Things had happened. Things that dislodged memories of other things, dark things, dark, nasty things he didn't understand.

He turned his back on it all, made his way to the station and a life left behind. He had no fucking choice, no fucking choice at all.

He called Jen from the hotel room. The phone rang at her place. Rang and rang until a male voice answered.

'Hello?'

He didn't say anything.

'Prick,' said the voice on the other end. The phone went dead. For the fun of it, to antagonise the bastard, he called the number again.

'Hello?' The same voice. Alert now. Angry.

And again, he didn't say anything.

'You're a wanker, John Finch,' said the voice. 'A fucking dead wanker.'

He heard the receiver slam on to its bed.

He waited a moment, mulling it over. Fuck it. He called a third time. The phone rang and rang.

Nobody answered.

9th April 1988
FA Cup Semi-Final
Liverpool 2 v 1 Nottingham Forest
Hillsborough

Sheffield on a Saturday.
    Sheffield on the Kop.
    An impenetrable memory.
    There are only snippets.
    A John Barnes penalty.
    That fucking Aldridge volley.
    Clough scrambling a futile lifeline.
    It's all lost in shadow.
    Forgotten.
    Misplaced in the other.
    Were you there?

He woke to the sound of thunder, came up groggily from some dismal, floundering dream. He heard a voice, someone shouting his name. The thunder was the sound of fists pummelling the hotel-room door, a prelude to pummelling his fucking head. He remained perfectly still. He could hear the bastards hissing in the corridor.

'I told you. The prick's at her place.'

'He can't be.'

'She hid the cunt.'

'No, the slimy fucker's in there.'

More shouting.

'Oi! John fucking Finch. Come out, you piece of shit!'

He slithered out of bed, scuttled across the room on his hands and knees, bollock-naked, a primordial organism. Silently, he flicked the security bolt across, just in case they got a fucking key card from somewhere, just in case they were that fucking bright. He rose to his feet and stared out through the little spyhole. The same two as the other evening for sure, only this time he could see their faces. A mad bastard with huge fucking knuckles adorned with signet rings. A Polish fucking accent. The other shorter, all angles and sharp edges. It took him a moment to connect the face with the past. Jen White's little fucking brother. In with blokes that relished beating the shit out of strangers. Now they wanted to beat the shit out of John Finch. So he hunkered there, naked in the bedroom, staring out of the spyhole at the two of them, watching them hop from one foot to the other. They looked like they were on something. A fist came flying at the door. Finchy ducked backwards as it hammered against the wood. He couldn't help imagining the punch landing, couldn't help imagining his front teeth caving in, making dinner of his own fucking enamel.

'I know you're in there, cunt.'

The brother.

'You can't fucking stay there forever.'

The big Polish bastard. Bent out of shape.

Finchy pressed his eye to the lens again, witnessed the shift manager appear at the end of the corridor weakly flanked by two chambermaids. All three of them looked terrified but the poor fucking shift manager had to do something.

'Excuse me. Excuse me. What's the problem?'

He heard the brother say,

'Don't fucking speak to me, you prick. Don't you dare speak to me.'

One more hammer blow crunched the door.

'We're on to you, Finchy,' shouted the brother. 'You're fucked.'

And then they were gone, down the corridor, shoving the shift manager into the corner, shouldering the chambermaids out of the way, all swagger and posture, but he knew the big bastard would give it even if the brother was a twat. The first round had been a fucking warning and that had hurt enough. The big fucker was hard as nails.

Finchy retreated across the room and into the bathroom, stepped in the shower, shaking with nervous tension, scared shitless. He looked down at his gouged chest, at the scratch marks Kelly had given him when she'd launched herself at him.

John Finch, human fucking punchbag.

He got dressed and packed, calculated how long he ought to leave it before making a dash to the station and away from the place. He went to the window and stared out at the street-lamps, the noiseless evening. He sat on the end of the bed, staring at his mobile, thinking of Jen and thinking of Kelly, wondering if either of them would pick up their phones if he called, if that were even possible, thinking about mute living rooms and silent halls, dark stairs and locked bedrooms full of secrets, wondering what the fuck to do next.

A fucking fugitive in the town that raised him.

He undressed again, dropped back into bed. There was nothing he could do, nowhere he could go.

Summer on the streets. Summer with his shirtsleeves rolled high. Summer in the village with Jen. Summer walks. Summer sunshine.

Jen White and John Finch.

John Finch and Jen White.

England struggling at Euro 88.

England returning home in shame.

Long-drawn-out evenings on the yellow sofa, sultry nights in his room, the window open, cool breeze on bare skin.

'Lisa met someone,' says Jen. 'She says he's the one.'

'Great,' he says.

'Kevin.'

'Kevin?'

'That's his name, Kevin.'

'Sounds like a bundle of laughs,' he says.

'You know him. From when you were kids … or something.'

He sorts through his Kevins, realises he only knows one.

'Aye, he's alright,' he says. 'He's sound.'

'Saahnd as a paahnd,' she mocks.

They laugh. It's easy to laugh.

But Lisa's met Kevin.

A thing slips between them. An imperceptible thing.

The summer meanders ever onward.

Finchy and Jen.

Jen and Finchy.

But on some days, after his round is done, Finchy watches the girls in the park, the girls in their summer clothes. On some evenings, when he's out with the lads, Finchy watches the girls in the bars.

There's a gentle tug at his shoulder.

It's almost unnoticeable.

He feels it all the same.

The Football League receives £44 million for a four-year TV rights deal.

Liverpool, Everton, Manchester United, Tottenham Hotspur, Arsenal, West Ham United, Aston Villa, Sheffield Wednesday, Newcastle United and Nottingham Forest, your Nottingham Forest, have threatened to form a breakaway league in order to secure more of this revenue for themselves. You vow to stop going to football if it happens.

You are an advocate of the pyramid.

You will always be an advocate of the pyramid.

August bank holiday weekend brings Norwich away, the first game of the season.

August bank holiday weekend brings defeat at Carrow Road.

Forest draw at home to Sheffield Wednesday, to Aston Villa and Luton Town. They draw away at Derby and Everton.

Forest are six games into the season and yet to register a league win. Forest are 16th in Division One.

There's just the League Cup, a 6–0 win at Chester. You travel on Bob's bus to get the ground in, to tick off another of the ninety-two. Some bloke gets nicked for drinking on the bus so you travel back one lighter.

Forest pick up their first win of the season at Loftus Road. Forest complete their demolition of Chester City.

You are nine games into the season. You have watched every minute of every game. You are determined to keep your one hundred per cent record this season.

Pride demands it.

The lads demand it.

But the next game is away.

The next game is at The Den.

The next game is against Millwall.

And Millwall are second in Division One.

'You're not going there,' says Jen. She has no idea about football but she knows about Millwall.

'You're not going there?' asks his dad, averse to all risks.

'Of course I am.'

'You must be mad.'

'We're all going.'

'Train or bus?'

'Train.'

'You are mad.'

'It's all hype,' he says. 'Don't worry about it.'

'Let's hope so. How's the flat?'

'Alright. Cold. Needs a clean.'

'I expect it does.'

A pause.

'Is there any dinner? I'm starved.'

'There's something in the oven.'

'Great.'

'What time's the train?'

'Ten. Something like that.'

'You'll have your work cut out.'

'Harcross is sorting it. He's a Millwall fan. He's off himself.'

'I won't ask how much it's costing.'

He shrugs.

'It's what I spend my money on.'

His dad, eyes half on the paper, licking his fingers to turn the pages. Him at the oven, taking out the dinner his mam left there. He sets the plate down on a mat, tucks in. Pork chops, mashed potatoes, peas. The only proper meal he's had all week.

'How's work?'

'Best not to ask.'

'Don't go upsetting anyone.'

'How's that?'

'Don't go losing it.'

'I won't go losing it.'

'Right. How's the car?'

'Okay. Needs a clean...'

His dad at the worktop with the paper, him at the table, his brother upstairs at the computer, his mam at work, cleaning, bringing in the extra pennies. Local radio station in the background, a phone-in about the state of this and that.

'You get some funny buggers on here...'

His dad, laughing to himself.

'How's it going with Jen?'

A bolt out of the blue.

'Okay.'

His dad nodding. Relief all around. Glad to get that out of the way.

'Are you staying for your mam?'

'I'm off out. Tell her I'll be over Sunday.'

'Well, go careful tomorrow.'

'I always do.'

Out of there. The car heaters blowing a gale. His dad in the door. The warm glow of home. A father's wave to a son.

And so three daft bastards head to Millwall, keeping their heads down, keeping their mouths shut. Bellies churning. The myth working its way in. Even BJ quiet. King's Cross, New Cross. The curious cage leading down into the Lion's Den.

'You're gonna get your fucking heads kicked in...'

Heartbeats running ten to the dozen, eye to eye contact with the baying fuckers on the other side of the fence.

Into the corner, into the shadows of the away end, watching Forest take the piss for eighty minutes. A Steve Hodge double. 2–0 and cruising. The Den a fucking mortuary. Twenty thousand mute lions with nothing to roar about.

Giving it some from the away end.

Safety in numbers.

'Can you hear the Millwall sing, I can't hear a fucking thing...'

Until the home fuckers score.

And twenty thousand lions find their tongues.

The Den lifting out of itself.
Miiiiiiiillllllllwwwwwwwwwwwaaaaaaaallllllll.
Miiiiiiiillllllllwwwwwwwwwwwaaaaaaaallllllll.
Forest quaking.
The Den shaking. Rocking and fucking rolling.
Millwall on the charge. Forest in retreat. Lions and lambs.
Hodge for Forest. Cascarino and Ruddock for Millwall. Two
fucking two. Grateful for a point.
Back into the walkway. Millwall fucking loving it. Out into
the streets. On to the High Street. Into the station.
Three daft bastards not making a squeak.
All the way home.
It's tipping it down when he gets up for work on the
Monday. Harcross is full of it. He greets Finchy with a great
fuck-off smile, Finchy drenched from the ride in.
'Thought your boys had us there.'
'Missed too many chances.'
'What about our humble home?'
'Shithole.'
Harcross raises his eyebrows.
'Awesome,' says Finchy. 'One of the best.'
'No trouble?'
'Nope. Southern softies.'
'I'll bet you were shitting yourself all day.'
The depot oddly quiet, full of men but quiet.
'Who died?'
'You'd best go look at your frame.'
'Awww shit.'
His frame piled with mail, electric on top of poll tax, letters
on top of fucking letters.
'There's three days' worth of shite here.'
Spence's frame rammed too, but Spence somehow in
control.
A metronome.
'More haste less speed...'

Hushed voices of men with too much to do and not enough time to do it, the sound of the rain pummelling against the roof of the depot, the sound of too little sleep hammering inside Finchy's head. Another day, another pound of flesh.

'Listen to that shit. It had better stop,' he says.

'It's not going to,' says Spence.

'Since when were you made weather prophet?'

'Since I watched it on the news this morning.'

'Seriously?'

'You'd best get your waterproofs on.'

His fucking waterproofs, stuffed in the bottom of his locker. Creased to buggery and smelling of damp and fuck knows what else. He pulls the sad fucking things out and hangs them from the peg, then he heads back to the frame. Pig sick.

6 a.m.

7 a.m.

8 a.m.

He's normally at his mam's by now, stuffing his gob with biscuits, reading the morning paper. Instead he's stood in the doorway of the depot in his manky waterproofs, watching the rain sile down. Three tight bags of mail. Bundle on fucking bundle. Two bags already off to the pick-up, the third strapped to the bike. He stands there for a good five minutes, willing the rain to lay off, but it's set, incessant, tipping from the grey sky on to a grey town.

Grey in every fucking way possible.

He takes a deep breath, steadies himself and launches himself into hell, manoeuvring the bike through morning traffic, the hiss of tyres on wet tarmac, a dizzying maze of headlights and brake lights, gutter puddles three inches deep, potholes bubbling like geysers, heading out of the town centre and uphill to the walk. It's 8.30 a.m. He hasn't started. Five hundred and ninety-eight bastard houses. Not one single fucker to go without. The street full of miserable kids trudging to school. He watches them through the rain dripping off his hood. They don't smile. They don't take the piss. They don't respond in any way.

They just trudge.

9 a.m.

10 a.m.

11 a.m.

He delivers to the school, the steamed-up windows, feels a pang of longing. The reception's warm, inviting. The smell of the place triggers something inside of him. He wants to curl up there in the foyer, nestle himself against a radiator and sleep. The receptionist offers him a cup of tea but he declines. Instead he drops off the bundle of letters, turns around and steps back out into the abyss.

12 p.m.

1 p.m.

2 p.m. Fingers numb from cold. The walking dead.

3 p.m.

3.30 p.m. The same fucking kids, trudging home.

He flops through the sorting office door at 4 p.m., a soaking wet rag, a drowned fucking rat. Men on the afternoon shift eye their watches, grin at each other, take the piss. Sarcastic bastards.

Harcross emerges from the office.

'What are you still doing here?' asks Finchy.

'Waiting for you cunts.'

'Plural?'

'You're not the last. We're sending out a search party.'

'Great. Take a fucking boat.'

'You know you're back at five?'

'I was going to talk to you about that.'

'Don't come in...'

'Really?'

'No. Go home, get dry, get some food. You can come in at 5.30.'

Harcross. Generous to the core.

He turns and walks back out into the rain, wondering if feeling will ever return to his fingers, his toes, his wrinkled fucking cock.

The season rolls onward.

Forest lose on live television at home to Arsenal but they beat Liverpool at the City Ground and Newcastle at St James' Park. You're late arriving at Selhurst Park for Charlton away and you miss the only goal but it doesn't matter because Forest win there, too. By mid-December Forest have only lost two games in the League. They've beaten Coventry and Leicester in the League Cup to reach the League Cup Quarter-Finals. There's a buzz around the City Ground, a buzz each and every match day, a consensus that this is the best Forest side since the turn of the decade, a sense that big things are around the corner.

You are part of it.

You are part of every living, breathing moment.

And it is part of you.

7th January 1989
FA Cup Round 3

Nottingham Forest 3 v 0 Ipswich
City Ground

Here you go again. The Tractor Boys half decent. A potential threat. But the Reds are on a mission and the job is done to perfection.

The Tractor Boys are mown down.

A week later Forest trounce QPR 5–2 in the League Cup to reach the League Cup Semi-Finals.

It is the most exciting time of your life.

28th January 1989
FA Cup Round 4

Nottingham Forest 2 v 0 Leeds
City Ground

The fucking club gives up the lower tier to Leeds. Leeds fill it and a home game feels like an away game.

Eight thousand Leeds caged at Nottingham station. Escorted up Queen's Road. Led like cattle along London Road, through the Cattle Market and over the Lady Bay Bridge. Eight thousand Leeds arrive at 2.45 p.m. on match day. There's mayhem outside the turnstiles. They want to watch the fucking game.

Leeds and the police.

The police and Leeds.

Their magnificent support spreads along the whole of one touchline, urging the yellow-shirted fuckers on.

The whole of the lower tier.

All of it.

Leeds building steam in Division Two. Howard Wilkinson at the helm.

Leeds who will win the Division Two title a year later.

Leeds who will win the Division One title three years later.

Leeds on an upward curve.

But not today.

Forest too fast. Forest too slick. Forest 2–0 up at HT.

Nice one.

Drinks on Valentine's day in the village pub. Something in the air. The pub packed with family. Jen's sister and her bloke asking for quiet. Jen's sister and her bloke announcing their engagement. The room in rapture. The spotlight falling on Jen. The spotlight falling on him.

On John fucking Finch.

A rabbit in headlights.

After the party he drives Jen back to his flat.

They drive in silence.

He stares at the road ahead.

He stares at his white knuckles.

'Lisa wants us to go out with her and Kevin one night,' she says at last.

'Right,' he says.

'And they're off to Yarmouth for a break,' she says. 'We could go with them.'

'In the summer,' he says. 'We could do that in the summer.'

'She was thinking Easter. Bank holiday or something.'

He shakes his head.

'Derby away on the Saturday, United at home on the Monday,' he says.

She doesn't say anything else.

She turns and looks out of the passenger window.

And that's the end of the matter as far as John Finch is concerned.

Watford 0 v 3 Nottingham Forest
Vicarage Road

Sunday. On the telly. Through the allotments and up the walkway to Vicarage Road. Uninspiring but Forest out in numbers. A sense of momentum now, something building, gathering pace and weight and purpose.

Blow-up dolls and blow-up cocks and balls. A party on the shallow terrace that serves up a shit view of the game.

Forest exterminate the hornets, swat them dead, crush them underfoot.

It's too fucking easy.

An FA Cup Quarter-Final beckons once again.

Thursday

In the morning he took his bag to reception, asked the girl to change his room. The shift manager appeared.

'We don't want any trouble,' he said.

'I'm not giving you any trouble,' said Finchy. 'What trouble am I giving you?'

'Those men,' said the shift manager.

'I don't know who they are,' he said. 'I don't know who they are or what they want. I just want a different room, one with a window that opens, on the ground floor if you've got one.'

They gave him what he wanted. He half expected the police to come knocking, half expected to have to deal with that on top of everything else, but the shift manager obviously thought better of it. It was one thing getting the police involved, it was another making yourself a target. Anyway, no police came knocking on his door.

Kick up old stones.

Scuff your Sambas.

See what's underneath.

He staggered into town, seeking fresh air, keeping his wits about him, sidled into the marketplace, wondering if the sandwich van would still be there. And it was, a small bit of the past clinging to the present. He joined the queue, eager now for a taste of the old days in the form of a bacon and egg bap.

'Look who it isn't,' said a voice.

He wheeled about, expecting the big fucker, expecting a fist in the mush. But it wasn't the big fucker. It was a face he instantly recognised, a face he'd often thought about over the years, his old neighbour from the sorting frames.

Spence. Once of twenty walk. A piece of piss.

Spence. Cocky, self-assured, difficult bastard.

Finchy smiled all the same. He couldn't help himself. After all these years…

'I heard you were about town,' said Spence.

'Who told you?'

Spence shook his head.

'You should know I never reveal my sources.'

He winked.

'Back for a funeral but a non-attender. Staying at the North Hotel but not always in attendance there either. Likely to emerge from a terrace on Broughton Street in dawn's early light … causing much astir…'

'How the fuck…?'

'That's my delivery, you daft bastard. I saw you coming out of the place.'

'And the other stuff?'

'Common knowledge, mate, for a local postie with an ear to the ground.'

'Fucking hell,' said Finchy. 'Some things never change.'

'Nope,' said Spence.

'It's hardly headline news though, is it?'

Spence shook his head.

'It might be if those Eastern Europeans get hold of you.'

'Aye, well,' he said. 'They've got their facts wrong.'

'You should be used to that sort of thing, though,' said Spence. 'Remember that young lad's ex?'

Finchy reached the front of the queue, ordered his breakfast sarnie.

'Not sure, mate,' he said.

'Yeah, you do,' said Spence. 'Lad was only with us five minutes and you were on his missus.'

'He dumped her,' said Finchy. 'She was fair play. Besides, that was fifteen years ago.'

'And here you are again.'

It was ever thus. He couldn't read the bloke, couldn't tell if he was joshing or serious. And that was Spence. Spence all over. An expert at feeding a bloke a line and reeling him in. Finchy almost took the bait but this was Spence for fuck's sake, seeking a rise as always.

Even now.

'You're still at it then.'

Finchy looked Spence in the eyes, searched for a weakness, received only the same cocksure grin.

'Yep,' he said. 'Still at it after all these years.'

'Still bowling?'

'Still bowling.'

'Still enjoying a beer at the Nag's?'

'Every now and then,' said Spence. 'Perhaps we'll see you in there before you head back?'

'Perhaps,' he said. He took a step backward.

'You're not rushing off?'

'Going to meet an old friend,' said Finchy.

'You're not going to eat your sarnie?'

'Aye,' he said. 'I'm eating my sarnie.'

Finchy bit into the sarnie, felt the gritty texture of the bacon and the warmth of the egg yolk as it ran down his throat.

'Well then, don't be shy,' said Spence. 'Spill the beans.'

'Fuck off, mate,' Finchy said. 'Whatever I tell you I might as well sing from the rooftops.'

Spence shook his head.

'That hurts,' he said. 'That really hurts.'

And once upon a time he'd have fallen for that, back in the day. But he was older now, a little bit wiser, more used to giving it to the lads and lasses at school than receiving it.

The queue shifted forward. Spence ordered his sarnie, sucked the air in through his teeth.

'After all these years,' he said.

'Here we are all over again.'

'Not the same though, is it?' said Spence. He looked around him.

Finchy shrugged.

'The place has changed,' said Spence. 'It's lost something.'

'I'm not sure it had much to lose,' said Finchy.

'You don't mean that,' said Spence. 'You think you do but you don't.'

'You're right,' said Finchy. 'I don't mean it. I had some great times here. I wasn't unhappy, only at the end. What about the PO? Are the same blokes still working at the office?'

'When did you go? 90? Aye, a few. Some moved on to pastures new. Some went the other way. We lost a couple to drink, one to the big C. You should drop in on the place, say "hello", have a chinwag about those murders.'

Cunt.

Finchy held out a hand and Spence took it. They stood there locked together in the marketplace, the same location, the same people, a different time.

'Pop into the Crown,' said Spence. 'See who you remember and who you don't.'

'I will,' said Finchy. 'I will.'

Finchy turned to go, made it all of ten yards.

'They never did catch the bastard,' shouted Spence. 'Fucking strange that, don't you think?'

Finchy almost turned around, almost succumbed, but he held himself in check, walked away from the van and over the road between the traffic. He was a hundred yards further on when he saw the steps of the old pub in front of him.

Her pub.

It's after midnight on a Friday, the glasses washed and back on their shelves, the chairs on the tables, the bar wiped down, everything but the floor, a job for the morning staff. She has two bar jobs that keep a roof over her head. She has a boyfriend. She's getting somewhere. At last.

She shouts 'goodbye' and shoots her boss the finger for some sarcastic reply, then she's on her way.

She steps out into the night.

She's all legs. Her skirt barely covers her arse. And she wears heels. Always heels. They click on the pavement as she walks.

She marches under the railway bridge, down the Western Road, long legs striding, heels clicking, handbag clutched at her side. She has two choices now, to take the shorter route past the scout hut and industrial estate, cut across the little park with the kiddie's swings. It's overgrown up there, full of shadows. Or she can follow the Western Road, a route that takes her out of her way but one where there's traffic, well-lit pavements, signs of life. She's not thinking about these things though, not really. She's not afraid or thinking about being afraid. She's just walking home after a long evening. She's ready to crash out, rise in the morning, pick up her daughter, take her to the Saturday market, to McDonald's for a bite. It's a normal weekend in every sense.

This is her town for fuck's sake. Nothing happens here. She grew up on these streets, played on these swings, wandered mindlessly through the estate as a teenager, laughed, drank, necked in dark places.

It's her fucking town.

It's the blood in her veins.

If she isn't safe here, she isn't safe anywhere.

So many things were gone and so many things remained.

The scrub was still there, the bank, the ditch. He lingered a while, not knowing what the fuck to do, staring at a patch of grass, tangled weeds, unkempt shrubbery. No swings at least, the swings resigned to history, just the concrete foundation where they had once been fixed to the earth, fractured now, forlorn, crumbling to dust. On the other side of the car park, irony of ironies, a new health centre. He started towards it, head full, slipped down the alley at the side, expecting one world, discovering another.

No fucking rabbit runs.

No deadland to get lost in.

Not here.

A wire fence separated the scrub from the adjacent car park. He walked around its edge, knowing where he wanted to get to, knowing how it used to be, met a wrought-iron fence instead, a cluster of new buildings beyond, freshly tarmacked streets, a row of pleasant little dwellings. In 89 it had been the back end of everything, sandwiched between Edwardian terraces, sixties' council houses and an industrial estate floundering in its own decay. In 89 it had been a netherworld, a cut-through lined with trailing brambles, covert nettles, dumped baby carriages, tyres, petrol cans, shit. He'd navigated his way through it all on Saturday mornings, a grand way to start the day, to save himself five crucial minutes, to get to the station on time, to get to London and Birmingham and Liverpool and Manchester. A carrier bag full of sarnies, a bag of crisps.

Fred Perry polo shirt.

Stone Island jeans.

Adidas trainers.

A creased tenner in his back pocket.

Life and how to live it…

Staring about himself in the scrub he noticed it was raining.

He skirted the fence, searching for a way through, followed it to a factory yard, stood there as the rain fell like tears, looking fucking maudlin and mislaid until some bloke came out for a ciggie and spotted him. At thirty fucking three years of age he turned tail, embarrassed, retreated the way he'd come, anxious, upset, struggling to contain it all, another anchor lost to the tide.

He was half an hour late reaching the pub. Jeff was already at the bottom of his first pint.

'Ever the punctual Finchy,' he said. 'Ever the fucking punctual.' Then, 'What happened to you?'

'I took a short cut. It didn't work out.'

'They never do, mate,' said Jeff. 'Anyway, what're you having?'

A nervous fucking breakdown.

'Whatever you're having.'

Jeff drifted to the bar, left him damp and forlorn at the table, returned a minute later with a pint of draught.

'Give this a go,' said Jeffery. 'Our latest special. And sit fucking down, for Christ's sake.'

He listened to Jeff for an hour, listened to his talk about beers and brewers, the difference between one and the other, the miles on the road, the changing landscape of the hospitality business, but he wasn't fucking with it. In the end he just came out with what was on his mind, put it all out there for examination.

'Earlier on I spent fifteen minutes staring at a patch of earth. I might have stayed there all day if I wasn't meeting you.'

Jeff shifted in his seat.

'A patch of earth?'

'Where they found that lass.'

'Lass?'

'For fuck's sake, that barmaid, Tracey what's her name?'

Jeff shrugged.

'You know,' said Finchy. 'Around the corner from your mam's gaff. It was big fucking news at the time…'

'Seriously?' asked Jeff.

'Seriously what?'

'You want to talk about that?'

'Aye,' he said.

Jeff shook his head.

'For fuck's sake.'

'What do you remember about it?'

'Fuck all, mate. Barmaid at The Bell. Found in a car park. Boyfriend a suspect…'

'It wasn't the boyfriend. He had an alibi.'

Jeff shrugged again.

'I can't remember jack shit about those days if I'm honest, not unless somebody reminds me.'

'I'm reminding you. We were set for holiday. National Express. Newquay.'

Jeff laughed, perked up a notch.

'I remember Newquay, mate. Crazy golf. Footy on the beach every fucking day. Chasing around the bars after fanny at night. Some bird from Bristol in the sack. Dirty cow...'

Jeff grinned, lost in a moment.

'Fucking hell,' said Finchy. 'You remember some random tart but you can't remember a thing about a murder on your doorstep.'

'I remember the tape across the street. I remember that. And I remember every fucker in town on about it. She used to walk past my front window every fucking day. I remember those legs. Every fucker remembers those legs.'

'Do you remember what you were doing that night?'

He laughed.

'Fuck me, are you serious?'

'Yes,' said Finchy. Deadpan. Dead straight.

'It was a Friday,' said Jeff. 'I was probably rat-arsed some-where with my old boss. Friday nights straight on the piss after the office shut. If I was anywhere I was there.'

'Not with the lads...'

'Not on Fridays. It was out with the boss or home for some nosh and a good night's kip. Saturday was my day with the boys. One session a week with them was enough.'

A look across the table.

'What's all of this about, anyway?' asked Jeff. 'One minute it was Forest, now it's a fucking murder mystery. We were meant to be having a good old spot of reminiscing.'

'I started thinking about how we used to play in those bushes when we were kids and how I used to cut through that way when I was trying to catch up with you fuckers on a Sat-urday morning. It's all fenced off now.'

'You're a mad fucker. No wonder you're piss wet through.'

'I wanted to have a wander, get a feel for it all.'

'It's a business park, mate. One or two new builds thrown in for good measure.'

'Maybe,' he said. 'But it wasn't, was it? It was never a fucking business park.'

Jeff shrugged.

'You hark on about those times like they were better, like a bit of scrub's more appealing than some level-headed invest-ment. Anyway, fucking hell, let's get back to football before I top myself. What else have you got on the list?'

Finchy swallowed a mouthful of ale. Perhaps Hopper was right. It was no fucking good and it wasn't fucking fair either, springing shit like that on whoever he came across. He wiped the spittle from his mouth.

'The incident at Donnie station?'

'Fuck me,' said Jeff. 'Fuck me in a British Rail toilet.'

Back from the north somewhere. Travelling the main artery, the train full to bursting. Cocksure little bastards, ready to let go for the first time in a week, rowdy as fuck as always, drawing attention, drawing complaints from Joe Public in the age of the train. The guard coming down the carriage, having none of it, some tough Scottish fucker with a point to prove. One after the next giving the guard a mouthful, the guard giving it back, meaning business because he was a Scotsman and he didn't give a fuck.

Donnie Station. The guard holding the train, calling the transport police, having the lot of them chucked on to the platform. In the car park, Jeffery and his knowledge of the sta-tions of the north. They hop over the fucking wall, slip through the goods yard and clamber back on the train before it pulls away. Jeff leads them to the mail car. The lads pile in, hide in the dark, keep their heads down in case the fucking guard comes back, not knowing what the fuck they'll do if he does.

Forty-five minutes in the dark, splayed out on mailbags, Donnie, Retford, Newark, the old town, the church a fucking beacon, drawing them home. The guard's face a picture as they run down the platform and out into the night.

Bolshie bastards. Little fuckers. Pissed-up wankers.

'Gaaaaaaaaaaaahhhhhhhhhh!'

The two of them laughed their sorry arses off talking about it.

'Aye, we had some fun, mate,' said Jeffery.

The smile drained from his face.

'But I don't know,' he said. 'Those days are long gone.'

A moment dropped between them.

'So?'

'So I'm wondering why you're putting yourself through all of this.'

Finchy shrugged.

'I didn't intend to,' he said. 'I'd buried all of it. Or at least I thought I had. BJ's phone call kicked it all up. That and Cloughie's departure.'

'Still, I'd try not to dwell,' said Jeff. 'Most of the past, most of that stuff, probably deserves to be left where it is. There's not much to say about it really. We were just lads. We had fuck all else to bother ourselves with.'

'That's what Hopper said.'

'Aye, well, you just have to deal with it.'

'I haven't dealt with it though, have I?' he said. 'I thought I had but I hadn't.'

'I'm not talking about finishing it all up. None of us have done that, mate. We deal with it by not dealing with it, by getting on with everything else, getting through each fucking day...'

He supped his pint. He stared about himself, lunch over now, the pub inhabited by drawn men and half-finished pints of ale.

'I'm not sure that's enough,' said Finchy.

'Of course it's not enough. Of course it's not. But that's life, me old mucker. That's fucking life for you.'

Finchy stared at his own half-drunk pint on the table, the dregs of beer sticking to the side of the glass.

'Maybe I deal with it by dragging my arse along to watch the cunts play week after week,' said Jeff. 'Maybe I deal with it like that. And maybe BJ deals with it by kicking off every now and then. I'd rather do those things than deny it ever happened. There's one or two of the fuckers who've done that, just buried it as if it never was.'

'And Stimmo?'

'He dealt with it his way. Perhaps that's where we're all heading. We just don't know it yet. At least the soft bastard's out of it all now.'

A shadow shuffled past and said goodnight. Jeff nodded in its direction.

'No more bad dreams for Stimmo, eh?'

Finchy shrugged.

Jeff, staring into the depths of his pint glass, sluicing the remains around and around and around.

'Okay, I'll tell you this one thing,' he said. 'I have this recurring dream. Remember Newquay? Fistral beach? That fucking lifeguard dragging me out of the rip tide?'

'Aye,' said Finchy. 'I remember that.'

'I have that fucking dream,' he said. 'Over and over. I'm in the water and then I'm under it. I'm thrashing about in the blackness, lungs burning, head fucking exploding. And here's the thing. There's a flood of blue light and I'm not on my own any more. I'm still fucking drowning but I'm in a sea of bodies, me and a thousand other fuckers packed into a space that's too small. I can't fucking move. I can't struggle. I can't do anything. And I can't fucking breathe either. Fuckers are dying all around me, just going limp, staring off somewhere. There's this bloke. His face is pressed against mine. I can feel his fucking stubble on my cheek. His eyes are open but they're not fucking looking at me. He's not looking anywhere. A bit of dribble runs from his blue lips. I can't breathe. I'm clearly fucking dying. And then some fucker grabs me and I wake up and I'm in bed, gasping for fucking air.'

Silence for a time. The two of them nursing their pint glasses, swilling the dregs.

'The same dream, every time.'

'Jesus.'

'The missus says I cry out. I don't know if I do but that's what she tells me. I haven't told her about the dream mind, I haven't told anybody except you, here, now. Shit, mate, can't we change the fucking channel? You're a depressing bastard. Talk about opening a can of fucking worms.'

'Aye, sorry.'

'Don't be sorry. Just keep schtum, that's all. Especially when her indoors arrives. We're all a bunch of fuck-ups when it comes down to it.'

Finchy smiled.

'It's just the past,' said Jeffery. 'Friendship groups naturally splitting apart, moving on to new things. Surely that's all this is about, moving from one life to the next. It's the same for all of us.'

Jeff fished in his pocket, pulled out a season ticket.

'Look. They're at home this Friday. I can't get there. Have it on me. Just don't lose the bloody thing. Drop it back here when you're done.' He placed the card on the table. 'As for the other stuff, do you seriously want to dredge all of that up again?'

Finchy shrugged for the hundredth time.

'It's like I'm on a fucking train,' Finchy said. 'I can see the stations passing and I know it's time to get off but the train doesn't fucking stop. It just keeps going...'

'Pull the fucking emergency cord. That usually does the trick. On second thoughts, don't.'

Jeff laughed.

A woman appeared in the doorway. Whatever the plan had been, Jeff changed it, got to his feet, cut her off before she got hold of what she was witnessing.

'I'll see you around, mate. Don't forget the game.'

'I won't, mate. Thanks.'

He stared at the ticket, at the Major Oak and the three lines, struggling to imagine himself back there, struggling to come to terms with something that ought to have been easy, hardly daring to touch the thing. And he remembered the rest of that evening after the Donnie incident, the rest of the story.

He didn't go into town. He left them on the High Street, made sure his programme was on display in his jeans and went to get food instead, a good old curry, carried it back to the flat, back to the darkness. He sat on the yellow sofa and watched TV until he collapsed there, woke at five on the Sunday morning with a fucking sore head, a carton of rice on his lap and on the carpet, an impression in his lower back where the programme had nestled. He heard his flatmate coughing in his sleep, cursed his fucked-up body clock, climbed the stairs to his room and fell on the bed. It was Sunday. He pulled the covers over himself and rested in the cocoon like darkness, wishing Jen was with him.

But she wasn't.

He'd opted for football, hadn't he?

He'd opted for that.

Again.

26th February 1989
League Cup Semi-Final, Second Leg

Bristol City 0 v 1 Nottingham Forest
Ashton Gate

A West Country Sunday in the sheeting rain. Ashton Gate rocking and rolling, pulsing and throbbing. Aggravation. Anger. Aggression. All fucking day. The Executive Crew out in force, a point to prove.

2–2 from the first leg. City rampaging in Notts town centre.

Everything to play for on the pitch and off it.

Stuff kicking off on every corner of every fucking street. Off the bus and straight into the thick of it. One hundred of the fuckers coming out of nowhere, a surprise attack. A cuff around the head for your trouble. You hop into some front garden, head ringing. A bemused woman stares out of a lounge window.

A piano, a cat, a set of silver ornaments.

Back on the street. Momentum reversed. Forest running the Robins now, chasing them down. On another corner, a burger van is tossed about in a sea of bodies, some poor cunt in chequered chef whites trying to clamber free. Hot fat, ketchup, five hundred burgers and bread rolls spill into the Bristol puddles. The burger van goes over with the bloke inside. Every fucker cheers. The guy crawls away from the van, mired in fried onions.

Poor fucker.

To the ground. To the game. Another packed terrace. February sleet. A barrage of noise. A barrage of coins. Some cheeky twat clambers on to hoardings and goads the City fans to do their worst. Coins rain in from the home end. Coins batter the advertising hoardings. Every fucker flinches.

A barrage of spite showers down on the Ashton Gate terraces.

The rain turns to drizzle, clings to the skin. Sweat and fucking drizzle.

The ebb and flow.

The blood and guts.

Football on a brown quagmire.

The great leveller.

In injury time City force a corner and Alan Walsh strikes the post.

Be still your beating heart.

One hundred and sixteen minutes of torture.

One hundred and sixteen minutes of pain.

One hundred and sixteen minutes in the rain at Ashton Gate, daring to dream, not daring to dream.

And then Clough's layoff finds Webb. Webb's hoists in a cross. Clough swipes his boot at fresh air but Garry Parker is in the box. Garry Parker has the ball at his feet. Garry Parker's shot hits the roof of the net.

Every fucker goes mental.

Twenty seconds of madness.

Twenty seconds of ecstasy.

Twenty seconds where nothing else in the world matters.

Que sera, sera, whatever will be, will be…

Shattered boys and shattered men.

On the pitch and on the terraces.

Bricks and bedlam on the Bristol streets.

Another bus window bears the brunt of Cup frustration.

It doesn't fucking matter.

Forest have defeated Bristol City 1–0 at Ashton Gate.

Forest are going to Wembley.

And you are going with them.

'You're always at football,' says Jen.

'You knew that when we met,' he says.

'That was over a year ago,' she says. 'We never see each other.'

'We see each other all the time,' he says.

'Lisa and Kevin are still going to Yarmouth.'

'We talked about that,' he says.

She gets up off the yellow sofa, coughs.

'Your flatmate's smoking shit again,' she says. 'I can't stand it.'

She reaches for her jacket.

'Where are you going?' he asks.

'Home,' she says.

He sighs.

'When the season's done, we'll go away,' he says. 'I promise.'

He grips her hand. She tears herself free.

'I'm sick of Lisa and Kevin,' she shouts. 'I'm sick of football and I'm sick of you.'

And then she's slamming the door, gone from the place. He doesn't get up to follow her. He doesn't do anything at all.

18th March 1989
FA Cup Quarter-Final

Manchester United 0 v 1 Nottingham Forest
Old Trafford

Monday lunchtime. The Cup draw on the radio.
Not United away. Not United away. Not fucking Manchester United away.
Manchester United will play … Nottingham Forest.
Highbury one year, Old Trafford the next. Forty-five thousand baying for blood but Forest impregnable. The classic away day. Franzie Carr jinking, twisting, turning, freeing himself on the right. Franzie Carr to the byline, Franz Carr squaring the ball, Garry Parker in the middle, Garry Parker in the centre of the goal. The simplest of tap-ins.
One Garry Parker.
One fucking nil.
The second half. Forest under the cosh, the Stretford end in full voice but ten thousand mighty Reds giving it back. Ebb and flow, end to end. Hodge off the goal-line. Sparky Hughes in the referee's face. Thirty-five thousand in the referee's ear. Ten thousand voices singing their boys home.
Wembley, Wembley, we're the famous Cloughie's army and we're going to Wembley…
Fuck me, you might be going three times.
The Simod Cup.
The League Cup.
The FA Cup.
Nottingham Forest are in the Semi-Final hat.
Norwich are in the Semi-Final hat.
Everton are in the Semi-Final hat.
Liverpool are in the Semi-Final hat.

Norwich (let it be Norwich).
Everton (you'll take Everton).
But not the fucking Scousers again.
Not fucking Hillsborough again.
Not the fucking Kop again.

The same fucking arguments.
    In the boardrooms and corridors.
    In the pubs and clubs.
    Behind closed doors.
    The SYP.
    The FA.
    The strategy and the struggle.
    'I'd be happy with Leppings Lane.'
    'They had the Kop last year.'
    'Share and share alike.'
    It doesn't matter.
    Because this year you'll have the bastards whichever end you're in.
    It's written in the stars.
    You're a believer.

15th April 1989

The thousands in a crowd move as one,
with no shared intelligence.
Prof. Dr G. Keith Still

It's dark when he wakes, dark when he cycles through the streets, dark when he arrives at the sorting office gates on this Saturday in April.

It's dark when he steps away from his frame to check the boxes.

At 6 a.m. he goes out to the ramp and waits there, knowing he can't bundle up yet, can't bag up yet, knowing eyes are on him, knowing the limits. It's too fucking early so he stands on the ramp and watches the black sky shift to cobalt blue, watches it brighten into a cloudless morning.

Back inside he readies the round. By 6.30 a.m. he's out of the place, not hanging around, not looking over his shoulder as he slips out of the gates, not caring about Webster or anybody. He's set on one thing today, one thing only. In six hours' time he'll be on the football special. In seven hours he'll be on the Penistone Road, Sheffield. In eight hours he'll be at Hillsborough, him and twenty-eight thousand Forest.

His heart skips a beat.

There's a spring in his step as he makes his way up the path of the first call on Hope Close. There's every fucking reason for it. Forest are flying, beaten just twice in twenty-two games since the turn of the year. They've won at White Hart Lane, Highbury, Old Trafford and the Baseball Ground. They've won the League fucking Cup at Wembley.

Everything comes easy on this morning. He glides from letter box to letter box, street to street. By 9 a.m. he's back at the office. Harcross gives him the thumbs-up and ushers him out of the place before Webster and his cronies get an opportunity to stick their oar in.

At 10.30 a.m. he's on the train, him and all of the others and then some. It's an FA Cup Semi. Every fucker who is any fucker has a ticket for this one.

And every fucker who isn't.

Nottingham station rammed with red and white, the football special awash with beer and song.

Langley Mill, Alfreton, Chesterfield, Dronfield.

Beer and song, all the way to Sheffield.

He loves it and loathes it in equal measure. Twelve hundred of the fuckers at Plough Lane two weeks earlier, twelve hundred diehards. Today there will be twenty-eight thousand at Hillsborough, four thousand more than the average home gate at the City Ground.

The station at Sheffield is top heavy with SYP. There's nowhere to go except where the SYP want them to go, no chance of slipping the net. There's a fleet of double-decker buses lined up outside the station and he files aboard the upper deck. It's 1 p.m. on match day, zero minus two hours. There's alcohol in the air but no sign of it anywhere. Not now. The top floor of the double-decker is manned by two members of the SYP. Some of the lads crack jokes but the SYP aren't laughing. The SYP never fucking laugh. Not on match day.

It's slow going through the city of Sheffield, slow going on the Penistone Road.

'We could have walked there quicker,' says BJ.

Finchy nods. Finchy looks at the old bill. The old bill stare back.

Finchy looks out of the window instead. There are fans streaming up the Penistone Road, fans draped in red and white. There are fans spreadeagled on the grass of Hillsborough Park. The sun is shining. The sky is blue. It's the perfect day to watch a football match.

The bus crosses the River Don and pulls in outside the Kop end turnstiles. It's 1.30 p.m. A year ago they were straight in from here but they're older now and some of the lads are looking for a drink. They mill about on the pavement outside the Kop, choices to be made. There's talk of this pub and that pub, talk of time to enjoy themselves. He's not up for it. There's the SYP for starters. There's the fucking part-timers.

'I'm going in,' says BJ.

'I'm with you,' he says.

Finchy hands over his ticket, shoves through the turnstiles and makes the steep climb up the concrete steps to the back of the Kop. He buys a programme, moves through the clusters already in place to locate a view similar to the year before. It means the others might find them later, if they're not too fucking late. And then there's fuck all to do but wait, room still to sit on his arse on the Kop and flick through the programme, to breeze over the message from the Sheffield Wednesday Chairman describing his 'perfect venue' overlaying a photograph of Leppings Lane, to glance at the 'Flashback' article of a year before, to enjoy the photograph of Garry Parker turning in Franz Carr's cross for the winner at Old Trafford and Bobby Robson's article suggesting the match 'could be a classic'. He feels it too. Fifty- four thousand souls are feeling it, but there aren't fifty-four thousand in Hillsborough, not yet, not by a long shot. The Kop is filling up, as are the North and South Stands but the Leppings Lane end is all wrong. The pens to the left and the right are only sparsely populated. Just the central pens are truly occupied.

'What the fuck's that all about?' asks one voice to his left.

'They've not sold their tickets,' laughs another to his right.

He's thinking the same, that there's been some enormous fuck-up, that none of what he's seeing makes sense.

And nothing changes as the clock ticks onward, except that the central pens become fuller, tighter, become a mass of heads and bodies and that some fans clamber over the lateral fencing from the central pens to the wing pens.

But he doesn't know anything. He only knows that it's 2.40 p.m. on match day, just twenty minutes before the biggest game of the season.

Outside the ground, in the narrow elbow of Leppings Lane, more than five thousand fans are still trying to get in.

And the Leppings Lane end has not reached capacity. There is room in the wing pens. Plenty of room.

But the wing pens will not reach capacity.

Not on this day in April.

Not on this day.

15th April 1989
Semi-Final

Liverpool v Nottingham Forest
VOID

You're always there.

5.20 p.m.

He's traipsing his way back to Sheffield station, casualty numbers drifting from the open windows of cars trapped bumper to bumper on the Penistone Road, finding his ear.

Thirty dead.

Fifty.

Sixty.

Seventy.

Over seventy dead.

There are queues of lads lined up outside the phone boxes at the station. Pick a queue, any queue, wait your turn. He waits forty minutes. His dad answers. His dad tells him to get home safely. It's okay because he's safe. Everything will be okay.

But it's not okay. It will never truly be okay.

He doesn't call Jen. He's only got one ten-pence fucking piece. There are queues of lads behind him. His own crew have already fucked off to the platform.

6.10 p.m.

The 'Special' inches out of the city and through the peaks. Some lads are talking about it. Some lads are telling jokes about dead Scousers. Some lads are picking fights with the blokes telling jokes. Some lads are worrying about the football, about the FA Cup, if the game will be replayed, if the whole thing's been ruined. Some lads are staring out of the train windows at England's green and pleasant land, their eyes filled with tears.

Some lads aren't anywhere at all.

Dronfield. Chesterfield. Alfreton. Langley Mill. Nottingham.

Lads alight the train.

Lads drift away.

Lost souls slip back into lives they no longer own.

Lives removed.

Forever.

Finchy calls Jen when he's back on his terrain, back in the flat, pacing the hall, unable to settle.

'You're alright?' she asks. 'Do you want me to come over?'

'I need to be out,' he says. 'With the others.'

'But you're alright,' she says. 'You're safe.'

'Aye,' he says. 'Aye, I suppose I am.'

There's a cool breeze blowing when he steps out of the flat. He sets himself against it and heads into town. A chill runs through him. The hairs on his arms stand to attention.

The sun is dropping beyond the trees that border the river. The sunset is a pink wash that darkens and thickens as he makes his way in. By the time he reaches the pub the sky is the colour of blood.

It's 8 p.m. on 15th April 1989.

9 p.m.

They're all out but no fucker's really out. They're six hours and seventy miles away, on the Spion Kop at Hillsborough. The same lads as a year ago, the same location, the same beers on the table. The pool table's there but no fucker's on it. Music's playing but no fucker's listening to it. Fanny coming and going. No fucker gawping. Amidst all of this, they pick through the cost of it.

'They'll cancel the fucking Cup.'

'Fuck that. It's a Semi-Final.'

'We'd have won today. I fucking know it.'

'It'll be all Merseyside now. The papers'll be all over it. Fucking Scouse bastards.'

BJ offers his two penneth and everybody listens.

'Listen to yourselves,' he says. 'Fucking listen to your-selves. People are dead. It's over.'

'Fucking hell,' say the others.

'Fuck me.'

'It's well and truly fucking over.'

BJ slams his fist on the table. Beer sloshes on to the carpet, the dirty sticky carpet that has seen five hundred nights like this.

But never like this.

'You're all cunts, do you know that? All a bunch of fucking cunts.'

He picks up his bottle and fucks off, leaving them there. Finchy watches him go, knowing BJ's frustration will turn into something else before the night is through, force its way upon some poor unsuspecting fucker that doesn't know any better. It's guaranteed.

Finchy observes Stimmo pick up his own pint and slip away towards some lads that don't go to football. Finchy sits thinking about Jen, wanting to catch up with her now, to tell his story, not sure how the fuck he's going to tell it. He doesn't realise it will be that way for the rest of his life. He sits marooned, a pile of fresh shit to deal with, a new understanding about the workings of the world on his plate. And from this day forward no fucker will speak about it. No fucker will offer to help. The boys will all be stuck with it, guilty as fuck for living. And the response will always be the same if they ever get up the nerve to mention it, forever a look, a shake of the head, the fear of dwelling in that place. He'll want to talk about it. He'll fucking need to talk about it. But no fucker will be interested. And in the end, they'll stop talking about it with each other, too. It will became a thing they share without sharing, something to bury at the bottom of a fucking pint glass. For fifteen years.

He thinks about his grandfather and the army days, how each time the old guy brought those days up the family would move on from it. Will it be the same, him trying to talk about things and everybody else ducking and weaving?

Of course it fucking will.

And that poor guy had to carry it for fifty fucking years.
Mention it in passing. Drop a line in. Measure a reaction.
But no fucker reacts. Ever.
So bury it then. Bury it deep.

He drives to Jen's on the Sunday, turns up for Sunday roast,
for beef and Yorkshire pudding, for Brussels fucking sprouts.
He's got no appetite for any of it, their sombre faces, their
furtive glances over the table, their attempts at light conversation. After the charade he and Jen go for a walk through
the village.

'You didn't call,' she says.

'I couldn't,' he says. 'There was nowhere to call from.'

'You called your mam's.'

'Eventually,' he says. 'Eventually. There was a queue a
mile long for every fucking phone in the city. That's how it
was.'

'I just thought you might…'

'I called you when I got home,' he said. 'I called you then.
That's all there is to say about it.'

And Sunday bleeds into Monday.

Nobody speaks when he walks into the sorting office.
Nobody looks him in the eye. Spence is unnervingly quiet,
focused on slotting the letters into his frame. Robbie Box is
nowhere to be seen. Harcross comes over with the barrow,
hands him another bundle, pats him on the shoulder and
trundles away. In the locker room, Jack Stanley, ex-Fire
Brigade and one of the old boys, pipes up without looking in
his direction.

'How are you, lad?'

'Alright,' he says. 'Alright.'

'Good,' says Jack Stanley. 'That's what we like to hear.'

That is all.

The newspapers are full of photographs. He catches them on his round, finds himself pulling the things out of letter boxes where they've been stuffed by the paperboy, standing on the doorsteps of his people reading about the thing that will come to separate them from him. Images of men, boys and girls, terror, pain, panic, an unforgiving compression. Eyes and cheeks and noses. Bloated faces press against wire-mesh fencing.

The living and the dead.

The dead standing up.

There's a list of names in the paper too, a list of the deceased and their ages. He can't look at the list, can't bring himself to read it. He will never be able to read it.

Tuesday bleeds into Wednesday. An endless flow of misery.

He writes a note to the local rag, fan to fan, works on the words for hours, changing this, changing that. Something to do with them all being united, Liverpool, Forest, across the miles. He takes the note down to the newspaper offices and hands it over. It appears on the Friday, at the foot of an article about some bloke who was there. No fucker asks him for his story. No fucker wants to know.

Middlesbrough 3 v 4 Nottingham Forest
Ayresome Park

You travel out of duty, out of respect for the dead and for the game you love. And you travel for the lads too, your brothers, to be with them.

Grey April skies. *You'll Never Walk Alone* ringing from the terraces as the teams take the field. One minute of silence while a solitary car alarm cries a forlorn lament for the lost. Black armbands, eyes on the turf, a drawing of breath and then they're off again, football picking up the pieces, trying to mend things.

Middlesbrough 3 v 4 Nottingham Forest.

The game is a homage to football, a nod to better days but the game is an afterthought. You and the boys on the terrace in the corner, still numb from it all, not knowing when to laugh, when to cheer, when to sing. Not knowing what the fuck to do.

Middlesbrough away.

Seven days after tragedy.

Wanting to be there. Not wanting to be there. Having to fucking be there. Numb with shock. An undigested thing in the gut. An indigestible thing. A fucking tapeworm. A parasite feeding off your guilt and shame. And nothing to be ashamed about. Nothing to be guilty about.

Guilty of nothing.

Guilty of everything.

Finchy and Jen.

Jen and Finchy.

There's talk that they're not getting on so well, that he's been seen out on his own more often, that she's been seen heading straight from college to the bus station instead of his flat. There's talk that he dumped her and then begged her to come back to him. There's talk that he doesn't know what the fuck he's doing, what the fuck he wants.

There's talk of things like that.

Liverpool 3 v 1 Nottingham Forest
Old Trafford

Twenty-two days since the horror of Hillsborough.

It's an FA Cup Semi-Final but it isn't.

It's a game between two sides but it isn't.

Everton await the winners. An all-Merseyside final is in the offing.

So only one side can win today.

Forest are on a hiding to nothing.

There are thirty-nine thousand in Old Trafford yet the atmosphere is stilted, tainted with inevitability, tinged with sadness, touched with loss. There are gaps on the terracing. There are people saying the game shouldn't be played. You feel it, too, but you go out of duty, out of necessity, out of habit.

Because it's in your blood.

You're there with T-Gally and Gav and Hopper and Jeff and BJ and JC and Sharpster. All of you are there except Stimmo. Stimmo is not there. Stimmo is somewhere else.

You don't know where Stimmo is.

An exemplary minute's silence, Laws and Crosby in a mess, Aldridge nodding home the opener. Webb equalises. Aldridge strikes the crossbar.

It's an FA Cup Semi-Final but it isn't.

On fifty-eight minutes Aldridge makes it 2–1 but the worst is still to come. Houghton's throw finds Aldridge who lays off to Beardsley. Beardsley crosses and Brian Laws turns the ball into his own net. Aldridge ruffles the hair of Brian Laws. Brian Laws who is the Nottingham Forest representative of your supporter's branch. Brian Laws who

visited your gaff to play darts and pool. Brian Laws who brought the
League Cup trophy along for the ride.

Aldridge grins and spins away.

Aldridge takes the fucking piss.

And Forest are out of the Cup.

They've been out of the Cup for twenty-two days.

You'd like to say you care but you don't.

You really don't.

10th May 1989

Liverpool 1 v 0 Nottingham Forest
Anfield

You travel because you love your club.
You travel because you love your players.
You travel because it is Anfield.
You watch Brian Laws foul John Aldridge in the box.
You watch John Aldridge score the penalty for Liverpool, the only goal of the game.
You clap the players from the pitch at full-time.
You clap the Nottingham Forest players and you clap the Liverpool players.
But you do not clap John Aldridge.

Friday.

The phone rings. He's expecting Jen and another bout of soul-searching but picks up to Gav instead.

'How's it hanging?'

'Okay,' he says. 'Yourself?'

'It's been another bastard week,' says Gav. 'But it might get better.'

'How's that?'

'There's a party tonight. Some farm in the sticks.'

'A farm?'

'Aye, mate. It's buzzing. Every fucker I've seen this week's been on about it. It's a big fucking thing apparently, the latest fucking happening.'

'Jesus,' he says. 'Everybody's a step ahead.'

'What's that?'

'Never mind,' says Finchy. 'I'm not sure. I was all into going to town.'

'Fuck that,' says Gav. 'There'll be no fucker out. Trust me. I've got my ear to the ground. You don't want to miss it, mate.'

He blows out his cheeks.

'There's Jen,' he says.

'Fuck that,' says Gav. 'With respect, like.'

'I'll call you back.'

'No need,' says Gav. 'We're heading off at ten from the Hound. If you're there, you're there. If you're not, you're not.'

Fifteen minutes later Jen comes knocking at his door. He lets her in, leads her upstairs to the living room.

'I've not come to talk,' she says. 'I've just come to see you.'

'Are you staying?' he asks.

She shakes her head.

'I can't,' she says. 'I have to look after my brother.'

'Might as well go now then,' he says.

She grimaces.

'You don't have to be like that,' she says. 'You could come back with me. We could get a film out.'

He doesn't speak.

'I'm watching the game,' he says. 'And I'm tired. I need a kip.'

She sighs.

'I'll leave if you want,' she says.

He nods his head.

'I think I need an early night,' he says.

'I can stay for a bit,' she says.

'If you like,' he says. 'But I really need an early night.'

She goes to the kitchen. From the sofa, across the landing, he watches her as she rifles through the fridge.

'There's nothing,' he says. 'I've not been arsed to fetch anything.'

'You should have told me,' she says. 'I'd have brought something.'

He shrugs.

'What now then?' she asks.

He shrugs again.

Ten minutes later they're in his bed, naked between the sheets but it's awkward, uncomfortable. They struggle to fit together.

When it's over he closes his eyes. He thinks he hears her crying, or trying not to cry, but he's not certain and he doesn't ask. He doesn't say a fucking thing, just keeps his eyes closed tight shut. In the end she gets to her feet, gets dressed, walks across the room and closes the door behind her. He listens to her footsteps as she descends the stairs. He listens to the door slam, to her feet on the pavement outside.

Eventually he slips The Stone Roses out of their sleeve, sets them on the turntable, turns up the volume. He closes his eyes.

He's still in bed when his flatmate bursts in carrying a pack of pills.

'What the fuck?' he asks.

'Just saw your bird at the bus stop,' says his flatmate. 'She didn't speak to me.'

Finchy shakes his head.

'Don't ask,' he says. 'What have you got there?'

'None of your fucking business and nothing you could fucking afford,' says his flatmate.

'Pills?'

'Beans.'

'I thought you were purely a weed man,' says Finchy.

'I'm branching out,' says his flatmate. 'These are the future. You mark my words.'

'Are they any good?'

'Are you kidding? These are fucking legend, mate. Not that you'll ever know. I need a fucking Tupperware box. Something airtight. Then I can bury the bastards in the garden.'

He gestures towards the postage-stamp yard and the shed the Scottish fucker never opens.

'Don't you think you should ask him first?' asks Finchy.

'Are you fucking kidding me? Just remind me to nick a fucking Tupperware box from work.'

'You're a real entrepreneur,' says Finchy.

'You have to start somewhere. Speculate to accumulate, that's my motto. Now what's the fucking time, I need to get ready for work.'

When he's gone Finchy falls out of bed, makes his way to the bathroom, runs himself a bath and festers there for an hour until the water is tepid and his skin as mottled as his brain. He thinks about Jen cooped up on the bus, the country lanes, the stillness of the village, the garden path, her mam at the window. He thinks about what a cunt he's being these days. He thinks about Gav and the party. A party on a farm. He wonders what the fuck it's all about. He clambers out of the back and stands in front of the bathroom mirror. He puffs out his chest, takes three deep breaths, places his palm on his ribcage, feels for confirmation of his beating heart.

26th May 1989
Liverpool 0 v 2 Arsenal
Anfield

Liverpool have won the FA Cup, beating Everton 3–2 at Wembley. You watched it thinking about what might have been. You watched it with a lump in your throat.

Guilty of nothing.

Guilty of everything.

Now Liverpool are playing Arsenal to decide the Division One Championship. Arsenal have to win by two clear goals at Anfield. It's unlikely to happen.

It's more unlikely to happen when half-time comes and the score is still 0–0.

But something happens in the second half. Smith scores for Arsenal. The Kop goes quiet. You watch the TV and you watch the Arsenal fans. They sense it and you sense it. Every fucker senses it.

The clock ticks on through sixty minutes, seventy, eighty. The clock reaches ninety minutes. The Kop comes to life. Shrill whistles material-ise from three and a half sides of Anfield. Liverpool are virtually home and dry, done and dusted with the Division One championship, done and dusted with the double. Again.

And then Barnes loses out to Richardson. Richardson returns the ball to Lukic. Lukic throws to Dixon. Dixon finds Smith. Smith finds Thomas.

In your flat, in the room with the yellow sofa, on the edge of the yellow sofa, you watch with wide, wondrous eyes. You watch the Arsenal fans on the North West Terrace. You watch the ball ricochet off Nicol back to the Arsenal player's feet. You watch the ball hit the Liverpool net.

You look for John Aldridge.

You imagine walking up to him at this precise moment, ruffling the fucker's hair.

You can't see him anywhere.

Finchy heads into town where the blood is up.

There are fights in the pubs. There are police in the pubs. Finchy skirts around the people massed on the pavements.

He watches the police drag some idiot in a Liverpool shirt out of the pub.

He wonders why the cunt's not at Anfield.

He laughs.

Into the Hound. Out of the Hound. Into some fucker's car. Six lads crammed in the back. Finchy prone across the fucking seats.

Tunes on the stereo. Pounding tunes. Too fucking loud.

Keep yer fucking head down.

A blur of street lights.

The cunt driving too fast. Too fucking fast.

Tyres grappling with the tarmac.

No fucking street lights.

Tyres grappling with gravel.

The night fucking sky.

Pulling up. Piling out. The car speeding off.

A field. A fucking field.

And beat.

Beat. Beat. Beat. Beat. Beat. Beat. Beat. Beat. Beat. Beat. Beat. Beat.

And people.

People he knows. People he doesn't know. This town and that town. Every fucker gathering.

Gav grinning. From ear to ear.

He wanders about in the darkness, into the mass of bodies, into the movement, into the pulse, becomes part of the pulse, part of the beat.

No fucker talking. No need to talk.

No fucker drinking. No need to drink.

Every fucker dancing. Every single fucker dancing.

It might have been a Saturday on the terraces. It might have been but it wasn't.

No aggro. Just the beat. Just the music.

Some girl he's never met. All legs. All legs and smile. She hands him a pill. She laughs. He thinks of his flatmate. He doesn't look down. He pops it home. Of course he fucking does.

And now he's dancing, in the pulse. He's dancing and dancing. And everything is racing. Everything is racing. And everything is perfect. Everybody is perfect. The girl is fucking perfect. The stars are on fire. They're fucking on fire and they're beautiful. The girl is beautiful. Everything is beautiful.

He's dancing with the girl and the girl is dancing with him.

Later, somehow, fuck knows how, he's dancing with her in the living room of his flat. She's taking another pill. He's taking another pill. They're crashed out on the sofa. He's laughing. She's laughing. He can't stop laughing. The yellow sofa is liquid gold. He's sinking into it, sinking into a river of gold. The girl's naked skin is gold. The girl is a river of gold. Everything is a river of gold.

Later still he's on a black street. The girl is ahead of him, all legs. He follows the legs. He kisses the legs goodbye. He follows the legs. He follows the legs. He kisses the legs goodbye. He's alone under the railway bridge, alone by the river.

The river.

The river.

The river is full of legs. The river is full of eels.

The narrow street is a river, a river of liquid. His front door is liquid. The stairs are liquid. He can't climb the liquid stairs. He's marooned on the liquid stairs.

He wakes at five in the morning in a crumpled heap at the foot of the stairs, his body clock primed even when he abuses it. He gets dressed and falls out of the front door, his head a fog, the whole fucking street spinning. The streets are lathered in fog. Everything is a fog. He can't remember a thing about the previous evening, not a fucking thing. He leans over a garden wall, pukes into a patch of daffodils.

The lights in the depot are too bright. He has to shield his eyes.

Harcross comes over.

'You're late,' he says.

Finchy raises his hands, surrenders.

'Worse for wear?'

'Leave it, please,' says Finchy.

'Don't blame me for burning the candle,' says Harcross.

'It wasn't a candle.'

'I guessed as much.'

The first hour of his round is bathed in fog, a void with him at its centre. He tries to recall the previous evening but there's nothing there, nothing for him to cling to except an American accent and the most beautiful legs he's ever seen, the most beautiful body he's ever seen.

For some fucking reason he feels like crying.

The fog burns off as the day grows into itself. His head clears a tad. The air is warm, the trees in full leaf, insects on the wing. He's in the flats, in no fucking rush, the flats rank in the sunshine, him sweating in rolled-up sleeves. Kids are roaming the estate before breakfast, gone for the day. Some bloke is hanging around outside block six, a great fuck-off tattoo on his neck.

Loitering.

Waiting.

For the postie.

'Al-alright, mate. G-got anything for twen-twenty eight?'

Fuck. He hates this shit.

'I've to deliver it, mate,' he says, forcing a smile. It's the best he can muster on a difficult morning.

'It's okay. You can just give me it.'

Finchy punches in the code for the door, shakes his head, feeling sick in the stomach. He thumbs through the bundle.

'There's just a giro,' he says. 'I can't give you that.'

The guy shifts in his stance, eyes wide, all pent up.

Cunt.

'But it's mine.'

Finchy shrugs, tries to look apologetic.

'So I've got to climb the stairs, let you deliver it, let myself back in and then get it?' says the bloke with the tattoo.

Finchy nods.

'Those are my orders,' he says.

'What are you? Fucking army?'

'There are people that hang around waiting for the postman to come along. I'm not saying you're one of them.'

The guy's cheeks flush red.

'Come on, mate, I'm going out. I'm late.'

'I would if I could. If you climb the stairs, let yourself in…'

'Fuck it,' says the bloke.

It will come now, if it's going to come, the blow to the face, the bloodied lip, the broken nose. Finchy closes his eyes and waits.

'You're a prick.'

The sound is further away. He opens his eyes to see the bloke on the mucky grass. Lying bastard.

'Cunt,' shouts the guy, at the other flats, at the morning, at life itself. He kicks a wall. A brick comes loose so he kicks it again. He kicks the fucking wall like he wants to break somebody's head.

Finchy pushes his way through the doors, climbs the stairs. When he reaches the top floor he looks out of the window. The bloke is nowhere to be seen.

Ten minutes later and his bag's empty. He freewheels down the road, enjoying the sun on his face, done for the weekend, wanting to go home, shower, clear the shit out of his head, collapse on his bed, sleep until lunchtime.

But something's going on at the top of the lane. There's a police car parked across the white lines, deflecting the Saturday morning traffic. There's a crowd of people hanging around the road block, topless blokes, skinny guys with cigarettes on the go, fat women in T-shirts and leggings, sweat-stained armpits, kids milling about, tugging at the blue-and-white tape.

'Can I do the box?' he asks.

The policeman shakes his head, goes back to watching the kids and the tape. Finchy looks at the crowd, spots Porn Billy amongst them. Porn Billy, the man who can get anything, for a price, in 1989.

'Alright?' he says. 'What's going on?'

'A body,' says Porn Billy.

'What?'

'A body in the hedge. Down by the swings.'

'Fuck off,' says Finchy. 'I was there not three hours ago.'

'Been there all night.'

'No.'

'It was on the radio. Body of a woman discovered in hedge bottom. Some kids found her.'

'I'd have fucking seen,' he says.

'Obviously not,' says Porn Billy.

'Did you hear who it is?'

'They've not said. Woman over there says she's a barmaid.'

'Local?'

'Aye.'

'Fuck.'

'Aye.'

A series of images form in Finchy's mind, photofits of the

barmaids who've served him on Saturdays like this one. Blonde. Blonde. Red head. Short hair. Long hair. Thin. Fat. Pretty. Not so pretty.

He races back to the office, cutting through the primary school, through the rat-run behind the mental unit, through the industrial estate, eager to get back, to let the fuckers know the news.

But they know already. They always know. If you want to know anything about anything in the old town, ask a fucking postie.

'Barmaid from the Crown,' they say.

'Worked the Bell at weekends,' they say.

The Crown. Postie pub. Mainly the older blokes, the ones who leave the office at lunch to wander straight in, the ones who emerge from the place before the evening shift, the ones that reek of alcohol at the facing table, at the sorting frames, the ones who can't do the job without a few pints in their bellies.

An image forms in his mind, a face, a body, a smile. But it's not clear, not yet. It will take a photograph in a newspaper to plant the indelible image in his head, a grainy face staring back at him, for a moment, for hours, for fifteen fucking years.

Murder.

On his twenty-one walk.

Fuck.

He walks back to the flat, taking the path along the river's edge, the sun well up now, sunlight flickering and flexing on the water, insects skimming the surface.

Across town, a body in a hedge bottom. It's hard for him to set the two things against each other, in a town where nothing ever happens.

A body in a hedge bottom.

In the summer.

In the sunshine.

Despite the warnings.

Despite the doubts.

Despite himself.

Out of duty. Out of shame. Back to the two-up two-down, back to the living room and the TV. Back to the past.

Jen White's place. Dredging through the mire.

There was tea with milk this time. He supped at it, stared at the steam rising from the surface.

'You drove me to the woods,' she said. 'I was babbling on about college and you cut me off, told me you wanted to break up...'

He shifted in his seat, knowing what was coming. 'I remember that,' he said.

'You were so fucking deadpan about it. You sat there staring out of the window, telling me it was over, that you couldn't carry on with any of it.'

'I remember,' he said.

'I was heartbroken, in floods of tears, a right mess...'

She walked across the room until she was standing in front of him.

'You didn't say a fucking word. You just turned the car around and took me home. You pulled up outside my house and you waited until I was climbing out of the car and then, you fucker, *then* you told me you didn't mean any of it...'

He remembered all of it, the engine idling in the woods, the shivering trees, her face streaming with tears.

'That was you,' she said. 'That was the person you became.'

He tried to reach back to that person. Fucked-up, frustrated, floundering.

Always fucking floundering.

He shook his head. He shrugged. He didn't say anything. There was fuck all he could say.

'You spent two weeks begging me to forgive you for that, calling and calling, turning up at the house, posting letters...

'Jen...'

'… and everybody was telling me not to bother, to fucking ignore you until you went away…'

'Jen, listen…'

'… but you didn't fucking go away so I took you back. And all of that, all of that just gave you fucking licence to do what you did next, to give me the fucking runaround for months and months.'

He got to his feet, made for the door. She blocked his path. When he went to step around her she pushed him back down on to the settee.

'No, you fucking well don't,' she shouted. 'You were going to say something. So say it. Say it and then it's done.'

'I just don't think we should be talking about this.'

'Why? Because of him? Because of that selfish prick?'

She grabbed a photo frame off the television and threw it to the floor.

'Fuck him,' she said. 'Fuck the both of you.'

He moved to get up again.

'Sit the fuck down,' she said. 'Stop fucking thinking about yourself. You deserve this. You deserve to sit there and listen until I've said what I've got to say. Then you can fuck off if you want. You can fuck off and never come back.'

Silence.

'Because it's the same,' she said. 'You fucked off and he fucked off. Both of you left me fucking treading water, both of you are selfish bastards.'

He leant forward. With his elbows on his knees he buried his head in his palms. It was the drink, of course it was the drink, night after night in the hotel room with the minibar for company, but it was still difficult to sit there, to sit and take it all and not be able to explain himself. And yet what the fuck was there to explain? He could hardly deny any of it, or try to make out she had it wrong. He'd been an insecure, jealous fucker and those things had dominated him for a time, then he'd changed, become somebody else, lost interest, looked for others. He'd fluctuated like that for months and months and she'd been the one to live through all of that with him. She'd shared the fucking journey, or been dragged along for the ride. And he knew when it had all started, when it had all changed.

It was hardly a fucking mystery.

He looked at her. He thought about Stimmo. He thought of her coming down for breakfast one morning to find two police officers at her door.

Sombre faces.

Sad, sympathetic faces.

Bearers of bad tidings.

Fuck.

Fuck. Fuck. Fuck.

He stopped listening to her, closed his eyes and blocked her out somehow, or perhaps she wasn't speaking any more, perhaps she'd run out of things to say or collapsed on the sofa beside him. Yes, that was it, he could feel her weight against his, feel her chin digging into his back. She was out of it.

They were both out of it.

Hillsborough. Hills-ber-rer. A loose thread flapping in the wind. Something attached to him. Something he couldn't rid himself of. More than a memory. A fucking burden.

Hillsborough. Hills-ber-rer. A shadow. A dark mass. A tumour. Riddled with it. Fucking riddled with it.

All of them riddled with it.

Was it fucking terminal?

Was it?

'That shed,' he said to nobody. 'We played there as kids.'

And he could see them all, lost in the white space behind his eyes, see them clambering through the hole in the fence, pushing through the deadland, traipsing through the scrub to the tracks, forcing the door of the shed open, letting the light in. Him and Spridge and Minx and Hanratty, sprats each one, sprats he lost touch with when they reached eleven years old, when the grammar school sent him the letter. Marshy was there too, Marshy who killed himself on his motorbike when he was sixteen. And Stimmo, the quiet one. He was there too, lagging behind. He could see them all in their fucking summer rags, him in his yellow Forest shirt, Minx in his red Liverpool shirt. He could feel the sun on his back, the heat from the tracks, hear the far-off ghosting of an approaching train, the track screaming in the sunlight. He closed his eyes against the harsh edges. But nothing was harsh-edged then, not really. Everything was softened, by youth, by summer, by the haze that melted the tracks into molten ripples of silver.

They were ten years old.

Innocent fuckers, the lot of them, until that fucking afternoon.

Some shopkeeper from town, some poor bastard with nothing left to offer the world. The rope swinging in the swell of a passing HST. The five of them staring up at the corpse for a minute or more, none of them uttering a fucking word. The sun beating down. The bloke's shoes shining in the cracks of sunlight. Everything cracking thereafter.

Ten years old.

His mam fussing over him for a spell, until it seemed he'd forgotten about it, put it behind him, stomped on into the 1980s with the rest of them, changed schools, left the deadland and its many guises to those trapped by circumstance coming up behind.

They should have torn the hut down after that day, done the bloke's memory some justice, or burned the fucking thing to the ground.

But they didn't.

He was still ten years old when the banging woke him. He dragged himself upright, felt her stirring beside him, spotted the shattered picture frame on the grate, felt the sunlight strike his eyes, blinked himself into the present.

And everything fell into focus. Jen's brother at the window, distorted fucking face pressed against the glass, the big Polish fucker behind him, the two of them hammering at the door, threatening to break it apart.

Fuck me, he had to wake up. He got to his feet, felt the room shift on its axis, almost fell back into the grate, planted a foot down to steady himself, felt the crunch of glass and plastic, saw Stimmo staring up at him from the carpet, caught her eye for the first time, rising from the sofa to see what the fuss was about, saw her heading for the door handle in some sort of trance.

Some ancient part of himself kicked in.

Fight or flight.

Fucking flight, mate.

He didn't hang about, was out the back door, over the fucking wall and away in a blink. He heard Jen screaming at them to fuck off, heard her brother yelling back at her. But they weren't there to mess about or to listen to what she had to say.

Were they fuck as like.

They were here to batter the fucker vaulting over the back wall.

Finchy reached the end of the alley, looked back over his shoulder to see the big fucker hurdling the wall and coming after him. Back in the day he'd have left them for dead, shot off fleet-footed into the distance, but it wasn't back in the fucking day. His knees were fucked from too much Sunday football on gruesome pitches and his head was clogged with whatever shit he'd poured down his throat in the previous days.

The big fucker gaining with every step, shouting after him in Polish. He didn't need a fucking translation to get the drift of it or what the cunt would do to his skull if he caught him. He still had the fat fucking lip from the week before.

Thirty-three years old. Teacher of English. Pillar of responsibility. On the sick. Tearing up the High Street of the old town to save his fucking face from a mashing. Big Polish fucker at his heels. Daydreamers on the pavement, daydreamers and spacers, carrying on regardless. Some not seeing him at all.

Vacant cunts.

Always vacant.

A vacant fucking place.

He was no good in a foot race, not today. He ducked into the bus station instead, where folks were gathered in little throngs, burst through one set and then the next, trying to lose himself amongst them.

But he was too animated.

He stood out like a sore fucking thumb.

Across the tarmac instead then, dodging great fuck-off buses. The sorting office on his left. He thought about crashing inside, imagined the doors swinging shut behind him and everything being as it was fifteen years earlier, Harcross in the office, Robbie Box at the facing table, the lads coming together to kick the Polish fucker out of the joint. But the red doors were closed. It wasn't fifteen years previous and it was no fucking good wishing otherwise. He could hear the big fucker's slapping steps on the tarmac behind him, ever closer, could almost feel his stinking lager breath on his neck. He shot over the road through the mid-morning traffic, the Crown ahead of him, praying that BJ was inside the joint.

He didn't get that far.

As he reached the door BJ stepped out of it. A guardian fucking angel. BJ filling the pavement, forming a barrier of belly and great fuck-off fists. Finchy too knackered to run any more. He stopped, turned around, to see the big fucker try to barge past BJ, to see him ram his nose against BJ's fist instead. He saw the bloke's nose implode, saw everything below his neck continue in a forward direction while his head stayed put, saw the big fucker collapse backwards and hit the pavement. His hands came up to his face. He started mewing like a fucking kitten.

Jen's brother stopped short behind him.

'Fuck off, mate,' he shouted at BJ.

Big fucking mistake.

'Who are you telling to fuck off?'

BJ stepped over the Polish guy, barrelling down the street in the brother's direction.

'He's the one we're after.'

'And you're the one I'm after,' said BJ.

The big fucker scrabbling backwards and away, no longer a factor. Jen's brother backing away too. He pointed at Finchy.

'You're fucking dead,' he shouted. 'Fucking dead.'

Finchy stood behind BJ, not knowing what to do with himself. Half the fucking old town had woken up at last. A semi-circle was forming around them. It was only a matter of time until the old bill came along. Beyond BJ, Jen's brother and the big fucker retreated around the corner, one supporting the other.

When they were no longer in view BJ turned to face him.

'Don't I keep saying you're a daft cunt?'

He twatted Finchy on the chin.

'What the fuck?'

'That's for not listening,' said BJ. 'And you lot can all fuck off.'

He turned back into the Crown as the onlookers recoiled.

It was good to have friends.

When he gets home the flat stinks of greasy fry-up and burnt toast. His flatmate's in the kitchen munching away. There are baked beans on the lino, great smears of beans.

Finchy retches.

'Look what the fucking cat dragged in,' says his flatmate. 'What the fuck were you up to last night?'

'Eh?'

'This morning. On the stairs. I had to climb over you to get in the door.'

'Fuck knows.'

'You went to that all-nighter, you cunt. I fancied that. How was it?'

'Fuck knows,' Finchy says again. 'I don't remember.'

'You don't remember?'

'I took something.'

'You took something. One of mine?'

'No. I don't know. Someone gave it to me.'

'You lying cunt. I thought I was missing some. That's a tenner you owe me.'

'It wasn't yours.'

'Fuck off. You can take it from my rent.'

'There was this Yank bird. It was a mess. I walked her back to the college dorms. I can't remember anything else.'

'Sounds like one of mine. They're not designed for light-weights. Did she have one, too?'

He shakes his head, shrugs.

'Lying bastard. That's twenty you owe me. I have to get off nights. That's my fucking scene right there. I should have been there. Fucking hell, raves are where it's at!'

'Is that what it was?' asks Finchy.

He goes to the bathroom, splashes water on his face, the fog descending again, his stomach cramping.

Smears of beans.

He collapses to his knees, vomits at the toilet bowl. Some of it reaches the target.

Some of it.

He vomits again.

When he earns some relief he drags himself in the direction of the hallway, the stairs, his fucking bedroom.

'Did you fuck her?' shouts his flatmate.

'Who?'

'The American bird.'

'I don't know,' he says.

'You fucked her.'

'If you say so,' says Finchy.

'What about Jen?'

'What about her?'

'When are you seeing her?'

'I'm not.'

'So it's off?'

'It's complicated.'

'She just comes over and stays the night a couple of times a week?'

'What's it to do with you?'

'Nothing,' says his flatmate. 'Your morals are nothing to do with me.'

Finchy begins to negotiate the stairs, stops, grips the banister to steady himself.

'Pass me the bowl,' he says.

'You're fucking joking,' says his flatmate but he empties the contents of the washing-up bowl in the sink all the same, slides the thing across the lino in Finchy's direction.

'I want my twenty quid,' he says.

'I don't owe you twenty quid,' says Finchy. 'Did you hear about the murder?'

'Yeah. Barmaid from the Crown. Found in that car park off Hope Close. Fucking ironic that – hey, isn't that your patch?'

'You know fucking well it is.'

'Fuck me,' says his flatmate.

He throws his plate in the sink, takes his mug of tea and wanders into the hall, starts up the stairs behind Finchy who is trying to climb the fuckers again.

A desperate ascent.

'Is that it?' asks Finchy.

'Is what it?'

'Is that your response to them finding a murdered woman in a hedge bottom?'

'No,' says his flatmate. 'No, it isn't. Sometimes I dream my life's as exciting as yours.'

He pushes past Finchy, reaches the top landing, enters his room and clicks his bedroom door shut.

Once a sarcastic cunt, always a sarcastic cunt.

BJ and Finchy in the Crown.

BJ and Finchy totting up the odds.

'You realise that's it,' said BJ. 'The end of your fucking adventure.'

Finchy didn't say anything. Sat in the Nag's with his tail between his legs, his chin smarting from BJ's fist, there was nothing he could say.

'You're a jammy bastard,' said BJ.

'I know.'

BJ supped his pint.

'Because on any other day I'd have been at home getting some well-deserved shut-eye. I've been up since five, on site since six. But I thought I'd come for a pint first, see who was about. Only nobody was about…'

'Perfect timing then,' said Finchy.

'Don't get cocky. Like I said, you're a jammy bastard. Now, tell me you're not going to see her again.'

Finchy shrugged.

'It wasn't a fucking question,' said BJ.

'I'm not sure I can just fuck off.'

'If I were you I'd not even bother getting your things from the hotel. They'll be all over it. Them and the rest of their cronies. All the more determined to give you one.'

'I have to. There's stuff I need.'

'Well, I'd like to say I'm finished with this business. But I won't be. There'll be payback after this. You wait and fucking see. The things we do for our pals, eh?'

'You can handle yourself.'

'Against one or two for sure, but those pricks will sort it so there's five or six of the bastards. They'll be tooled up too. Mark my words I'm in for a pasting.'

Finchy looked BJ in the eyes.

'It's appreciated,' he said. 'For what it's worth.'

A moment. The barmaid at the glasses. His face in the mirror behind her.

'But I can't just fuck off,' he said. 'I owe it to her not to do that again.'

BJ puffed out his cheeks.

'For fuck's sake, mate, what are you hoping to achieve?'

'I don't know,' said Finchy. 'Something more than this.'

He pressed his finger against his chin, winced with pain.

'She's in a real mess,' he said. 'She needs someone to help her through it.'

'And you think that's you? Fucking hell, mate, you caused half of it in the first place.'

'Exactly.'

BJ shook his head.

'Do me a favour,' said Finchy.

'Another one?'

'One more. For old time's sake.'

'What do you think this was for?' BJ shoved his swelling knuckles into Finchy's face.

'I owe you,' said Finchy. 'I know I owe you. But I can't fuck off. Not yet.'

'What then?'

'Let me stay at your gaff. Just until this is sorted. Just until I know everything's finished and put to bed.'

BJ downed the rest of his pint.

'You're a cunt,' he said. 'A soft southern cunt.'

'So I keep hearing.'

'Tomorrow,' said BJ. 'Not tonight. I'm busy.'

BJ rested his hand on the bar, displaying his swollen knuckles.

'This needs a nurse's attention,' he said.

'And you know a nurse, I suppose.'

BJ grinned an impish grin.

'What am I going to do tonight then?' asked Finchy.

'I don't give a shit,' said BJ. 'Lock yourself away and don't come out?'

Sunday afternoon in the flat. He spends the time sprawled on the sofa, absorbing a western he's seen a dozen times. Sunday afternoon recovering from the debacle of Friday, drifting in and out of consciousness.

A fucking train wreck.

When the phone rings he ignores it. He knows it's Jen but he has nothing to say. He can't find the words. He can hardly fucking think for fuck's sake. When the film ends he walks to the window, looks out at the darkness, at the orange street lights, at the dullness and drabness.

He drops back on the sofa, flicks through the channels, one – two – three – four. The phone rings again and he ignores it again. He can feel the change in himself but he doesn't understand it. He doesn't know what to do with it. He pulls on his jacket, walks down the stairs and out into the night. He makes his way to the Chinese, orders a takeaway, makes his way home again. He thinks about the barmaid, about Hope Close, about blue-and-white tape flickering in the breeze. He thinks about the all-nighter, the rave.

And still there's nothing on the TV. He takes the food to his room, sticks the stereo on, picks at the takeaway. He's not fucking hungry. He looks at the clock. 7 p.m. He picks up the phone. Some of the lads are heading to the pub, then to T-Gally's for a smoke. He doesn't want to go but he doesn't want to stay in either. He can't go to Jen's. He hasn't got what it takes. He drags his sorry arse to the pub and then he drags it home again. There's a fracture in his landscape. He can feel it widening. It's the same with how he feels about Jen.

Perhaps.

Maybe.

He isn't certain.

He isn't certain about anything.

He's done next to nothing all day. He climbs into bed, sticks the TV on and lays there seeking out something to occupy his busy mind. And there's nothing, just him in darkness, thoughts of Jen in his head, thoughts of the American girl, legs, dancing and dancing and dancing. For the first time he feels the aching in his thighs and calves.

The minutes tick into hours, Summer rain falling on the dark town, running in torrents from the guttering, flooding the street.

CID in the office when he turns up on Monday morning, a great herd of the bastards milling about the place, taking blokes off left, right and centre for statements. He waits his turn, struggling to focus on the frame, the street names and numbers collecting in black clots, his nervous hands quivering, his heart a fucking jackhammer.

He notices Spence looking him up and down. Spence, ever the observant.

'Bloody hell,' says Spence. 'You'd best confess and put them all out of their misery.'

He shakes his head, grits his teeth.

'It's not something to joke about,' he says, knowing he's waving a great fuck-off red rag, inviting an onslaught.

But Spence doesn't say anything. He doesn't do anything either. He just leans back on his perch, sucks in his cheeks, starts humming a little tune.

Boot fucking Hill.

Finchy tries to switch off to it, takes one breath and then another but it's no fucking good.

'What are you going to say?' he asks Spence. 'What are you going to tell them?'

'About what?'

'About who she was seeing, who she was involved with.'

'Nothing to do with me,' says Spence.

'So you're going to say nothing? What if no fucker says anything?'

'There's nothing to say, unless you know something I don't.'

'I don't know anything…'

'Tell them that, then,' says Spence.

'But I've heard stuff. We've all heard stuff.'

'Not me.'

'Bollocks.'

'All I know is where they found her and who delivers up that way. I'll have to tell them that, I suppose.'

Spence grins.

They turn up in the row then, four of them. Two minutes later Finchy finds himself in a side office with a big moustached bastard and his pal, tells them what he knows, tells them more than he knows, tells them stuff he doesn't have a fucking clue about. He can't help himself. Everything just drops out of his mouth. Through the window he sees Spence leaving the office down the hall, sees Robbie Box head in after him, sees Robbie Box come out and Dave Hunt go in. Through all of that the big moustached bastard asks him questions, checks his notebook, treads over the facts. He tells the bloke none of it is fact, just hearsay, just office chatter. He tells him until he's blue in the face but the bastard goes over it anyway, again and again and again.

It takes him forty-five minutes to get out of there.

When he arrives at his frame the place is empty. There's just him with his back to a dozen CID, sharing jokes, sharing notes, sharing their discoveries. He is physically shaking from top to toe. It's all he can do to prep the rest of the round, all he can muster to bag up and make his way down the row of frames to the exit, where he stands shivering on the ramp, his head a swirling fucking vortex.

Throughout the round he goes over it all, trying to piece together tiny smithereens of memory, unable to see any patterns, any configurations at all. The previous weekend is a black hole. Friday into Saturday. Pills and thrills. And then what? Everything sucked into a fucking black hole.

Except dancing and beat, an American girl with perfect skin. And legs, he can remember the legs.

He'll never forget the fucking legs.

Finchy made his way back to the hotel, eyes on the darkness ahead of him, eyes on the darkness behind, looking out for the big fucker and anybody else Jen White's little brother might have attached himself to. His head was spinning from too much drink. Again. He'd never been able to keep up with BJ and the others. He'd learned that fucking lesson long ago. But somehow he'd had another bellyful. His head was pounding. The trees bordering the sloping avenue that led to the hotel were tilted, in danger of toppling over. Or so it seemed. The street lights were tilted too. Everything was fucking tilted.

Between bouts of shuffling footsteps he kept looking over his shoulder, just in case. But the avenue behind him was deserted, the blinking traffic lights at the bottom of the incline the only movement in his vision.

Nothing else stirred.

He runs into Spence at the breakfast van, him with his bacon and egg bap, Spence with his coffee. Part and parcel of the morning these meetings, when the mail's not too heavy, when Finchy can get down there. Not Spence. Spence is always there. It's written into his daily schedule. Just like the ribbing he delivers Finchy every fucking morning.

'Eh up,' says Spence. 'Look who it isn't.'

Robbie's sat on the steps of the market cross, newspaper on his knees, grease dripping from his sarnie, his lips smeared with egg. He hardly bats an eyelid.

'You were in there a long time,' says Spence.

'What's that?'

'In the office, with CID. Must have had a lot to say.'

Robbie perks up. Robbie grunts. Robbie senses something.

'They kept asking me questions,' he says. 'Everything I told them led to another one.'

'Aye, well I told you to keep your mouth shut.'

'I didn't tell them anything important,' he said. 'Just the

same things over and over. It was my walk after all. They wanted to know what I'd seen.'

'But you didn't see anything.'

'Exactly.'

'And you didn't tell them anything?'

'Why are you so bothered?'

'I'm not,' says Spence. 'I'm just watching out for you. You open your mouth it's you who'll get it.'

'Who from?'

'From the fuckers you land in the shit, you daft bastard.'

'Fuck me,' says Robbie. 'You've not been snitching.'

'Have I fuck,' says Finchy. 'I don't know anything to snitch about.'

'No fucker knows anything but some bastard knows everything,' says Spence.

'You know more than me,' says Finchy.

'Judging by this morning I'm not so sure,' says Spence.

'I didn't tell them anything,' repeated Finchy.

'I'm not saying you did,' says Spence. 'I'm not saying you did.'

All of this outside the breakfast van in the market square. All of this.

The lobby was deserted. He lurched across the hall into the corridor, made it to his room and then stopped himself. Not tonight. Not fucking tonight. He wandered back to reception. There was no fucker there. He reached over the counter and grabbed a bunch of keys, nabbed the bastards and hopped in the lift, took himself up to the top floor out of the way. He thought about letting himself in a room but didn't have the bottle to do it. Besides there were no door keys on the bundle, just doors that unlocked cleaning cupboards and routes into the stomach of the place, into the boiler rooms and the attic. He didn't know what the fuck he was looking for but he knew when he found it. Somewhere at the back of the hotel, somewhere stuck out of the way he found the service elevator and next to it a linen store. It would fucking do. He let himself in and then hurled the keys down the corridor so the staff would find them when they came looking, then he slipped into the far corner of the room, to a great barrow filled with freshly dried bathrobes, imagining the big fucker and Jen's brother turning up at his room with a crowbar and a hammer, forcing the door open at 3 a.m., wielding the fucking things in the direction of the bed to find him a step ahead of them once again. Stupid bastards. He shut off the light and flopped into the barrow, grinning to himself in the darkness, recalling the moment the big fucker's nose exploded.

Fucking hilarious.

And somewhere amongst it all, amongst the darkness and the smell of fabric conditioner, he found himself opening his eyes to see his old teacher in front of him, six foot six of bone and sinew stooped amongst the sheets and towels, his shoulders draped in a Union Jack with the words 'Nottingham Forest – Champions of Europe' emblazoned across its centre. Before he could comprehend this vision the ceiling disappeared to be replaced by a tapestry of stars.

The constellations.

His teacher stared up at them, pointing to a shape amongst the heavens, pointing and smiling in wondrous adoration. It was the Forest badge. He could see it clearly. The single oak, nestled there between Orion and the Plough.

Ludicrous, but he found himself grinning as his head swam. The linen room, transformed now, became his old teacher's observatory. He could see the books on the shelves, specks of dust dancing in the starlight. He was ten years old. His body filled with a tingling sensation. He laughed as a child in the darkness. The future was an endless horizon. He was in a classroom at his old primary school, sat on the carpet in the reading corner staring up at his teacher's knees, crammed in place between Judith Jackson and Louise Wallace. In the corner, beside the bookshelf was Stimmo, there with a far-off look on his face, staring down at the carpet, picking at it with his fingers, muttering, silently muttering, fucking miles away. Rain was pouring down the windows in great torrents. The sky was black. The sky was falling. The sky was a ceiling in a linen room in a hotel in the old town a quarter of a century later.

Stimmo was gone.

His teacher was gone.

He closed his eyes and curled himself into a ball in the barrow full of linen, more alone than he had ever been.

The flat's quiet, dead of sound until the news kicks in with his alarm clock. Finchy wakes slowly, dragging himself from dark places, hearing a doorbell ringing, dreaming of bare white flesh, tangled red hair, slugs and snails. Fucking spiders. He walked right past the spot, right fucking past it and was oblivious, too comatose to take anything in. He isn't ever going to take one of those bastard beans again.

'… barmaid who had just finished her shift…'

He can see her as clear as day in that short skirt, white legs that go on forever, marching home in the early hours, always with somewhere to go, not fucking knowing, not seeing.

But why would she know? Why would she see?

Nothing ever happens here.

Not here.

Everything happens somewhere else.

'… police following several leads…'

A stranger's hands at her neck, her heels kicking and flexing, her fingernails scratching and scraping. Running out of breath, running out of time, running out of life.

He hears the doorbell, realises he hasn't imagined it, pulls himself out of bed and over to the window, yanks it open and looks down on the street. There are two of them. One is the moustached fucker who interviewed him at the depot.

They're in the street outside his flat, in their suits, the moustached and the non-moustached. His heart rate doubles despite himself.

Fuck.

What are they doing at his flat?

He imagines a pair of hands dragging the body across the car park, into the undergrowth, into the slugs and the snails, the spiders and the flies. He imagines happening across her on the way home from his shenanigans with the American bird, him with his blood up, his head, his body, his whole being at the will of a substance he has no control over, his own hands doing those things. It's fucking absurd but they're here, aren't they, here to see him again, to ask their questions and scribble their notes.

They spot him.

'Inspector Mayhew and Inspector Ritson. Can we come in?'

Fucking shouting that in the street.

Curtains already twitching.

He nods, doing his best to look nonchalant, shitting himself. There are two detectives from the murder squad on his doorstep for fuck's sake.

'I'll come down,' he says. He grabs his jeans and polo shirt, wets his hair, his face, tries to look casual. Casual is best. Casual is always best. He descends the two floors to the foyer, hears the clocks, the dozens of clocks, chiming half past the hour. He opens the door. The bird across the street is at her window. He shoots her a glance and she backs away.

Into the shadows.

'Through here,' he says to Mr Moustache and Mr Notebook.

He leads them up the steep stairs, on to the first-floor landing.

'Nice place,' says Mayhew, says Mr Moustache. 'Really nice.'

It isn't a nice place. It's a fucking flat above a clock-menders. It has orange lino flooring in the kitchen and a sink that's seen better days. The living room sofa's bright fucking yellow, something he picked up for free from a bloke who was skipping it. The carpet has stains on it. The windows don't fit properly. They rattle in their frames when the wind blows and upset the neighbours. The paint needs a fresh lick. And it's always too cold or too hot, never just right.

'A few questions. On what we spoke about,' says Mayhew.

He nods. His throat's parched. He can feel himself trembling.

'You said you knew the victim…'

'Knew of her. I said I knew of her.'

'What do you mean?'

'She was a barmaid in the Bell. She served me drinks. I recognise her from there. And the Crown.'

'You frequent the Crown.'

A statement, not a question. He has to clarify that. Slippery bastards.

'No. I've been there. It's the postie pub, right opposite … you know where it is.'

Mr Notebook scribbling. Mr Moustache staring out of the back window, down into the yard.

'Is that yard attached to this place?'

'No, that's for the flat downstairs.'

'So that's not your shed then.'

'No.'

'And you can't access it from this flat?'

'Not unless you climb out of the window or over the back gate.'

'And do you?'

'Do I what?'

'Climb out of the window.'

'No.'

'What about the gate?'

'No. I've no need to be out there. I store my bike in the passageway. That's all.'

'Right. And how long have you lived here?'

'A few months. Since January.'

'Nice place,' says the other one, says Mayhew. 'I could do with a place like this myself. How much?'

'£400.'

'For a room?'

'For the whole thing.'

'Got a bathroom?'

'Of course.'

'Can I have a look? I like a bathroom.'

'Down the hall,' says Finchy. 'I'll show you.'

'No need,' says Mayhew. 'I'll find it.'

Mr Notebook hovering about the place, while Mr Moustache waffles on about the benefits of a bath over a shower from somewhere deep within the flat. Somewhere deep within 'his' flat.

'The first pub. What did you say its name was again?' Mr Notebook adds, pen poised.

You know fucking damn well what its name is.

'The Bell. Everybody's favourite.'

Mr Notebook scribbles away.

'Were you there last Friday, then?'

Finchy shakes his head.

'Blokes at the PO say you're there every weekend.'

Fucking tossers.

'I stayed in,' he says.

'On a Friday. A young lad like you.'

No. I went to an all-nighter. I took a fucking E, possibly two. I might have fucked an American bird from the college but I don't think I did. I can't remember a thing about Friday. Not a fucking thing except waking up at the bottom of the stairs in a fucking heap. And legs. I remember legs.

'I was knackered. I wanted to watch the game in peace.'

'What game would that be?'

He raised his eyebrows.

'Liverpool Arsenal...'

'Right,' says Mr Moustache. 'Classic.'

Finchy nods in silence.

'You're a fan then?'

He stares at them blankly.

'Of football,'

He nods.

'I'm a Forest fan,' he says, to clarify, to set the fuckers straight.

Mr Notebook grits his teeth.

Mr Moustache grits his teeth.

'So you stayed in, on your own, all evening?' asks Mr Moustache.

'Yep.'

A lie. A barefaced lie.

'No girlfriend?'

'Not at the minute.'

'Right. Because...'

'We broke up.'

'You're not still seeing her?'

'Sometimes. She comes over. It's complicated.'

Does he look as guilty as he feels? Are they serious? Do they really suspect him of strangling a barmaid and dumping her semi-naked body in a patch of undergrowth beside a kiddies' playground? Do they really suspect him of that?

Fuck fuck fuck fuck fuck.

'Blokes at the PO say you arrived at work looking like shit last Saturday.'

'I told you. I was knackered.'

'Looked like you'd had no sleep.'

'I slept. I slept too long. That was the problem.'

Mr Moustache reappears.

'How many bedrooms?'

'Eh?'

'This place? How many?'

Mr Moustache, still going on about the fucking flat, about the benefits of a two-bed, one-hundred-year-old shell in some dark side street of some floundering town.

'Two,' says Finchy. 'Both upstairs.'

'Just you?'

'No. There's my flatmate.'

'Was he in last Friday?'

'No. He works at the supermarket.'

Raised eyebrows at that little fucking detail.

'Nights,' he says.

'On weekends?'

'He does all sorts.'

'Nights?'

'Nights.'

'Rough hours?'

'Nine till six, something like that.'

Mr Moustache looks at Mr Notebook, then he looks at the stairs

'Right.'

More fucking scribbling as they climb the second flight of stairs, to the landing, the little space outside the bedrooms. One door open, one door closed.

'Is he in?'

'I think so. I don't know. I haven't looked.'

'And this is your room?'

He nods.

'May I?'

He nods again, thinking 'No, you fucking can't, you moustached cunt. Why the fuck would you want to?'

'Not en-suite then.'

'Er, no.'

The bed a mess. His postie uniform heaped on the chair. The room stinking of sweat and farts and day sleep. Teacup on the stereo, tea stains, a few scattered biscuit crumbs.

'Did we get you up?'

'It's the early mornings,' he said.

'What time do you start work then?'

'Half five, something like that. Depends on the job.'

'Rather you than me,' says Mr Moustache. 'I'm all tucked up then.'

He turns to Mr Notebook. 'Aren't you?'

I bet you fucking are. Tucked up together. You moustached bastard.

'And you deliver to Hope Close?'

He nods.

'You said there was nothing in the bushes when you cycled past?'

'I didn't see a … I didn't see anything. No.'

'So there might have been something there but you didn't see it?'

'There might have been. I don't know.'

Silence.

'That row of houses. That's where your round starts, isn't it? By the kiddies' swings?'

Finchy nods.

'I can't remember what number was first that day. I might have skipped a few. I wish I hadn't … you know … to save those kids from…'

Mr Moustache tries the door to his flatmate's room. It's locked. He knocks. There's no answer.

'He must have gone out,' says Mr Moustache. 'Isn't that a pity?'

They descend the stairs again, head to the living room, to the yellow fucking sofa.

'It was free,' he says, to explain.

'Nice,' says Mr Moustache.

No, it fucking isn't. It's a fucking embarrassment.

Three blokes. One yellow sofa. Mr Notebook endlessly

scribbling. Over the same ground as before. White skin.
White legs. Always striding. Always purposeful. In a fucking
rush. Bar job to bar job.

The Bell and the Crown.

The Crown and the Bell.

Blokes bored of their wives. Drinkers. Smokers. Dirty bastards.

'These men...' says the one with the notepad.

Dirty drink-addled bastards.

He looks up, puzzled.

'When we chatted at the depot. The men you mentioned...'

'Common knowledge,' he says. 'I don't know any details.'

'Only she lived with her boyfriend. You know that?'

He shrugs.

'Rumours, then,' he says. 'Blokes talking in the canteen.
The blokes are always talking. You must know yourself.
Nothing but rumours...'

'These were ex-boyfriends?'

'I don't know. Yes. Probably. Like I said, it's mostly just talk
and rumour. Bravado. You know.'

The cunt knows but he isn't saying anything.

'You mentioned some names.'

'Yes, but...'

'Arnie Burrows?'

'So I heard. Maybe. Ages ago.'

'Ages?'

'A year.'

'A year. Not ages then. What about Bob Harris?'

'Nobber? Definitely a rumour. He's got kids. And he's
been ill.'

'We heard. Heart attack at his age. You wonder how these
things happen.'

The fucking kings of inference.

Nobber Harris. The Crown, before a late, after an early.
Each visit totting up.

Veins hardening. Liver shrinking.

Pint upon pint. Fag upon fag.

'And the other?'

'Some bloke who left the depot. I don't remember his name.'

Another silence. Just the pen, scribbling.

'So you didn't go out Friday?'

'No.'

'You stayed in and did what?'

He shrugs.

'Watched TV?'

'I'm asking you.'

'I think so.'

'Anything good on.'

'I don't remember.'

Porn in the corner, stacked under the newspapers, if they care to take a peek.

Tell them about the American bird. Just fucking tell them.

Tell them what? Tell them he walked her back to the college. Tell them he's no idea what her name is. Tell them she's fucked off back to the States already. Fucking convenient that. Tell them he wandered back through town in the early hours, that he doesn't remember how he got home or what the fuck he did on the way. Tell them about the legs? Tell them those things?

'You didn't go out on Friday and you didn't see anything on Saturday morning?'

'No.'

'And you can't throw any light on these boyfriends?'

'Only what I've told you. But not boyfriends. Just rumour.'

'Well then. Thanks for having us.'

'And thanks for showing me around the place. Just what I'm looking for.'

Right. Sure.

Down the stairs, to the door. The clocks in the shop chiming the hour. The dozens of clocks. He watches them climb into their blue Sierra, watches them sitting there, talking, Mr Moustache at the wheel, Mr Notebook scribbling into his little black book. He closes the door and climbs the stairs to the kitchen, sticks the kettle on. His flatmate appears in the doorway, hair lank, eyes bloodshot, skin as white as a corpse.

'Good fucking job they didn't see you,' says Finchy. 'They'd have arrested me for your murder instead.'

'Was that the fucking police? I thought it was the fucking police.'

'CID,' says Finchy.

The kettle's coming to the boil, steam clouding the window.

'Fuck,' says his flatmate. 'Fuck me.'

He turns and heads in the direction of the bathroom then he turns around again.

'Are they coming back?'

'I hope not.'

'Right. Because I've got a pot of beans on my fucking stereo.'

'I thought you were going to bury them.'

'Not much point now, eh? They'll be digging up out back looking for clues.'

Finchy chucks a tea bag in a mug and pours in the water, the steam licking at his face, tiny splashes scalding the backs of his hands. Then he repeats the process for his flatmate because what else are friends for? He drifts across the hall to the lounge, rests the mug on the fireplace and drops down on to the sofa. They have to get a new one. Fuck me do they. And they need to get rid of the porn and the fucking pills. They most definitely need to get rid of the fucking pills.

His flatmate reappears, the mug of tea in his grip.

'Is this for me?' he asks.

Finchy nods.

'Cheers,' says his flatmate.

'Listen,' says Finchy. 'If they come back, if they ever ask

you, there was no fucking American college bird. When you left for work I was settled on the sofa in front of the telly. When you got home I was not paralytic on the stairs. Do you understand?'

'You want me to lie to the police in a murder investigation?'

Finchy nods again.

'In that case,' says his flatmate. 'There are no pills. There were never any pills, not here, not at the all-nighter, nowhere.'

'They don't know about the all-nighter,' says Finchy.

'Fuck me,' says his flatmate. 'You really are on thin fucking ice.'

Friday

He hauled his suit and sports bag down the avenue to BJ's.

'I've the one bedroom,' said BJ. 'You're fucked if you think you're kipping in there. You can have the big sofa until the weekend and then we're done.'

The big sofa in BJ's living room. The big sofa nestled between stacked 'twenty packs' of lager and boxes of football programmes amassed over twenty aggravated years.

For fuck's sake.

He milled about the place, waiting for evening. He took the season ticket out of his back pocket, turned it over in his fingers, put it back. He wondered if he could do this thing, drag back the years like this, expose himself to the new while mired in the old.

Could he do it?

Could he really fucking do it?

He had to do it.

He had to.

He passed the old pub at five, the old pub where so many nights started, moved on up the High Street, the Guildhall and the green, the trees shedding their leaves in the bitter wind, darkness coming on.

Ever-repeating patterns.

To the corner, the PO yard, the iron gates, vans parked up on the ramp, strangers in those vans, strangers on the ramp, just a single smoker there, shuffling his feet to keep warm, the bright lights of the sorting office beyond the clear plastic doors, men gathered at the sorting table, blurred misshapen men pushing barrows in one direction and then the other, feeling it, smelling it, connecting with it, and yet separated from it. No longer a part of it.

Somebody else.

He was somebody else.

The long ascent to the station, the lights bright and harsh on the platform. He felt a stirring in the air, a distant tremble. A train came hurtling through, heading north, buffeting him, rocking him on his heels, creating its own vacuum.

Everything was a vacuum.

He watched the single light diminishing, made his way over the bridge to the isolated platform linking West to East, insular Midland towns to coastal resorts for one week of respite. He found himself a seat, waited, stared across the tracks, beyond the sidings, beyond the remnants of scrub to the housing development. Warm light crept from the windows of the new houses and spilled on to the station yard.

The old and the new.

A remnant of one, an infiltrator of the other.

The train was quiet, just a handful of people, too early yet for the Forest faithful, too soon after tea. He watched the lights of the old town slip past, studied the unaltered profile, stared once again at the brightly lit church, felt the drag of the long left-hand bend as the train turned in its westward arc. And then there was nothing much at all outside the window except black fields, the ribbon lights of the trunk road in the distance, the glow of the next town beyond the flat horizon, the quiet rocking of the train in motion.

And a thousand memories.

The city station. Busy. Him against the tide, taking his time, more uncertain of himself with each step. Meadow Lane masked in darkness, the black river, silent, toiling, the flood-lights of the City Ground aglow, forming a washed-out reflection on the water. He stopped and stared from afar, feeling it now, the fluttering in his belly, the first signal that it all still remained, coiled deep inside of him, deep in the gut. A part of him really, of his inner workings, the fragments that shaped him. He wondered how he'd ever come to doubt that, to forget it, to live without it.

But he had, for fifteen years.

He walked down the steps and along the river path, up behind the Trent end, no longer a squat fucking shed but a great hulking two-tiered structure teetering on the riverbank. He took the ticket out of his wallet, felt it in his fingers, folded it back in place.

Precious fucking cargo.

He walked a circuit of the ground, seeing what else had changed and what had not, took himself off behind the Bridgford end, picturing the old open terrace, the waves of sound drifting away, the packed away end when United visited in 85 and 86, the day the scoreboard became a perch, the floodlight a climbing frame, United crammed on top of each other, making room where they could find it, throbbing and surging, him watching from the Trent end, watching the visiting end fill to overspill, the stewards opening the adjacent pen, the United hordes growing like bacteria in a fucking petri dish. He'd fallen in love with it all in that moment, become energised by the electricity building around him, energy that charged his days and nights for much of his teenage years.

It was all just yesterday, a fleeting moment ago.

He moved on until he was stood beneath the Executive Stand, got to thinking about the lower tier, of season-ticket Saturdays, of the lads together all in a row, close to pitch side, close to the away end.

Friends and enemies.

Enemies and friends.

And then a different feeling engulfed him, the sense of

something dying, of something taking its final painful breath, of 96 final breaths.

And Tracey Carlton. And Janet Allen. Two more sets of final breaths.

Soon he was back where he started, on the bank beside the river, looking up at the Trent end, looking back towards the bridge, dark shapes crossing the water, hunched silhouettes against the headlights and tail lights, becoming clumps, becoming a throbbing mass at the turnstiles, the newly fledged creature revealing itself.

It was cold and he was feeling it. He drifted back along the riverbank against the flow of the water and the flow of the gathering crowds, bought a tea from a burger van, crossed the bridge to the far bank and sat himself down, sensing something missing, a void that couldn't be filled.

Or was it terror? Was that the thing turning his stomach inside out?

He sat on a wall, arse on cold stone, looking at the Trent end brightly lit against the night, and he saw the Trent end as it used to be. He was fourteen again, paying his £1.50, pushing through the turnstile, feeling the cold metal against his stomach, turning right, to the end of the terrace and the corner flag, moving along the front of each pen, ducking and diving from pen to pen, to the middle section behind the goal, moving towards the pulsing heart of the beast, attaching himself, singing and singing and singing, swaying, rocking, raising his hands, singling out each player, greeting each one in turn.

Players and fans.

Fans and players.

Feeling the ebb and flow of the game, its beat, being part of the game, part of the ninety minutes, riding each wave and surge of energy that came down upon him from above, riding it forwards and riding it backwards, him and the boys filled up with adrenalin, with living something that was not the old town, something none of their fucking mates lived, knowing a secret world, the simple joy of being part of something bigger than themselves.

Every fucking Saturday.

He sat on the far bank, separated by the river, in the same place he'd wound up in in his nightmares. He could hear the crowd, the gentle ripple of applause as the players entered the pitch. But it wasn't the same. It wasn't the fucking same.

And it wasn't enough.

He mulled about for a bit, weighing things up, more uncertain than before, the fluttering in his stomach becoming cramps that threatened to turn him inside out on the banks of the Trent, reveal all that was him. He imagined his inverted cadaver slipping silently into the black river, disappearing forever.

He searched for some resolve, wrestled with what had been and what was gone, forced himself to cross the bridge again, made his way to the gates, heart beating nineteen to the dozen, feeling sick, feeling drained, knowing he had to go through with it for the sake of BJ and Jen White, for Jeff and for Kelly.

And for Stimmo. He had to do it for Stimmo.

The click of the Trent end turnstile was the same but well oiled. He had to apply no pressure at all to get it turning. He climbed the steps to the upper tier, emerged above the pitch. A steward glanced at his ticket, pointed him in the direction of his seat. He disturbed people by pushing his way along the row, twelve seats from the gangway as the steward instructed, slid on to his plastic perch.

A mixed bunch around him, blokes in pairs, blokes with their dads, blokes with their women, blokes on their own, no groups of lads, the game played out to a polite murmur, punctuated by moans and groans, by the occasional wave of sound, the occasional ripple from the away end. But he could hear the players calling out to each other, could hardly believe his ears.

Was this it? Was this what it had become?

It went on that way, songs forming and dying.

Ghosts of songs.

When the home team scored, when the ball hit the net, when the player turned his back and pointed with his thumbs to the name on his shirt, when that happened he realised how much he'd come to loathe it all. The people around him were on their feet, the stewards already urging them to sit down again.

Music sounded out through the tannoy.

Fucking music.

'No,' he shouted, to nobody. 'No.'

He forced himself clear of the row, ran down the steps, pushed past the steward who tried to slow him down and shot away from the place.

He thought of Goodison in 85, FA Semi-Final, United and Liverpool slugging it out, the packed terraces, fans perched astride walls and fences, limpets clinging to extremities. Fifty-one thousand Scousers and Mancs riding every tackle, breathing every breath.

Euphoria at every goal.

Something deep within the soul.

Fans and players.

Players and fans.

He thought of Ashton Gate and White Hart Lane and the Baseball Ground, the frenzy of a goal. He thought of Highfield Road, that fucking cage, his ribs close to breaking under the strain of his jubilant peers.

He thought of Hillsborough 81, 87, 88, the unheeded warning signs.

He thought of that day in April 89, blue skies, the football special fringing pastel peaks, boarding the bus outside Sheffield station, great swarms of red and white on the pavements, the green splash of Hillsborough Park, the old brick turnstiles, the steep steps leading up in zigzag pattern to the back of the Kop and the darkness beneath the roof, the pitch in sunlight, Leppings Lane in sunlight, his life in sunlight.

Endless contradictions.

Blind alleys and dead fucking ends.

Black clouds rolling in.

He turned his back on it all, made his sullen way towards the station, back to the old town, reeling, wishing for the hotel room and the bed in the room with no windows, wishing for that but knowing he had to go to BJ's instead, curl up awkwardly on a sofa, wake to cramp and the smell of damp and share this fucking tragedy with someone who already knew the game was up.

He needed to go back down south, back to the life he'd built from the ruins of the one that had collapsed around him. If it was still there. If it still existed.

Because.

Because.

Because.

Just because.

Just another Friday evening after another week of flirting with the girls on the High Street, the girls that want to know when he'll be out next, when he's going to buy them a drink, make good on his promises.

Jen at home, waiting for him to make his next step. But he's unable to take a step in her direction. He can't do it. What he wants is to be out with the others, free of the shackles. What he wants is another all-nighter to come around, to take another pill and float away on its magical ride, swap this life for another. He can't fucking help himself. Everything builds and begs for release.

And it's seven already. Her mam and dad will be poring over the takeaway menu in anticipation. Friday night's curry night. He has the responsibility of depositing it in front of their faces.

Because Jen and him are not over, not really, because he doesn't have the courage to cut the rope. He doesn't have the fucking balls.

Such a cunt.

Such an ungrateful cunt.

So here he is, still in the flat, neither ready to head over with the food or to go out on the fucking town with the boys. He picks up the phone, puts it down, picks up the phone, puts it down, wanders the flat, a caged fucking animal. It won't be long before he wears footprints into the fucking carpet.

His flatmate surfaces, spruced up, no longer a fucking walking zombie.

'I thought you were off to see Jen...' says his flatmate.

'Yeah, so did I,' says Finchy.

'What's the score, then?'

He looks his flatmate up and down. He smiles a wry one.

'You've got her from over the way on a promise, haven't you? You've called a sickie.'

'What of it?'

'Then I've got to fucking go out.'

'It would help,' says his flatmate. 'It would definitely fucking help.'

'I'm sure it fucking would,' he says.

It's no good. He has to sort things with Jen, find some common ground. He picks up the phone, dials the number. She answers on the second ring, voice shaking, uncertain of herself, uncertain of him. He feels a terrible weight fall upon him.

He's fucking damaging her, wringing her out.

'You should be here by now,' she says, trying to act casual, trying to act like there isn't some great unspoken shadow hanging over them.

'Yeah, I know,' he says.

'What's up, then?'

He sighs, hoping his silence will do his work for him, hoping not to have to say anything.

'You are coming?'

Further silence, genuine this time, the words stuck in his throat.

'I can't,' he says.

A different type of silence.

'You said you'd come over tonight.'

'Andy's got a date.'

'So?'

'So we can't come back here.'

Pathetic. Scraping the barrel. Not even a reason.

'You can stay here,' she says. 'I thought that was the plan.'

He doesn't say anything.

'Are you seeing someone else?' she asks.

'Eh?'

'Are you?'

'Fucking hell—'

'Well?'

'No,' he says.

He can hear her mam and dad in the background now.

Where's the food? I'm bloody starved.

Hasn't he left yet? Tell me he's on his way.

'I can't stay at yours,' he says. 'I've work tomorrow. I thought you were coming back here.'

On and on and fucking on. Weaker and fucking weaker. Running out of options. Running out of room.

'I don't believe this,' she says.

'I'm going out for a bit instead,' he says. 'With the others. Then I'm coming home to sleep. I need sleep.'

Silence on the other end. The sound of further voices. The sound of the TV. The sound of shouting. The phone slamming about.

Jen's distant voice.

'Pills! I hate those things. I fucking hate them.'

Trailing away.

Her mam's voice on the line instead. Seething. Tanked up.

'Hey. What are you playing at?'

'Nothing,' he says. Weakly. Tragically.

'Do you want to be with my daughter or not?'

Jen's voice in the background. Screaming. Grappling for the phone. Terrified of the question. Terrified of the answer.

'Mam...'

'If you do, get your arse over here. If you don't, then fucking well leave her alone.'

'I can't,' he says. 'I do. I don't...'

He doesn't know what the fuck he's saying. He doesn't know what the fuck he's doing.

The phone goes dead. He stands holding it limply in his hands. His flatmate scoots past him, reeking of aftershave.

'Thirty minutes,' says his flatmate. 'Thirty minutes and then you're gone.'

His flatmate heads down the steep stairs and out of the front door.

Finchy makes his way upstairs instead, shuts his bedroom door and slumps on the duvet, the life knocked out of him. He's a shambles. It's a shambles. And suddenly he doesn't want to go any fucking where, not to Jen's, not to town, not even into the hall. He doesn't have the energy or the interest. He locks his door, switches off the light, buries himself in darkness.

He spends the evening listening to his flatmate and the woman from over the road, listening to them pant and groan, listening to the bed creak under the shifting weight of their oblivious fucking.

The phone rings three times before midnight. He ignores it each time. He doesn't have the guts to speak to Jen and he doesn't have the patience to speak to any fucker else.

He doesn't speak to Jen for two fucking weeks.

He doesn't call.

She doesn't call.

He thinks about calling.

He thinks it's best to leave it.

He thinks about calling.

He thinks it's best to leave it.
He imagines her with another.
He imagines himself with another.
He imagines her with another.
He imagines himself with another.
These are the things that circulate in his head.
Around and around and around in his head.

Back at BJ's. Back with the one soul who could link it all together.

The past and the present.

The present and the past.

'I could have told you you'd hate it. Don't you watch the TV?'

'It wasn't top flight though, was it?'

'No, mate, but this thing's bleeding down through the ladder. Ten years from now it'll be in park football and then we're all fucked.'

BJ rummaging in the fridge for a bite. BJ humming to himself.

'And if you know your history, it's enough to make your heart go...'

'Fucking hell,' he said. 'You'll have to go.'

'What for?' asked Finchy

'You're eating me out of house and home.'

'I've had one fucking biscuit and a beer,' said Finchy.

BJ stood up. He laughed. They both laughed. There was fuck all to laugh about, fuck all funny about any of it.

Finchy picked up a Forest programme from 84. UEFA Cup. Sturm Graz at home.

'I went to this game,' he said. 'My dad took me.'

'Quarter-Final,' said BJ. '1–0. Paul Hart header.'

Finchy grinned, a grainy image in his head, his dad not yet turned forty, the two of them high in the upper tier of the Executive Stand.

'One of the first games I went to,' he said. 'I remember looking around for the TV replay when we scored.'

'Daft bastard,' said BJ. Then he said, 'You remember Anderlecht?'

Finchy nodded.

'Cheating cunts,' said BJ.

'The ref was killed in a car crash.'

'The dirty cheating bastard ruined one of my fucking childhood dreams. I can still feel the hurt, my dad saying "It's only football".'

'He fucked up with some real estate.'

'So fucking what?'

'I'm just saying. He was ripe for suggestion.'

'You know the best thing about all that?' asked BJ. 'The Anderlecht president getting blackmailed by the gangster who arranged it all. I love that. Mess around in things like football, you deserve a good fucking from all sides.'

BJ chuckling to himself.

'Fuck me,' said Finchy. 'You've got it worse than I realised.'

'Not really,' said BJ. 'Cloughie said it himself. The game was corrupt in those days. That's why all the old school took a little bit. The game fucked them so they fucked the game.'

Finchy stared across the poky room, at BJ, spread out on the opposite sofa in his boxers, all belly and balls, empty lager tins on the mantelpiece, crisps on the carpet.

'I should call Kelly,' he said. And then he hesitated. 'What do you think?'

'Me? You're asking me?' BJ laughed. 'Don't look to me, mate. I'm a complete fuck-up. I got sent down due to a woman.'

Finchy looked at the tin of lager on the table, thinking for the hundredth time *Why the fuck am I here?*

'Caught my missus with some Polish prick. Or thought I did, daft tosser that I am. Went to Forest, cheated the ban. Lads convinced me to go for a pint when we got back to town. Found her in this pub. All tarted up. He was a cunt. Started giving it some. So I battered the fucker. Turns out he was a workmate. Innocent stuff. Looked pretty fucking cosy to me though.'

For a moment he stared off into a distant place only he could see. Finchy leafed through the programme, busying himself the only way he could.

'I got eighteen months,' BJ said at last. 'She threw me out. Now look at me. A one-bedroom pisshole on Radley Street. Fucking dump. Thirty-five years of age. Shit job. No prospects. What a wanker. She doesn't talk to me any more. Tell you something, mate. Fifteen years and fuck all has changed. The same blokes. The same casuals. The same pubs. The same shit.'

He reached down and swilled the beer cans at his feet in turn, until he found what he was looking for. He lifted a can to his lips and took a swig. He grimaced. Finchy grimaced.

'Thank fuck for football,' said BJ. 'It's a fucking lifesaver. Don't know where I'd be without it, where the fuck I'd be headed. Saturdays. I live for Saturdays. You should see me in the summer. I'm a fucking coiled spring.'

He rolled off the sofa, sat up on his haunches.

'Solved that, though. I go on fucking tour. It used to be England. Now I tour with the Reds.'

He trailed off, the way BJ always had, trailed off into the blackness that devoured him. What Finchy wanted to do was grab the cunt and give him a great fucking hug, for being what he was, for not fucking changing when so much had changed.

What he wanted to do was cry his fucking eyes out.

'Thanks, mate,' he said.

'What for?'

'Being honest … and the other stuff.'

BJ shrugged, shot him a wink.

'Like I said the other day, mate, what are friends for? But you're coming tomorrow, right? One last crack before you go?'

'Aye, mate,' he said. 'After tonight, I think I need a dose of reality.'

'For old time's sake,' said BJ. He raised his tin of lager.

'Aye,' said Finchy.

Clashing fucking lager cans.

'And those gone by the wayside,' said BJ.

'Aye.'

'One and then the next and then the next, like fucking dominoes. I've started to wonder when it's going to be my turn.'

'It's not age though, is it? It can't be our fucking age.'

'Stimmo did what he had to do,' said BJ. 'He took control. The fucker made up his mind not to fester. He'd had enough of all that. Not like old Nev. Nev capitulated in a different way. I know which one I'd go for, given a fucking choice. Mind you, Nev knew where the crack was. He knew what all this shit was about. He lived three lives in the time cunts like us manage one. It's just his kid I feel for. She deserved to know her dad better. One fucking day I'll tell her all about him, if I'm still about, if I haven't fucked off on his coat-tails.'

Finchy raised his glass.

'He was a top bloke,' said BJ. 'Quiet sometimes. Off in his own world. Nothing fucking wrong with that. I just wish I'd done more to help him at the end.'

Finchy nodded, thinking *we're all off in our own worlds, every single one of us.*

'Jen White doesn't feel that way about Stimmo,' he said.

'Aye,' said BJ. 'Well, she has a right to her opinion, I suppose. But I'd rather go out like Stimmo, in my own way, than let things take me.'

Another bout of silence. It filled the room.

'Do you think about it?' asked Finchy, at last.

'What?'

'Being next.'

'Aye, mate, all the fucking time.'

'Me too,' he said. 'Every day.'

'The curse of the survivor,' said BJ.

'Do you think so? We were hardly survivors though, were we? We were in the opposite end. No different to witnessing a car crash.'

'That whole day was a car crash, mate.'

'So now we're burdened. Forever.'

'Not forever. Just until we cop it, then who gives a fuck?'

'I thought I'd moved beyond it,' said Finchy. 'I thought I'd found it a place to rest.'

BJ shook his head.

'No,' he said. 'That's just fucking kidding yourself. That's no good to anyone. You have to face it down. Or try to.'

'Hopper?'

'You think he's buried it?'

'He just about said as much.'

'Fuck off, mate. It's in that house he lives in. In that fucking pristine lawn of his. It's in that fucking missus of his, too. And his kids.'

'I hope not, for all of them.'

'It's simmering, mate. You mark my fucking words.'

'Fucking hell…'

'I fucking hope so, mate. I fucking hope so.' BJ laughed.

'What happened with you and Hopper anyway?' asked Finchy.

'Eh?'

'You two were like that.'

Finchy pinched his finger and thumb together.

BJ shrugged, smiled his quiet smile, diverted his eyes to the TV.

'Life, mate. Life's what happened. He got married. I didn't. He stopped flirting with the old bill. I didn't. That's about the sum of it. I got nicked at Bramall Lane, he wiped his hands. Fucking SYP again.'

'I remember how hostile they were. I remember that. On the bus up from the station, on the Penistone Road…'

'That's the SYP for you. Those bastards fucked everybody over, just like they fucked the blokes at Orgreave.'

'Some of them, mate. Not all of them. I saw police in tears that day.'

'Aye, some of them. And some of them lied ... anyway, fuck it. I don't want to talk about that any more. I'm done talking about it. I thought you were going to call your missus.'

Finchy thought about Kelly, of the early years, the life they had then, their social circle, the travelling, the two of them in catering jobs they forgot about the moment they came off a shift. Everything easy. He thought about Hopper in the cul-de-sac, the freshly cut lawn, the cosy shape of his missus beyond the frosted glass, the way she'd looked at him when he turned up on the doorstep. He looked at BJ laid out on the sofa, at the piles of match-day programmes on the carpet. He looked at the stacks of DVDs, the row of coffee mugs on the TV, the tin cans. His mind drifted once more to Kelly, the circle forever completing itself, the look on her face when she told him the test result, the fucking joy there, and he thought of how he'd well and truly wiped that fucking joy off her face, how he'd crushed that joy with his reaction. He was suddenly full of self-loathing.

Not for the fucking first time.

'Just gonna borrow your phone, mate,' he said.

BJ barely stirred.

'Stick your cash in the jar,' he said.

There was no jar. He dialled home, thinking how fucking strange that word was. He really didn't know what home was any more, where the fuck to lay his hat or plonk his backside. Still, a phone rang in some distant fucking place, rang and fucking rang, rang some more.

It's me. Don't hang up. I love you.

Ha fucking ha.

I want the same things you want.

Pull the other one.

I've been a coward.

Now you're talking.

I had some problems but I've dealt with them.

Have you? Have you really?

I'm coming home.

Where the fuck is that then?

Seriously, I'm coming home.

Do what you fucking like, I won't be here.

The phone rang and rang. He pictured the empty house, the phone sounding out in the hollow kitchen. He pictured Kelly standing beside it, waiting for it to stop, waiting to see who was calling, if it was him, too fucking stubborn to speak to him. And he imagined the other thing, the house colder than cold, exactly as he'd left it, the same mug on the side, the same unwashed pans in the sink, the bedroom door closed, hiding a diabolical secret.

His life on a fucking precipice.

The present and the past.

The past and the present.

Kelly in their early days. Kelly all arse and attitude. Right up his street.

The two of them in the corner of the club, him with one eye on the place, petrified of running into his sixth-formers. The two of them at her place. Six months of untethered fucking until the novelty wore off, a year of settled solidarity, another of soul-searching and somnambulism.

And everything that came after.

Everything that had happened since.

Another Friday evening. Him and Kelly on the sofa, pile of shite on the TV.

'I'm pregnant,' she said.

Fatal hesitation. The weight of a moment.

'You can't be...'

He watched her face fall.

Such a cunt.

'I took a test.'

He got to his feet, walked into the kitchen, left her sitting there.

Such a fucking cunt.

Him pacing the lino, lost in the fuzz of information, floundering in his own terror.

It was dark out. The garden was just a black vault beyond the window. Panic black. Breathing shallow, head pounding, part of him wanted to tear into it, tear off like a mad fucker and never look back. He stopped at the kitchen door instead, turned on himself, stared across the living room to the place where he'd left her staring at the wall. And he understood what he was, what a bastard. Years of daydreaming about this moment, half a fucking lifetime and this is what she got, the cold fucking shoulder, a bloke that couldn't see past his own arsehole. He stepped back into the living room, sat down opposite her again.

'Sorry,' he said.

She shook her head.

'I get it,' she said.

He raised his hands.

'No, I really do get it,' she said. 'I've been there the past week.'

She shifted across on the sofa.

'Sit down next to me,' she said. When he didn't move she added, 'please.'

He placed himself next to her. She leant against him.

'I'm sorry,' she said again.

'It's alright,' he said.

'Is it?'

'Yeah,' he said. 'I just need a while.'

It wasn't alright. She miscarried at twelve weeks. She was away when it happened, visiting her folks. Like a cunt, like a self-centred fucking cunt he measured his relief in pints at the local. It was two days before he went to fetch her, until he met her zombified form on the doorstep of her mother's place.

Hard going after that. A year of toil, pathetic shots at tenderness and understanding until she started talking about trying again.

'We didn't try the last time,' he said.

'I want to try now.'

'Soon,' he said.

'How soon?'

'Christmas,' he said. 'Let's try after Christmas.'

And Christmas came and went. Winter became spring. Spring became summer. He got his two banks of four in place, fended off wave after wave of pressure, happy to keep the fucking score at 0–0.

Such a fucking cunt.

And now it was October, the months grating away, a great fuck-off elephant with them in everything they did. One great fucking elephant and then another. It was all fucking elephants. A great herd of the bastards.

They were miles from each other.

In all sorts of ways.

Or worse.

When he came out of himself BJ was standing beside him.

'What?'

'You need to see a fucking doctor,' said BJ.

'Yeah? Why's that?'

'You've been muttering away to yourself for the past two minutes. You were in another fucking world.'

'Chance would be a fine thing.'

BJ laughed.

'Nobody's keeping you here, mate,' he said. 'You know where the fucking door is. Maybe then I'll get my favourite sofa back.'

Finchy planted a palm on the wall to steady himself.

'These last few days have been a trial.'

'You're alright, mate,' said BJ. 'You can fuck off down south when it suits, put all of this shit behind you.'

'I did that once already.'

'Aye, and you'll do it again. Not like us sad fuckers trapped here, forced to wake up to it every fucking day.'

'It's not so bad, mate.'

'What?'

'This place. It's not so bad.'

'Isn't it? What do you fucking know about it? Seriously?'

'I know there are worse places.'

'No doubt, but it's not the place I'm talking about, it's the life, the sameness, the history on every fucking corner. It's not fucking healthy to stay in one place. It wears you down. I should have got away like you. I didn't have the balls.'

'It's never too late.'

'Do me a favour and shut the fuck up,' said BJ. 'I'm talking about a decade ago.'

BJ downed the rest of the can, chucked it on the carpet.

'Fuck this festering shit,' he said. 'Let's go for a quick pint before bed.'

The office still buzzing. Blokes whispering, blokes shaking their heads, blokes being blokes. Spence on a roll.

'The barmaid.'

'What about her?'

'You know they interviewed Harris about it?'

Finchy takes off his jacket, rests it on his seat.

'Six fucking hours. Right through the night.'

Finchy. Numb in the legs and in the belly and all the way up and down his fucking arms.

'What do you think?' continues Spence. 'Do you think it's him?'

'Rumour says he was knocking her off…'

'Not lately. Word is she'd settled down with that bloke of hers, sorted herself out.'

Spence, setting the letters in the frame. Never fucking rushed or flapping about. Never chasing the clock. Always a step ahead. Bastard.

'Don't fucking joke about it.'

'I'm not joking,' says Spence. 'It's hardly something to joke about.'

Finchy picks up his first pile of letters, starts the day, hands moving on autopilot to one corner of the frame and the next, not reading the numbers, just the names, knowing every fucking name on the route now. Maybe the cunts in time and motion are right. A more personal service, they say. Except it's shit boring. A fucking machine could do it.

'I can't see it,' he says at last.

'What?'

'Harris. I can't see it being him.'

'Give me a reason.'

'Fucking hell. You know the bloke. We all do. He might be a pisshead but he's not a fucking murderer. He's not going to strangle some girl, strip her half-naked and dump her in a fucking hedge bottom.'

Spence chews his bottom lip.

'Why not?'

'Do you think it's him?' asks Finchy. 'Seriously?'

'No,' says Spence.

'Well then?'

'Well then, what?'

'Why the fuck are you asking me if you don't think it yourself? What the fuck is all this about?'

'I'm just making conversation. But then I'm not CID, am I?'

'What's that meant to mean?'

'Well, they know what questions to ask. Take the other evening at your gaff for instance...'

Finchy nods. Finchy laughs. Finchy understands now. He doesn't ask Spence how he knows or where he gets his information. He's given up trying.

'It was just routine,' he says. 'They were ticking boxes.'

'Still,' says Spence. 'I don't expect it was very pleasant.'

'It was just routine,' says Finchy again.

'A routine murder investigation…'

'They were clearing a few things up from last week.'

'And visiting a few of their suspects, no doubt.'

'It really wasn't about me…'

'Still, can't have been easy to have the murder squad at your door.'

'Fuck off,' he shouts at last. He can't help himself.

'Is he off on one again?' asks Jack Stanley.

'Aye, Jack,' says Spence. 'All set on the hair trigger…'

'Youth of today…'

Blokes are laughing now. Blokes are taking the piss. Everything's firing in his direction. He tries to switch off from it, to get on with his prep, but it's no good. He's surrounded. They appear from the rows of frames, mischief in their eyes, eager to be part of the wind-up. Harcross appears with a fist full of mail, dumps another hundred letters on his frame.

'You missed some.'

Harcross turns and ushers the men back to work.

'Fuck me, you'll be out until lunch again,' says Spence, bundling up already, bundling up and packing his fucking bags.

Finchy stares at the frame, at the numbers and the letters, at the thin black segments. Five hundred and ninety-eight bastard gates, five hundred and ninety-eight bastard pathways, five hundred and ninety-eight bastard snapping letter boxes. He closes his eyes, thinking of Hope Close, thinking of Nobber Harris in an interrogation room. A chill runs up his spine.

Will they come for me?

'Fuck,' he whispers to himself.

Two hands swoop across his vision and lift a pile of letters in their grip. Stubby fingers shape the pile into a manageable form.

'Shove over, you daft bastard,' says Spence. 'I'll give you ten fucking minutes and then I'm out the door.'

'Cheers, mate,' says Finchy.

Four hands at the work of two.

'They didn't charge him, then?' asks Finchy.

'Of course not.'

'What's his alibi?'

'Home with the missus.'

'Six hours to sort that?'

'I don't think they believed her.'

'Right, like his missus is going to protect him from that sort of thing? How do you know all this?'

'Robbie's been over there. Can't keep a fucking thing to himself.'

He laughs.

'Surprised they haven't had you in,' says Spence.

A lurch in the belly.

'Why the fuck would they do that?'

'It's your patch.'

'So what? What's that got to do with anything?'

'Maybe you saw something.'

'I didn't see a thing.'

'You're a Bell man.'

'So are half the lads in the town.'

'Single male. Desperate for a bit. Sexy barmaid…'

'Desperate? Fuck off.'

'… no alib—'

'I stayed in. That's an alibi.'

'Well, that's what you told them.'

'It's the truth.'

'Of course it is, mate. Of course it is. Then there's trying to implicate others…'

'Eh?'

'Telling all and sundry her personal history…'

'Fucking hell. It's common knowledge. I didn't tell them anything they didn't know. Three blokes I mentioned. Three blokes.'

'Old Arnie's well fucked off with you.'

'What for?'

'Telling them he'd had a bit…'

'What makes him think I told them?'

'They told him. They asked about you…'

'Fuck off. They knew about him already. They asked me what I knew.'

Spence, laughing away, a source of amusement to himself.

'You're a prick,' says Finchy. 'You know that?'

'Fucking hilarious, though,' says Spence. He slips the last letter into its slot. 'There. How's that?'

Spence in shirtsleeves, heaving his bag over his shoulder.

'Four,' he says.

'Eh?'

'You said three. It's four.'

'Four what?'

'Four blokes.'

'Who?'

Spence shakes his head.

'I'm not a stirring bastard,' he says. 'You know me better than that.'

Spence winks in Finchy's direction.

'Who is it?'

He shakes his head again, taps a finger against his nose.

'Not so long ago, either.'

And then he's away, down the line of frames, around the end of the row and out of sight. Finchy turns back to the frame, to sorting the bundles, finds a rogue fucking letter in the first slot, another and another and another.

Spence. Practical fucking joker.

Finchy jumps from his seat and runs out the door. No sign of the cunt at the bike sheds. He hops off the ramp, jogs across the yard to the gates. Spence is a hundred yards away, ped-alling furiously in the direction of the railway bridge. Spence looks over his shoulder and waves.

Cunt.

Finchy turns back and heads inside. Harcross gives him a look and taps his watch. He goes back to the frame and works his way through the bundles rectifying Spence's wind-up, thinking about the lads, trying to decipher who number four might be, trying to remember what the fuck occurred in the hours with the American bird and afterwards, how the fuck he wound up crashed at the bottom of the stairwell sporting bruises to his arms and legs, covered in shit, cursing his flatmate for keeping dodgy fucking beans and the American lass for making him bite off more than he could chew.

In the locker room, sorting his bags, he doesn't hear Arnie Burrows come up behind him, doesn't know he's there until the little bastard has him cornered.

'Oi, what the fuck have you been saying about me?'

'Eh?'

'You fucking know. To CID. What the fuck have you been saying?'

He tries to speak, to explain, but he can't get a word in.

'I've got a wife and kids,' says Burrows.

Red face. Wide eyes. Dark black circles.

'I didn't tell them anything,' says Finchy.

'Well, you fucking told them something. Because at 3 a.m. this morning I was in the nick answering their fucking questions and now my wife thinks I've been dipping my wick where it doesn't belong and she's took the kids to her mam's, so you said fucking something.'

'Rumours,' he says. 'I told them they were rumours.'

'You didn't have to tell them anything.'

'They already knew.'

'Is that right? Is that the fucking case? That's not what they told me. They said you'd been naming names, pointing the finger.'

'Arnie,' he says. 'I didn't tell them anything. They're

chasing shadows. They don't have a fucking clue...'

Jack Stanley comes in to get his bags. He stops at the door, leans against the frame, folds his arms.

'Aye, well, it doesn't matter,' says Burrows. Then he starts laughing.

Finchy steps away, steps back.

'One piece of advice,' says Burrows. 'If you're going to tell tales, make sure your own story holds together, eh? Because I told them a few things myself. About what you were up to that night. About where you were and where you said you were. I'd be expecting another visit if I were you.'

Then he turns and leaves the locker room, leaves Finchy staring at Jack Stanley and Jack Stanley staring at Finchy.

'Having some trouble?' asks Jack.

Finchy shakes his head.

'No,' he says. 'Everything's fine and dandy.'

When he reaches Hope Close, it's all he can do not to stare at the hedge bottom, the car park, the remnants of blue fucking tape still strung from the trees. There's a car parked on the kerb, a blue fucking Sierra. There's some fucker sat in it. He can't tell if it's Mr Moustache or Mr Notebook and he doesn't dare look too closely in case it is. He keeps his head down, wanders his route, spends the rest of the morning going over and over it all in his head, what Burrows might know, what Spence might know, how any of them could know anything. He tells himself the answer is nothing. He tells himself Burrows is on a wind-up, desperate to get his own back. He tells himself these things but what if Burrows does know something? What if he knows about the American bird, about the pills, about what happened in the dark and black fucking hours, about the streaks of dirt and shit on his jeans.

What if Burrows knows about those things?

What the fuck happens then?

The blue Sierra appears outside his flat that evening. He's staring out of his window when he spots it across the way. The blue Sierra sits there for nearly an hour. He closes the bedroom curtains, shuts out the light and peeks through the gap, watches the blue Sierra, half expecting at any moment for Mr Moustache and Mr Notebook to appear, to inform him they've had some new information, to ask him to go over the Friday evening again. The woman across the way is wandering around her flat in just a T-shirt. When she goes to the kitchen to fix tea he can almost make out the pert curves of her backside. He thinks of her fucking his flatmate, screaming the fucking place down. He's meant to be watching the Sierra but he can't help watching her. When he looks back down at the road, the Sierra is no longer there.

Days come and days go, days of blue Sierras, twitching curtains, rooms cast in shadow, disturbed sleep. Jen's a distant figure, a captive in her own home. When he tries to call he can't get at her to talk. When he waits in for her to call around she doesn't appear. But they're not over. They're still not over.

Despite everything.

The weekends are different. The weekends are his time. Finchy and the boys on the town. Finchy and the boys on their weekly meanderings, pub to pub, bar to bar. Finchy and the boys, then just Finchy. He heads to the club alone, queues up alone, takes to the dance floor alone. In the toilet cubicle he takes one of his flatmate's beans from his pocket and swallows the fucking thing.

He returns to the dance floor and throws himself about.

He's out of control. He doesn't give a shit.

He takes up with some brunette, leads her out of the door and into the night. There's the ungainly scrape of her heels on the pavement as he pulls her through the sheltered housing, waking the oldies with her giggles and laughter. He doesn't give a monkey's toss.

On the bridge above the river, the dark allotment behind, he has her pressed against the rail, her hands in his jeans, his hands on her tits, his hands on her arse, his mouth on her mouth, her tongue on his tongue. Breathing hard he pulls her up the narrow street to the flat, up the slope between the terraced houses, fumbles for the key, fumbles at the door, stumbles on the steep stairs. Her skirt's riding up. Her with no knickers in his flat, in his room, his mouth on her neck, on her tits, on her nipples, his teeth on her nipples, the black dress peeling away. On the floor, naked, his face on her cunt, his tongue in her cunt, his boxers around his ankles, her mouth at his cock. And then the two of them fucking, her squatting on top, her underneath, her on all fours. No fucking condom. No fucking sense. Just fucking.

Her skin against his skin in the single bed. Her soft skin. The wondrous texture of her bare backside against him in the single bed. The glow of the alarm clock. Him pressed against her, feeling the excitement and clarity of it, the relief and release.

Guilty of everything.

In the morning things are stirred up again, skin against skin, mouth against mouth, sweat against sweat. He goes about his business whilst thinking about Jen. They're over in every sense of the word and yet they're not over.

Even now.

He takes the brunette home, drops her off, heads to work, knackered, thinking he should take a sickie, not able to, all that three strikes and out bollocks.

Fucking beans.

He wants to be back in bed but he's at the frame instead, a country route he hardly knows with its farms and its cottages and its nonsensical place names. He has a headache, a deep, throbbing headache. He's feeling sick in his stomach. Thoughts of the night before jostle for attention. His cock stirs despite the rest of him.

He's out on the High Dyke, him and the van. With no fucking sleep. Everything's a fog. And everything's coming at him. The droning fucking engine. The monotonous drone. The monotonous landscape.

The thin black ribbon road is a causeway through the nothingness. There are only the drainage ditches and the droves and the nothingness.

And the grey, smothering sky.

The smell of cabbage.

No fucking sleep and no fucking radio.

Drifting. Pictures in his head. Indelible. Wire-mesh fencing. Faces pressed against wire-mesh fencing. A tangle of limbs. A mass of bodies. The dead standing up.

The road. The fields. The sky. The drone of the engine.

The car park. The hedge bottom. Wet foliage. Pink fucking panties. Skin like polished bone. Red hair. Matted. Tangled. Slugs. Black fucking slugs and snails. The hedge bottom. A body in the fucking hedge bottom.

Spiders. Fucking spiders.

Smudged and rubbed out.

A faint remnant.

There and gone.

The monotonous drone filling his head. Coming in waves. Drawing him down. Down amongst the shit. And no fucking radio. No fucking radio. An empty black place. Calling him in. Two wheels on the grass. The steering wheel shuddering against his palms.

Snapping out of it. Too fucking late.

Gripping the steering wheel, white knuckle tight, bracing himself, feeling the world slow to a crawl. But not the fucking van. On the grass verge now, the dial reading fifty miles an hour, the dial stuck there. No fucking chance. And now the van is careering across the grass verge. The van is heading for the drainage ditch. There are tree branches striking the windscreen. There is a sound of thunder all around him. The steering wheel dances in his grip. The van hits the ditch. There's a crashing and tearing of branches. The sound of thunder. The van in the ditch. Him in the ditch. Eighteen years flashing before his eyes, his mam and dad, his brother, his grandparents, the garage block, the estate, the school. The TV at his mam's place, the living-room carpet, his bedroom, his cot, his mam's fucking womb. Over in a blink of time.

Staring into the laughing faces of the living, seeing only the bones of the dead.

The van rattles to a halt in the ditch. The van fills the ditch. But the ditch is shallow, thick with summer vegetation.

He stares at the blackness behind his eyelids.

The soothing blackness behind his eyelids.

He stares at his palms. He stares out of the van window.

He's lucky. He's so very, very lucky.

He clambers out of the driver's window, clambers up out of the ditch to the edge of the road, into the road. A car swerves to avoid him.

Coming to his senses he gets off the road, stands in the long grass, wanders along the verge to a lay-by, stares back at the van. The van's nose is buried in the ditch. The windscreen is fractured.

There's a pheasant in the field.

He stares at the pheasant.

The pheasant stares back.

A still moment with him at its centre. A moment of absolute clarity. He's still alive. He's crashed the van, buried it in the good earth but he's alive.

And he knows now.

He knows for certain.

He has to start again. Start again in a new place, put all of this shit behind him.

Put the beans behind him.

Put Hope Close behind him.

Put every fucking thing behind him.

He doesn't have a clue where to begin the process, what the fuck to do.

BJ in the corner of the Crown, one eye on the TV. Some League of Ireland game. Sectarian bragging rights and all that. Something to bite on. BJ in a Celtic shirt that had seen better days. A game of darts going off in the lounge. When Finchy sloped off for a piss at half-time, he stopped to watch some bloke slamming in ton forties like they were going out of fashion.

'Have you seen him over there?'

'You're a daft cunt,' said BJ.

'Eh?'

'You're a daft cunt who's been away too fucking long to know his arse from his elbow.'

'Who is it?'

'You know who it is.'

'I'm not seeing...'

'You're not fucking looking.'

'Not Forest...'

'No, but of our time...'

Finchy watched the guy step up to the oche once again, watched the way he caressed each dart before the automatic motion kicked in, before the dart thudded into the board front and centre. And he watched him lean away again immediately afterwards, somehow lessened in that moment, weakened by an absence of tungsten.

'Leppings Lane,' said BJ.

'No fucking way.'

'Serious.'

'What's his name?'

'You still don't recognise him?'

'How about you tell me? How about we do it that way?'

'Doddy...'

A trip switch somewhere in the back of his head.

What's in a fucking name?

Everything.

Doddy.

Doddy. Dodd. Jamie Dodd. They played together as kids, went fucking fishing together in the long-drawn-out summer before secondary school.

Every fucking day.

Doddy lived at the top of the road, had a sister, was forced down the other educational pathway aged eleven so that they hardly spoke to one another save jokes about football when their paths crossed in the pubs and clubs. The Semi of 88 top of the list, the 5–0 drubbing at Anfield a close second.

The match of the fucking century.

And here he was all these years later. So much fucking fatter. So much balder. Back at the oche, garnering another smattering of applause for another ton forty, shrinking back, standing to one side, a separate being amongst a pub full of blokes and a dartboard that had seen better days.

And worse.

'He looks half decent.'

BJ smiled.

'District champion since fuck knows when. Blokes tell me he's good enough to move up a notch or two, but he doesn't fucking bother.'

'Isn't that the fucking way around here?'

'Aye, mate.'

Finchy stared at Doddy, watched him sink the double he needed to win the match, watched his opponent shrug in resignation, watched Doddy slip his darts into their case. The guy at the scoreboard was still wiping the thing clear when Doddy slipped out the pub door.

'Thirty-five-year-old bachelor,' said BJ. 'Thirty-five-year-old nobody. He's gone in the head.'

'You think he'd talk to me?'

'What do you want to talk to him for?'

'Dunno. Old time's sake. What do you fucking think?'

'What do you want to talk to him about *that* for?'

'I don't. You're fucking right. I want to forget it ever happened like the rest of you.'

BJ pushed his pint glass to one side.

'What is this, John?'

'Eh?'

'What is this? Some sort of fucking therapy? If it is you can fuck off. I'm not a shrink. Jen fucking White's not a shrink. Doddy certainly isn't. None of us are. We don't have any fucking answers.'

BJ stared Finchy down and Finchy stared back. Because it mattered, didn't it, to talk to people, to share things. Surely it fucking mattered.

'I'll see you later,' said Finchy.

'I thought we were watching this.'

BJ pointed to the TV, at twenty-two blokes lining up for the second half on a freezing fucking night in Belfast.

'I'm going after him,' said Finchy. 'I'll see you at yours.'

He raced out of the door, knowing he was a mad bastard for leaving the confines of the Crown, opening himself up to all sorts of trouble if Jen's brother was about, or any of his crowd come to think of it. All it would take was to be spotted. All it would take was one fucking phone call.

In the kebab shop on the corner he shifted himself alongside Doddy, waited to catch his eye.

'I knew it was you,' said Doddy, without turning his head, without looking at Finchy at all. 'I saw you when you came out of the toilet. I never forget a face.'

'BJ pointed you out,' said Finchy. 'I've been away a while.'

'Ah, the Forest faithful. The Hillsborough hoodoo. I suspect the likes of him think I'm emotionally scarred. The fat fucking Scouse fan who never got over the horrors of Leppings Lane.'

'That's pretty much the sum of it.'

'Aye, well. It's a convenient untruth.'

'It's the reputation you've gained,' said Finchy.

'Ironic that, seeing as I've spent much of the last decade trying not to have a reputation.'

Finchy forced a smile.

'The darts keep you in the spotlight.'

'Yeah? Well these are the only thing I do that gets me out.'

He patted his pocket where the darts were snug and warm.

'Nothing to do with Leppings Lane, mind,' said Doddy. 'I dealt with that years ago. I told myself rather than dwell on what didn't happen that could have, I'd concentrate on what might have happened that didn't.'

'Aren't those two things the same?'

Doddy shook his head.

'Are they fuck! I stood in Leppings Lane, got shoved around a bit, fell to the ground, broke a couple of ribs and got pulled out of the place. There were seven hundred like me and ninety-six a whole lot worse. The other stuff, the things I saw, the things happening around me, I put them all to bed.'

Finchy wondered how that could be.

'I came up for Stimmo's funeral.'

'Aye. I heard all about it. Bit of a shame. He was half decent with the arrows himself. Can understand it though, living with a bird like that.'

'How do you mean?'

Doddy laughed to himself.

'Living with a bird that didn't love him, mate. I know something about that. If your mates really want to know why I keep myself to myself they should try barking up that tree.'

The guy behind the counter presented Doddy with his food, a great fuck-off pile of kebab meat and chips. Finchy ordered the same for himself.

'Where are you staying?' asked Doddy.

'North Hotel. Or I was. I'm at BJ's now.'

'BJ,' Doddy chuckled to himself. 'Now there's a character. We can walk together. I've a flat on Cyril Street.'

'Just you?'

'Fuck me,' said Doddy. 'I made that clear as mud.'

They started down the High Street, two souls reconnected after twenty-five years.

'You remember the reservoir?' Doddy asked. 'Biking out there day after day. Morning, noon and half the fucking night?'

'Good days,' Finchy said.

'Never fucking bettered,' said Doddy. 'Not that I hark back to it. I don't do that either. I just know we had it good then, had it simple. Not like the kids today. You got kids?'

Finchy shook his head.

'And you're not married either?'

'I live with my fiancée. We've reached a crossroads…'

Doddy laughed.

'To the left happiness, to the right drudgery. Straight on for abject failure.'

'You're a wordy cunt, do you know that? You should take up teaching.'

'Not for me, mate. I don't fancy anything that involves those bastards in government. Where is your missus wanting to go that you don't then?'

'She wants kids,' he said.

'That's usually the way,' said Doddy.

'I'm not convinced.'

'Yeah, that too. But what's the alternative? Give her up and start again with Jen fucking White?'

Finchy kept his mouth shut, started wondering if Doddy was one of Stimmo's lot after all.

'My ex didn't want kids,' said Doddy. 'Now she's shacked up with some bloke and three of the little bastards. So what she meant was she didn't want kids with me. What's your missus up to now you're here?'

Finchy thought of the dark stairwell, the bedroom door. He thought of Kelly fucking some stranger behind it, one of her call-centre toy boys, gathering his seed. He thought of the other potential scenario, the one he'd almost managed to suppress. Fucking Doddy and his questions. He shrugged.

'Do you remember that summer after Hillsborough?' he asked. 'Do you remember the killings?'

'Fuck me,' said Doddy. 'Are you sure you're carrying enough baggage around the place?'

Finchy shrugged.

'Let's just say I've been turning over a few stones,' he said.

'I remember one better than the other,' said Doddy. 'It was the talk of the fucking estate for long enough. Right on the bloody doorstep. Nasty fucking business that. Nasty horrible business.'

'I walked past the scrub the other day. I got thinking about it. It was on my delivery.'

'I remember,' said Doddy. 'I remember you plodding up and down our path.'

He wrapped up the rest of his kebab and chips, chucked it in a wheelie bin.

'Didn't some bloke in the nick own up to that one?' asked Doddy.

'Eh?'

'I'm sure he fucking did. Some bloke already in for murdering women. Linked himself to a load of other cases.'

Finchy grunted. Was it that simple, after all?

'I didn't hear about that,' he said.

They walked on, neither of them speaking.

'I played fucking darts the night we got back from Hillsborough,' said Doddy at last. 'Just me and a couple of mates who don't give a shit about football. Played darts and got pissed at me mam's gaff. Played for hours. Normally me mam would have come down and caused a stink about us keeping her up but she didn't. She left us to it.'

'My parents heard it on the radio,' he said.

'Aye, well, our mam knew fuck all except that I was in Leppings Lane. Because I told her that morning. I showed her the fucking ticket. So she knew nothing about how I was until I walked through the door at nine in the evening. It didn't cross my fucking mind to give her a ring. I was too spaced out. My error that. She's just about forgiven me.'

Doddy stopped walking, felt his back pocket for his darts.

'I'm off this way,' he said.

'Right, mate,' said Finchy. 'I'm down there.'

'Do yourself a favour,' said Doddy. 'Don't get mired in it all because it could have been you. I bet there were days you were so close you didn't realise it. At Upton Park for instance, somewhere like that. Crowds, mate. They go where they go. You think you can get out but you can't. And you wanted Leppings Lane, remember? You thought it was only fair. A bloke died at Hillsborough because my forearm was pressed across his neck. I couldn't fucking move it. I had no fucking option but to stand there and watch him fade away. Except I didn't fucking watch. I looked up to the heavens and prayed I wouldn't be next. When those cunts start on about bringing back terracing, think of the days you spent when you nearly had your own Leppings Lane. All those crowd surges. Forward and back. In Leppings Lane we all went forward but nobody went back. No fucker's died since then, have they? That's reason enough to keep things the way they are. If they don't like it, nobody's forcing them to go.'

He turned away. Finchy could see the dim lights of BJs flat at the bottom of the road. He scoured the shadows for hidden figures. He thought about spending the night at BJ's, cramped on the sofa amongst the detritus. He thought about Jen White's bed. Not tonight. Not fucking tonight.

He shook Doddy's greasy hand.

'I'll see you about,' he said.

Doddy laughed.

'I doubt it,' he said. Then he said, 'But do me a favour anyway. Keep your mouth shut about me. I prefer the mystery. It helps me get out of stuff I'm uncomfortable with.'

'Will do,' said Finchy. 'If you're ever down my way...'

Doddy laughed again.

'I won't be,' he said. 'I never fucking go anywhere.'

He turned down Cyril Street, an overweight shuffling figure, settled in his own unique solitude.

Finchy headed down the hill. There were no figures in the shadows. He let himself into BJ's place, took a beer from BJ's fridge, propped himself on BJ's sofa with the TV and pondered his next move. There were other scenarios for the murder of Tracey fucking Carlton than the stupid thing he'd been cooking in his brain. The water should have been clearer but somehow it was murkier. He realised he'd never be truly free of that one. There would only ever be things and his ability to cope with them, or not cope. As was the fucking way of the world.

But they weren't all infected with Hillsborough, because Doddy had said as much. He'd stood up to the thing and faced it down. He was doing okay, trotting on towards his own sunset.

It didn't have to be terminal.

None of it had to be terminal.

He fell asleep with a half-drunk bottle of beer nestled in his palm. Somewhere in the night he spilled the fucking thing. He woke to the stink of that, uncertain if he'd pissed himself, spent the first ten minutes of the next day trying to prise a piece of kebab meat free from his fucking teeth while BJ shuffled about the kitchen in his boxers like one of the walking dead.

After the hospital, after the checks, after his meeting with the boss to discuss the dangers of tiredness, he wanders across the sorting office yard and into the everyday. His head is sore. His wrists are sore. His legs are trembling. He arrives back at the flat, climbs the stairs, goes to his room. The bed is unmade. It smells of perfume. It smells of sex. He tears off the bedding, opens the windows, sprays the place with deodorant. He puts the bedding in the washing machine and steps into the hall. He recalls the pheasant in the field, a beady eye looking him up and down. He stares into the mirror.

After all of this, after all that has happened, he calls Jen.

'It's me,' he says.

'What do you want?' says Jen.

'To talk,' he says. 'To see how you are.'

Nothing. Or a choked-back sob. It's hard to tell, hard for him to hear.

'Hello?' he asks. 'Hello?'

There's a disturbance on the other end of the line. Someone shouts.

'You're not talking to that wanker.'

The phone falls silent.

The phone falls dead.

Saturday

BJ out early, off on some labouring job, cash in hand, of course.

'I'll see you at the station. 12.04 train.'

Finchy heard the door slam, lay in the half-light for a time staring at the ceiling, shifted on to his side and grabbed a couple more Forest programmes from the late eighties, flicked through them, searching, seeking, trying to link statistics on the page to events in his head. Some came easy, vivid pictures forming in his mind, a slide show, Psycho punching the air and giving it some after pummelling in a free-kick at home to Coventry, the lads piling together on the away terrace at Villa, marching across Stanley Park at dusk or through the decayed streets of a forlorn northern city; Manchester; Middlesbrough; Newcastle; it didn't fucking matter which. Giving a fuck about nothing and nobody.

Others slipped away, nothing but forgotten dates, dead moments, records of a life lived and disremembered.

A well to fall into.

He had to get up and out.

He pulled on his jeans, headed through the front door and into town, recognising the onset of further melancholy, knowing the signals, hearing Doddy's words in his head, trying with every sinew not to fall back into the fucking trap each and every time he dragged himself to the brink of safety.

He found a greasy spoon off the High Street, ordered a full English, sat with his back to the wall watching the window, on the lookout for Jen's brother and his cronies, not taking any chances, knowing he was taking a chance just by being there, by not fucking off back down south like they'd suggested, like BJ had suggested and Jen and every fucker else he'd come across on this mission to redemption. But he wanted to see Jen again, clear the last remaining dregs from the bottom of the glass, leave with a bit of dignity perhaps, a bit of fucking pride, despite everything.

And it was no good just fucking sitting there. He swilled down the last of his toast with a mouthful of tepid tea and skulked across town, stopping off at a sports shop where he swapped his boots for a pair of Sambas, true survivors, black with three white stripes, better for running, better for being, better for everything. He chucked the battered boots in a bin, strolled through town to her street, milled about on the corner for a time, plucking up the courage, thinking about being ten years old and doing this sort of thing, riding up and down Canal Avenue on his fucking bike in a bid to catch a glimpse of the girl of his dreams through her mam's net curtains. Sad, romantic little bastard. Now here he was, thirty-three years old, daring himself to walk up to his ex-bird's door, daring himself to have the courage of his fucking convictions. He sucked in a lungful of air, another and another, set off down the street with a swagger, his brand new Sambas flashing in the morning sunlight, trying to look the fucking man. But when he reached her door he lost his nerve, knowing that knocking on it might bring all hell raining down upon him.

'She's gone out, love.'

He wheeled about, a cat on hot tiles, to see some woman calling in his direction from an upstairs window. She looked down at him and repeated what she'd already said.

'About half an hour ago.'

And then she added, 'You're not from the paper, are you?'

He shook his head.

'Er, no,' he said. 'I'm not from the paper.'

'Good,' said the woman. 'She doesn't want to talk to anybody from the paper. It's no bloody business of the paper...'

The fucking paper?

He nodded, thanked her, walked away at a hundred fucking miles an hour. Or it felt like that. It fucking felt like that, marching down the street, his confidence crushed, not daring to look back in case they were lying in wait someplace, keeping his head down all the way to BJ's, shitting himself until he got inside and locked the door behind him.

The fucking paper?

There was one on BJ's doormat, local rag, free to everybody who didn't want one. He picked it up to see the Big Fucker plastered on the front page, the big fucker with his nose spread across his face, Jen White's brother too, both of them staring back at him sporting the solemn expressions of victimhood.

He looked at the hastily compiled headline.

VICTIM OF SAVAGE ATTACK. And underneath: *Foreign Nationals Fear for Their Safety as Unprovoked Violence on Immigrants Escalates.*

Unprovoked bollocks.

He pictured the editor a week from now, there with egg on his face when the police showed him the CCTV footage. He wondered if the editor gave a fuck.

Doorbell at three in the afternoon. He crawls from his pit, opens the curtains, sucks in his prerequisite lungful of fresh air. No blue Sierra. He lets the air out. Jen? He feels the familiar stirrings, his cock swelling, and the immediate guilt surfacing along with these things.

He shuffles down the stairs.

It isn't her, though. The outline's wrong, the hair the wrong colour.

Lisa. Jen's sister.

What the fuck does she want?

He opens the door, flutterings of a different nature in his belly now, abruptly nervous, cock retreating.

'Hi,' she says. There's no smile. He can hardly look her in the eyes.

'Can I come in?' she asks.

'Sure,' he says, feeling like a school kid, knowing what's coming to him. He is, after all, the biggest bastard the world's ever known.

She sits on the yellow sofa in the living room, sits there waiting for him to plonk his arse down.

'How's life?' he asks her.

'Fine.'

'How are the wedding plans?'

'They're fine.'

Because you two started this. You two with your whirlwind romance. Putting stuff in people's heads, backing me into a fucking corner…

'I've come about Jen,' she says.

There's a turn-up for the books.

'You've got to stop.'

He almost comes out with them, his million excuses, almost plays through the routine, but she's looking at him in a certain way, imploring him and he knows, he fucking knows.

'I know,' he says.

'So why don't you? This has been going on for weeks.'

'She keeps turning up,' he says.

'Tell her to go away.'

'I try,' he says, thinking 'I don't fucking try one little bit. I fuck her and then ask her to leave when I'm spent.'

She shakes her head.

'She's not coping,' she says. 'She may act like she is but she's not.'

'I know,' he says.

'Then why the fuck do you keep doing it?'

He shrugs. He rubs his chin. He tries to look past her and out of the window but wherever he looks she's staring back at him. She has a look in her eye, the protective, shielding gaze of the older sibling. It bores into him, stripping back the layers, exposing his fragile places.

'Please stop,' she says. 'Please end it. For good.'

'I will,' he says.

She gets to her feet then, makes her way past him and down the stairs, through the door, out into the street.

'Do me a favour,' he says to her. 'If you think she's going to come over…'

'Fuck off,' she says. 'Why the fuck would I want to do you any favours?'

And then she's gone.

He shuts the door, climbs the stairs, knowing she's right, knowing he has to sort it once and for all. And then he wonders what it would be like to fuck Jen's sister, if she's that fucking cold under the fucking duvet, imagines bending her over the yellow sofa, greasing her up a bit and fucking her from behind, doing them both a fucking favour, the shit-scared bachelor, the inevitable wife.

He trots upstairs to the landing, places his ear against his flatmate's door, listens for signs of life. He silently opens the door, holds his fucking breath. His flatmate's dead to the world. He creeps across the carpet to the pot of beans on the dresser, twists open the cap, steals a couple, twists the cap back on and retreats into the hallway.

He's not becoming addicted to the things.

It's nothing so serious.

Of course it fucking isn't.

He was crashed on the sofa letting his brekky settle when the doorbell went. He stiffened, held his breath, waited. The doorbell sounded again. He rolled off the sofa and crawled across the carpet to the hall, poked his head around the corner.

Not the fucking police.

Through the frosted glass he could see a solitary figure,

bulky but not shaped like the big fucker. Not police either. Still he waited, keeping out of sight. But the figure at the door didn't move, just stood there, pressed the doorbell again. It wasn't trouble, it couldn't be. Those fuckers weren't exactly schooled in patience.

He got to his feet and shuffled to the door.

'Hello?' he shouted through the glass.

'Post, mate.'

A familiar voice.

'And?'

'And what?'

'There's a letter box. Use that.'

'Needs a signature, mate.'

He inched the door open to find Spence there, a Jiffy bag in his hand.

'Well, well, well,' said Spence.

'Who are you,' said Finchy. 'PC fucking Plod?'

'North Hotel not grand enough for you?'

'It's my mate's place,' he said.

'I know,' said Spence.

'He's not in.'

Finchy reached for the Jiffy bag. Spence pulled it away.

'Right,' said Spence. 'You'll have to give him this then. Otherwise I might get in trouble.'

Spence passed him a card. 'He'll have to collect it,' he said.

'Fuck me,' said Finchy. 'Since when were you so particular?'

'It's more than my job's worth,' said Spence, grinning. Then he turned to go.

'Wait,' said Finchy.

'I can't hang about,' said Spence. 'I'm late already.'

'Late for what?'

'Late back,' he said. 'They don't give out docket like the old days.'

'I wanted to ask you a few things,' said Finchy. 'That stuff we were talking about the other day.'

Spence sucked in the air through his teeth. Just like old times.

'What about a pint when I'm done?'

'I dunno,' said Finchy. 'I'm trying to keep my head down.'

'I heard. Beating up innocent foreign workers.' He winked. 'How about it, though? Somewhere quiet?'

'Like?'

'The Social? It's members only. Safe as houses. No fucker even knows it exists.'

Finchy hesitated.

'Up to you…' said Spence.

'Okay,' said Finchy. 'How long?'

'Give me an hour,' said Spence. 'I'll meet you out front.'

Thursday morning. He's at the frame when Spence slips alongside him, the same fucking look on his face as always, the same mischief in his mind.

'There's been another.'

'Eh?'

'Housewife. Indoors this time.'

'Where?'

Spence reaches out an arm, extends a finger, places the finger on the frame.

'Just … there.'

'Longwood?'

'Longwood.'

'You're fucking kidding.'

'I wish I was. Strangled. Yesterday morning.'

Robbie Box appears at the frame. Robbie Box and his policeman's voice.

'Could you confirm your whereabouts at 10.00 hours yesterday?'

Blokes laughing now. Blokes coming to life. Robbie and Spence. A class double act at taking the piss in front of their adoring public.

Cunts.

Blokes heckling, chuckling to themselves, chuckling to each other.

He's been working the walk all week, on holiday rota. Highwood. Westwood. Long fucking wood. Him and the bike. One house and then the next. Jewels of dew on late summer lawns. The previous day a bastard. Two full bags of mail. A long fucking morning on a route he's still getting to know. Nothing out of the ordinary, though. Nothing suspicious. But what were the chances? Forty-eight fucking walks, him two for two.

Robbie at his shoulder, sensing a bite.

'Did you deliver to 61? Did you try to deliver a package? Did you take your little package to 61?'

Spence on one side, Robbie on the other. Him piggy in the fucking middle. He tries to picture 61 Longwood. No fucking good. They're all the fucking same up there, big fuck-off four-bedroom detached places, black tarmac drives, double garages.

Lawns and flowers.

Flowers and lawns.

An image crashes into his head, Mr Moustache and Mr Notebook. A million fucking questions coming at machine-gun speed.

'You again,' says Mr Moustache.

'Now there's a coincidence,' says Mr Notebook.

He rears up, chucks his mail down, makes his way across the floor towards the locker room. Robbie in full flow behind him.

'Hello, hello. He's cracking, lads. He's cracking.'

In the locker room. In the quiet. Fuck all to tell them. Fuck all to say. He can't remember a thing about the day before save for it being a bastard. Two bags of mail. Or was that Tuesday? He can't remember, can't get a foothold. He's all over the place.

Bastard flatmate.

Bastard beans.

He splashes cold water on his face, desperately trying to shock inert parts of himself to life.

Bastard, bastard beans.

Fully loaded, he works the delivery with his head somewhere else, seeing the event in every face.

Up the paths and down the driveways, in between the shrubbery.

The upper estate in the summer.

Leaf and lawn.

Insects and flowers.

His head a maelstrom.

Police tape flickering in the breeze at 61 Longwood, a policeman standing guard at the door, four cars parked up, one squad car and three unmarked. One of them a blue Sierra. The rest of Longwood, the rest of the upper estate deathly quiet. A sense of something in the air.

A weight.

A burden.

Janet Allen is her name, was her name. Thirty-three. Married. Husband in marketing, commuting to London each and every day. At work. Always at work. And an alibi. Distraught. Coming home for dinner and finding his wife in the kitchen. Face down. Asphyxiated. Another fucking tragedy.

Finchy glances at the house as he passes by, and beyond to where the fields start, where the main-line embankment runs across the back of the estate.

A fierce division.

A tender scar.

There's no mail for 61. He pushes his bike past the driveway, hardly daring to look that way, visions of Moustache and Notebook embedded in his brain, visions of them staring out of the kitchen window, seeing him there. And in that moment, a vision of Janet Allen appears, a face in a kitchen window, a shape beyond the patterned glass of the front door, bending to pick up her mail in a pink fucking nightgown, permed blonde hair, pink slippers. He doesn't know if such things are real or figments of his fucked-up imagination.

He cycles back to the office in a daze of colours, shapes and shadows.

He's fucking losing the plot.

He gets himself signed off work.

For three days he remains in the flat, alternates his hours between the yellow fucking sofa and his pit of a bed. He stares at the ceiling, stares at the floor. He stares into the faces of the living, seeing only the bones of the dead.

For three days he sees nothing else.

It doesn't matter if he closes his eyes. The images are printed on the backs of his eyelids.

It doesn't matter if he sleeps. They're present in every dream.

It doesn't matter if he stays awake. They crawl out of the shadows.

It doesn't fucking matter.

For three days he thinks about Janet Allen and Tracey Carlton, about beans and black holes in fucking time and space. For three days he waits for Mr Moustache and Mr Notebook to come knocking at his door for another round of tit for tat.

But nobody comes.

Nobody at all.

Not even Jen.

Keeping time in BJ's poky flat, the minutes dragging, anxious, ill at ease, unable to sit still. He stared about himself at BJ's debris, the programmes scattered about the floor, the lager cans on the TV and every other fucking surface. He wandered through to the kitchen, to a table piled high with bills and newspapers, flyers for takeaways, till receipts. The work surface covered in crumbs, metal cartons lined with half-eaten meals, unwashed plates, the sink full of the same, used cutlery, mugs with dregs of tea in the bottom, forks stuck in glutinous remnants of long-since digested meals. The washing machine was full, blinking away, the wash basket overflowing with BJ's work clothes, the kettle furred on the outside. There was an open box of cereal sat next to an open packet of biscuits, a lone tea bag separating the two.

Finchy turned his back on it all, overwhelmed, thinking about doing BJ a favour and tidying the place. Maybe. Possibly. Later. After Spence.

He took himself through to the hall instead. One side of the stairs piled high with boxes. He skirted past them, climbed to the first floor, not daring to look at the bathroom, moving instead to BJ's bedroom, an inquisitive, nosy bastard.

The bed wasn't made. No fucking surprises there. The sheets were discoloured with an off-white stain, the pillows too. The windowsill cluttered with old deodorant cans, aftershave bottles, dust on every surface.

The father left to rot in his own failings.

One last place, though. One last hope. A gut instinct. The wardrobe in the middle of the wall. Finchy approached it, drawn by compulsion, a need to know. He reached out and took the handle in his fingers. He slid open the door.

And there they all were, squarely folded in careful piles as they might have been in a store, hung to perfection in neatly arranged rows, BJ's casuals, his labels, his identity. Label upon label showing. Where the money went and the care and the legacy.

The history of a dresser.

Finchy stroked the fabric, breathed in the quality.

He stood there for an inordinate time indulging in the magnificence of each and every item.

Then he closed the wardrobe and bowed in reverence.

An hour later he was sat in the Social bar with Spence, just the two of them and the barmaid, no fucker else in the place.

'They never did catch the bastard,' said Spence. 'Fucking strange that.'

'I heard some bloke confessed. Some bloke in the nick.'

'Bollocks.'

'That's what I heard.'

Spence took a lengthy mouthful of ale.

'Remember Hillsy?' he asked.

'Derek Hills?'

'Aye, that's it. He went down.'

'In the nick?'

'Aye.'

'Fuck off.'

'Straight up. They caught him stealing the post. Went off the rails when his missus walked out.'

'Wasn't he a suspect back in the day?'

'No more than you.'

'I wasn't a fucking suspect.'

Spence grinned.

'They came to your flat.'

Finchy closed his eyes, refusing to be drawn.

'Hillsy was giving the barmaid one,' said Spence. 'Or he had in the past. He always denied it. But I heard differently.'

Finchy shook his head. Was Hillsy number four, the missing jigsaw piece?

'It doesn't mean he had anything to do with it.'

'No,' said Spence. 'No, it doesn't. But it explains why the police had him in custody for two bloody days when they got wind of it.'

'Poor bastard. What happened to him?'

'He fucked off. Derby or somewhere. Died last year.'

Finchy shrugged.

'Want to know what I think?' asked Spence.

'Not really,' said Finchy.

'It was either Arnie Burrows, Nobber Harris or Derek Hills.'

'It might have been a stranger.'

'It might have been, but it wasn't.'

'How the fuck do you know?'

'I don't. But I'd put a few quid on it,' said Spence 'Or it was you...'

'Well, it wasn't me,' said Finchy. 'Fucking hell.'

'I reckon Hillsy did it.'

Finchy shook his head, laughed.

'No chance,' he said.

'He was forever on the piss. I reckon he did it and can't even fucking remember doing it. That's what happens, isn't it? People drink too much, take things they shouldn't, forget who they are, do things out of character, wake up not remembering anything about the night before, where they were, who they were with, what they were doing?'

And now Spence was staring right at Finchy, straight-faced, unblinking. Finchy stared back, held his own, fought to hide his rattling heartbeat.

Spence. A cunt. Always a cunt.

'And the other one?' asked Finchy at last. 'Janet Allen?'

Spence's mouth creased upwards. He smiled, showed his perfectly white teeth, shook his head.

'We'll never know,' he said. 'Maybe that was just a coincidence, eh? Two unconnected events. One and then the other.'

Tracey Carlton.

Janet Allen.

One and then the other.

One and then the other.

And everybody looking at every fucker else.

A summer laced with paranoia.

In the pubs.

In the clubs.

Even at the all-nighters.

In the parks and alleyways.

In the summer.

In the sunshine.

In the shadows. In the trees. In the darkness.

Every Friday in the local paper.

Every Friday on the local radio.

The blue Sierra parked across the street.

The blue Sierra parked up on his walk.

An endless string of customers at the flat, all hours of the day and night.

His flatmate no longer at the supermarket, guarding his beans like a dog with a bone, Tupperware box stashed behind a loose brick in the passageway.

The flat a venue for endless visitors.

His flatmate up and down the stairs.

His flatmate up and down the passageway.

The Scotsman losing patience, threatening to lose his rag.

The Scotsman screaming blue murder in the foyer while the clocks chime midnight.

The Scotsman hammering on the walls and ceilings, baying for blood.

Finchy popping back the beans.

His room bending and stretching in all directions.

The ceiling pressing down upon his chest.

The ceiling pressing down upon his cheek.

Suffocating him.

Smothering him.

Summer bleeding away.

The year bleeding away.

Unable to stem the flow.

'At least you got out though, eh?' said Spence.

'I didn't do anything.'

'Aye, you did. You made the break. Look at this place. It's full of lazy bastards. They moan about the immigrants but at least those fuckers get off their arses and get the job done.'

'And you?'

'I've not long until retirement. Just counting the mornings as they come, ticking each one off the list.'

'I miss it sometimes,' said Finchy.

'No, you don't. You think you do but you don't.'

'I miss the blokes. I miss the banter.'

'Fair enough, but you wouldn't miss the job if you knew it. The job's shit these days. They tampered with it until it was fucked. They'll privatise it one day and that'll be that. We'll all get our golden handshakes and then they'll break it into pieces.'

Finchy looked around the room, at the four wooden-clad walls of the Social, at fading photographs of football teams and cricket teams and darts teams and pool teams, at the empty chairs and tables, the velvet cushions, the dark carpet.

'This place is on its last legs,' said Spence. 'I give it a year tops.'

'And then what?' asked Finchy.

'And then nothing,' he said.

An old bloke shuffled in through the Social door. He nodded at Spence and ordered a beer. Spence turned to Finchy and whispered.

'Do you remember him?'

Finchy shook his head.

'Jack Stanley,' he said. 'He used to work at our place.'

Finchy smiled, stared over at the bent-up figure supping his pint in the corner, newspaper spread on the betting pages. Good old Jack. One of the old guard. One of the best.

Spence spoke.

'I envy you,' he said.

'Fuck off,' said Finchy.

'Seriously,' said Spence. 'You got out just in time.'

You got out just in time.
You got out just in time.
You got out just in time.

11.50 a.m. He stepped out of the Social and moseyed up to the old town station, waited for a train to carry him north, him and BJ and a crowd of other blokes he'd never seen before, all of them dressed for the day in their labels, some of them already tanked up, already reeking. He separated himself from the throng, shimmied up the platform, retreated his ten yards.

Lincoln City v Grimsby Town. Yellowbelly pride at stake, on the field and off it.

The Imps versus The Cods.

BJ withdrew alongside him.

'Smart,' said BJ noticing his resplendent Sambas. 'Now you're talking my language.'

'And that lot?'

'Fucking idiots, mate,' he said. 'They'll not get in. Not today. They wanted to know who you were. They wanted to know why you stopped going to Forest.'

'What the fuck's it got to do with them?'

'They don't trust you, mate. They think you're old bill. But they trust me so you're alright.'

They found themselves seats at the front of the train, well off the radar, years of experience coming in handy. Finchy sat and listened as half-remembered songs drifted down the carriage from the half-cut souls at the far end, the window framing the old town until they descended into the cutting north of the station and the black tunnel beyond. Then he was staring at his own reflection. He turned away.

'There'll be carnage today,' said BJ.

'Reminds me of the Baseball Ground,' he said. 'Reminds me of Filbert Street.'

'This'll be worse,' he said. 'Less police. Less protection. More action. Not inside. Outside. Mark my words.'

'And you'll be in the thick of it...'

'We'll see what happens, mate. We'll see what happens.'

BJ rubbed his hands, grinned his boyish grin.

It wasn't carnage, at least not beforehand. BJ took him to a pub away from the ground, away from the police, away from the madness. They sank a couple of pints, one eye on the TV in the corner and one eye on the window. When kick-off approached they headed in, skirting the Catchwater and the river, traipsing along Sincil Dike, blood up now, blokes and plods clotting the pavements, the narrow terraced streets, trooping up to Sincil Bank, distant chanting drifting on the breeze, the squawk of a police tannoy, the wail of a siren.

The sweet sonata of match day.

Tension in the air.

Grimsby at home.

And something he recognised, something he knew, an old fucking friend come to say 'hello'.

The game as he remembered it.

Sincil Bank rocking, packed to the rafters, twenty-two players slugging it out on the pitch, eight thousand slugging it out off it, honours fucking even in every respect. He spent most of the game watching the lads in the away end. They'd been lads themselves, full of some inner fury. They weren't lads any more but it was the same all around him, lads starting out at a level they could afford, lads in the thick of it and older blokes, blokes like BJ, who'd seen it and done it and never moved beyond it, blokes in their thirties yet still in their casuals, blokes with kiddies at home and bills to pay, dressers let loose on a Saturday to do what they'd always done, blokes with bald heads and tired eyes, blokes who'd been about a bit and never found anything to replace it. So they fucking carried on doing it, where they could, when they could, sidestepping the banning orders that came their way. And why fucking not? What else was there? What else could compare to it? Who was he to judge BJ and the rest of his fucking throng? What right did he have to pretend to be any better? The bloke had stepped up when he was ripe for a pasting. He owed BJ the courtesy of not belittling him for what he was.

Fuck that.

He was better than that.

Afterwards, they paraded along Scorer Street, to the same pub as the Dale game. He knew what was coming but couldn't drag himself away. He'd reached the end, though, he knew that much. He knew he'd be heading back in the morning, back to the life he'd forged from the scrap he'd started with.

BJ, serious in his drinking now, downed his pint in great gulps, wiped his mouth and ordered another. He was talking a lot. His eyes started to go.

'Those cunts don't understand. Those bastards just don't get it.'

Finchy nodded his head, wondering who the cunts and bastards might be.

BJ. Once a mad fucker, always a mad fucker.

'I'll be seeing my kids tomorrow,' said BJ.

Finchy thought of Kelly. He thought of the arguments, the serious talks, the elephant lodged between them.

'I'll take them out somewhere. Somewhere nice.'

Finchy nodded.

'Some cunts grow out of this,' said BJ. 'At least that's what they say. But I don't know how that's possible. How the fuck can you grow out of it? If you can grow out of it you were never part of it to begin with. That's my fucking understanding. I read this thing the other day. '*Kids holding hands with their dads, picking up pace as the ground looms into view.*' Breaks my fucking heart that does, mate. Breaks my fucking heart. So fucking beautiful. Because I still feel that. I felt it today. And one day I want my boy to feel it. I want him to have what we had. But he'll never have what we had … not the way it's heading.'

There were police outside the pub. Finchy spotted them

through the frosted glass. And then, in a fluid movement, the blink of an eye, carried by the momentum of others, he found himself moving towards the door. The line of police was on the far side of the street, linked arm in arm, forming a barrier. Finchy and the other blokes spilled out of the pub, where they were buffeted and barged into an ever-decreasing space as the police sealed off the road.

Or tried to.

Finchy sensed what was coming before it happened. He was there with BJ on the street corner, listening to the sound of a baying and yelping crowd. He could see BJ sniffing the air, sniffing out some Codhead aggro. Whatever the police had planned, whatever their ideas were, they were too few in number to prevent what was coming. One great cock-up just waiting to happen.

The Grimsby escort came marching down the street on the opposite side of the police line, seven hundred mariners heading for the station.

Thirty-six miles on a map. The same fucking county.

Half a world away.

Two fucking tribes.

Somewhere in the chaos of those moments, BJ started shouting.

'It was ours, mate. It was ours and they stole it. They kicked us when we were down and then priced us out of our own fucking manors. Never fucking forget that.'

Finchy nodded.

'Take these,' said BJ. 'I'll see you later.'

BJ chucked him the keys to the flat, then he turned away. A brick went careering over his head, then another and another. Pint glasses went flying back. Finchy wanted to disagree with the daft fucker but he couldn't. He was fighting back tears. His head was a mess, riddled with half memories and uncertain tomorrows. BJ was in the melee now, pushing against the police line with the others, moving ever onwards towards some final destruction, his boys all around him.

He turned around one last time.

'They fucking stole it,' shouted BJ. 'Tell that to your lads at school. The bastards fucking stole what was ours! Tell them that for Nev and Stimmo and every fucker else!'

The police line broke. Everything kicked off then. Lads piled into lads. Blokes piled into blokes. The police scattered. The melee swallowed BJ in its midst.

Finchy wheeled away, ran to the corner, ran down the next street. He lost it then. Tears came in floods. A grown fucking man blubbering on a fucking street full of terraced houses, in the shadows cast by molten floodlights at dusk on a Saturday. He heard the wail of a police siren. A riot van came shooting up the street. He watched it draw to a halt, watched eight baton-wielding policemen clamber out. Another van pulled in behind it. He tried wiping the tears from his cheeks but it was no fucking good. He wasn't one for crying, not in public or private, not fucking any place.

But he was crying now.

And it wasn't just Stimmo or Jen White or seeing BJ again or being in the old town for a spell. It wasn't the fucking trouble he was witnessing. It wasn't even that one day in April. It was everything, being a man, being a dresser, having a past to hark back to, having one life and then another and then another, a box full of broken threads and loose endings.

He'd had more than enough. He wanted to go back and deal with the Kelly business. He wanted to sort it, get it all on the table, find her there and tell her some truths he'd kept buried for too fucking long.

One broken thread he might mend.

If she was there. If he hadn't throttled the life out of her.

He spent the night in BJ's flat listening to the local radio phone-in, listening to bloke after bloke and woman after woman have their say on the aggro of the afternoon; the disgrace; the shame; the thuggery. He listened to the presenter lap it all up.

Animals...
Worse than animals...
Put down the lot of them...
He'd heard it all before.
And still they didn't understand.
They would never understand.

Sunday

When he woke the next morning there was an envelope on the mat in BJ's hall. It had his name on it. He opened it with anxious fingers, knowing it would be from her. He read the contents and sucked in a lungful of air, readied himself for one last rendezvous.

He climbed the stairs and peered into BJ's bedroom. The bed was empty. Wherever BJ was, he wasn't home.

She was waiting at the bandstand, sat undercover out of the rain. He sat down next to her, careful not to get too close, one eye on the park, nervous that she'd been followed, that at any moment he'd find himself cornered by the Big Fucker.

Out for pulverising revenge.

'Please don't,' she said. 'Either you're here or you can fuck off.'

He halved the distance between them, stretched his legs out, folded his arms. He thought once again about how she'd changed, how there was no trace of the meek creature of fifteen years ago, the wreck of a girl he'd left behind.

'We didn't have to do this,' he said.

'You came to me,' she said. 'You started it.'

'I didn't start *this*,' he said.

He pointed to his head, at the scrapes and bruises.

'Big fucking deal,' she said. 'You can have that for fifteen years ago.'

'That big bastard's off his nut.'

'Am I supposed to give a shit?'

'I don't know,' he said. 'Are you?'

A pause.

'His name is Roland. He's one of Stimmo's mates, not mine,' she said. 'And my brother's a prick. His heart's in the right place but he hangs around with the wrong sorts. He always has…'

'I'm not fussed about your brother.'

'The two of them got a hammering the other day.'

'Oh yeah?'

'Roland had his nose smashed in. Know anything about that?'

He shook his head.

'Not a fucking thing,' he said.

'Short bloke. Curly hair?'

He shook his head again, shrugged, smiled. She smiled back. She knew. Of course she fucking knew.

'Did you sort it?' she asked.

'What?'

'Whatever it was you came back to sort?'

He stared through the veil of rain and across the park towards the river. There was nobody about, just the raindrops dripping from the branches, the park strewn with fallen leaves, a solitary thrush busy amongst the debris of autumn.

'I came for the service and failed to make it,' he said. 'So no, I haven't sorted it yet. There's more to it than expected.'

He heard the sound of the church bell calling the faithful to worship. It drifted across the rain-smeared morning, reminding him of the school bell, the choked corridor, that whole business.

'And when you do, then you're off back?'

'I guess so,' he said. 'I've a job down there.'

'Is that all?'

He shook his head.

'No,' he said. 'No, that's not all.' Then he said, 'That's the first time you've asked me…'

'It's none of my business,' she said. 'I'm just not stupid.'

'I don't think you're stupid,' he said. 'I've never thought you stupid.'

'But all's not well, is it? Otherwise you wouldn't be here.'

'No,' he said. 'But this has nothing to do with that.'

He changed the subject.

'I'm just sorry I turned up like I did. I had a lot on my mind. I needed some answers.'

'We all need fucking answers,' she said. 'You should see somebody, a professional. Stimmo should have seen somebody. Maybe we all should, eh?'

'Maybe,' he said.

'But you won't.'

He shrugged.

'I know you won't,' she said.

'I'll deal with it,' he said.

'That's not the same,' she said. 'That's not what I'm talking about.'

'I know,' he said. 'I know it's not.'

The two of them in the bandstand. The two of them in their own worlds.

'It's like fifteen years never happened,' he said. 'This week. That's how it's made me feel, like I never went anywhere, never did anything. I feel like I could walk through the sorting office doors in the morning, pick up my mail and step right back into the life I was living.'

She turned to him, on her own tangent.

'I don't feel guilty,' she said. 'Sitting here, feeling these feelings, I don't feel guilty about any of them. Just shame. I'm ashamed of myself for not feeling the guilt I should be feeling…'

'Nothing happened,' he said.

She looked at him.

'Between us, I mean,' he said.

'You never change,' she said. 'You still think everything's about you when nothing's about you.'

He opened his mouth but she cut him off.

'No,' she said. 'Don't fucking bother. You'll only make things worse.'

She sighed, got to her feet.

'I need to walk. I can't sit here.'

She started along the river. He followed a pace behind. They meandered through the oldest streets of the old town, each of them burdened by memories of each other, places triggering new memories; the patch of green where he used to wait for her after college; the bridge where they'd stand watching the swans on the water; the bar where they first met, places that remained, places that were lost, replaced by other places that meant nothing to either of them. He caught up with her and they walked together, sometimes leaning against one another, sometimes laughing. In stray moments he thought of Kelly, of the answerphone that refused to yield its secrets.

Somehow they reached the end of her street.

'I missed you so much when you left,' she said. 'I didn't think it was possible to miss somebody the way I missed you. But then I realised I'd been missing you for a long time, ever since…'

He looked down at the river to see a fish flick against the surface. He noticed the flash of scales.

'Did I really change?' he asked.

She nodded.

'Yes,' she said. 'Yes, you did.'

He started to speak, cut himself short.

'Before that day I was everything to you and after it I was nothing. I'd say that was changing, wouldn't you?'

When he still didn't say anything, she smiled, at him, to herself, he couldn't tell.

'Small things at first,' she said. 'Then bigger things. You were with me before. Afterwards you were against me. Or it felt like that.'

'I'm not saying you're wrong,' he said. 'Just that it wasn't deliberate.'

'Thank fuck for that,' she said. 'God knows what sort of person you are if any of it was deliberate.'

He turned towards her.

'I'm sorry,' she said. 'I didn't mean that.'

'A lot happened all at once,' he said. 'I woke up to the world. Or I thought I did.'

He could see how that might register, what that might do to her to admit such a thing, but there was nothing he could do about it then and there was nothing he could do about it now.

She looked past him, down the street. His eyes followed hers to her front door. Then she turned to look directly at him. He realised he couldn't read her. He didn't know what she wanted, only what he imagined she might want from him.

'It's all wrong,' she said. 'I know it's all wrong. I'm just not sure I care any more.'

She held his gaze, refusing to yield. The two of them stood like that, locked in position. Here was that need he'd argued with Kelly about, the thing neither of them could allow in themselves. Here was that nakedness, that rawness, here in the old town. Here it was exposing itself to the fucking bone.

He imagined himself following her down the street, entering the house, imagined making love to her, her making love to him. He wondered where that might take them, what wounds it would heal, what wounds it would open. He imagined all of this in a microsecond of time.

'You should leave,' she said. 'You're right. You were right then and you're right now. Because if you don't go you'll be here and I don't think that's the answer...'

She turned her back on him, started down the pavement.

He shouted after her.

'I need to ask you something,' he said.

She stopped. A sudden breeze buffeted her jacket. She stiffened against it, turned to face him.

'I never hurt you?'

She puffed out her cheeks.

'Physically, I mean. I never did that, did I?'

'You want to know if you beat me? You want to know if you did that?'

He nodded.

'You don't remember?'

He shook his head. She paused. He felt the weight of fifteen years on his shoulders, forcing him to buckle.

She laughed quietly.

'No,' she said. 'You never did that. Do you think you'd be standing there if you had?'

'Not even at the end?'

He was thinking of that spring and summer, of a pitiful white corpse in a ditch, a housewife strangled in her own kitchen, stories in newspapers, shattered husbands revealing their secrets to shattered wives, blue Sierras and blue pills, every fucker looking at every fucker else.

'Never,' she said. Then she said, 'Fuck me, is it really such a fog for you that you can't remember a thing like that?'

He felt the relief coursing through his being.

'Some of it,' he said. 'Not all of it, just some of it.'

She turned on her heels.

He felt a rising desire to go after her, but he knew that fucking scenario, how all of that shit worked. So he let her go instead, let her walk away from him, watched her from the corner until she reached her door, watched her look back at him. She didn't wave. She simply opened the door and disappeared inside, gone from him. Again.

A new season.

A new beginning.

Murder drifts away on the autumn breeze.

The blue Sierra stops haunting your waking hours.

For a while everything settles.

And you?

You're back on twenty-one walk, back to the grind.

A new season.

A new beginning.

The same seat in the lower tier.

The same lads all around you.

But it's not the same somehow, even if everything is the same.

And so begins the separation.

Lads at the pool table. Lads at the bar. Talking about those boys from the pub team, taking a fucking minibus, stopping off for one too many, every fucker needing a piss. Stopping for a piss. Taking off again, the driver not looking, not fucking seeing the car coming the other way. One great fucking mash-up. Bodies scattered in the road, in the field, in the ditch, bodies every fucking where. The minibus driver dead at the scene. One player paralysed for life. The rest of them fucked up in all sorts of ways.

And now the cunts want to take a minibus to Southampton, to the Dell, a right royal piss-up, one hundred and eighty miles each way. He isn't having any of it.

And so begins the separation.

The parameters have changed. It isn't about the football in 89–90. It isn't about anything. Their souls have been sucked out of them. Nothing matters except the moment and no fucker's sober when the moment happens.

He sits in the pub listening to their stories, taking the flack for missing this game and that game, thinking 'this is what it is now, a chance to get rat-arsed.' Half the fuckers don't remember where they've been.

He's sick of their glazed expressions, the way they can't hold a conversation past Saturday lunchtime. When he wants to talk tactics and football they want to talk shit. And they're unpredictable, forever pushing the fucking envelope, getting into scrapes. It's only a matter of time until a scrape turns into something else. He isn't sure half of the fuckers, the sheep, will be able to handle it when it comes. There are only two or three that can. He isn't one of them, doesn't want to be.

When the lads down their pints and up sticks, move one pub along on their weekly Sunday night route, he slips away. He calls Jen from a phone box, begs her to come over and then he sits on the yellow sofa to wait for her, thinking things might be better if he takes a step away from the football for a while, goes back to playing perhaps, picks and chooses his games a little more, saves a few quid. That things might be better if he stops popping the beans, if he stops going out, if he stays in and concentrates on Jen and nothing else.

It's not as if she doesn't deserve it.

Jen arrives in a taxi. He pays the driver.

'You said you were working tomorrow,' she says.

'I am,' he says. 'But I wanted to see you.'

'I thought it was a lads' night,' she says.

He shrugs.

'It was,' he says. 'It was shit. A shitty lads' night.'

'Sunday,' she says.

'That's not the reason,' he says.

It's past eleven already.

He pulls her to him, feels the warmth of her, the soft flesh.

'Is this what you got me over for?'

'It's an added bonus,' he says.

'Okay,' she says. 'But please promise me something?'

'What?'

'Please let things be normal again. Call me when you say you're going to call me. Turn up when you say you're going to turn up. Stop taking the pills. That's all I'm asking.'

'Okay,' he says. 'I'm sorry. I will.'

They kiss. The room is dark. He undresses her and she undresses him. They drop into the bed, disappear into the warm folds of the duvet. He feels comfortable tonight. It suits him. He feels good about it. Her sister is right. It's time he made a choice and stuck to it.

And the other stuff, the doubts, he forces them down. She doesn't deserve those things, this girl who opens herself up to him on a mournful Sunday evening, offers him shelter from the worst of it all. She doesn't deserve anything but his graciousness.

But the next morning is a bastard, laden with phone bills. It's 7.50 a.m. when he reaches Hope Close. He's an hour behind before he starts, an extended morning stretching ahead of him, threatening to break his spirit. The night before with Jen is already burdensome, a conflict between her soft white flesh and his black fucking heart. And there's something in the air on this morning, an electricity building. There's no sunshine. It's just fucking muggy. He's sweating like a prick as he works. Dark clouds roll in over the estate. He watches them swallow the school and the row of shops near his mam's place. He watches them consume the whole town, watches them turn the day to night.

He's on Foxton Avenue when a bolt of lightning strikes a house not four doors from where he's standing, strikes so close he feels the pulse of electricity in the air all around him. The explosion of thunder is instantaneous. He drops to his haunches, reduces himself instinctively to something lesser than his being. And then he waits under the porch of the house he's delivering to, waits there while the rain tumbles down and the storm passes over the town and away. He watches it as it recedes, in awe of its power. He looks down at his own two hands, at his palms. He raises them to his cheeks to check he's still in the land of the living, feels the sensation of his skin on his own skin.

He looks across at the school, at blue sky encroaching and gathering beyond its rooftops. He imagines a different future for himself.

Again.

You go to games and you don't go to games.
You see Jen and you don't see Jen.
You're unwelcome at her place but she comes to yours.
Against her sister's will.
Against her mam's will.
Somehow you drag yourself through Christmas.
Somehow.

7th January 1990
FA Cup 3rd Round

Nottingham Forest 0 v 1 Manchester United
City Ground

The suits give up the lower tier again, shift the Forest fans into the upper tier.

Idiots.

United bring their hordes. United fill the lower tier.

A home game feels like an away game. Again.

Ferguson is on the rack. Some say Ferguson is one game from the sack. But United are up for this one, up for revenge for 89. Pallister sticks Crosby on his backside. Martyn outmuscles Örlygsson. Hughes clips one in towards the penalty spot and Robbins heads home the only goal.

You watch from the upper tier of the Executive Stand, separated from the action by circumstance. It is not the end, not quite, but you can feel it coming, something shaking loose, setting you free. You do not want to be free but it is happening all the same.

A late Nigel Jemson equaliser is ruled out by the referee for fuck knows what and Forest lose at home to Ferguson's Manchester United. United will go on to win the FA Cup.

You will go to Wembley anyway as Forest successfully defend the League Cup but it's the FA Cup you want. It's the FA Cup that Clough wants.

In 1990 it's what everybody wants.

But you will never have it.

And Clough will never have it.

Snow comes to the old town, smothering it, making a slow job slower. Finchy wakes to a silent, muffled morning, traipses to the office on foot, leaving virgin footprints behind him. A solitary car passes by, creeping through the fall, hardly managing it. When it's gone, the silence settles once more.

Like a tomb.

The older boys on the vans are stood on the ramp discussing routes, which places they might reach, which places are beyond them. Then they head inside and pull out their selections. No such luck for the townies. He frames up and bags up, trudges to the bikes, no good to ride on but a packhorse to push up the hill into the softened bowels of the estate. And then he's out in it, pressing onwards, the soundtrack to his morning the muffled clacks of gates and letter boxes, the crump of his boots, the song of a solitary robin. Hope Close is dressed in virgin snow. The hedge bottom is a white linen shroud. There's just him and his ghosts. Every fucker else is inside, not bothering.

The old town at a standstill.

He props the bike against the wall outside the flats and keys in the security code, carries his bundle of letters into the echoing stairwell, the discarded rubbish in the windowless foyers where the lazy bastards can't be bothered to negotiate a flight to the bins. He delivers the giros and the court summonses, the fucking *Reader's Digest* videos. When he emerges from the fifth block his bike's gone. The bag of mail's gone. There's just a set of cycle tracks in the snow, snaking away, disappearing into the estate. Ridiculously he sets off in pursuit, manages twenty steps and then stops. He turns back to the flats, stands there marooned amongst them, a pathetic figure.

Someone calls down at him from a bedroom window, points a finger.

'He went that way, mate.'

He shrugs his shoulders.

He wanders to a phone box, sticks his ten pence in the slot, calls the office.

'Someone's nicked my bike,' he says.

Harcross on the other end. Sounding fucked off.

'Where from?'

'Canal Court.'

'What are you doing there already?'

'I wanted to get it out of the way.'

'You daft bastard. You'll just have to walk the rest.'

'Eh?'

'Walk the rest of the delivery.'

He gulps in a lungful of air.

'They nicked the mail too.'

'You left your mailbag outside the flats?'

'Aye.'

'You're in the shit then, aren't you?'

'Shall I follow the tracks?'

'Don't be a twat. Go and deliver your second bag. I'll head up there and find you. Carson's going to go fucking mental.'

'They nicked my box keys.'

Silence on the line. Harcross taking a deep fucking breath of his own.

'Right. Meet me at the box. Carson's going to have my balls over this. Do the fucking route how it's designed. Fuck me. I was just sitting down for some brekky. Told myself to fucking ignore the phone. I've a good fucking mind to make you wait and freeze your bollocks off.'

Harcross puts the phone down, leaves him standing in a phone box suffocated by snow. Beyond the glass some kids are packing snowballs. When he steps out they hurl their ammunition at him.

'Special delivery!'

Then they leg it.

Little bastards.

And later that morning, during the grilling that comes from Carson, a warning light flashes in the back of his head, that this is how it will always be.

'Are you listening?' asks Carson.

He snaps out of it.

'I'm just thinking,' he says.

'We're not paying you to think,' says Carson. 'All you have to do is take the mail and stick it through a letter box. It's not rocket science. It isn't any type of science.'

Finchy nods. There's nothing to do but nod.

As he's leaving, Harcross pulls him to one side.

'Do yourself a favour,' says Harcross. 'You can't spend the next forty years living for Saturdays and football.'

'So my dad keeps saying,' says Finchy.

'You should listen to your dad,' says Harcross.

31st March 1990

All Britain Anti-Poll Tax Federation 6 v 0 Thatcher
Central London

The tax burden shifted from the rich to the poor.

Two hundred and fifty thousand in Kennington Park.

Two hundred and fifty thousand on the streets.

Sit-down protests in Whitehall. Mounted police. Scarves and staves. Shields and batons.

There are pitched battles on the streets of London.

There are burning vehicles on the streets of London.

One hundred and thirteen people are injured. Three hundred and forty are arrested.

You deliver the letters because that's your job. You deliver the telephone bills and the electric bills, the gas bills and the water bills.

You deliver the community charge letters too.

You deliver the community charge letters and then go to the postbox, open it to find half of the fuckers have posted them back where they've come from. This goes on for weeks and weeks, to and fro, to and fro. Some people take to ripping the bastard things up and throwing them back at you on their doorstep. It's like that for a time.

But you're not their enemy.

You're really not.

In Cheltenham, at a Conservative Party Council Conference, Thatcher is confronted about the poll tax.

There are questions and more questions.

There are rumblings of disquiet in the rank and file.

Thatcher's days are numbered.

The knives are out.

He headed back the way they'd come, back along the river, up on to the High Street and across town, scanning the faces coming his way.

Ten minutes later he was back at BJ's, reaching the end. The house was empty, no sign of the daft fucker anywhere.

Finchy packed his bag, folding and fitting what little he had into the corners and compartments. He made himself a mug of tea and sat on the sofa amidst the piles of programmes, resisting the urge for one last look. It was over, wasn't it? There was no need to dig any more. There was nothing left to discover. He thought about what Spence had said to him the previous day. He ran the names through his head. Spence had said there were four but he'd named only three and Finchy. He wondered what drove Spence to bring all of that shit up the way he did, what the bloke was trying to prove. He wondered if Spence had something to hide, if Spence could be number four.

Of course he fucking couldn't.

And it didn't matter.

It really didn't matter.

He thought about Mr Moustache and Mr Notebook all those years ago. He wondered what they'd learned and what they hadn't been able to prove. He wondered what the fucking truth was.

It was half an hour until his train, time to get his arse into gear. He took the mug to the sink, rinsed it and placed it on the draining board. He stood in the entrance to the kitchen staring about himself. He pulled out his suit, felt in the inside pocket and took out the little enamel Forest badge. He thought about BJ. He climbed the stairs and entered BJ's bedroom, opened up the cupboard and worked his way through the rack. He picked out one of BJ's polo shirts and lifted the hanger out of the wardrobe. Carefully, very, very carefully, he unclasped the badge and pierced the right breast of the polo shirt. He closed the badge. He bent to kiss the badge and then he turned away, walked down the stairs, picked up his bag and shut the door to BJ's flat behind him.

4.30 p.m. Friday. Another dusk.

The doorbell sounds in the flat, an angry, distant echo in the stairwell. Prone on his bed he doesn't move. He doesn't do anything. The doorbell rings again. He rolls out of bed, aching, his shoulders tight, his back protesting, He creeps to the window, peers down into the street. The street is dirty with melting snow. The cars are covered in black salt. There's no blue Sierra across the way. There's no shifty-looking fucker after a bag of beans. Those days are a distant dream.

Her then.

He thinks about not answering the door, about hiding, wishing her away, but his car's on the kerb, the landing lights are on in the flat, there's no way she's going anywhere. He moves to the mirror, checks himself over, rolls on some deodorant.

Vain, arrogant bastard, even still.

His flatmate's out, the door to the bloke's room wide open, the stink of a thousand fags and tokes permeating the air. He slams the door shut and makes his way down one flight, two, to the foyer and the glass door, sees the disproportioned shape of her beyond. Guilt surges through him, and the other thing, the thing he can't beat into submission. His fucking nemesis.

He opens the door to the smell of her perfume. She's made up, smiling that forced smile. It's become routine. This is what they are.

'Alright?' she says.

'Alright.'

'I've come to see you ... to make sure you're okay, to see if you need anything.'

He's thinking 'Remember her fucking sister. Remember what you fucking told her. Remember what you promised. Months ago.'

He thinks this every time.

But he's saying, 'Come in if you want' without comprehending how those words have come to arrive at his lips, fall from his mouth, exist in this moment.

Because he's still fucking at it.

He follows her up the stairs. Her in the tightest jeans. Those fucking black boots. He has a face full of her arse which moves just so on this evening, coaxing him.

The whole thing happens as he wills it not to happen.

She turns left, into the kitchen, drops her bag on the table and turns to face him. The kitchen smells of her perfume. He offers her tea but doesn't make it to the sink. He has her pressed against the wall instead, his mouth pressed against her mouth. He feels her stiff nipples against his chest, grips her arse through the denim, kisses her, teeth bashing teeth, has her moaning in the hollow shell of the kitchen. Her shirt's open, her heavy tits are falling out of her bra, her hands are busy at his flies, her hands are on his cock and balls, his fingers are inside her, deep in her wetness.

And then he's lifting her against the wall in the kitchen, fucking her against the wall in the kitchen, fucking her in her boots whilst she bites his neck.

Pain and pleasure.

Pleasure and pain.

His back's protesting, his cock begging for more. Her jeans around her ankles, he's fucking her because it's easier than not fucking her, because he can get away with it, fucking her with his unprotected cock. When he's getting close he turns her around, bends her over the kitchen table and fucks her that way instead, pulling her on to him until he's ready to burst. He whips it out and sprays his cum over her arse, feels the need and desire and all of those things drain away in an instant, until he's simply stood in the kitchen of his flat with a limp cock exposed to the world, his trousers around his ankles, the kitchen smelling of spunk and perfume and fucking, and she's slipping away to the bathroom, all of that over in an instant and he's already watching the clock and listening for the clocks and wishing her gone from the place.

She's hardly fucking arrived.

When she returns he's on the yellow sofa in the living room. She drops down beside him, wanting more than he can give, no longer a potential receptacle, just an ex-girl-friend, someone he's dumped and then gone on fucking because it's easier than not fucking her, someone he doesn't want to have to care about, something he wants to be free of. If only she'll let him.

Spineless bastard.

'College was rubbish,' she says.

He grunts.

'Lisa's set a wedding date for the summer.'

He pulls away from her.

'Sorry,' she says. 'I was just saying.'

'It's bollocks,' he says.

She falls into her own silence. He imagines what she's thinking, that she's pushing her luck, that she mustn't mention the two of them, that if she just keeps her mouth shut he might let her stay for the night. He thinks he might too.

He has no other plans.

It's dark when he wakes. She's asleep on the sofa beside him, her cheek resting on his shoulder. He moves away from her, trying not to disturb her, watches her for a minute or more, wondering what he's doing to her and why the fuck he feels he has to fashion an escape route from someone so pretty and so fucking dedicated to him despite the bastard he's turned out to be. And then he imagines himself five years hence, stuck in this flat with her, stuck in the postie job, stuck in the old town. He imagines wedding bells, her family and all of that shit, imagines the two of them forever one step behind her sister through forty years of married pur-gatory, through maternity wards and christenings, and any lingering doubts he has crawl away down the steep stairs and out into the night.

He skulks through the flat to the bathroom, turns on the hot water and runs himself a bath. He strips naked, pulls off his crusty underpants, delicately detaching his foreskin from the fabric. He locks the fucking door and slips down into the water, trying not to think about the fuck from earlier, unable to think about anything else, picturing her arse bent in front of him, his cock in her cunt, her tits dangling, gripping them from underneath and squeezing those stiff nipples. He watches his cock harden again in the fucking bubble bath and laughs to himself, at his own feebleness, closes his eyes, imagines the next morning, the M62, the Pennines, Stanley Park, Anfield.

One he can't miss.

Some of the lads had been up there since Hillsborough, to lay flowers, to pay their respects. Not him, not yet. He imagines it will be alright though, just a fucking football match, but surely it will be so much more than a fucking football match this time, so much fucking more. He closes his eyes, tries to think about fucking her again, but it's no use, his mood's shattered. All he can think about is three hundred and sixty-four days ago and everything, every single bastard little thing that's presented itself in the interim, the life he knew before, the life he knows now. He becomes acutely aware of the ticking clock in the bathroom, the ticking clocks in the shop below, the fucking ticking clocks, leading him inexorably onwards towards some final, inevitable destruction.

He's still lying there, in tepid water, when he hears the doorbell go, some fucker hammering like crazy on the door, someone screaming up at his window, screaming the fucking street down. He clambers out of the bath, bollock-naked. Jen's mam and sister, the two of them in the fucking street, the car blocking the fucking road. Engine running, lights on. Her mam screaming like a fucking banshee, screaming his name, her sister hammering on the door like she means to break through it. He gets himself dressed, meets Jen in the hallway, her looking mortified and terrified, not knowing what to do with herself. Her mam still screaming, howling that he's a 'prick' and 'cunt'. And she's right. She's fucking right. He's ashamed to be living. He feels pathetic standing there with this beautiful thing in front of him, every bit the fucking animal he is. He looks Jen in the eye and he realises that she truly doesn't see it.

But she will, one day.

She fucking will.

'I'm staying here,' she says.

He shook his head.

'No, no, no,' he says. 'You can't.'

'They're an embarrassment,' she says. 'I can make my own decisions.'

He shakes his head again. He steps towards her, steps away from her.

'They're right,' he says. 'I'm a cunt. I've been doing this to you for months.'

She starts to panic then, starts to tremble and cry and beg him not to open the door and all he can do is shake his head and tell her he's sorry. And still she isn't angry with him, only desperate for him to change things. But he can't change things. He's incapable of changing anything.

'I'm sorry,' he says. 'I need to man up.'

He starts down the stairs, gets halfway before the glass window smashes. The Scotsman appears, steps into the lobby. Finchy watches as he's bundled out of the way by Jen's mam. Then she's on the stairs, energised by plain fucking fury, shoving him to one side. They start going at it, Jen and her mam, on the first-floor landing, Jen shouting that she isn't going anywhere, her mam having none of it. He stands there in the stairwell, weak and pathetic, trying to sink into the shadows that are too delicate to protect him. Her sister follows, shoots him a look, spits words in his direction.

'You fucking bastard,' she says.

'She just turned up,' he says.

'Fuck off.'

She pushes past him too, climbs the stairs. And then Jen's sister and mam enter the stairs again, heading downwards this time, Jen locked between them, Jen reduced to a kicking, screaming child. They have to pry her off every fucking surface to get her from the flat to the car and she won't go and now the neighbours from over the street are out to witness the fucking spectacle and he's reduced yet further to a mere scrap of a man, weak and pathetic. When she's finally trapped in the back of the car, her mam comes for him, swearing into his fucking face, telling him to fuck off and to never, ever speak to her daughter again and there's nothing he can do but stand and take it. Because he fucking deserves it.

For what we are about to receive…

Jen's mam slams the door behind her, causing what's left of the glass to fall out and then she launches herself at his car, giving it a flying kick, denting the bodywork. He catches one last sight of Jen, turning to look at him through the rear window, tears streaming down her face, make-up smudged, hair a mess, a wreck of a girl.

And may we always be mindful of the needs of others…

And they're gone, the show over. The Scotsman stands staring at the hole where the glass panel used to be.

'Fucking hell,' he says, 'better than *EastEnders*.'

Finchy turns around and heads upstairs, leaving the foyer exposed to whatever, leaving the dent in his car, not wanting to step into the street. He gets himself a beer and carries it to his room, sticks the Carpets on full fucking blast, collapses on the bed feeling like a fucking scolded teenager, lays there until the Scotsman starts banging on the wall and telling him to shut the fucking noise up.

He fucks off out instead, drives through the old town until

he reaches the car park by the canal, pulls up there, sits with the engine idling, staring at the spot in the hedge where they found Tracey Carlton, wondering how he'd come to miss a body in a hedge, white skin in green foliage, sitting there in the driving seat with all of it racing through his fucking head.

Again.

Nine months. Nine fucking months.

He sits there for ten minutes, the engine turning over, his stomach performing somersaults. It takes him that long to notice the car sat in the corner of the car park, the driver hunched in the driver's seat, much like he's hunched. He might be staring at himself, at some all-revealing reflection. He stares across the car park, stares right into the cunt's eyes and the cunt stares back at him. There's no reason for anybody to be parked up in the car park of a boarded-up business, no fucking reason at all, but here they fucking are, the two of them.

A moment passes, a moment where Finchy feels himself folding inwards on himself, and then he makes a move to step out of the car. As soon as he does the other car pulls away. He watches it turn left down out of the car park, disappear into the evening. Finchy sits there, half in, half out of the car, thinking only of the bloke's eyes.

Dark eyes.

Furious eyes.

The same as the pair staring back at him now in the fucking rear-view mirror.

Exactly the fucking same.

14th April 1990

Liverpool 2 v 2 Nottingham Forest Anfield

You would like to go to the World Cup with England but you don't. You would like to be there when it all kicks off in Cagliari but you won't.

But you're at Anfield on this day of remembrance, on this day of mourning. You visit the gates and the memorial to Hillsborough. You place your palm on the metal and close your eyes.

But you do not look at the list of names.

You will never look at the list of names.

You're there when the Kop pays you its respects and you pay your respects in turn.

There are tears in your eyes when you see the flags bearing testament to ninety-five lost souls. There are tears in your eyes when the Kop sings 'You'll Never Walk Alone'. There are tears in your eyes when you wander in the direction of the coach and the life you no longer recognise as your own.

It has been three hundred and sixty-four nights of turmoil.

It has been three hundred and sixty-four days of waking to another morning.

You are guilty of nothing.

You are guilty of everything.

There is April, there is May.

There are Mondays and Tuesdays and Wednesdays and Thursdays and Fridays and Saturdays. An ever-spinning wheel.

There are patterns.

There are routines.

There are fixed fucking duties.

There are no pills.

There is no Jen.

Not any more.

There are no surprises.

There's no football either.

Italia 90

The press have predicted a summer of blood. The government have fanned the flames. The Italian authorities fear the worst.

Sardinia is a fortress.

Alcohol is banned.

There are limited ports of entry and restricted movement.

There is a stop-and-search policy at the border.

Moynihan in his element.

Moynihan the opportunist.

Moynihan.

Thatcher's poisonous dwarf.

Leading the war on football.

Fucking revelling in it.

Those fans that get in risk summary deportation just for being.

It's a crime to be English.

11th June 1990

England 1 v 1 Republic of Ireland
Cagliari

The old town cinema showing the game on the big screen. Big John Robertson guest of honour. Big fucking mistake. Lads barrelled up, barrelling in.

Beer in the aisles.

Beer on the seats.

Puke on the seats.

Puke in the aisles.

The owner fretting and fussing.

England 1 Rep. Ireland 1.

Forest fans like lapdogs in the post-match Q&A. Robbo slagging off England. Every fucker slagging off England. Half the Irish players from the best fucking English teams.

Heroes and villains.

Villains and heroes.

You're not having any of it. You're on your feet, making your point to a bloke you'd once worshipped, the bloke you used to pretend to be on a Tuesday evening at football club, on a Saturday in the park, you in your yellow Forest away shirt with the blue trim.

And Robbo is playing to the crowd, taking the piss. The crowd are lapping it up.

Cunts.

The boys are lapping it up.

All cunts.

You want the earth to swallow you and you are a laughing stock.

But England make it out of the group.

He moves across to cover the old boys, a different route each week, mental stimulation, delivering to the country, a fucking day off midweek, a chance to do something less boring instead. Eight walk, pushing his barrow up the High Street, flirting with the shopgirls. Thirty walk, on his bike, nice and easy does it, roasting in the summer sunshine. Nightingale in the van, job done by mid-morning, parking up in the woods, munching on his sandwiches, having a kip, the best fucking job in the world.

The rough with the smooth.

The smooth with the rough.

Thirty-three walk, his old favourite but growing with the new estate, becoming a pain in the arse, fourteen walk, with the schoolgirls' 'Morning Mr Postman', twenty-two by the old canal, twenty-one's dirty sibling, the rabbit warren estate, alleyways and dogs, broken fences, broken houses, broken lives.

The deadland.

Two walk, nipping into his flat for tea and biscuits, terraced houses, easy fucking money. And every day throughout the summer, each and every time he delivers to a school, he feels the pull of it, hears a calling, wonders how that might be, how he might get there, if it's too late for that already, at nineteen, if the chance has passed him by, if he's earmarked for this life and no other for the next forty-five years. When he brings the subject up in the canteen the blokes have a field day.

'A fucking teacher?'

'Don't you need a brain to do that?'

'You just want to shag the girlies.'

'Fuck me, I couldn't do that job. I'd murder the little bastards.'

'I couldn't keep my dick in my pants.'

'Bollocks, I hated school.'

Only Harcross truly listening, delivering a quiet word in his ear.

'Do it. You're too fucking intelligent for this place.'

He doubts that but he listens to Harcross all the same because he loves the skinheaded bastard.

He doesn't know it yet but he always will.

England 1 v 0 Belgium
Bologna

One hundred and nineteen minutes. Penalties looming. Gascoigne free-kick. Platt volley.

One fucking nil.

The lads in the living room at Gav's place, piling on top of each other, piling in. And you on the sofa, strangely out of it.

Thinking.

Weighing things up.

Loving it and hating it.

Thinking it's coming to an end, feeling that and not knowing what to do, thinking about journeys, about new beginnings, about endings and partings, saying goodbye to nineteen fucking years of growth in the old town, thinking about your college application, thinking about the lads, about leaving one life and starting another, thinking about all of that in the slice of time it takes for them to get to their feet and call you a miserable bastard.

And so you're dancing.

Dancing in the living room at Gav's place as England book themselves a place in the Quarter-Finals.

She was standing outside with her back against the brick wall of BJ's house.

'I thought I'd walk you to the station,' she said. 'Then I'll go. For good this time...'

He felt it then, a terrific surge of sadness. He didn't want to leave but he knew he couldn't stay. There was no way in the fucking world he could stay. He'd grown apart from the old town, grown into a different person in another place. Not a better person, not a more accomplished individual, none of those things, he'd simply changed from the person he was into the person he'd become. It was natural. It could happen to anybody. But the old town would always be with him. She would always be with him.

And so they walked the labyrinthine alleyways one last time, him with his bags, her trotting along beside him, heels clicking on tarmac, to the station foyer, the platform. Somewhere along that journey they took to holding hands.

'You're a daft bastard,' she said. 'You always were a daft bastard.'

'Maybe,' he said.

People were filing inside the train when they arrived, passengers gawping from the windows, not having a fucking clue what they were witnessing, him out of kilter on the platform, her awkward beside him.

'I'll take a seat next to them,' he said. 'Tell them the whole fucking story.'

She smiled.

'They wouldn't believe you if you did,' she said.

'They fucking would,' he said. 'The way I'd tell it...'

He picked up his bag and stepped on board.

'You take care,' she said.

'You too,' he said.

And then the door was sliding shut, hissing out air and she was lost to him for good. He watched her from behind the window, watched her diminish in size and shape and texture, held it in until the train pulled away, choking it all back, and he failed a little in that and had to hide his face from the other passengers by keeping it pressed against the window, exposing himself to the old town as it slipped away. He turned around. He didn't bother with a seat in the end. He sat on his bag by the parcel shelves, not wanting to look at anybody, not wanting to watch the old town disappear, not wanting to see any of it or feel it or have to deal with it.

But he would have to, he would fucking well have to.

He sat there wondering if he'd achieved anything except to stir up fifteen years of sediment, and flee before the sediment had time to settle.

He wondered if one day, out of the blue, he'd come back to stir it all up again.

Sometimes he dreams of pouring petrol on the yellow sofa, lighting a match to it and watching it burn.

Sometimes.

He switches on the stereo. The Blue Aeroplanes. Swagger. He listens to Gerard Langley spout his poetry, drags his body out of bed and over to the window, gazes out at the quiet street.

A movement in the bathroom opposite. He catches his breath, shuffles into the shadows, watches the vague outline of the woman opposite struggle out of her clothes, watches the red sweater come off, the blue jeans, the black underwear, revealing pink skin, the dark patch between her legs, all of this a suggestion through frosted glass.

The woman opposite, single mum, no bloke on the scene, his flatmate providing the interim entertainment whenever the two fancy it.

Bizarre.

Not his type, truth be told, but he watches her anyway, watches her step into the shower and pull the curtain across, watches the frosted glass mist over, so that when she steps out of the shower he can barely distinguish the shape of her at all. He waits for her to move from the bathroom to the bedroom, her in a towel, black hair pushed back, watches her do all of those things then draw the curtains across and shut him out.

Selfish cow.

He drifts to the kitchen, sticks some toast under the grill, goes to the phone in the living room, drops on to the yellow sofa and calls up Gav.

'Half seven?'

'Sounds good.'

'I'll pick you up.'

'Is that it?'

'What else do you want me to fucking say?'

'I don't know. How was your day, something like that.'

'Okay. How was your day?'

'Shit.'

'Right. See you at half seven.'

He puts the phone down, smells the fucking toast burning, races into the kitchen to save it. Too late. He goes back to the packet. Just the crusts left. He takes out a knife and starts scraping the burnt edges of the toast into the sink.

'Bollocks to this,' he says.

He drives to his mam's, hoping to strike lucky, to stumble in on a hot pot, sausage and mash, something wholesome. Six-thirty on a Tuesday evening, the streets emptying of traffic, the dead day of the week, no fucking football, no fucker in the pubs, early to bed and early to rise.

There's no hot pot, no sausage and mash, just the dog end of a steak and kidney pie. His dad throws some chips in the oven to go with it. He sits at the kitchen table, the radio in the background, the local news, the same locked-in places, the same dull stories. He stuffs himself, talks about the job and football and when he'll be around again.

He drives back to the flat as the long summer day comes to an end, unlocks the boarded-up door, steps into the dark foyer, climbs the steep stairs. He hates coming home to the flat as much as he hates going home to his mam and dad's to steal a meal.

There's just him and the twilight again, him and the alarm clock, him and the dark hours counting away towards another day in paradise.

And a World Cup Semi-Final.

4th July 1990
Germany 1 v 1 England
Turin

The Hound packed to the rafters. Shilton flat-footed on that deflection. Jammy German bastards. Lineker levelling. The place erupting.

Beer on the walls.

Beer on the ceiling.

A right fucking mess.

Extra time. The landlord weighing up the damage against the dough. Waddle off the post.

Jammy – German – bastards.

The fucking penalty shoot-out.

The cheers and the tears.

Blokes spitting blood at Pearce. Your Stuart Pearce. But he's not yours, he's England's and England are out of the World Cup. Blokes spitting blood at Forest all the same, Forest spitting back with fists and foreheads, everything kicking off in the pub, spilling into the street, the throng joined by other throngs from other pubs.

Police on the High Street and the Market Square, barking their orders and sticking the boot in but not enough police, not on this evening. Lads and lasses drunk on the drama. A horde marching up the High Street towards the clock tower.

Bottles exploding as grenades.

Shop windows shivering.

Car windscreens.

Everything a fucking target.

The Guildhall decorated with scaffolding, the throng gathering there, nowhere left to go except home and no fucker going home, not yet.

Blood still up.

Some mad fucker on the scaffolding, clambering up the outside like Spiderman. Police on the tannoy. No fucker listening. Spiderman at the clock tower now, turning to the massed ranks, tearing off his T-shirt to show his bulldog tattoo, raising his fists to the cheers, climbing onwards, upwards, fearless. A gaggle of police urging him to come down, booze and bottles raining down. The police issuing their ultimatums.

No fucker adhering.

England at war with itself.

Not for the fucking first time.

You watch the drunk on the scaffolding, the crowds of lads, the boys and the men, the lasses too. You watch the bottles hurtling through the air, some finding their mark, others falling short. You look across at the police vans and you listen to the fuckers spitting and spouting their anger at nobody and nothing. You stand there under the trees, a way off from it all, watching it unfold.

You aren't pissed. You're not devoured by it any more either. And you want no part of it. You turn away, slip into the alley, thinking about getting your boots dirty on a Saturday, discovering something else about yourself that isn't all of this.

Thirteen million viewers.

Mothers and daughters.

Fathers and sons.

Thirteen million.

For many it's the beginning.

For you it's the end.

But you don't want to go to the flat. You can't face the emptiness. You venture through the estate instead, past the kiddies' swings, past the fucking car park, the hedge bottom, through the folds of darkness, feeling the separation, the past unravelling, the old town loosening its grip, loosening its hold, letting you go.

At last.

The lights are off at your mam's. You let yourself in, steal some ham from the fridge. You fix yourself a sandwich. Your dad comes down to check who's in the house and then heads back upstairs without saying anything.

There's nothing to say.

You need sleep. You crash on the sofa. You're thinking about getting out of the flat, getting some money together. You have one eye on a future, sorting yourself out, putting the things you've been mulling over into action before the old town drags you back into itself, cuts off your air supply, suffocates your spirit.

Forever.

You're just in time.

Kelly wasn't home. The house was dark and empty. He clicked on the kitchen light, filled the room with brightness. He rubbed his eyes. Everything was the same, the condiments where they were meant to be, the cutlery resting in the cutlery tray, the place mats on the dining table. Everything was how he'd left it.

He moved through the kitchen. The pad and pen on the table, the washing-up in the sink. He passed his inverted reflection in the kettle, glanced meekly at his distorted form.

And yet there had been a shift, in the fabric of things, in his perception of them, something slight, almost intangible. The house was cold and silent and absent of the feeling of home.

It was all untouched. All of it.

He wandered through to the living room, musty, occupied by tired light, the curtains closed, the TV remote perched on the arm of the sofa. He pulled back the curtains, opened the French windows, got some air in the place. He thought about going upstairs to the bedroom but he couldn't do it. Not yet. He wrestled away images of a lifeless body draped over the bed, of pillows, of electrical cords coiled around sickening white flesh, of fury and frenzy and incandescent rage.

Instead he stood looking around the living room, at the photographs, the ornaments and trinkets, the pictures on the wall, their favourite picture, a village in winter softened by snow, the orange glow of home in windows, a lone horse standing upright in a field of white, stoic, resilient, locked in time. He imagined, as he had many times before, wandering into that scene, becoming part of it, resting his palm on the horse's broad neck, hitching up his jacket and trudging down the lane to the house that was his own, pushing open the door, feeling the warmth hit him, shaking off his boots, brushing himself down, heading deeper into the house, deeper into a home. And here he was in his own home, still in his jacket, feeling the cold against his cheeks, feeling marooned within its walls, uncertain of what the next few minutes might reveal, uncertain of everything. He took off his jacket and sat on the arm of the sofa. He picked at the backs of his arms.

The blinking light of the answerphone caught his eye. He reached over to it, looked at the red display indicating half a dozen untouched messages.

Another bad sign.

He took a deep breath and pressed the button, listened to his own distant voice calling from a vacuous nothingness, from faraway hotel rooms, from BJ's hallway. He choked back tears.

The last message was from Chris, inviting him back to work, suggesting they put it all behind them, suggesting that everything was sorted. Good. That was good. He had a fucking job to do after all, lives to steer in this direction and that, dreams to deliver. There was just his own life to pilot, his own fucking future to secure.

The message clicked off. He stood staring into the blackness.

Later, eventually, he climbed the stairs, holding his hands out to keep himself upright, feeling his world tilt on its axis, causing him to feel sick in the stomach, dragging himself from the brink of vile places, clinging to the real world, or at least his perception of it.

He reached the dark landing. The doors were all closed, a further signal that he'd been the last person to leave the house, because Kelly wasn't like him, Kelly didn't care about doors and windows and lights and plug sockets.

The little window in shadow. The silent stillness of the house. Not even the quiet drip of the cistern. One thing and the next and the next.

He stopped at the bedroom door, straining to listen beyond it. He placed the palm of his hand on the cold wood.

He pushed the door open.

The room was stuffy, full of shadows, but the bed was empty, the duvet neat and tidy, the cushions placed just so. He stood there, breathing in the familiarity, breathing in his own forgiveness.

It was alright.

Everything was alright.

The phone rang. He could hear it in the furthest outreach of his mind. It was far off, hardly audible, but it was ringing for sure. He knew it would be Kelly, that she'd taken off as he'd taken off, the two of them more compatible than they cared to understand, the two of them one and the same. The evening came back to him in that very moment, the fight in the bedroom, the scratching and the tearing, her slamming the bedroom door, descending the stairs, dragging her car keys across the kitchen unit, leaving the house, starting up the car and speeding away, leaving him there. He remembered all of it. He remembered spending the next hour setting things straight, locking doors and windows, tidying, organising, putting everything in its place, as he always did, as he had to do. Everything except the washing-up. There had been no time for the washing-up.

And then he'd left.

Neither of them had returned since.

He crossed the threshold of the bedroom and sat on the edge of the bed, his eyes streaming with tears.

Somewhere beyond the walls of his home he could hear a train pulling out of the station. And he could hear singing, all the boys together on some glorious away trip. He could hear BJ and Jeff laughing at some mad moment, hear Spence and Robbie Box laughing too, taking the piss. He heard the soft thud as one of Doddy's darts hit the board, the quiet murmur of the TV in Hopper's cosy living room. And then he heard the sound of Jen crying into a pillow, Tracey Carlton screaming in a car park, Janet Allen gasping her last breath in her modern kitchen. He heard the weakening cries of a solid mass of people, heard them slip, one by one into unconsciousness. He stared helplessly into the dark void surrounding him, stared through wire-mesh fencing at lives slipping away. He heard the creak of a rope swinging from a beam in a tired old railway hut, Stimmo's final moments on this good earth.

He saw all of those things and heard all of those things as if they were happening all over again.

He would always see them.

These things were his burden.

But they were only echoes.

The Lads

The lads were Forest and Pompey, Wednesday and Everton.
The lads were Notts County, Lincoln City and Liverpool.
And the others.
All the others.
Connected through one common bond.
The pull of Saturdays.
The pull of away days.
This story and that story.
This adventure and that adventure.

Every single fucking week.

My blessings and respect to each and every one of you.

Notes and Acknowledgements

This novel was written almost entirely to the sounds of Ian Brown and The Stone Roses.

Other notable musical accompaniment:

The Inspiral Carpets
The Wedding Present
The Blue Aeroplanes
The Brilliant Corners
Cud
Happy Mondays
Depeche Mode
The Weather Prophets
Ian Prowse and Pele
The Bridewell Taxis
The Popguns
Talk Talk
The Smiths
    and
The Cure's enduring album *Disintegration*, released on 1st May 1989

Plus many, many, many more.

A soundtrack to an era.
A soundtrack to a life.

It was the end of the 80s, the end of our youth
Ben Graham

This has been an emotional journey, one full of melancholy and magic, blessing and burden.

Much thanks to the many old friends who have lent me their memories and reinstated my memories of a period of my life that had been locked away for many a year. I am eternally grateful.

To Mike Nicholson for his incisive comments and expertise on the Hillsborough sections. I hope I've done all that were there justice.

To Martin Odoni for his thoughts on various details concerning Liverpool FC and for pointing me in the direction of Chris Rowland's book on Heysel, *From Where I Was Standing*, an excellent read.

To the members of the Facebook group 'Lost Football League Grounds of England, Wales and Scotland'. They know where this book's heart is. Speak to them, listen to their stories.

To Karen (for her boundless positivity), Martin, Malcolm and all at Arcadia Books, particularly Gary Pulsifer for supporting this project from its germination. I hope I've done the idea, our idea, justice.

To Al Needham for lending me his words and wisdom on Notts dialect and all at Left Lion for their support.

To Jeremy and Sue Rodwell, for Chania.

To all at Café St Pierre and Café Boho, Canterbury for not hurrying me on each time the cups and plates were empty.

To Bruce Springsteen and the E Street Band for keeping the fire burning both in themselves and in me. May it never be extinguished.

To all of the players, management and supporters of Nottingham Forest Football Club during the 1980s. Thanks for the many wonderful hours spent in your company.

To Justin, Dan, Bruce, Scott and anybody who has made a creative contribution to this novel.

To my wife and children for putting up with everything the writing of this novel has thrown at us, and for allowing me the hours. I am eternally grateful for their enduring patience, understanding and support. Without them this book wouldn't exist.

Finally, to all of those who need to listen, a simple message: Give the game back to the fans. That's who it belongs to.

Danny Rhodes, February 2014